MOMENTS IN TIME

MOMENTS IN TIME

CHRONICLES OF ETERNITY I

J. A. GORDON

DERWEN PUBLISHING

PEMBROKE · DYFED

First published in Great Britain by Derwen Publishing 2009.

Derwen Publishing
3 Bengal Villas,
Pembroke, Dyfed
Wales, SA71 4BH

A CIP catalogue for this book is available
from the British Library.

ISBN 978-1-907084-00-3

This is a book about the people who fall between the cracks of history. Much of
what appears here is recorded history and the names of those persons, places and
events have been used unaltered but the names of the other persons are not
necessarily those which they used at the time.

Design and production by David Porteous Editions.
www.davidporteous.com

Printed and bound in the UK.

PROLOGUE

The fire sat low in the grate, keeping the chill of the early evening at bay, and sent long shadows flickering over the closed cream shutters. It was an old house and the draughts playing in the room made the candle flutter but her voice was comforting and firm.

'I want you to clear your mind and let your body feel very heavy. Now, imagine you're standing at the top of a flight of ten steps,' she said. 'Now go down the steps, one by one, and as you go down, you're going deeper and deeper into your consciousness. Ten, nine, eight, seven, six, you're going deeper and deeper, five, four, three – your breath is getting deeper and deeper'.

The subject lay on the sofa breathing slowly and steadily.

'Two, one', she said, 'You're standing at the bottom of the steps and there's a corridor in front of you stretching as far as your eye can see, stretching into eternity. There are doors on either side of the corridor and I want you to walk down the corridor for as long as it takes – until you get to the door you need to go through. Do you understand?'

The voice came through strongly, 'Yes, I understand and I'm walking down the corridor past the doors but I know that the door I want to open is so far away that I need to run'.

'Go ahead, run as far as you need'.

There was an expectant pause in the room while the subject raced towards the door to understanding but the silence was punctuated by the gentle snoring of the dog lying across the subject's lap.

'Are you there yet? Have you found the door you need?'

'Yes, I'm there. I have my hand on the door knob.'

'Good. Open the door, look around and tell me where you are'.

'Um, I'm standing on a grassy knoll overlooking a lightly wooded valley. It's evening time and it's beginning to get dark. I'm in a sort of camp. There are camp-fires and funny looking tents'.

'Are you alone?'

'No, no, there are men with me, quite a few of them, actually…..

men in uniform. They're dressed more or less like me but my clothing is a bit different from theirs'.

'Are you male or female?'

'I'm male and I think that I'm a soldier. Yes, that's right, I'm a soldier but it's a long time ago….. I, I…. I'm a Roman soldier.'

'How old are you?'

'For some reason, I don't really know how old I am but, looking at me, I would say that I'm in my late twenties, or thereabout.'

'Who is with you?'

'My men are with me…. I mean that the men with me are from my century…….mmmm, looking at my dress, I see that……crikey, yes, that's it…. I'm the centurion. I'm the commanding officer of these men'.

'Who are they? What sort of men are they?'

'Well, they're my soldiers but they're also my family ……I mean, they're the people I live with day in and day out and they're the people I really know and trust.'

'What's your name?'

The voice was strong and resonant, coming from somewhere very deep, 'It begins with a 'G'. It sounds like 'Greek'. My name is……my name is……. Graecus. Yes, that's it, my name is Graecus.'

CHAPTER ONE

The Feast of Saturnalia was over by some weeks but it was still a cold foggy day when the two men stood on the top of the hill looking down on the little town in Germania Inferior. From the position of the sun in the sky and the shadows on the ground, they knew it was about two hours short of the midday and they increased the pace of their steps down the hill as today was the day of the slave market and they did not wish to be late for the best of what was on offer would quickly be gone.

Graecus and Felix covered the stony ground quickly and easily in comfortable silence; they were old friends and comrades and had marched together many times, in many places. They were auxiliary soldiers in the Roman Army and today they were looking for manpower at the market. By this time, over a hundred years after the death of Julius Caesar, the Roman Army was spread across most of Europe and North Africa but few of its soldiers had actually been born in Rome and many of the Legions and auxiliary cohorts were drawn from Italians and conquered peoples.

Graecus was not a Roman. He spoke Greek as well as he spoke Latin and that accounted for the nickname he had been given in his century but, although he was olive-skinned and had dark brown hair, his grey eyes showed that his Mediterranean blood was mixed with that of an ancestor from elsewhere. Graecus was ignorant of where and when he had been born but, from the good state of his teeth, his straight back and his usually robust health, he and others reckoned he was about 27. Felix had also been lost or abandoned as a child but his name had been given to him on account of his extreme good humour – a quality which made him popular in tight corners.

Had they been less lucky, they could easily have suffered the same grisly fate as others but they had been taken into Army as young recruits and could now remember only that life. Graecus had recently been promoted to Centurion in recognition of his organisational abilities but there was no rancour between the two men; Felix had not wanted the job anyway.

As they entered the town, the men knew that they drew the stares of its inhabitants. They were curiosities to most of these people who lived a narrow life and probably never ventured much beyond the pastures where they took their pigs and cattle. Now, the two young men made their way through the rubbish-strewn streets to the town centre.

What passed for the town square had today been commandeered by the slave-master who was standing in the middle hawking his wares and Graecus immediately saw this was the usual depressing sight of a motley collection of wretched people who had nothing in common other than that they all profoundly wished they were somewhere else. Graecus recognised the slave-master, having already seen him on several occasions and having marked him down as one of the more unscrupulous of his trade.

The soldiers surveyed the ragged bunch of slaves as they stood, bound and shackled together, on the stone platform. They were an unprepossessing lot – broken down old men and women, sad-eyed girls and, distressingly, a beautiful pregnant girl who was so terrified that she had noisily relieved herself, standing up on the stones.

Graecus and Felix swiftly concluded that there was nothing there which could be of interest to the Roman Army and this was a pity because they had been walking since dawn to be at the market on time. Graecus approached the slave-master, a greasy man in his forties in a stained tunic, asking him in his own tongue if the people on show were all that he had. The man, knowing from his dress that Graecus was a Centurion and would have good Roman money to spend, became over-eager to please and said, 'Apart from those on show I have only a few children at the back of the tavern but, sir, surely you and your colleague would like to see the beautiful girl?'

At this point, his servant, knowing that his master was indicating that the soldiers were interested in this girl, released her bonds and pulled her forward by the arm. Seeing that she had dropped her head, he pulled her up by the hair so that they could see her face.

She was, indeed, very beautiful. Her hair was light gold and her eyes were green. She was about 15 years old and heavily pregnant. There was about her something fine and delicate hinting that she was of noble birth and had probably spent most of her young life in privileged surroundings looking forward to a gilded adulthood as the wife of a rich man. But now she was here in a filthy marketplace, in a tiny town, pregnant – no doubt as the result of rape – in thrall to a slave-master on sale to any man who had enough money to buy her.

Graecus stared at the girl for several minutes as these thoughts occupied him. The slave-master, misinterpreting Graecus's stare for lust, said, 'I could have her taken to the tavern and stripped, sir, so that you could more easily make up your mind' but Graecus felt irritated by the man's tone and said sharply, 'That is neither desirable nor necessary. I am looking for recruits not a wife.'

At that moment, the noisy bustle of the square was rent by an almighty bellowing coming from behind the tavern and the master, sensing that the noise was coming from the slave children, hurried away to see what was going on. The servant let go of the girl's hair, but this was all that had been holding her up and she fainted, crumpling to the floor like a discarded cloak. Graecus signalled to Felix to go to the tavern to fetch some beer and some bread whilst he sat her up and gently patted her cheek, trying to revive her. She came round after a few minutes and was surprised to find herself in the arms of the young Centurion. She started to struggle to free herself but Felix came and offered the bread to her which she snatched from his hand and stuffed unceremoniously into her mouth. Felix gave her the beer and she drank deeply. Colour was returning to her cheeks and Graecus asked Felix to go back to the tavern to see if there was meat or fish for her as she appeared to have been starved for some time.

The girl was now more curious than frightened and Graecus tried to speak to her in the local tongue but was met with incomprehension. He knew a little of the language spoken by the Gauls, so he tried that. Again he was met with a blank stare. He knew a little of the language spoken by the Franks, so he tried that. Again, nothing. Now running out of ideas, he tried addressing her in Latin and was met with a small smile of recognition. He asked where she came from and she said, 'Sir, I am from Ierne, a beautiful island far away from here, where the grass is very green and the mountains are white with mist. I lived with my father, a nobleman, and my brothers and I had a soft life but I was captured by raiders who killed my family – running them through with their swords in front of my very eyes.'

Now she began to cry and Graecus gave her his neckerchief so she could dry her eyes before going on, 'Then they took me for their plaything. They stole my maidenhood and raped me time and time again but, when I became pregnant, they sold me to the slave-master.' And she sobbed again, great gulping sobs which contorted her beautiful face as tears dropped onto her coarse brown dress. Graecus knew that unless this girl's luck changed soon, she would end up at best destitute and at worst dead. He could not buy her for himself but he thought that if he bought her and left her in the town, perhaps working at the tavern, then at least she and her unborn child would have some chance of survival. He quickly calculated how much money he had and decided how best he would bargain with the slave-master who was rapidly reapproaching, beaming, showing his yellow teeth at the sight of Graecus holding the girl's hand.

Graecus put down the girl's hand and said, 'I do, after all, wish to buy this girl but I am not willing to pay the asking price. It is too much. She has been on the market for some time and she is losing value by the day as her confinement approaches. I will give you two thirds of the asking price, and I do not wish to haggle. Take it or leave it.'

The slave-master was not having the best of days and he agreed almost immediately. So, within minutes, Graecus was the proud owner of a beautiful, dispossessed noble girl pregnant by an unknown raider. The girl began to weep again but quietly this time. Graecus hoped she was weeping with relief and then she said, 'I am pleased, sir, to have been sold to such an upstanding person as yourself and I am yours to command as you wish but may I now say goodbye to the slave children who were my companions?'

Graecus gave her his arm and they walked slowly to the back of the tavern where there stood a wagon containing children of all ages ranging from about three to thirteen. They were mostly dark-haired and dark-skinned but there were a few with lighter colouring and now as the little throng began to pulsate from the middle of the wagon and the air ring with nether-wordly cries, he saw a very different looking child.

He was about ten years old with white-blonde hair and strikingly blue eyes. He was very, very dirty and, as he was bellowing his head off, he was beating the daylights out of a much older, bigger boy who had a piece of bread in his hands which, it may be assumed, the blonde boy thought was his by rights. Graecus was amused by this and asked the slave-master to show him the boy. The slave-master raised his eyes heavenwards and said, 'Sir, you are welcome to view the boy, in fact, you are welcome to take the boy, gratis, if you can get him out of the wagon without severe injury to yourself,' and Graecus signalled to Felix that they should enter the wagon and extricate the dirty boy.

As they entered the wagon, the other children gave way to the soldiers who were then left as observers of the melee between the Dirty Boy and the Supposed Thief. As fighting men themselves, Graecus and Felix enjoyed watching a good scrap and stood for several minutes as Dirty Boy kicked, bit, punched, scratched and clawed at Supposed Thief who was by far the larger and heavier of the two. Sensing that he was being observed, Dirty Boy, who clearly liked an audience, gave a final uppercut punch to Supposed Thief's jaw and laid him out on the wagon floor before retrieving the piece of bread from his outstretched hand. He was smiling triumphantly, and so was off his guard, when Graecus and Felix grabbed him from either side and carried him kicking wildly out of the wagon.

Dirty Boy lay on the ground punching the air as Graecus held down his legs while Felix took from the pouch at his waist a small piece of rope and tied the child's ankles together. This made him squirm all the more but Graecus now sat on his legs while Felix

11

found more rope and tied his wrists while sitting on his belly with his back to the boy. This exercise had left them all breathless and so, for a few moments, the two men sat on the child. They thought they had tamed him until Felix felt a searing pain when the boy sank his teeth into his left buttock which made him jump up in pain and Graecus laughed until the child managed to disentangle himself enough to knee him quite hard in the chest.

This was serious business and Graecus and Felix informed by decades of fighting together, moved by instinct and without thought to grab the child by his testicles and throat and hold on until he gave up the struggle. When he seemed to have gone quiet, Graecus pulled the boy to his feet. He now stood – towering over the child – and looked him squarely in the eye and was astonished to see not fear or respect but only curiosity.

Graecus was intrigued and, summoning the slave- master with a glance, he asked where the boy had come from. The slave-master said, 'All I know, sir, is that the child was found in the ruins of a village sacked by vandals. He was about eight years old at the time but he gave his captors such a run for their money that, grown men though they were, they were shamed by a mere child. Since then, he has created mayhem wherever he went and I shall be glad to be rid of him'.

Graecus was impressed by this child's instinct for survival and carefully appraised him, taking in his stature and his utter fearlessness. The child was sturdy and looked capable of hard work. Felix seemed puzzled and Graecus asked what was in his mind and Felix said 'I am wondering why you are so interested in this boy'. Graecus took a few moments to answer and said, 'I feel that, properly trained he will make a good soldier and, as he has been offered to us for nothing, it would be an insult to the gods not to take him.'

This was all well and good but there remained the practical matter of how to transport a very strong, angry, child all the way back to camp. There was also the problem of what to do with the pregnant girl who was now officially Graecus's property.

Graecus felt that circumstances had overtaken him but it was time to regain control of the situation so he told the slave-master that his servant must help Felix keep the child quiet while he went back to the tavern to try to make some sort of future for the beautiful pregnant girl.

Graecus entered the tavern through its back door and came face to face with a handsome woman of about thirty who told him that she was its proprietress. He gave her his best smile and, after telling her his name, addressing her in her own tongue, he said, 'Madam, I see from your face that you are a woman of great compassion and understanding. I also see that you may need willing hands to help you in the running of your business.'

The proprietress, who had very fine piercing dark blue eyes and dark blonde hair piled on the top of her head, said, 'Centurion, whatever you wish to say to me would best be said over a drink. Please sit and allow me to pour you a cup of beer' and, truth to tell, by this time, Graecus was in need of sustenance so he accepted the beer from the woman and sat on the bench at the big table in her warm kitchen where the smell of baking bread mingled with the scent of the drying herbs hanging from the rafters.

Graecus gratefully drank some of the beer and, wiping the corners of his mouth with his fingers, was about to speak of his dilemma when the lady tavern owner said, 'Sir, you are a stranger to these parts. My name is Arminia, my family have lived in this town for many generations. We do not often see so fine a man as yourself in the town. What is the purpose of your visit here today?'

'Madam, I am here to try to find extra manpower for our century which is encamped in the woods several hours' walk from here, but I have not been successful.'

'Sir, I would not wish you to leave this town disappointed by what it has to offer in the way of hospitality', and, as Arminia said this, she drew near to Graecus and, to his surprise, bent down and kissed him on the lips.

Graecus had been shut in camp for most of the winter, away from female company, so he kissed Arminia back with great warmth and enthusiasm and he was just considering whether the lady could be persuaded to give herself to him when she raised him to his feet and manoeuvred them towards the door so that she was leaning backwards against it and Graecus was facing the door, kissing her. They kissed for some minutes and, when they came up for air, Graecus found his nose pressed into Arminia's hair. He was pleased to notice that it did not smell of the rancid butter with which most of the local people dressed their hair – rather it smelled of chamomile and her neck smelled of lavender. She was altogether delightful and Graecus could not resist her. Finding his way into her skirts, he inched his hand up her leg and, casting about to find her undergarments, he discovered that she wore none and this so increased his ardour that it was not long before they were pleasuring each other hard up against the back of the door so as to deter incomers.

Graecus had been in a man's world for most of his life but loved women, he loved their softness and the fact that they were bringers of life not its destroyers and now that he was engaged in the act which makes life, he was exultant and his enjoyment was matched by that of Arminia who was skilled in the art of love but was charged with an unexpectedly pure energy and tenderness. Their crescendo was loud and spectacular and, when they had finished, they stood breathless against the door, shaken by the experience.

Then they dusted themselves down and went and sat at the big table. 'Now Centurion,' Arminia said, 'What is it you came here for?' Graecus pondered how best he could make a case for the girl and then said, 'Madam, I find myself in the strange situation of having today bought a female slave because she is, I think, of noble birth but she is young and very heavy with child. I feared for her future but I cannot keep her myself. She requires sanctuary and I wish that she could find it here.'

Arminia leaned forward and raised an eyebrow before Graecus tactfully continued, 'She is beautiful, madam, in a way not normally found in these parts. She has light gold hair and green eyes and she would make a wonderful addition to your tavern. Just think of it, madam, customers will come from miles away drawn by the twin delights of her beauty and yours'.

'Soldier, your tongue is as graceful as those parts which I have recently enjoyed. Bring the girl immediately so that I can make up my mind while I am still heady from the pleasure of your embrace'.

'Madam, I am very fortunate this day to have met you.'

Graecus rose from the table and leaned over to Arminia and kissed her again with a lingering softness. Then he stood and went to the door and, opening it, called for Felix to bring the girl.

Felix bustled into the kitchen holding the girl who was looking much better. They all sat at the table then Graecus said to her, 'I wish to explain to you that I cannot keep you myself, but if you will promise to work hard and honestly I may be able to persuade this lady to put a roof over your head and that of your child when it is born'.

The older woman smiled at the girl, sympathetic to her plight and said, 'What is your name dear?'

And the girl answered, 'My name is Aoif and I have today been rescued from a terrible fate. I will work hard for you madam and I will be honest. All I ask is for you to treat me and my child with kindness'.

Arminia said, 'The life here is sometimes lonely for a woman in business on her own and I would welcome your company', and the matter was settled.

There remained the problem of the very dirty boy and how to get him back to camp but Graecus had a brainwave: it would make matters very much easier if the child were blindfolded so he asked Arminia if she had a piece of cloth which could be used for this purpose. The lady smiled and left the room only to return moments later with large piece of cloth from which she cut a strip long enough to go round the child's head.

It was time to say goodbye and Graecus, wishing to keep his adventure with Arminia to himself, took her to one side and said, 'Madam, you have been sent by the gods to me today. I am deeply grateful for your assistance'

And Arminia said, 'Sir, we do not know when we wake each day what the Fates will bring us.'

15

Then Graecus turned back to Felix and motioned to him that it was time to leave. The two soldiers bade them farewell and wished them a long and happy association before retrieving the child from the slave-master's servant who complained bitterly that they had left him for so long in charge of the ruffian.

Graecus took the strip of cloth from his bag and, with difficulty because the boy kept moving his head and butting him, tied it over his eyes before releasing him from the rope binding his ankles. He raised the boy to his feet and, holding him by the arm and addressing him in Latin, he said, 'You now belong to me and to the Roman Army. You will be trained to be a soldier and you will be treated with fairness and respect as long as you behave yourself and uphold the standards required of a Roman soldier.'

Graecus knew that the boy did not yet understand the language being spoken to him but he wished to start as he meant to go on and he felt that, if he spoke to the boy in a kindly way using a measured tone, the child would at least understand that no harm was meant to him.

Then the odd-looking trio began their long walk back to the army camp with Graecus setting as smart a pace as possible with the blindfolded child as he wished to regain camp before sundown.

As they walked, he and Felix each held one of the boy's arms guiding him over the stony terrain and up and down the hills, talking all the while about the day's events and how surprised the men would be by this addition to their camp.

Many miles later, they saw the smoke of the fires rising from the hill-top above them and, as they drew nearer, the almost square wooden palisade surrounding their camp came into view against its backdrop of the cliff-face which rose above the hill-top on which they had laboured to make their camp.

They had been sent to this isolated place some months before as a satellite camp to a much larger legionary fort several miles away and this plateau had been chosen for their site as giving good visibility while being easy to defend on account of its being backed up against the 150 foot cliff-face.

Graecus's century had been sent there as it was often the auxiliary forces which manned frontier posts. Although the posting had been described as being temporary, they had already been there longer than anticipated and, even though they were still camping in tents, there was as yet no sign of their being moved on.

Graecus and Felix started up the hill which was lightly dotted with trees and quickened their steps at the thought of taking their ease with their comrades and the hot food that would await them although in Graecus's case, the food would be less welcome than usual as Felix would not have cooked it and no-one else in camp was his equal with the cooking pot.

As they approached the camp, walking through the wooden gates, they were met with the incredulous stares of their fellow soldiers who were wondering why they were dragging a blindfolded child and, by the time they approached the main part of the encampment, they were accompanied by a curious crowd.

They took the child into the largest tent and tied him, seated, to a stool while Graecus gently explained to him that he was about to remove the blindfold reckoning that, even though he could not understand the language, he would understand its tone.

But he was wrong. As soon as the blindfold had been removed and Graecus bent down to peer at the child, Dirty Boy spat at him full in the face. The curious onlookers gasped and wondered what Graecus would do in retaliation to such disgraceful conduct and Graecus's immediate reaction was to want to slap the boy very hard but he decided that this would not be appropriate as the child was tied to the stool so he contented himself with saying sternly to him, 'Your behaviour is unbecoming of a Roman soldier and you will have to learn that colleagues and rank must be respected'

The onlookers did not think much of this as they felt that the child had been let off too lightly and there was a general clamour to know what this was all about.

Graecus then told his men, 'There were no obvious recruits to be had at the slave market but we saw this boy fight and were so impressed by his strength, fearlessness and determination that we decided that he would be as good as anybody and, being so young, he could more easily be schooled in the Army's ways'. He then told them the story of the beautiful pregnant girl and of his leaving her with the tavern owner (carefully omitting his encounter with her in the kitchen). The other men had not had such an interesting day and there was so much ribaldry exchanged about the beautiful girl that Graecus was extremely thankful that he could keep the secret of his coupling with Arminia to himself.

Meanwhile, the child sat sulking on the stool, glowering at anyone who looked at him but now it was time for supper which today had been cooked by Illyricus (who had been given that nickname because he came from Illyricum) and consisted of rabbit stew with root vegetables and herbs. The dishes and spoons were brought in and put on the table and the men helped themselves to bread and stew.

A dish and spoon were placed in front of the boy and food put in the dish but he did not eat. Graecus wishing to en-courage him, made faces to him seeking to indicate that it was delicious and, to show that it was not poisoned, he helped himself from the child's dish.But still the boy did not eat even though he must by then have been very hungry and thirsty having used up a great deal of energy in fighting and walking back to the camp.

Another of the men, Litigiosus, (so named because of his love for a good argument) asked Graecus what was the boy's name and, after considering for a moment, Graecus said, 'I shall name him Germanicus because of his blonde hair and blue eyes. That is undoubtedly his lineage'. So it was that Germanicus arrived at Graecus's century in the transit camp in Lower Germania.

But days went by and Germanicus still would not eat. It was beginning to be a cause for concern; the child had been in the camp for a week and, as far as they were aware, had eaten nothing. He was beginning to lose weight and had dark circles under his eyes. They had managed to clean the boy up by covering him in oil and using the *strigilis* before throwing him in the river to rinse off. He had drunk deeply from the river water and had since sipped beer and wine but no-one had seen him eat.

Graecus tried to make him eat by sitting next to him at mealtimes and tried to tempt him with tasty morsels of meat but to no avail. Felix had taken his culinary skills to new heights by preparing special pies and pates, soups and sweetmeats which the men enjoyed but still the child would not eat.

Nor would he speak. Graecus was attempting to teach him Latin by speaking to him constantly and pointing to things, giving their names. He tried to get the boy to accept his new name by pointing to his own chest and saying 'Graecus' and then pointing to the child's chest saying 'Germanicus' and although he was sure that the child understood, he having shown signs of intelligence in other areas, still he would say nothing. And eat nothing.

It was galling to say the least. Here he was in the company of some of the best men it was possible to know, having kindness and attention lavished on him, being tempted with good food, having a clean bed and being taught the most important language in the known world, and all he could do was sulk. Graecus assumed that the child would have to give in at some point and that he would, eventually, eat and, after that, he would speak but more days passed and still the child did not eat and he grew thinner and yet more days passed and he grew thinner and thinner and then he became ill.

It started with a mild fever which did not at first seem too serious although in his weakened state it was still worrying but then he collapsed while watching some of the men undertaking weapon training and they knew he must be very sick as he was too stubborn to give in to mere hunger.

So they put him to bed in the big tent and Graecus called for Magnus, the century's medicine man. Magnus carefully examined the boy's tongue, felt the pulse at his neck, looked in his ears and eyes, asked to see a sample of his urine and pronounced himself – baffled. He recommended that the child be given a thin gruel made from pig offal to try to replace the strength he had lost and that cold wet cloths be placed on his head and belly to bring down the fever. Felix was only too happy to make the gruel and Graecus sat patiently on the boy's truckle bed holding him up spooning it into his mouth whilst speaking softly to him in Latin, repeating his name over and over again. This went on for three days with the boy getting weaker and weaker and Magnus still not knowing what was wrong with him.

Then the child developed an angry red rash all over his body, including his eyelids and was seen to be scratching it constantly. This caused him great discomfort and it distressed both Graecus and Felix to see the child so afflicted but not be able to do anything to help him other than feed him the gruel and keep him in bed.

The fever grew worse. Graecus again asked Magnus what would become of the child and the big man said, 'I fear for his life because he is so weak and, worse, he appears to have lost the will to live.' Then Graecus said, 'Is there anything else, anything, you can think of which would help cure him?', and Magnus said, 'My knowledge of childhood illnesses is not great but I think that the child has given up fighting the illness and that he will die'.

That evening, the Centurion sat on the child's bed and looked at his poor tortured face and now saw not stubbornness and anger but only a small boy who may never have known kindness or friendship before and whose short life had seen much hardship and tragedy and Graecus did something he had not done in many years – he wept. He wept for the boy because he had come to admire his spirit and would miss the challenge of trying to teach him but he wept also for himself as a boy who had known neither his parents, nor where he had come from and had never known normal family life.

Germanicus lay on his bed and, somewhere in his feverish brain, registered the fact that Graecus was crying and that he was crying because of him and Germanicus had an epiphany – he realised in his dormant heart that this man had treated him with much kindness and respect and that he liked the life he had seen in the past few weeks and his heart leaped in his sick body and gave way to a feeling of pure joy that life could, after all, be worth living and he, too, began to cry.

Hearing him snuffling behind him, Graecus turned to see tears coursing down Germanicus's cheeks and felt that a corner had been turned; here was the child beginning to behave as a child; healing could begin.

Graecus called for Felix and asked him to concoct the most delicious but easily digested dish he could think of so that the boy could be coaxed to eat and Felix ran to his pots to fulfil this request returning a half hour later with a pudding made from milk, almonds, raisins and spices to find Germanicus sitting up and Graecus sitting on his bed repeating over and over again, 'My name is Graecus, your name is Germanicus', as he pointed firstly to his own chest and then to the child's. When Felix came into the tent, he pointed to Felix and said 'His name is Felix'.

Felix handed the dish of posset to Graecus who leaned towards the child with the spoon in his hand in the hope that the child would open his mouth and allow himself to be fed and each of them was misty eyed when the boy opened his mouth and swallowed the first real food he had had in weeks. Once he had tasted the excellence of Felix's food, Germanicus ate greedily and the cook was dispatched to find soup and bread to fuel the hungry boy.

He began to recover, slowly at first but gradually regaining his colour and strength over a few days and then Magnus allowed him out of bed for a few steps and then for a few more. By now, he was eating for Rome and his wasted body was filling out.

Gradually, he began to take an interest in those around him and was eventually well enough to sit for several hours at a time wrapped in a wolfskin watching the men take their exercise and practice their weaponry skills. He seemed at his most content watching the men and this was soon the way he spent his days although Magnus insisted that the child must be back in bed before sundown and not be allowed to sit at the campfire listening to the men tell campaign stories and jokes and sing their campfire songs.

And so the days passed and Germanicus grew stronger and stronger, nourished by Felix's wonderful culinary concoctions and the care and attention of Graecus and the century.

CHAPTER TWO

And then it was the Feast of Lupercalia, a very special day when the men celebrated with a banquet and much carousing. Graecus felt that it was now time for Germanicus to begin to observe other aspects of Army life and asked Magnus if it would be bad for his health if Germanicus were to be allowed to stay up and eat and drink with the men. Magnus said, 'I think it will do no harm as long as the child is in bed by midnight and he is not allowed to drink too much, nor eat all of the very rich dishes. He has been very ill and although I am sure that he is naturally strong, we must not allow him to overtire himself'.

So Germanicus took his place at the table with the rest of the men sitting between Graecus and Magnus. Felix, who was extremely gifted in obtaining supplies of unobtainable food-stuffs, had surpassed himself and produced dish after dish of boiled fowl, roast boar, grilled pigeon, compotes of vegetables, pates and puddings made from nuts, figs and honey. All of this was accompanied by wines, mead and beer and the men ate heartily and drank freely enjoying the wonderful food, the unexpected balminess of the February night and each others' company.

It was the custom on these occasions in their cohort for the Centurion to make an address and Graecus rose looking solemn as he prepared to give a eulogy about Rome.

Graecus did not relish public speaking but he took his duties seriously and so had spent many hours wandering in the woods around the hill-camp practising his speech. He was now quite proud of it and felt that it was composed not merely in the spirit of Cicero but also captured the lucid and persuasive style of that great Orator's prose.

As Graecus stood, he felt the full weight of his new rank and the men fell dutifully silent as he began, 'Brothers, this is the Feast of Lupercalia, a feast long established in our history. I am sure that I do not need to remind you that Lupercalia is connected with the revered she-wolf who suckled Romulus, the founder and the first ruler of our great city. But I must remind you of the great sacrifices made by our city's early citizens – those men who were dedicated to Rome and found solace in hard work. I wish to remind you of Lucius Quinctius Cincinnatus who was famed for his devotion to the Republic in times of crisis and was regarded as the ultimate Roman statesman. He was called from tilling his land to take command and having fulfilled his duty, went back to his farm, shunning personal glory.'

At this point, Graecus cleared his throat and there was a general shuffling of feet among the listeners. Then he went on, 'I wish to remind you of the virtuous qualities which made Rome mighty – thrift, duty to the state and lack of personal ambition. But now, I shall progress to the real subject matter of my address......' and had just opened his mouth to continue when Pneumaticus, whose name means 'Belonging to the Wind', shattered the peaceful throng by letting forth a loud, fruity, trumpeting............................ fart.

Normally, in a camp full of men who all know each other well, this would hardly be a cause for comment but, given the solemnity of the moment, the men were all wondering quite what Graecus's reaction would be and many of them, looking at his face and the dark clouds gathering on it, began to be grateful that they possessed better digestion than Pneumaticus.

But, all of a sudden, Germanicus, who seemed to have been trying to stifle a cough, gave up the struggle and laughed out loud and, having begun to laugh, was unable to stop.

Soon, all the men were laughing and, in the end, Graecus too appreciated the humour of the situation and joined in. But then the mood changed as they all realised that this was the first time they had heard the child laugh and his unaffected mirth, after weeks of worry, so touched their hearts that many of them were constrained to wipe their eyes and noses in an elaborately casual way and others were overtaken by a need for several seconds to look down and inspect their sandals for minute specks of dust.

Pneumaticus, mightily relieved, stood and said, 'Brothers, I offer a toast to Germanicus – the century's newest and youngest member' and all the men joined in raising their vessels to the boy who did not know exactly what had been said but knew that he had done something to please them, that he was accepted........ and that he was at home.

It was just a few days later that the dog appeared. It was a small dog, grey and hound-like in appearance with a long nose, pointy ears and a deep chest but it looked thin and, when it arrived at the camp, it was limping.

The dog first appeared at about two hours short of midday and contented itself with sniffing about first the latrine area, then where the rubbish was being piled up prior to its being buried in the ground and then it went and had a look at where the men were exercising and doing weapon training and this was where Germanicus first saw it, limping around the perimeter of the ring they had described in the dirt as being a sort of arena. The men doing sword practice in the arena shooed the dog away and, as it looked as if it were all too accustomed to such treatment, Germanicus felt sorry for it and called the dog to him by whistling softly to it.

The dog came over to the boy who was sitting on a stool, wrapped in the wolfskin because it was a chilly day, and the two regarded each other candidly for a few moments before the dog, making its mind up more quickly than Germanicus, put its paw on the boy's knee and looked at him with bright intelligent eyes. This was enough for the boy who immediately fell deeply in love with the animal and wished to keep it.

The dog looked hungry and Germanicus decided that he would find Felix to get some food for him so he set off in the direction of the clanging sounds and delicious smells. When he found Felix, the cook, covered in bits of feather was concentrating hard on plucking and gutting chickens and was surprised to see both Germanicus and the dog. Even though he knew the boy did not yet understand much of what he said, he felt moved to ask him what he was doing with a stray dog and Germanicus, well knowing what the gist of the question had been, showed him that he had adopted the dog by patting its neck and stroking its back while the dog, in whose life so far affection had been in short supply, wagged its tail furiously.

Germanicus then rubbed his belly with his hands indicating hunger and pointed to the dog trying to get Felix to understand that the dog was hungry and Felix, who knew about feeding all sorts of creatures as well as humans, saw for himself how thin the little animal was and, being a kind-hearted sort, stopped what he was doing and went to fetch some scraps of pig fat, skin and chitterlings which he threw on the ground in front of the dog.

Neither Felix nor Germanicus had seen anything disappear as quickly as the scraps so the cook went to get some more while the boy stroked the dog and made encouraging noises in its ear. Then Germanicus noticed that although the animal was clearly a dog, he had only one testicle but, although this might have mattered to some, it did not matter to Germanicus one bit.

Felix returned with more scraps and the dog dispatched them with the same rapidity while Germanicus looked on fondly as the little animal's eyes widened in disbelief at its good fortune.

Germanicus knew that if he were to be able to keep the dog, he would need Graecus's permission and felt that he would need to show that he could look after it so he begged a length of thin rope from one of the men and tied it round the dog's neck thus fashioning a crude collar and lead. That was the easy part – now he had to face Graecus having the twin disadvantages of not speaking his language and not knowing what his attitude to dogs might be.

As he was a straightforward child, Germanicus felt that an open approach would be best and he decided that he would seek Graecus when the men had their noonday meal when he would be more at his ease than when attending to his duties and would be in good spirits due to partaking of one of Felix's tasty dishes but it was still about an hour before the noonday so he took the dog for a walk around the camp's perimeter.

They had been wandering aimlessly for about a quarter of an hour when the little dog saw something in the woods beyond the camp's perimeter and Germanicus being a mite bored and, in any event, being a boy, decided to let the dog off its leash and observe events. Once freed from its constraint, the dog sped off into the undergrowth at an amazing pace and then stopped dead with its nose in the air, scenting its surroundings.

It stayed in that position for about thirty seconds and then was off again at breathtaking speed, this time running out of sight so that Germanicus was afraid that he had lost his new friend and was desolate at the thought when the dog reappeared with something in its jaws. The dog looked very proud as it approached Germanicus and dropped its prey at his feet before sitting on its haunches looking adoringly at its new owner.

Germanicus looked at what the animal had killed and was surprised to see a big buck hare which he picked up and examined carefully. There were no visible marks on the hare and no skin broken, so, as it might be good for the pot, pausing only to put the dog back on its lead, he went to look again for Felix to show it to him even though he knew Felix would be very busy.

Felix was indeed busy, red in the face, stirring something over a big fire but he smiled as the boy and the dog came into view as, truth to tell, he was now becoming fond of the boy and amused by his antics.

Germanicus went over to where Felix was stirring his concoction and showed him the buck hare. Felix, thinking that Germanicus had trapped it was about to congratulate him on his good work, but the boy pointed to the dog and by imitating a dog running fast and then catching something by the back of its neck and shaking it, indicated that the dog had caught the big hare. Felix was very impressed by this and smiling in an encouraging way, bent down to pat the dog and scratch his ears. The dog, thinking that truly his luck had turned, gave Felix his most winning look and wagged his tail thereby converting the cook to his cause.

It was now the noonday and the men were congregating in the middle of the camp, hovering about waiting for Felix to appear with their repast. There was the smell of sweat and leather, good natured banter, laughter, and the sound of voices deep in conversation as Graecus entered the scene looking, Germanicus was relieved to see from his vantage point behind a tree, as if he were in good spirits.

So far, so good but Germanicus thinking it best to wait until all the men were gathered together and Graecus had at least had something to eat before he made his appearance with his new friend, stayed behind the tree stroking the dog for a few minutes.

But by now his presence had been missed and the call had gone out for Germanicus so he had no choice but to appear complete with his scrap of a dog on the makeshift lead and go to sit at the table.

On seeing Germanicus, Graecus's face was a picture of competing emotions: on the one hand he was relieved that the child had appeared but on the other he was not pleased by the fact that the child now had a small, pathetic-looking, limping dog on a dirty bit of string.

As the Centurion struggled to master his thoughts, Felix appeared wreathed in smiles and made his way to the trestle table, pausing only to pat the dog on the way. Germanicus had seen the dark thoughts pass through Graecus's mind and felt that it would be harmful to his cause to say or do anything at this point so he just sat at the table quietly and, with as much nonchalance as can be mustered by a ten year old boy, ate his food, trying to foster the impression that it is a common occurrence for boys to find dogs in the course of the morning and bring them to the table as fully fledged pets at midday.

Graecus felt he had been manipulated and that his command had been undermined by this boy who, in such a short time, seemed to have taken over the camp and was pondering how to deal with the situation when his old friend Felix, sensing what was perturbing him, leaned over and said, 'He is a child still. He understands neither our language nor our ways but he has a good heart and he wishes to keep the dog. Can he not be allowed to have something of his own?'

Graecus was now ashamed of his earlier thoughts but was still unsure how to accommodate the animal without losing face and Felix, again reading his friend's thoughts, produced from under his apron the big buck hare saying to Graecus, 'Look here. This magnificent buck was killed by the dog this morning. It is cleanly killed and good for the pot. Is the Army so well-fed that it does not need more meat?'

Graecus knew when he was beaten; the dog would stay and be Germanicus's pet but also part of the century so, holding the dog by its lead with one hand and the big buck hare in the other, he said, 'Brothers, I present this animal to you and I welcome it to our ranks as 'Hunter-in-Chief'.

Germanicus did not know what was being said but he knew that the dog was his and could stay and he ran to Graecus and, much to Graecus's surprise, threw his arms around him. Litigiosus then asked what the dog would be named and Graecus said, 'As he is so small, his name will be Exiguus'.

So it was that a small, unremarkable limping dog became Exiguus of the Roman Army.

The days wore on becoming longer and warmer and Germanicus slowly settled into army life gradually becoming accustomed to its rhythms, nuances and ways. As Germanicus settled in so did the dog. Now that its limp had been cured by Magnus, it was having two square meals a day and was getting large amounts of love from Germanicus and attention from the men, it began to thrive and proved itself in its role as a hunter bringing in game which it had dispatched so carefully that it was always good for the pot.

Life for Germanicus began to acquire a discernible pattern and meaning. As a result of the Latin lessons he was having with Graecus, he was beginning to understand what was said to him and, haltingly at first, but with increasing confidence, he could reply in the language spoken by his companions.

The daily lessons took place sitting with Graecus under a tree with Zig ('Exiguus' was too long a name for a small dog) sitting beside them and Germanicus stroking Zig's ears for inspiration every time Graecus asked him a difficult question. The advantage of this was that the dog learned Latin as rapidly as the boy and was soon answering to commands of 'sede' (sit), 'remane' (stay), and 'adveni' (come).

Graecus was teaching him about Rome and its history so that

he would understand that being part of the Roman Army was an honourable calling and that helping to keep the '*Pax Romana*' was something in which any man could take a pride. Germanicus enjoyed these hours alone with Graecus who, although he could on occasion be a harsh taskmaster, treated him with patience, courtesy and understanding.

Felix also was taking part in the boy's education and was teaching him the secrets of his kitchen on the basis that there can never be too many good cooks in a camp. So Germanicus could sometimes be found peeling onions, chopping garlic, gutting game or plucking fowl and at other times he would be listening to Felix as he told him about the use and properties of different vegetables, herbs and spices and where they could be found either in nature or in the market-place.

Learning with Felix was a different matter from learning with Graecus as he was a more light-hearted character, much given to bursts of uproarious laughter interspersed with wheezing and coughing as, in his huge enjoyment of whatever joke it was he had just made, he would often inhale the smoke from the fire on which he had placed his pots.

And then came the incident of the mysterious fruit.

Felix had managed to acquire a dozen fruits very similar to those we nowadays call 'pineapple'. These were very precious to him as they were rare and he planned to use them in a special pudding as part of the banquet he was making in honour of the visit to the camp of a Roman Senator and his wife, and some other senior officers. So Felix was bustling about, whistling, singing, wheezing and coughing, entirely in his element because he was doing that at which he was best – creating a wonderful feast which would be the talk of the Legions and the crowning glory would be the pineapple puddings which would be spectac-ularly served in the actual pineapple shells, one for each of the twelve very important guests.

Germanicus, lessons over for the day, accompanied by Zig, whose nose was twitching excitedly at the sensational smells coming from the various pots and dishes, wandered into the field kitchen in search of Felix but Felix, busy discussing with Graecus what was to be the seating plan at the banquet, was nowhere to be seen so Germanicus began rooting around.

First he looked in the pans to see what was boiling, then he looked in the tins to see what was roasting, then he looked on the preparation slabs to see what else was being made ready and then he spotted the pineapples.

Not surprisingly, Germanicus had hitherto been ignorant of the existence of pineapples so he was astonished to see a host of them with their wonderfully green spiky hats and their glorious yellow and green criss-crossed skins. He approached with caution and something like awe thinking they might bite or spit at him but took a grip of himself and realised that they could not be harmful as they were in Felix's kitchen.

Then he became bold and picked up one of the strange beasts by its spiky hat, wondering at its weight and the prickliness of the spikes. He now felt brave enough to give the beast a quick sniff and was again surprised to find that it smelled sweet but with a sweetness different from any other sweetness he had experienced before. He gave it another sniff, but much deeper this time, trying to decide just what sort of smell this was. He then gave himself up to the sensation and stuck his nose right up to the diamond patterned skin and inhaled deeply of the heady perfume which makes the pineapple the 'King of Fruits'.

Germanicus was intrigued and very, very curious. What on earth could this strange and wondrous thing be? It was probably not an animal, it did not smell like a vegetable yet it was bigger than any fruit he had ever seen. He again weighed it in his hands and had another deep inhalation of its scent but was none the wiser, albeit more greatly intrigued and impatient to know what was inside the yellowy-green skin.

Since Germanicus had come to the camp, he had been encouraged to pursue his thirst for knowledge and had not been discouraged from eating anything. In fact, he had been rather spoiled by Felix who indulged the boy's appetite and loved to see dish after dish of food disappear down his throat like morning mist on a hot day. Germanicus may not, therefore, have been entirely to blame in thinking that it would not matter if he took a knife to this foodstuff and tried it for himself – after all, there were so many of them how could a person count them all and know how many there were?

So, without more ado, he took a knife and cut the beast in two to expose the juicy yellow flesh inside and immediately understood that it was a fruit. Now, emboldened by this discovery, he took one of the halves in his hand and licked the exposed flesh.

His tongue exploded with joy at the flavour so he licked it again and decided that he needed to take a slice and actually eat it which is what he did. Followed by another slice and another until he had eaten the half he had licked and was just starting on the second half when Felix returned to find Germanicus sitting on the ground with the butchered remains of one of his treasured pineapples scattered around him.

Poor Felix was horrified. Horrified to think that his plans for the important banquet had been ruined and horrified to think that he wanted to kill Germanicus with his bare hands for being so thoughtless and selfish. Germanicus, realising that Felix had returned saw the look of horror on his face and froze, the remaining half pineapple in one hand and the knife in the other. He saw that in some way he must have done a terrible thing in eating the pineapple and realised with a horrible lurch of his heart that he had hurt one of his best friends.

Felix had to pause and think what to do. Firstly, what should he do about Germanicus who had, unquestionably, behaved very badly and secondly what could he do about twelve very important guests and only eleven pineapples?

Well, as far as Germanicus was concerned, there was only one thing for it, he must take him to Graecus and tell him what had happened and, as their officer, he must decide what would be the best punishment and as far as the pineapple was concerned, that would have to wait until later. So he approached Germanicus who was still frozen in mid-gesture and silently beckoned him to rise to his feet and to follow him which

Germanicus meekly did followed by Zig who, ears back, knew that something was up.

They quickly found Graecus who saw the look on Felix's face and said, 'My friend, what in the name of the gods is wrong?'

Felix said, 'I found the boy eating one of my precious pineapples without permission and now my plans for the spectacular puddings for our banquet are ruined and I have no idea how I shall solve the problem.'

By now, Germanicus's understanding of Latin was good enough to know that he had transgressed badly – he understood the words 'without permission' and began to comprehend what he had done. Graecus was looking grave and his grey eyes were troubled when he turned and spoke to him saying slowly so that the boy would understand, 'You have heard what Felix has said, do you wish to deny this?' and on seeing Germanicus shake his head he continued, 'You have today behaved not in accordance with the standards we expect of you. You have behaved selfishly and dishonestly in taking something which was not yours and in preventing Felix, who has always treated you with kindness, from properly showing his prowess as a cook, you have dishonoured him'

Germanicus, whose earlier life had been lived among people whose philosophy could most neatly be described as 'every man for himself', could not bear this; he was stricken to the core by the words 'selfish', 'dishonest' and 'dishonour' as he knew enough by now to know that putting one's comrades before oneself and treating them with honour were cornerstones of discipline and good order in the Roman Army.

He had failed; he had failed the very people who had probably saved his life. He felt ashamed and all the more so because Graecus's words were spoken not in anger but in sorrow and disappointment. He did not know what to do so he did what he had always done in the past...............he ran.

He ran out of the camp, past the barricaded rampart and ditch, down the hill, followed by Zig whose ears were pinned flat to his head. As he ran, hot tears of self admonishment coursed down his cheeks and splashed on the turf beneath and as he ran he kept on asking himself how he could have thought that it was acceptable to take the pineapple. He ran and ran and kept on asking this question until he had run out of breath and had exhausted himself with grief.

Germanicus fell to the ground and lay with his face in the grass and the dust while Zig licked the back of his neck.

Meanwhile, at the camp, Graecus having thought about following the boy and having decided that he should have time to contemplate the consequences of his actions, went with Felix to see if anything could be done to save the century's culinary reputation. Back at his post, the cook, surveying the wreckage of the pineapple, quickly saw that one half of it remained intact and calculated that it would be possible to serve part of each pudding to each of the dozen guests in half a pineapple shell if he put the rest in the middle of the table in a dish which he could decorate with the remaining shells.

The afternoon wore on and Graecus was torn between wanting to go and look for Germanicus as he wished to know that he was safe, and wanting to teach him a lesson. The later and the nearer to darkness it got, the more he was tempted to try to find the boy but he kept reminding himself that he was a formidable fighter and had Zig with him so he should stick to his principles.

Graecus was becoming more and more frantic as the shadows lengthened as it would soon be time for the guests to appear and he would not himself be able to search for Germanicus. Delicious smells were coming from Felix's pots and dishes and the rest of the camp was in a mood of expectation, keen to set eyes on the Senator and his wife and the high ranking officers but the much vaunted feast was turning to ashes in Graecus's mouth because he so wanted the child to return in one piece.

Graecus stood at the side of one of the camp fires turning over in his mind time and again whether he should have said something different in his condemnation of the boy's behaviour and concluding each time that he said the correct thing.

Then he turned his attention to all the changes which had recently happened in his life........feeling that it had been enriched by the sudden addition of the child...... how it could not be the same again without him and.........how it was unlikely that he would ever have children of his own and...... was that a good thing and.........what is the meaning of life? By now, Graecus was so distraught that he did not hear the small feet running into the camp and the soft sound of the dog's paws in the dust so when he looked up he was surprised to see Germanicus standing in front of him.

The relief crossing Graecus's face was enough to tell the boy that he was truly valued and it was with gratitude that he knelt before the man who had saved his life and given him a code of honour by which to live the life thus saved. Germanicus knelt and in the best Latin he could muster said to Graecus, 'Domine, I am sorry that I have let you down. I ask for your forgiveness'.

Graecus gently raised the boy to his feet and said, 'You are forgiven', and seeing the look of thankfulness and respect on Germanicus's face, in that moment, he realised that something terrifying and wonderful and entirely unlooked-for had happened – he had become a father.

CHAPTER THREE

Graecus now needed time to think and he told Germanicus that he should go and help Felix prepare the banquet.

Alone, Graecus tried to understand his feelings and spent some time examining these new sensations. This was uncharted territory and it was necessary for him to look at the situation from several angles before he could identify what he felt. Then he decided that it was joy. It was joy because he had never dared hope that he, fatherless as he was, would himself become a father and, once he had decided that this was his true reaction to recent events, his heart felt lighter than it had done in many a year and, smiling to himself, he turned his attention to the other major worry of the day.

But he need not have worried for Felix was in the thick of it, stirring pots, tasting dishes with a spoon, raking the fires, chopping herbs and generally being the calm cook he was while infusing the situation with his great good humour, laughing and wheezing all the time.

Germanicus was sitting on a little stool with Zig at his side watching intently as Felix bustled about. From the look of affection on the boy's face, it was clear that he and Felix had made their peace and normal relations had been restored. Satisfied that Felix had everything under control, Graecus ruffled Germanicus's hair and went to oversee the setting up of the dining table and the lighting of the torches.

Going to the centre of the camp, where six men were working putting together the large trestle table which would be tonight's dining table, here Graecus encountered Impedimentus, the century's Baggage Master, who was struggling to carry two large pieces of wood which when lashed together would form one half of the large table.

Graecus greeted him warmly as they were old comrades and Graecus knew that, just as he relied on Felix to make sure that his men were well-fed, Impedimentus was one of the men on whom he relied to ensure that they were well-equipped as it was his job to look after all the century's equipment. So it fell to Impedimentus to make sure that there were enough beds, cooking pots, tables, blankets, spoons, knives, cups, dishes, etc, as well as all the other things that an itinerant army needs together with enough vehicles and beasts of burden to carry the baggage from one place to another.

Alone among his comrades in the century, Impedimentus was a pure Roman, having been seconded to this auxiliary cohort for operational reasons. He had been born in the Imperial City thirty years before and his wavy black hair, coal black eyes and olive skin were testament to this proud ancestry. In contrast with the rest of his comrades for whom Rome was an embodiment of an ideal, for Impedimentus it was very real – he constantly received news of home from his family, travellers and visitors and, in doing so, learned much about the daily politics of the city and about changes in its fashionable circles.

Graecus was not interested in politics, he was far too simple a man to involve himself in a pit of vipers and preferred to leave matters of state to those who liked the sound of their own voice rather more than he did, so he was not especially attentive when Impedimentus began to talk to him about the Senator, Tarquinius Pompeius Rubicundus, who was to be their guest that evening.

Impedimentus loved to gossip and had recently seen one of his distant cousins who had given him news of Rome which was only two months old and he was anxious to tell Graecus what he had learned about the Senator, 'He is not from one of the old families. Indeed, he is one of that new breed who have entered public life through being rich. He made his money from property investments in the overcrowded parts of the city where the plebs live and has risen to prominence by sponsoring some of the Games and Circuses which keep the mob amused.'

Graecus grunted at this, thinking to himself that he would probably not have much in common with the Senator and responded to Impedimentus by saying, 'Yes, obviously he has not experienced military life for himself and it is necessary for his political advancement to have a working knowledge of the Army, so Rubicundus is having to tour some of its outlying posts. I hear that he's bringing his wife.'

Impedimentus's face now broke into the grin which usually signalled that he was about to impart a particularly juicy piece of gossip and this occasion was no exception as he proceeded to tell Graecus about the Senator's wife, Drusilla.

'Oh yes, I've heard *all* about her.' said Impedimentus and stopped what he was doing before continuing, 'Well, it is a matter of record that she is the daughter of a fishmonger from the wrong side of the city and that she was very lucky to marry the ambitious young Rubicundus who was a cut above her in the social stakes. Her good luck continued when he demonstrated a genius for making money and a name for himself. To be fair, she performed her part of the bargain by producing four strapping sons and a daughter. But now it's said that there are many in Rome who could strap a pair of the cuckold's horns to Rubicundus's head and that he occupies himself with slave girls and ladies of the night.'

Graecus nodded wearily at this but Impedimentus took it as encouragement and went breathlessly on, 'Clearly, it's not love which binds them together but an ambition for power, status and money which each realises will more easily be achieved with the other as an ally rather than an enemy. It is said that Rubicundus is henpecked but that is not exactly true; he is in thrall to his wife because he is too weak to control her but he does have his own interests and sometimes it suits him to allow her to think she has the upper hand'.

Hearing all of this through half closed ears, Graecus's heart sank – he had proved himself in battle many times but he was not good at making small talk with people whose main interests were self advancement and politics. It was going to be a long evening.

By this stage, the men had assembled the big table and had put chairs around it – these had been borrowed from the main camp nearby and were the Legion's best as were the good plates, cups, flagons and dishes which were now being placed on the table. Other soldiers had been busy lighting the torches and were putting them in the ground around the dining area and, as they finished their work, Graecus stood for a few moments thinking that they had done a good job and that it all looked very handsome with the torch light glinting off the metal objects on the table and the soft light giving everything a glow.

All that now remained was for Graecus to make himself presentable and for the guests to arrive. Graecus's toilette was thorough without being elaborate – he washed his face and hands in a basin of clean water and scrubbed at his teeth with a twig specially cut for the purpose and a paste prepared by Magnus but he knew he was a well-made man in the peak of health and that he looked impressive in his soldier's garb. As he tweaked the fastening of his scarlet cloak at his shoulder, he heard the sound of horses' hooves and knew it must be the guests arriving.

There was one face among the arrivals which was very welcome – that of Flavius, who had been in command of the nearby Legion some years before, a man in his mid-forties, greying at the temples and a soldier to his fingertips – a General of the old school for whom it would be anathema to treat an honourable enemy with disrespect. Flavius was a soldier's soldier. Unlike many of his rank he had risen through the Legions on merit. He was thus a great favourite with all the men who would follow him straight to the Underworld if that was what he ordered them to do.

Although not a Roman, Flavius was an Italian and had entered military life as a career because he was unlikely to inherit a fortune, but he had found that the open air life suited him and he had proved to be intelligent, courageous and a great leader. Unlike some of his colleagues who contrived to live a life of luxury even on the battlefield, Flavius was renowned for never asking his men to undertake or tolerate anything he would not do himself – a principle which Graecus much admired and himself practised to a minute degree. Graecus was, therefore, light of heart as he stepped forward to greet him, clasping him warmly by the hand interlacing his fingers with those of Flavius so that they were interlocked in the fashion which was peculiar to

Graecus's cohort and a representation of which appeared on his century's Standard. Graecus and Flavius exchanged warm smiles and the General clapped Graecus on the shoulder several times laughing and exclaiming that it was good to see one of Rome's most trusted and reliable Centurions.

Then the Senator and his lady descended from their chariot and Flavius turned to face them to give them the proper precedence in accordance with their rank. As they approached Flavius, Graecus was able to have a good look at these visitors who were the first important Roman civilians he had seen in a long time.

Sadly, Graecus was not impressed. Tarquinius Pompeius Rubicundus was aptly named, being very red in the face on account of being very portly and somewhat out of breath as if he, not the horses, had drawn the chariot. He was probably about forty but looked older because of his bad posture and little piggy eyes lost in the folds of his fat cheeks. He was, however, of above average height which lent him some dignity and did have a warm smile which was more than could be said for his wife.

Drusilla was very short and, from what Graecus could see in the torchlight, was not enjoying her visit to the camp as, although it could be said that she was smiling, her smile was a death's head grimace. She was wearing a hooded cloak, which even to Graecus's unpractised eye, looked to be of the finest wool and the dress underneath was similarly a manifestation of her husband's wealth.

More horses arrived carrying the other military guests and Flavius now turned to Rubicundus and asked if he could introduce him to one of Rome's best Centurions, gesturing to Graecus to come forward. Graecus mustering his most diplomatic phrases, said, 'Senator, I and my men are greatly honoured to have such distinguished guests at our humble camp' and Rubicundus, who was, after all, a politician, took this in good grace.

Flavius then turned to Drusilla, saying, 'Graecus is also one of our most chivalrous officers and I know that you will feel safe being protected by such a gallant young man.'

Graecus was perfectly capable of playing his part as the

ladies' man and, leaning low over her hand, he assured her of his utmost attention. As he rose, his nostrils were assailed by the exotic scent coming from her bosom which, he noticed was somewhat exposed by her low cut dress but which, although well-supported, was surprisingly meagre. Graecus was now looking into Drusilla's face and, seeing that she liked looking into his face, wished that he could return the compliment.

Graecus gave Drusilla his best smile and hoped that it looked genuine enough but, in reality, his heart was not in it as what he saw, when he looked her fully in the face, was – there is no other word for it – evil.

She was about thirty-five with glittering brown eyes which were darting about all over Graecus drinking in the details of his person. Her smile now changed from one of sufferance to one of concupiscent appreciation, looking at Graecus as if he were a juicy piece of meat. Graecus collected himself and said, 'My lady, you will, indeed be safe out here in the woods as I and my men are at your disposal.'

The other military guests were assembling and Flavius busied himself making introductions. As he had been in the Army for many years, Graecus knew most of the other men but there were two officers who were new to him: Marcus Severinus Romanus and Gnaeus Claudius Verus. Impedimentus knew of them, however, and had told Graecus that although Romanus was a patrician Verus was an equites which meant that his family were of the new, rising and politically important merchant class who were now taking over many of the powerful positions from the older, landed patricians.

These men were introduced to Graecus by Flavius who told them, 'You will need to work hard to be better soldiers than this Centurion and you can learn much from him.' Romanus took this in good part, smiling at the Flavius's obvious affection for Graecus but Verus gave the older soldiers a withering sideways glance and Graecus allowed himself to reflect that, with his soft face and delicate looking white hands, Verus could not really be cut out for a life of active soldiery.

It was now time to sit at table and Flavius took Drusilla's arm to guide her to her place next to him with Verus at her other hand. Rubicundus was next to Graecus who had Romanus on his other side. All were now seated and it was time for Felix to demonstrate his genius. Drusilla let down the hood of her cloak and Graecus was astonished to see that her hair was blonde.

He was astonished because he knew that Drusilla was a true Roman but it was unheard of for a true Roman to have blonde hair and, covertly, insofar as he decently could and insofar as the torchlight allowed, he looked carefully at her hair only to see that its colour was due to art rather than nature. In fact, on this closer inspection, it became clear that whatever process had been used to produce this effect had tortured the hair into a dull brittle mass whilst leaving the roots their more usual colour. Graecus wondered what it was that made women do this to themselves and thought that it may have been that female slaves from Germania were now popular in Rome and that jealous wives wished to copy their blonde beauty.

He was thus occupied when Drusilla looked in his direction and, seeing him looking at her, misinterpreted his interest and gave him a wide lascivious smile but Graecus immediately realised what she was thinking and, disconcerted, looked quickly away.

The first dish arrived. Felix came proudly to the table bearing a dish containing honey roasted dormice, which, he had been reliably informed by Impedimentus, were nowadays a very popular delicacy in Rome. Flavius was delighted to see such an elegant dish for the important guests and there were appreciative sounds from all around the table except Drusilla who appeared bored and Verus who reviewed the dish with a contemptuous sneer.

The next dish was a soup of vegetables flavoured with *garum*, the fermented fish sauce which was much prized by Roman cuisine for its salty flavour and the body it gave to any foodstuff. The soup was again acclaimed by the guests apart from Drusilla and Verus but, Graecus noticed, even though the young officer appeared to think that the food was beneath his sophisticated palate, he ate heartily enough – indeed, he had gobbled the dormice with such rapidity that Graecus had had time to eat only one of the sweetened little bodies before the dish was empty.

Felix and his helpers danced attention on their guests, filling wine cups, bringing more bread, taking away empty platters and, taking their lead from their General, all the while, exuding good humour and camaraderie.

Rubicundus was asking questions about the cohort and Flavius was telling him about its organisation and its history. Just as Graecus was tuning his ears to try to hear what Flavius was saying to Rubicundus, the General tried to draw Drusilla into the conversation and Graecus heard him tell her, 'Madam, I know that you will be interested to know that the motto of this cohort 'Omnibus in Unum' means many things. On the one hand, it means that the men in the cohort are united in their loyalty to Rome, it also means that they are united in their loyalty to the cohort and each other – it is only by being able to rely fully on the man next to him that a soldier can go into battle with the stout heart necessary for doing his best.'

Despite being the wife of an ambitious Senator, Drusilla was clearly not moved by any of this – she yawned openly during Flavius's speech but Romanus leaned forward and asked about the cohort's peculiar greeting and was delighted by the enthusiastic explanation that the handclasp where each man, palms down, interlocks his fingers with those of the other, was yet another illustration of the motto because such a clasp, uniting the hands is almost unbreakable and demonstrates that unity is strength.

While this conversation was continuing, Drusilla and Verus were exchanging conspiratorial glances and gossip about Rome interspersed with giggles, silly voices and exchanges made behind their hands. Graecus, hoping it did not show on his face, viewed this with distaste; he was unaccustomed to soldiers who were such overt politicians and thought that a young man from a good-enough Roman family should have better things to do than flirt with a lowly born, over-scented, over-painted woman even if she were married to a Senator.

The next dish arrived. Jugged hare. It would probably have surprised the soldiers at the table and it would, no doubt, have horrified Drusilla to know that the three hare in the dish had been killed by Zig but it was the case and, with the little animal's customary care, he had ensured that the skin was unbroken and that the hare were perfect, albeit dead, when he had presented them to Germanicus.

Felix uncovered the dish of hare. Graecus saw Drusilla turn up her nose at what was revealed and saw that Felix saw her expression and his heart went out to his friend who had worked so hard. Verus intercepted Graecus's look but kept to himself his thoughts about these people whose outmoded ideas about military honour and trust were not in step with the ambitions of the new merchant class who were coming to power in the Empire.

Flavius served Drusilla with a portion of the jugged hare and then passed some to Rubicundus who began happily to eat but Drusilla amused herself with more whispered exchanges with Verus while so ignoring the food before her that it was cleared away untasted.

Graecus now had to answer the call of nature and, catching Flavius's eye and signalling that that was his intention, he rose from the table and walked steadily to a convenient point out of earshot of the party, the latrines being too far away.

Pausing only to gauge the brightness of the moon and the angle of trajectory sufficient to ensure that he did not wet his feet, Graecus had just taken firmly hold of his member and let out the small sigh of relief which often accompanies the beginning of the flow, when his enjoyment of the moment was shattered by a low female voice at his elbow, 'Soldier, if you would let me hold your member then it will be more interesting for us both'.

This posed Graecus with two problems – the first being to know what to do in response to this surprising statement and the second was to avoid pissing on his sandals which were still quite new.

Graecus was accustomed to thinking quickly on his feet in battle but, in those circumstances, he was not normally holding his member and having a piss. Various thoughts passed swiftly through his mind, some of them involving turning and pissing on the lady's sandals, but all of them were impractical, so he decided to try to make light of the situation.

Keeping his back to her, he said, 'My lady, I fear that if you were to take hold of my member, I should be unable to continue to relieve myself and I am sure that you do not wish me to suffer discomfort'.

Graecus hoped that this would be a sufficient hint to Drusilla that he was not willing to play her game but he had underestimated her boldness and the thickness of her skin and she replied, 'Soldier, it is our mutual comfort and delight which I seek,' while moving her hand round to try to grasp his member.

This was too much for Graecus who was taken aback at her effrontery and the thought that he actually might piss on her feet, so with a startled cry he pushed her away with his free hand whilst saying sternly, 'Madam, you forget yourself'.

It is possible that Drusilla had never been denied a man's attentions before, it is also possible that she was humiliated by being rejected by a soldier, it is also possible that she wished to avenge herself of some marital peccadillo but whatever her state of mind, her response to Graecus was terrifying as she turned to face him, curling her lip, and snarled, 'Soldier, you have just made a very large error of judgement. How dare you think that you can turn me down! Who do you think you are? I can and I will make very sure that you will regret this moment'.

Then she turned on her heel and walked away with such pounding steps that her heavy ornate sandals threw up little clouds of dust in the moonlight and her dress billowed behind her.

Graecus was left holding the offending member, the free flow from which he had been enjoying now sadly interrupted, and as he stood there he pondered the power of the rage of a scorned woman and hoped that time would soften the wound. As he cheered himself with this thought, the flow of urine recommenced and he was able to finish the job for which he had left the table but it was with a sense of unease that he re-approached the happy party.

As Graecus sat, Flavius asked him about the newest addition to the camp saying that he had heard that the century had acquired a blonde haired German boy who was a formidable fighter. Graecus, relieved that the conversation had returned to an uncontroversial subject, felt free to speak of the unusual circumstances of the boy's recruitment and to speak warmly of his talents, telling the General proudly of the boy's exploits and how he was learning both the arts of warfare and Latin with great aptitude. Rubicundus overheard this and said, 'Oh, this is just the sort of thing I like to hear. These are the real stories which my colleagues in Rome love to know about. I would like to see the boy. Can he be brought to us?'

Graecus felt that this would not be a good idea as it would mean rousing the child from his bed but he could think of no good reason why to deny the Senator's request so he dispatched Felix to bring Germanicus to meet the important guests.

In the meantime, Drusilla, no doubt smarting from Graecus's rebuff, was paying exaggerated attention to Gnaeus Claudius Verus who was regaling her with stories of life among Rome's noble families and the closeness of his cousin, Septimus Pomponius, to persons who had the ear of the Emperor, Nero. As the young man whispered to her, Drusilla's shrill laughter filled the night air and rang through Graecus's head driving out his thoughts.

Felix had hurried away in search of Germanicus and returned within minutes leading the child into the torch lit circle by his arm. Clad in his cream linen nightshirt (which had, in fact, been one of Graecus's but cut down to accommodate Germanicus's shorter legs) the child looked like an angel.

Felix had tried to smooth down Germanicus's unruly hair with spit moistened palms but had had little success – although as the boy stood there blinking the sleep from his eyes, his blonde hair shining in the soft light, he looked the perfect image of a holy child.

Germanicus was not in any way afraid of these strangers as he knew he was with those who protected him so he stood his ground staring openly, one might even have said brazenly at them. Flavius liked the child's steady gaze and gestured to him to come forward so Germanicus approached the General, who he knew was a very important person in the Army and gave him his best smile, which, as he had not yet grown all his adult teeth, was somewhat incomplete but nevertheless very charming and the old soldier was, indeed, charmed.

Flavius now addressed Germanicus in simple Latin asking him how he liked the Army, how he liked the camp and how he passed his days and Germanicus calmly said, 'Sir, I can think of no better life than to be in Graecus's century in the Roman Army. I am learning Latin and all about weapons and warfare and Felix is teaching me how to cook.'

The adults had listened to the boy in silence but there was laughter at this, especially from Flavius and Graecus and it may have been this that encouraged Germanicus to walk round the table to stand next to Drusilla.

Drusilla was mildly flattered by the child's attention as he seemed to have become the General's little pet and yet here he was conspicuously preferring to pay court to her so she smiled at him in what she thought was a suitably encouraging manner.

Unfortunately, Germanicus's education had not yet included the study of the female psyche with particular reference to vanity, so perhaps he may have been excused from not knowing that a woman's hair is her crowning glory.

Or perhaps he did know this and felt that Drusilla's hair did not pass muster for he moved closer to her and, taking a strand of her hair in his fingers, he inspected it keenly – firstly with a look of curiosity on his face, then disbelief and then, to Graecus's horror, amusement.

It was then clear to Graecus and, he assumed to Drusilla and everyone else at the table, that what Germanicus had thought was that her hair was a new type of hair that he had not seen before but that, once he had touched it, he had realised that it was achieved by artifice and, in the way children have of honestly expressing what adults do not dare to say, he had expressed his disbelief that a person should wish so to torture her hair.

Germanicus was now openly laughing at Drusilla's hair and the tableau of him, with his unruly but nevertheless beautiful blonde hair, holding the tawdry locks while the men fell silent in fear at her reaction was to be etched on Graecus's mind forever.

As it dawned on Drusilla what was the cause of the child's laughter, she firstly froze then grew very red in the face, redder in fact than her husband, then she squared her fat shoulders and setting her head forward on her short fat neck, in a voice straight from the Underworld but via the fish market, she bellowed, 'Get that fucking kid away from me!'

Germanicus beginning to realise that something was amiss and that it may have something to do with him, unceremoniously dropped Drusilla's hair and ran to stand next to Graecus who, bearing in mind his earlier exchange with Drusilla, wished for just a moment that the child had chosen someone else for his refuge but, remembering that he was in effect the boy's guardian, he collected himself and calmly told Germanicus that it was time for him to return to bed and asked Felix to take him away.

An uncomfortable silence followed in which the men at the table, some of whom wore many honourable battle scars, did not dare look at Drusilla whose rage could be felt pulsating through the thin night air. It fell to her husband, a braver man than he looked, to break the silence by saying that he had heard that Felix had prepared a very special pudding and it was surely now time to enjoy it. Flavius and Graecus enthusiastically nodded their agreement to this and Graecus signalled to one of the men attending them to fetch the pudding.

In fact it was Felix who brought the puddings proudly bearing them in their half pineapple shells on a big platter with the dish containing the second helpings in the middle.

The men all exclaimed at the sight of the puddings and Felix looked very pleased at their appreciation of his efforts but if Graecus thought that this dish would lighten Drusilla's mood he was mistaken for she sat immobile with such a look of disgust on her face that it might have been imagined that a bowl of steaming excrement had been placed before her. Taking his lead from Drusilla, Verus also looked down his Roman nose at the pudding but Flavius and Rubicundus began to eat theirs and were soon praising the flavour and the texture of the dish and congratulating Felix on its excellence.

At last the banquet was over and the guests were ready to leave. Paradoxically, as things had turned out so badly, Graecus was dreading this moment as he did not know whether to try to apologise to Drusilla or whether it would make matters worse. He decided that it was best not to say any more and so, in bidding her farewell, he contented himself with bending low over her hand but she, a woman well-versed in the keeping of a grudge, as he bent, whispered to him, 'Do not think, Centurion, that I shall forget you or your blonde boy. I have ways of heaping curses on your heads'.

Graecus shivered as she said this as he knew she meant it and that, in her own way, she was a woman with great power.

Flavius, sensing that Drusilla had said something vengeful to Graecus, in giving him his goodbye, held him by the arm and said quietly to him, 'Do not be harsh with the boy. He is unaccustomed to the ways of ladies from Rome and their vanities. There is something unusual about that boy. He is a fine lad and will be a fine soldier, look after him well – Rome will require some truly honourable soldiers in the coming years.'

As the chariots and the horses took the guests away and the sound of the wheels and the hooves disappeared into the night, Graecus was left pondering the events of this most disastrous of evenings and, perhaps most disturbing of all, Flavius's words concerning Rome's need for truly honourable soldiers.

Graecus felt that it was a great pity that the banquet in which he and Felix had invested so much, had turned out so badly – all due to the vainglory of a fishmonger's daughter from the wrong side of the Tiber and, with an involuntary shudder, that she was a woman who would make a bad enemy.

'Still', he thought, as he removed his tunic, 'I need never see her again'.

CHAPTER FOUR

Life went on. For Germanicus, there was much to learn. His Latin lessons with Graecus continued. With Zig at his side, he learned the declensions of the nouns and conjugations and all the tenses of the verbs, he learned the correct use of the subjunctive, the deponent verbs and the ablative absolute and he very quickly became fluent in the language.

Graecus was amazed at the boy's progress as his vocabulary grew at an astonishing rate and he, who was something of a pedagogue, thoroughly enjoyed his role as schoolmaster as it enabled him to expound on two of his favourite subjects – grammar and syntax. There are not many people for whom Latin Grammar holds a fascination but Graecus was one of these happy few as he appreciated its logic and clarity and he loved being able to impart this to such an enthusiastic and eager pupil.

Germanicus also enjoyed these lessons and loved speaking the new language. Indeed, with all the zeal of the convert, Germanicus became quite garrulous and could often be seen chattering away to the men in his bright clear voice as they listened patiently with an avuncular interest to whatever tale he was telling.

In fact, it became something of a problem for Germanicus was often stopping the men from getting on with their work and sometimes, if they saw him coming, they had to hide from him so that they would not have to listen to long, windy tales of Zig's exploits and what a good hunter he was or what Felix was teaching him to do in the kitchen or what so and so had said.

Germanicus was clearly a sociable soul and had probably never had the chance before in his life to chatter to people in this way – it seemed as if he had not spoken in his life before and there was a huge dam of language which had burst giving out this torrent of words which, although intelligible and fluent, were not necessarily fascinating to his increasingly small audience.

Graecus had noticed that the men sometimes tried to avoid him and had seen the glazed look in the eyes of those who had been subjected to one of Germanicus's longer stories and decided that he must explain to the boy that sometimes one must listen and it is good manners to let others have their say. Graecus explained this as gently as he could as he did not wish to discourage the boy's obvious desire to be friendly to everyone in the century and was pleased that he understood the mild rebuke and took it in good part.

Graecus also explained that in the century it was necessary to live in harmony with the other men as each man needed to be able to entrust his life to the man standing next to him and that having respect for each other was a vital part of maintaining that harmony. In saying this to him, Graecus was encouraging Germanicus to put other people before himself and to see that the morale of the century depended on no man being more important than any other and that each man depended on his colleagues as they depended on him.

At the same time, he was learning some basic arithmetic from Graecus who figured that if Germanicus thought that no-one would miss one pineapple out of a dozen then it was time that the boy learned how to count. There was also the reason that, if the boy were to be a good soldier, it was essential to know how to count as it was necessary to be able to check supplies, deal with money, know how many enemy there were etc. etc.

So Graecus could be found scratching numerals in the dust with a stick and Germanicus would sit scratching his head or Zig's ears as he tried to understand the unruly figures. Graecus soon found that Germanicus was a much more apt pupil when it came to words. In fact, the boy seemed to be incapable of understanding the decimal system and although he was willing to learn, he had no sympathy with numbers and Graecus would watch his face grow dark when he reached for the stick and the relief in his face when the lesson was over and he would bound away into the trees with Zig at his side, eager to bring back some game for the pot.

Both teacher and pupil began to dread these lessons and Graecus despaired of his ability to teach this subject until, one day, Felix who was passing by and saw the look of fearful incomprehension on Germanicus's face, had the idea of making the dusty numbers actually relate to something real and went to his stores and came back with a pouch full of dried beans.

The effect was dramatic. From not understanding the meaning of numbers and not seeing the point of them, in having them in columns of ten and moving them from one column to another, Germanicus quickly saw what was happening when ten became twenty and twenty became thirty and thirty became forty and so on and this realisation gave him some understanding of the subject so that it became easier for Graecus to teach him and to go on to the rudiments of geometry which was also needed as soldiers often needed to dig earthworks to secure the perimeter of the camp and were sometimes called upon to build roads and bridges.

Graecus was relieved that Germanicus was able to understand the mathematics he was teaching him, even if he did not enjoy the work as, in other respects he was such a keen student and had the makings of an officer. In his quiet moments, Graecus gave this much thought and realised how proud he would be if this boy were to rise through the ranks.

There was also the matter of cleanliness – Graecus was almost fanatically clean and insisted that his men follow his example. In support of this fanaticism, Graecus had sound reasons. For example, he required his men to look after their teeth using specially shaped twigs to clean them with the paste prepared by Magnus and Graecus's reason was that soldiers with toothache are less effective than soldiers with sound teeth.

Similarly, he required his men to have clean bodies as they were thereby less likely to catch diseases and, in any event, they would be less likely to attract unwanted attention. Indeed, if Graecus saw that one of his men was less than clean, the errant soldier would be subject to Graecus's withering comment, 'Sextus (or Septimus) (or Quintus), go wash yourself, the enemy will smell you long before they can see you'. He also required that his men be clean shaven and have short hair for the good reason that helmets can be lost in combat and facial hair and long hair can be caught hold of by an enemy who is then much better able to slit a throat or stab a neck.

Germanicus had been the dirtiest child imaginable but was

now transformed into an angelic presence by virtue of being taught how to keep himself clean.

And Graecus took steps to see that all his men were very well turned out with uniforms free of dust and with gleaming metal-work – he reckoned that, even though they were auxiliaries, his men were the best in the Roman Army and he wanted them to feel justly proud of that fact; it was all part of being a confident, efficient fighting force.

The men were also fit and strong as Graecus personally saw to it that they took exercise every day; he designed these exercises and supervised them so that the men did them correctly. What Graecus wished to achieve was that the men had superb balance and this bal-ance could be achieved by strengthening the middle body.

As a young soldier, Graecus had observed gymnasts training their bodies; he saw that their steadiness was achieved by having good balance based on a strong middle body achieved by con-stant working of the abdominal muscles and he insisted that his men followed this method by rolling backwards and forwards over barrels with their hands behind their heads.

The men good naturedly followed Graecus in this and did appreciate that it made them better fighters and safer in battle but, on occasions, for example, after a large meal the night before, especially when accompanied by much wine and beer, these exercises for the belly would be set to the music of men farting. This would be the cause of much mirth but no-one would wish to be next to Pneumaticus who could be relied upon to pro-duce wind of the most noisome kind.

Graecus greatly valued Pneumaticus as a soldier and as a man but his intestinal disturbances began to be the cause of com-plaints from the other men.

Within the Roman army a century was divided into 'contu-bernia' or messes of eight men who ate together, slept together, fought together and, sometimes, died together. The reason for this togetherness was that for the most part it gave the men a great sense of loyalty to each other and fostered a relationship akin to brotherhood among the members of any *contubernium*. In every century then, there would usually be ten contubernia and a century mostly comprised rather fewer than one hundred men. As a Centurion, Graecus took great care in deciding which men should comprise a contubernium and sought to balance different personalities, skills and fighting qualities within each group. Sometimes there would be problems and a man would need to be moved from one mess to another but, normally, Graecus's men were contented soldiers and were happy to be in his century.

But now arose the unusual problem of Pneumaticus and his wind. Well, Pneumaticus had always had wind, that was why he had been given his name and his tendency to trumpet had been regarded as a something of a manly virtue but, for some weeks his eruptions had been particularly vicious and, on occasions, downright poisonous, so much so that Graecus, having received various complaints, had been forced to move him from the contubernium he had been living in for the last three years and put him in his own tent with Germanicus, Felix, Impedimentus, Illyricus, Litigiosus and Magnus. This was all well and good but, as the farts got worse and worse, even Zig would move away and the men could not bear it any longer. And, there was another problem – Pneumaticus snored.

Something had to be done or they would all be gassed in their beds as they lay awake listening for the next snore, so Graecus decided to ask Magnus if there was anything he could do.

The opportunity to have a quiet word with his colleague soon arose when Pneumaticus was out of the way and Magnus was sitting on his bed in their tent mixing herbs for one of the soldiers who had earache so Graecus sat opposite him and said, 'Brother, there is an urgent subject on which I require your assistance. I am acutely aware of the fact that Pneumaticus is poisoning our air and I cannot put up with it any more. I am sure that you and our other brothers in the tent feel similarly injured by these vapours and I wish to know if there is a potion for his disgusting farts and a cure for his snoring'.

The ever helpful and knowledgeable Magnus knew immediately what to advise for the farting and said, 'The answer for the farts is a mixture of peppermint oil and charcoal but I have none of the oil at present and I can think of no answer for the snoring'.

Graecus knew that there would be a rebellion from his closest colleagues if nothing were done so he agreed with Magnus that he would go the next day into the little town and buy some of the peppermint oil so that the potion could be made up the following evening. Then Germanicus came into the tent and, on hearing that there was to be a journey into the town the following day, he asked if he could come as he wished to see his friend, Aoif, who would have given birth some time before. So it was agreed that the Centurion and the boy would go to the town and, because Zig went everywhere with the boy, the dog would go too.

They set off as soon as it was fully daylight and made an interesting sight – the tall, lean dark man, the sturdy blonde boy and the little dog which, after months of good food, plenty of hunting in the fresh air and many hours of Germanicus's loving attention, was far from the pathetic, wounded beast they had first seen and was now a glossy, muscular, surefooted and handsome animal with a spring in its step.

As they walked, Zig snuffled at the ground and kept his ears cocked for the sound of something to kill. The sun rose in the sky and the man and the boy proudly watched the dog as he lifted his head and sniffed the air, his nose twitching at the different scents. The day was warm and bright and Germanicus whistled as he covered the dry ground. In making this first journey back to the town since he had been taken into the Roman camp, he felt a sense of adventure coupled with deep gratitude that he now had a sense of truly belonging somewhere and that, for the first time as far back as he could remember, he mattered.

Graecus was similarly thoughtful as he strode along for this morning's walk gave him unaccustomed time to himself. The past few months had been among the most challenging of his life but also the most valuable. He had been a soldier for as long as he could remember, so the prospect of fighting and dying was something he had learned to live with a long time ago, but now there were new matters to consider.

Firstly, there was his command. Was he a good Centurion? Did he have the strength of character to lead men older and more experienced than himself into battle? Was he too hard on his men, was he too soft on them? He knew that his colleagues in other centuries used the vine staff regularly on the backs of their men but he had felt little need for this; Graecus's punishment for errant behaviour was to look very sorrowfully down his long aquiline nose at the miscreant who would see the hard steel in his grey eyes and he would know that not merely had he let Graecus and the cohort down but, much worse, he had let himself down and the shame of this would long outlast any quick flick of the lash.

Graecus now thought about whether he could expect to rise further through the ranks or would he just try to serve his 25 years and retire with his pension, his Roman citizenship and a piece of land?............ And then there was the boy. What was to happen to him? There was no doubt in Graecus's mind that he and the boy had formed a strong unit but it was more than that – he again searched deep in his brain for the right word to describe his feelings towards the boy and failed to find it but when his heart spoke the word 'love' he knew that it was correct.

This was both terrifying and amazing. Terrifying because of the responsibility and the novelty of it but amazing that a hardened soldier who had led a life untouched by the softness of real emotion, could find in himself a feeling of such purity and simplicity that, once he had realised that he did, indeed, love the child, and then he looked at him, raking the ground with a stick, throwing stones for the dog and singing tunelessly as he ran along, his heart turned over and he knew he would never be the same again. This realisation made matters all the more complex and it was a troubled Graecus who walked into the town with his two young charges.

The town was surprisingly busy and its streets and open spaces were packed with people, animals, food-vendors, jugglers, fire-eaters, fortune-tellers and hangers on, all of whom conspired to make Graecus conclude that something was going on. As, indeed, became clear when they entered the square and saw preparations being made for what was going to be the tenth rate equivalent of a Roman circus – seating was being arranged and barriers erected between the seats and the would-be arena which was being covered with sand in anticipation of an after-noon's bloodletting. Somewhere from the distance, came the smell of shit and the sound of large beasts and towards the back of the square could be glimpsed a cage containing people.

For some reason, Graecus had never liked the Circus and the thought of an afternoon of entertaining killing only added to his already fretful mind. However, there was work to be done and he gathered his thoughts trying to remember the best way to the apothe-cary's shop through the thronging streets. He knew that he must get the peppermint oil but Magnus had also asked him to get orris root and juniper berries for the tooth powder he gave to the men and for castor oil which he sometimes used as a cure for constipation.

And Felix had asked him to try to get various herbs and spices and, if he saw one, a strong cooking pot and, if there were a large one, he would like to have a new leather purse, etc, etc. Graecus also hoped to be able to see the green eyed girl and.........if he were truthful to himself, the handsome lady tavern owner. All of this in a horribly crowded town where he must not lose sight of Germanicus and Zig, who must, if he were to enjoy the company of Arminia, be provided with suitable alternative company.

As he made his way through the streets, forging his way through the numbers of people who were shouting at one anoth-er in the guttural local tongue, he heard a different voice, speak-ing perfect Latin in a beautifully modulated tone. It was truly a musical voice and, for a moment, he stopped elbowing people aside as he stood to listen to it in this most unexpected of places. As he listened he calculated that the voice must belong to a patrician lady in her middle years and that she must be very well educated and, just as he came to this conclusion, he saw such a lady who appeared to his eyes as a beacon of civilisation among a sea of peasants. And, as he saw her, she saw him.

Their eyes met and there passed between them a look of recognition – that each saw the other as something known and familiar where all else was foreign. The lady smiled at Graecus and he smiled back revealing his good teeth while giving her a small bow in deference to her high status. The lady beckoned to Graecus who, keeping a tight hold onto Germanicus' elbow whilst he was clutching Zig's lead, zigzagged his way across the crowd to get to her. As they approached the lady, she gave Graecus a dazzling smile as if she had known him for many years.

'Young man', she said, 'You are a sight to gladden the heart of a lady far away from home! How fortunate I am to see a gallant officer so many days' journey from Rome. Tell me your name and how you come to be here and who are your companions.' Graecus bent over the small, warm hand she offered him and then stood straight to address her. He saw that she was about 45 years old and was still very striking but must have been extremely beautiful in her youth. Her hair was coloured with some sort of red dye to disguise its having lost its dark lustre but her black eyes were glittering with intelligence and her face was animated. He told her who he was and explained that Germanicus was his young charge.

The lady then turned to the boy and the little dog, stooping a little to get a better look at them, gave them all her attention – taking Germanicus's face in her hands, turning it from side to side examining him in detail as one would a potential purchase were one in the market for a slave boy and then patting the little dog on the head while feeling its muscles under her hand as she stroked its back with her other hand.

Germanicus was staring at the lady with great curiosity and some apprehension as his last encounter with a female had been the unfortunate meeting with Drusilla and he was not confident in the company of high born Roman ladies. She sensed this and drew closer to him again with a curious look in her eye but he backed away and Zig, who was normally silent, feeling the boy's discomfort, growled at her. Yet again, Graecus was aware that the boy lacked social graces, but then it was hardly surprising, and he resolved to teach him how to behave in the presence of women but, in the meantime, tried to make light of the boy's behaviour and said, 'My lady, I must apologise for the boy – he has been schooled in the ways of the Roman Army for only six or so months and he has not met many ladies but could you please tell me who you are and what you are doing in this little town in the middle of nowhere?'

The lady said 'My name is Vulponia and I am a priestess of the cult of Isis. Like you, I come here to help the Empire defend its borders but my task is to appease the gods of this place and bring Isis here for our own people. I have set up a small temple in a grove just outside the town and am making sacrifices to our Goddess. Our meeting today is no coincidence; it has been arranged by the gods and I wish you to visit my temple and make offerings to Isis.'

This invitation was not necessarily what Graecus wished to hear as he felt that the day would be busy enough as it was but he also did not like to disappoint a lady so he agreed that he would visit the temple later in the afternoon and, once he had found from Vulponia where it was, he and his companions went on their way, Graecus assuring the lady of his wish to worship Isis as he left her.

The next task was to find the Apothecary and to purchase the medicaments. This entailed going past the tavern so it made sense for them to go there and enquire after Aoif, the beautiful girl with the green eyes. As Graecus pushed open the front door, Arminia was in front of him wiping a wooden table and, on seeing him, she immediately recognised him and, obviously recollecting the last time they met, she blushed in a becoming manner and gave him a little curtsy. Graecus was very pleased to see her also and thought that she had become no less handsome in the intervening period so he approached her and kissed her warmly on both cheeks.

'Soldier' she said,' You are come to visit me'.

'Indeed I am, Ma'am, and to enquire about the pregnant girl and her child as the boy here was fond of her and she was kind to him when they were both captives'.

'Oh, sir, she is long gone away from here. She gave birth in my bed upstairs to a strong boy and was making herself useful to me in the tavern when a rich traveller came along and was taken by her looks. He bought her and the child and took them to Rome.'

At this, Germanicus looked crestfallen and Graecus put his hand on the boy's shoulder to steady him. Germanicus decided to take the disappointment sitting down and found a seat at the wooden table where he sat with his chin on the top of Zig's head whilst stroking the dog's ears.

Arminia now came closer to Graecus and he could see lust in her eyes which was a relief to him as he was having much the same thoughts as her but the problem was what to do with the boy?

Arminia had already thought of this and said, 'Child, you look hungry, come with me to the kitchen where my slave will feed you and, if you feel sleepy after you have eaten, there is a couch in front of the fire where you can rest'. Germanicus needed no coaxing and followed her like a lamb.

When she returned, Arminia winked at Graecus and, taking him by the arm, led him upstairs to her chamber where they revisited the delights they had enjoyed at their last meeting.

About an hour later, Graecus descended the stairs humming one of his favourite songs feeling much lighter of spirit. Going into the kitchen, he saw Germanicus asleep by the fire, his blonde head resting on the dog's which was lying next to him. This was a picture of such domestic felicity that it pierced Graecus's heart and he felt an up swelling of love such as he had never experienced before in his life. The day was getting much brighter.

It was time to go to the Apothecary so Graecus woke the boy and, saying farewell to Arminia, the three left for the busy streets walking as quickly as the crowds would allow.

The Apothecary was a wizened old man who spoke only a little Latin but Graecus spoke some of the local language so, between them, they managed to understand what was wanted and the three left the shop in better time than the Centurion had thought.

As it was not yet time to go to the Temple of Isis, Germanicus, who had been intrigued by the preparations for the Circus asked if they might go to see some of the spectacles. Graecus was not especially in favour of this but, after some consideration, decided that he could not nor should he, shield the child from the realities of life and that they would go but not for the whole of the afternoon's 'entertainment'. So they proceeded to the makeshift arena and purchased seats near the front for just a few coins.

The crowd was a mixed bunch. There were the townsfolk for whom this mediocre affair probably represented the height of sophistication, there were also some persons who looked to be members of a merchant class who had probably travelled more widely but there were also a few people who were obviously wealthy and, although they were of local stock they had clearly taken to the ways of the Romans as they were dressed in the Roman fashion and were clean shaven, not bearded as was the local custom.

At the periphery of the crowd there were the usual tradespeople hawking their wares: a woman selling honey- cakes, a man selling nuts, a boy playing a whistle and a number of maimed beggars among whom was one legless man who, propped on a piece of dirty sacking resting on his arms, asked passers-by in a plaintive voice for a few asses, all of this perfumed by the smell of unwashed humanity, dirty clothing and the smoke from the braziers of the hot food sellers.

Germanicus had quickly become accustomed to the order and discipline of life at the camp and now, looking around him wide-eyed at the crowds of noisy ill-assorted people, he edged himself closer to Graecus on the rough bench.

Then, with the roll of a drum and the strangled sound of a battered horn, it was time for the Circus to begin and into the arena strode, or, as he was very fat, waddled the Master of Ceremonies – a man in his late forties or early fifties, dressed in a bizarre toga-like garment but made from a gaudy fabric which may have once been magnificent but was now torn and patched in places and covered in stains into whose provenance it was probably best not to enquire.

He was carrying a whip with which he smote the sandy ground making a loud cracking noise in an attempt to whip the crowd into a frenzy of excitement at the thought of the afternoon's activities. He said, 'Ladies and Gentlemen, you are about to witness great spectacles of human and animal endurance – the sort of spectacles that the good citizens of Rome regularly enjoy at the Circus

Maximus. I have travelled far and wide about the Empire finding the best men and animals to bring to you this very afternoon.' Here he smote the ground again before saying, 'I promise you blood tingling acts which will have you on the edge of your seats, and you will speak of this Circus long after it has left town.'

By now the crowd was restless and the old Showman knew it was time to leave the ring so he announced the first act – a cock fight.

In came the hooded birds with their handlers who removed the little head-dresses and went to stand at either end of the arena. The trumpeteer blew a short note on his instrument and the cock owners let down their birds which strode towards each other in the centre of the arena, the spurs on their legs catching the afternoon sunlight. The birds stood opposite each other for what seemed like long minutes and the crowd was beginning to murmur in complaint that nothing was happening when, all of a sudden one of the birds, a handsome yellow creature with an impressive black tail, took off into the air in the direction of the other bird and, hovering in front of it, gave it a blow on its breast with its spur and drew blood. This was the first blood of the afternoon and caused a roar of approval from the crowd.

The wound to its breast seemed to make the other bird, of a similar size to the first but all black, wake up because while the first bird was enjoying the crowd's applause and almost took a bow, the second flew behind it, landed on its back and tore into it with gusto. This pleased the crowd even more as both birds were now covered in blood and the various personages of the little town settled comfortably in their seats for a festival of gore.

For a few minutes the birds exchanged blow for blow but then they began to tire and seemed to lose interest in the fight and the crowd grew restive again but the Master of Ceremonies must have seen all of this before because, just as the crowd's mood began to be ill-humoured, quietly and without any fanfare, there was let into the arena.................a fox.

Or that was what it looked like at first but, when Graecus had given it a more careful look, he realised it was a vixen who was now padding around the inner edge of the arena sniffing the air, scenting the blood of the cockerels but sniffing also the smell of humans and many of them.

As the crowd fell silent, contemplating this newcomer, the vixen stopped her perambulations and stood still, looking firstly at the cockerels and then at the crowd. She did this several times, moving her head slowly then she put her head on one side as if she were trying to solve a particularly knotty problem, then she made up her mind and turning towards the middle of the arena, flew at the wounded cockerels and, within seconds, killed and dismembered them both.

The crowd was ecstatic. This was what they had come to see – nature red in tooth and claw and they whooped and laughed and slapped their sides and pointed to the vixen and jeered at the remains of the once strutting cockerels.

Cheered by this appreciation of his powers as an entertainer, the Master of Ceremonies came back into the arena accompanied by a netsman who calmly approached the vixen as she was still licking her chops and expertly put the net over her before bundling her into it and taking her away.

The Master of Ceremonies stood in the middle of the arena with his hands in the air acknowledging their applause and smiling in a modest manner. He began to speak and the noise died down as the audience strained to hear what the next act would be.

It was to be a dogfight. Graecus did not know whether Germanicus had been to a Circus before nor whether he had seen a dog fight before and assumed that the boy's short life had been full of incident, some of it violent, but now that Graecus loved him, he did not want him to be unnecessarily distressed and was aware that the child was fidgeting but had not said that he wished to leave and, in any event, this was life as it was lived in the towns and cities of the Empire and he may as well get used to it.

He was not, though, quite so confident about Zig who had been very alert during the previous act and had strained at his leash when the vixen appeared but had again lain down now that she had been taken away. The Master of Ceremonies was signalling the beginning of the next act by raising his arms in greeting to the dog handlers who came into the ring with the canine protagonists: a large grey hound of the breed which was now being imported from Britannia and was regarded as a status symbol and a smaller but fierce looking dog with a thick brown and black coat of a type which he had seen in Germania but not elsewhere.

The handlers walked the dogs around the perimeter of the ring close to the crowd so that the people could view the animals at closer quarters. They were both dogs and Graecus saw that the hound had the usual elegant loping gait of a sprinter and seemed languid and almost bored but the German dog had its hackles up and skulked rather than paraded round the ring showing off its powerful shoulders and bared teeth. It seemed as if this would be a battle of speed and nobility versus brute force.

The handlers unleashed the dogs and left the ring. The hound looked not in the least concerned while the German dog crouched low towards the ground, its belly almost touching the sand, the smaller dog clearly feeling threatened and ill at ease. The crowd was expectant and some people began to whistle which served further to unsettle the now panting German dog. Meanwhile, the contrast with the hound could not have been more marked as it stood yawning but keeping an eye on the other dog. After some moments punctuated by the whistling and calling of the crowd, the German dog took off towards the hound and made for its back end but the hound was too quick and was off in the opposite direction before the other dog was within sniffing distance so they now stood staring at each other, the hound looking a little more engaged in the proceedings and the German dog looking even more down in the mouth.

At this point, someone in the crowd close to the smaller dog took from a leather bag something which looked to Graecus as if it were a cooked chicken leg and proceeded to eat it. The smell from this delicacy reached the brown dog's nose and so distracted it that it ceased to gaze at the hound and looked instead at the man enjoying the chicken leg.

This was a big mistake for the hound galloped over to the

German dog which was still off guard and with one blow of its huge front paw made a gash all the way down one side of its face before cantering to the other side of the arena. The German dog could not believe this at first and for a few seconds did not react but then it turned in fury after the hound which allowed it to get quite close to it then sped to the furthest point away from the wounded dog.

The German dog stood for a while breathing heavily and then sat down. It was a more intelligent animal than either Graecus or the crowd had given it credit for because, for the first time since they had seen each other, this seeming lack of interest on the part of the brown dog had galvanised the hound which now looked fully alert and rather less haughty.

It looked almost as if the brown dog would go to sleep and the hound would take such umbrage at being ignored that this would be a non-event of a fight but then the man with the now eaten chicken leg helpfully threw the bone into the arena between the two dogs each of which immediately flew towards it colliding in the centre of the ring.

The hound got possession of the bone and had it in its mouth but the German dog took a bite out of the hound's leg and succeeded in getting it to drop the tasty treat. Undeterred, the hound had a go at the top of the brown dog's head and took a flap of skin away from its skull. Blood was pouring into the brown dog's eyes and enabled the hound to take the chicken bone from its mouth. The hound tried to turn away to make for the edge of the arena, presumably the better to enjoy the bone but the brown dog was not giving in and took the opportunity to snap at the hound's balls which were dangling down and managed to make contact causing the hound to howl very loudly and Zig to crouch under the seat with his paws over his eyes.

It looked bad for the hound and the crowd was whooping and cheering the local dog, probably feeling that the stuck up foreigner had got its just deserts but just when the brown dog felt victory within its jaws, the hound turned its long back and sank its teeth into the smaller dog at the back of its neck and held on.

It now looked like stalemate with the brown dog attached to the hound's balls and the hound holding it by the scruff of the neck but the brown dog was bleeding much more than the hound and, in the end, had to release its jaws which gave the hound the opportunity it needed to pick it up and shake it by the back of the neck until it was dead.

Curiously, the crowd did not seem at all happy with this turn of events and there was muttering and shuffling of feet when the lifeless dog was taken away. The hound looked nonplussed as it thought it had won and that it had done its job but there was hissing when it was taken from the arena by its handler.

Graecus looked to see what Germanicus was thinking and saw that he was uncharacteristically quiet and pensive. Zig, on the other hand, had reappeared from under the seat and seemed to be happy that the hound had won.

The Master of Ceremonies strode back into the arena with a big smile and the roll of a drum. He gestured for silence and the crowd, knowing that the main attraction of the afternoon was about to begin, obeyed his command.

'Citizens, friends, fellow countrymen, you are now about to witness the spectacle you have all come to see – the flower of the Gladiator's art, the sport which entertains our Emperor, the sport which delights Rome. You are about to witness a fight to the death between two matched men, two men who come here this afternoon to show you how real men can fight.'

The crowd was silent with anticipation while the Master of Ceremonies paused for breath before continuing, 'I now introduce to you for your inspection our first gallant fighter, all the way from the stinking marshes of Britannia, a noble warrior captured in battle against our Legions. Ladies and Gentlemen, I bring you Cartimanduus.'

At this a man entered the arena passing close by Graecus's left hand.

But 'Man Mountain' would have been a better description. He was tall, about a half a foot taller than most Romans and very heavily muscled, so heavily muscled in fact that his lower and upper arms were corded as were his thighs and calves. He was enormous and the crowd was delighted with him, whistling and calling and cheering as he walked to the centre of the arena, broadsword in hand.

Cartimanduus now stood still and straight in the afternoon sunlight, its rays bouncing off his large shaved head and oiled chest which was naked except that nearly all his upper body was covered in the blue tattoos favoured by the British – sinuous whorls sweeping up his arms, across his vast chest, over his shoulders and down his broad back curving towards the short leather kilt he wore over his lower body.

Cartimanduus acknowledged the crowd's attentions with a wave of his sword and a big grin showing teeth sharpened to vicious-looking points.

The crowd went wild with delight at the sight of this Man/Beast but he was such a caricature that Graecus almost laughed.

It was time for the Beast's opponent to appear and the drum rolled again and the crowd again fell silent as a new figure walked into the arena.

Graecus's heart sank. 'By Jupiter' he thought, 'Has the Roman Empire come to this?'

As he viewed the pathetic figure now reluctantly making his way across the sand, Graecus stole a look at Germanicus and saw complete incredulity on the boy's face which, on the one hand pleased him as it perfectly mirrored his own feelings and was testament to the child's sense of fairness and upholding the standard but, on the other hand, worried him as he knew there would be a bloodbath and this would be disconcerting for Germanicus.

The second 'Gladiator' was now in the middle of the arena but anyone less like a fighter would be hard to imagine. He was about seventeen, of medium height and very slightly built, so much so that when you looked at him, the words 'weak as water' immediately came to mind: in stark contrast with the Beast he had no discernible muscle, only pale thin limbs.

To Graecus's mind it would have been funny had it not been so tragic. To Graecus, the thought that someone could pit these two men against each other in a fight which was purely for entertainment and where they were so ill-matched, was an appalling indictment of the codes by which the Empire now lived. How could you think it was appropriate to put two men in a fight to the death where one more than anything resembled the other's breakfast?

The crowd clearly did not share Graecus's misgivings. They had decided that the best way to deal with this mismatched contest was to ridicule the newcomer by jeering and catcalling and the poor young man, in Graecus's mind 'the Sacrifice', shifted uncomfortably from foot to foot weighed down by the heavy sword, the feel of which appeared to be so unaccustomed to him that he was passing it from hand to hand, unsure whether he should hold it in his left or right.

The Beast was enjoying himself, flexing his muscles, striding about the arena, brandishing his weapon in an ostentatious display of his years of skill in using it to kill and maim – all of this to the delight of the crowd but not to the delight of the Sacrifice who, judging from the widening dark patch on the kirtle he was wearing, had wet himself. This fact, unfortunately, was not lost on the Beast who sneered at him, nor on the crowd which laughed and whistled in amusement at his public ordeal while Graecus and Germanicus shifted uncomfortably in their seats.

The Master of Ceremonies now stood between the two contestants and asked them to walk a number of paces away from each other while he held up his hand the fall of which would mean that the contest had begun. Graecus could only imagine the horror being experienced by the Sacrifice whose only prayer could be that his death would be swift and clean but Graecus knew this would be unlikely as it was the Beast's job to torment his prey before wounding it and then giving the crowd the vote on whether this pathetic stripling would live to pursue a life of misery.

The Master of Ceremonies dropped his hand.

Normally at this point, the two Gladiators in an arena would begin to circle each other, their knees slightly bent so that they could spring into action when necessary and this was exactly what Cartimanduus did, walking round the Sacrifice with a springy gait like a stalking animal but the Sacrifice did no such thing presumably because it was alien to him; he just stood there holding the broadsword tip down in the sand, as unready for combat as a person could be.

This was very bad form as the Beast could not, even according to the inhuman rules of the arena, just charge up to this youth and run him through – where would the fun be in that? No, the youth must first be shamed into making a stand and then, after a bit of showy swordplay, the Beast could run him through or injure him and give the crowd the opportunity to decide that his life was so worthless that it should end that afternoon, and, even if it did not, the alternatives would be so horrific that he might well wish that he had perished in pursuance of the mob's entertainment.

Graecus was musing on the tragedy unfolding in the arena and took another, closer look at the Sacrifice. True, he was thin and lacking in obvious muscle but there was something of a sinewy look to him and a light in his eye which hinted at intelligence. This was no horny-handed child of the soil and it could only be conjectured as to the circumstances which had brought him here.

The Beast, who bore the mark of a slave, the clipped ear, clearly knew it was his job to provoke The Sacrifice into some sort of aggression or, at least, self defence was trying to get a reaction from him by sneering at him and making feints with his sword but this had no effect despite the braying of the mob so he tried laughing at the young man and calling him names, saying that he was 'effeminate' and a 'ponce', each of which was a potent insult to any Roman male.

None of this had any effect; instead of hardening The Sacrifice's resolve to fight to retrieve his honour, all it did was make him drop his sword, burst into tears and fall on his knees, not in a faint but in supplication and because he wanted to be sick.

This was very, very bad. This was bad for the Sacrifice as The Mob would wish him to be skewered and then chopped slowly into pieces for cowardice and for spoiling their afternoon and it was bad for the Beast as both the Mob and the Master of Ceremonies would blame him for the lack of 'sport'. Summoning up his most powerful insults, therefore, in a final attempt to get the stripling to be a man and fight, the Beast went over to his genuflecting opponent waving his sword in the air and, taking in the crowd, he said 'Get up you snivelling heap of shit. How dare you insult these people by refusing to fight. You are a disgrace to manhood and a disgrace to Rome,' and then he spat noisily and plentifully on the youth's bowed head.

The crowd was turning nasty and baying for blood shouting to the Beast and saying, 'Kill the cowardly little bastard anyway! Run the little fucker through! Teach him a lesson!'

Graecus was disgusted by these events but not for the same reason as The Mob; he was disgusted that one of the fruits of the Roman Empire seemed to be that innocent, possibly fine people would be sacrificed to keep the plebeians amused and less inclined to question the excesses of the nobility and the rich and it seemed to him that this was a betrayal of the principles of the Founding Fathers of the world's greatest city and it was not for this that he fought with the cohort.

Germanicus was also unimpressed and was sitting with an expression of pure stone on his face which made him look like a grown man and Graecus knew that the child was thinking the same thing.

The Mob was now in a frenzy and the Beast was holding the edge of his sword to the young man's throat threatening to slice it if he did not pick up his sword. Germanicus looked aghast at the prospect that the unarmed man would be executed before their eyes and Graecus could take no more of this unedifying spectacle, feeling that it degraded everyone present.

So he stood – tall and imposing in his tunic, breastplate and cloak, his helmet held at his side. At first, only a few people looked at him, but as he removed the scarlet cloak, put down the helmet and then drew his sword, more and more of the Mob ceased to look at what was happening, or not happening in the arena, and to see what the handsome Centurion was up to.

Within a minute there was complete silence in the makeshift amphitheatre and all eyes, including those of the stripling who had lifted his head, were on Graecus who calmly and purposefully strode into the arena and, sword at the ready, squared up to the Beast and said, 'I see you wish for a fight this afternoon and I would wish that you are not disappointed. Our friend here has no stomach for it but I would be delighted to fight an ugly fat pig like you'.

The crowd realised what was happening and hollered with delight knowing that the Beast would have no alternative but to fight Graecus and that it would be a much better spectacle than what had been on offer.

The Beast knew all of this as well as The Mob so, shifting his mental alertness up several notches and flexing his muscles, he took his mark and faced Graecus.

The Master of Ceremonies, silently thanking Mithras for sending this Centurion who was saving the day's entertainment from being a humiliating failure for him, hurried into the arena and, shoving the Sacrifice off to one side, stood between the two men, his right hand held in the air, and counting to three, let it drop, signalling that the fight could begin.

The men began to circle each other, Graecus much lighter on his feet than the Beast but it was the Beast who made the first move, taking a wide-sweeping lunge at Graecus with his sword but missing him by several feet. Graecus now felt sufficiently warmed up that he could take a swipe at the Beast and did so but it was more of a practice than anything else and enabled him to calibrate the speed of his sword in the prevailing conditions.

The Beast was circling again, crouching quite low and Graecus was keeping his distance when the Beast suddenly stopped and turned so that he could the better make a surprise lunge at the Centurion.

Graecus was indeed surprised but not off his guard and, even though the Beast's sword missed him this time only by inches, his superb balance did not falter and he was able to move out of harm's way quickly but in doing so he made sure that he was on the balls of his feet with his knees bent slightly and, just when the Beast thought that he had routed the soldier, Graecus turned on him so swiftly and moved his sword with such economy of

70

effort that the Beast did not see what was coming, and Graecus was able to make contact with the Beast's shoulder and chop a chunk from it causing blood to spurt down his arm, covering the blue tattoos with a red efflorescence while the Mob roared its approval.

The Beast then made the silly mistake of looking to see what damage had been done to his shoulder, despite its not being his sword-arm which had been injured, and Graecus knew that he had never been in battle – it was a cardinal rule that a true warrior only looks at his wounds after the battle has ended. In seeing this, Graecus lost any respect he may have had for the Beast as a noble warrior who had had the misfortune to be captured and saw him merely as a bully.

This made Graecus determined to put the Beast on his mettle so he now crept up to him, nearing him at his sword arm and made a bold thrust for his chest. The Beast parried this thrust but was not quick enough to deflect the follow through which pierced him at about waist level and, again he looked at the wound as the blood spilled down his belly, saturating his kilt, and on to his leg. He seemed amazed that it was his blood was running into the dirt.

Graecus could have taken his head off with one blow at this point but did not wish to blunt the edge of his sword and, in any event, he sensed that the crowd had begun to get the measure of the Beast, and contented himself with merely nicking his hamstring so that he, too, would fall on his knees into the sand of the arena.

Graecus stood, towering over the kneeling Beast and, taking a handful of small silver coins from his purse, threw them on the ground and said, 'This is payment for the life of this young man whom I am taking with me. The afternoon's entertainment is finished – this man here has had enough,' and then he spat on the ground in front of the bully before going over to the Sacrifice and, gently grabbing him by the shoulders, raised him to his feet while signalling to Germanicus to bring his cloak.

They put the cloak over the Sacrifice's shoulders and, supported by the Centurion and the boy, he left the arena and the Circus, pausing only to get the dog.

Standing in a side street off the square, they made a strange tableau as Graecus wracked his brains thinking about what to do with this pathetic young man; even though his stock was high with Arminia, he could not see how he could persuade her that the stripling would increase trade and he could not see how he would be a useful farm worker so, for the moment, he was stumped..... and he must now visit the Temple of Isis.

But what to do with the others in the meantime? Well, he thought, his stock was probably high enough with the lady tavern owner that she would take in Germanicus, the young man and the dog and, probably, feed them, for a short while as he made his visit to the temple. So they made their way back to the tavern where Graecus was gratified to see the look of joy on the lady's face as they walked in. He hoped she would not be disappointed that he could not stay and, although she would undoubtedly have liked to have had his company again, she was a warm-hearted woman and readily agreed to give his charges shelter and food while he paid his respects to Isis.

So, off he set for the edge of the town and the grove which Vulponia had described to him.He walked quickly and found the place without difficulty. It was just beyond the outskirts of the town, set back away from the road and behind a clump of tall trees so that once you had penetrated the trees and they had closed behind you like a curtain no-one would know where you had gone.

This thought occurred to Graecus as he passed through the trees as it was a rule of warfare that you should try to be visible to your friends but not to your enemies but he dismissed it from his mind as, truth to tell, he was by now, after the somewhat distasteful events of the earlier part of the afternoon, looking forward to the company of an attractive, patrician Roman lady.

And here she was, coming towards him through the late afternoon sun, resplendent in a pleated white gown caught in a cummerbund under her breasts, her hair piled on her head but a few strands escaping becomingly at the nape of her neck and the side of her face. With the sun behind her, walking in a stately manner, she was magnificent and Graecus allowed himself to think that Rome and its people must, after all be safe, if this splendid woman was one of its figureheads.

'Ah', she said, 'You have found us. How clever of you! But then I felt I could rely on a gallant soldier to be able to find his way to our Temple. Tell, me where is the boy and his dog?'

Graecus explained that he had that afternoon acquired a new slave and that he had left all three of them at the inn so that he could all the more dutifully devote himself to Isis and this was met with a tinkling laugh from the lady which made him feel as tall as poplar tree and as powerful as an oak tree and as manly as a lion. Truly, he thought to himself, this lady embodies the best of the virtues of Rome and is living proof of the rectitude of the principles which motivated its Founding Fathers.

As he finished speaking, he smiled at her and was rewarded with a smile of dazzling brilliance which made him feel that he could take on the world for this woman.

'Now', she said, 'Please follow me' and led the way towards a rocky opening at one side of the grove and, as they passed between its portals and into a narrow passage, again it occurred to Graecus that he was choosing not to follow the rules about courting danger but, again, he dismissed his instinctive reaction as unwarranted and happily followed Vulponia down the long passage lit by the torch she had taken from its bracket just inside the cave's entrance.

After what seemed to Graecus to have been a very long, and increasingly airless, walk down the passage he suddenly felt a breeze on his face and, just as suddenly, the passage gave onto a large cavern in the rock. This was lit by more torches and was very beautifully decorated with statues and altars around the perimeter but, in the middle of the cave, was a fountain on top of a pond. The silvery noise of the fountain combined with the smell of incense and the sound of someone playing the cithara all conspired to produce a scene of surpassing peace and beauty which was balm to Graecus's somewhat frazzled soul.

Vulponia was standing next to the fountain and indicating a bench on the other side of it; 'Come and sit next to me and we shall share some wine and food,' she said. Graecus had not eaten since he had broken his fast at the beginning of the day and needed no further invitation to join Vulponia on the bench.

As soon as they were seated, a young man in a white tunic appeared carrying an amphora and two silver goblets on a tray which contained pomegranates, grapes, figs, dates and cold meats and bread and cheeses. He set the tray on the table in front of the bench and Vulponia signalled to Graecus to begin to eat.

Graecus was hungry and the food was delicious so he did not stint himself and when Vulponia poured the wine, he drank deeply from the goblet, showing his appreciation of its excellence by smacking his lips.

'Ah', said Vulponia, 'I am so pleased that my handsome new friend recognises good wine. Indeed, it is the best; it is Falernian, from the Campania region.'

Graecus knew nothing of this, merely that the wine had exhibited none of the acid harshness of the wines he usually drank but it pleased his sensibilities to be sitting here discussing wine with such an aristocratic lady.

Indeed, despite his lack of knowledge concerning his parents, Graecus loved to be in the company of those he regarded as the nobility and his very lack of a known pedigree encouraged him to think that he must have been of noble birth himself but, by some tragedy, separated from his parents at an early age – in his quiet moments, he would often muse on the extensive estate on which he must have been born, probably in Greece, and the beauty and grace of his Mother and the intelligence and valour of his Father.

So, Graecus was enjoying himself in the company of Vulponia and partaking of yet another goblet of the excellent wine and Vulponia was flattering him and putting her scented little hand on his knee and speaking to him in a low, seductive voice, 'Well, Centurion, you have come here to pay your respects to Isis.'

'Yes, my lady, and with all due deference.'

'That is as it should be but I wish you to know that I have

decided that you will pay your respects in a particular manner.'

'Just name it, ma'am and it shall be yours', he said expansively.

'Isis requires the boy to come here to be trained as a priest and the dog may come with him', she replied.

At these words, a shade from the Underworld stretched up and traced a cold clammy finger across the back of Graecus's neck and he was suddenly aware that he had drunk too much, said too much and was too far away from his friends.

Seeking to calm himself and to make himself clear, he summoned up the dregs of his best smile and said, 'I fear, my lady, that will not be possible. The boy is my son.'

'But, surely, that cannot be! There is not a drop of your natural blood in the child.'

'The boy is mine by adoption and I have no ambition that he should be a priest of Isis. Indeed, my ambition is that he should join the cohort.'

'But he would make a wonderful follower of Isis and I would personally sponsor him, not merely here but in Rome, and he could keep his little dog.'

Graecus heard all of this but he was not convinced. He knew, for instance, from the way that Vulponia had inspected the dog that it would not be long before the *Haruspex*, the soothsayer, would have his hands in the dog's entrails, using the hound's innards to make predictions but he did not understand why she should so want to have Germanicus as a postulant so he decided to be as firm as possible within the bounds of good manners and said to her, 'My lady, the boy is all I have, I have no other family and I wish to keep him with me.'

Vulponia was obviously trying to keep her temper and to be civil, for she sweetly enquired, 'But do you not see, soldier, that I could give him the better life?'

This put Graecus on the spot because if she were correct, then his wanting to keep Germanicus with him would be selfishness on his part and he genuinely loved the boy and wanted what was best for him so he spent some moments thinking carefully before he replied, 'No, madam, I do not. My son likes the outdoor life, he has the instincts of a warrior and he will make a fine soldier, indeed, I cherish the ambition for him that he should become an officer.'

Vulponia shifted impatiently in her seat and gave a testy sigh before saying, 'I think you do not fully understand the position. I am making an offer to you for your son of something which will give him much influence and a strong position in society, being a priest of Isis is sought after, yet you are throwing this back in my face – something of which people higher in the world than you would be grateful!' and as she said these last words, angry red spots appeared high on her cheeks.

This was all becoming very difficult for Graecus as he hated contradicting a woman and, *a fortiori*, contradicting 'A Lady' but he could not give up the one thing he had had in his life which he really loved and he did not, in all honesty, see why she was so set on the idea of having Germanicus for Isis.

So he said to her, 'My lady, I am conscious of the honour you do me to ask for my son but I do not see why you are so set on taking my child for Isis.'

At this, Vulponia felt that she had sensed a chink in Graecus's armour and that she could give vent to her feelings so she said, 'But he is so beautiful. He has such a fine stature and there is a noble quality to him. I must have him!'

This was the wrong thing to say to Graecus who now felt that Vulponia was not in the least interested in Germanicus's welfare but only in her own advancement and, looking her straight in the face, he said, 'Madam, I have made up my mind, you cannot have my son.'

At first she could not believe that he had refused her request and it took a few seconds for her fully to appreciate that she had been turned down, then she dropped all pretence of politeness and femininity and flew at him in a rage which would have done justice to any of the Furies. Coming in very close to his face, she bared her clenched teeth at him and hissed, 'You do not know what you unleash. You cannot be aware that I am a powerful woman with powerful connections with the Emperor at Rome.

My family are feared and respected in equal measure and no-one, I repeat, no-one, refuses me with impunity!'

At this point, her anger increased to such a pitch that with her right hand she reached towards Graecus's left cheek and scratched him hard down the side of his face drawing blood and, as she assaulted him she said, 'And a lowly soldier like you has no business mixing with matters of high state. You will regret this.'

Graecus sat stunned as much by the ugliness of her behaviour as by her tantrum and was beginning to consider what on earth she could mean by 'matters of high state' when he suddenly began to feel very faint and tired and tried to shake his head to clear his brain but this only made matters worse so he tried to straighten out his back and to breathe deeply but that did not help and, in the end, he was so tired that all he could do was stretch out on the bench and go to sleep. His last thought before losing consciousness was that the angry Vulponia had looked like the little vixen devouring the chickens at the circus – Vulponia indeed.

Graecus awoke to find himself lying on the ground, flat on his back and when he opened his eyes he was looking up at the moon which, he noted, was full. He tried to sit up but this movement was accompanied by intense pain in his head and a throbbing in his left cheek so he sat still for a while, trying to remember how he had come to be in this place. Looking very carefully around he saw that he was in the grove outside the Temple to Isis and, judging by his body temperature, he knew that he had been there for some time.

Thinking over what had happened, he felt that he should leave the grove as quickly as possible and make his way back to the tavern so he tried to get up but was able only to get to his knees and even this movement was such as to cause him to be violently sick which then made his headache all the worse but, gradually, he felt a little better and was able to get to his feet.

Graecus then staggered to a tree which he used for support while he noisily and lengthily relieved himself and, feeling the better for that, walked more steadily out of the grove and back to the town aided by the full moon.

As he walked, he tried to make sense of what had happened and was hard pressed to understand why Vulponia should have been so very angry and what she had meant but, even though he turned it over and over in his mind, he was none the wiser and, as he walked, he passed his hand over his brow, trying to clear his thoughts but to no avail..........except that...............a chunk of his hair was missing.

At first he tried to convince himself that he was mistaken but, no, it was the case that the lock of hair which normally (and, he usually thought, attractively) fell over his brow was missing.

This caused Graecus to ponder even more and to think that his recent brushes with Roman women were turning into the stuff of nightmares.

Eventually, he reached the tavern and was relieved to find that the door was unbolted and the room lit by a small lamp so that he could make his way to the kitchen.

And there in front of the embers of the fire curled up with his head on a bale of straw was Germanicus and next to him, curled within the folds of the boy's tunic, was Zig.

Graecus looked at them for some moments and felt a lump in his throat – his recollection of the day's strange and disturbing events mixing with his love for the child and the picture of innocence before his eyes. Then he recalled the other event of the day and looked across the room to see the stripling, (in his mind's eye now 'the Stripling'), lying on the floor with Graecus's scarlet cloak over him.

At this point, Graecus would have loved to have had sufficient of the milk of human kindness running through his veins to have been able to look upon the Stripling with some sympathy for, although it had undoubtedly been a bad day for Graecus it had unquestionably been a worse one for the young man but Graecus was feeling sorry for himself and all he could see was the huge problem of what in the names of all the Gods he was going to do with this additional burden.

As he was standing there thinking about this, the door behind him opened softly and in came Arminia. She had a quizzical lift to her brow so Graecus explained to her what had happened and she made him sit at the kitchen table while she brewed up something to clear his head and settle his stomach, all the while speaking softly to him about life in the town and asking him about life in the cohort. She was very easy company and he was forced to reflect that, in fact, she was far more 'the Lady' than was Vulponia.

When he had drunk the draught she gave him there arose the question of where he would sleep and it was soon settled between them that her bed was quite large enough for two and, so it transpired, that this strange day ended in a much better way than he could have anticipated.

CHAPTER FIVE

It was an unusual start to the following day for Graecus as he was not accustomed to begin his day in bed with a woman but he, nevertheless, found it very pleasant and he was whistling as he made a somewhat later appearance at the fast breaking meal than would normally have been the case.

When he sat at the table, Germanicus and the Stripling were already there eating copious amounts of bread and cheese and bread and honey and bread and cold meat. The Stripling looked less haunted than before and was so obviously enjoying his food that Graecus allowed himself a little warm-hearted feeling towards his fellow man and concluded that the only thing he could do with his new slave was to take him back to the camp until he had a better idea.

They set off after their repast and after Graecus and Arminia had bidden each other a lingering farewell.

Walking swiftly, the three males and the little dog left the town behind them and were soon out in the countryside with the sun shining on their backs and the air fragrant with the scent of wild flowers. It was a glorious day and Zig, now unleashed, was busy sniffing at holes and chasing birds.

Intriguingly, the Stripling spoke good Latin with an educated but foreign accent but was not willing to say where he had come from, merely that he was very grateful for having been rescued and that he would serve his master honestly and faithfully and, for the moment, that was good enough for Graecus .

They reached the camp some time after the midday and Graecus, bracing himself for the barrage of questions which the century would ask of him, was not disappointed for, as soon as they gained the camp, Felix was upon them berating Graecus for having been away much longer than he had said he would be and giving them all a fright that they had been kidnapped or murdered. This was echoed by Magnus but he was, at least, mollified by Graecus's having brought back all the medicaments he had asked for and set about making up the necessary potions for Pneumaticus.

Having vented his spleen, Felix reverted to his usually good-natured self and became curious about the Stripling asking what Graecus intended to do with him. This became one of the questions of which Graecus was heartily sick because it was asked time and time again and he soon tired of saying, 'I know not'.

The other questions which he came to find very irksome were, 'What has happened to your hair and who did that to your face?' These were difficult to answer in any way which was both truthful and flattering to Graecus's self-esteem for, if he told the truth – that he had allowed his head to be turned by the attentions of a high-born Roman woman and thereby found himself in a sticky situation, then he would inevitably look foolish, so he grappled with this for a while, contenting himself with a half-jocular, half-muffled response about how, 'you could never tell what a woman would do next,' and was succeeding in telling this half truth until Felix, ever able to read Graecus like a book, tackled him for more specific information and was able to winkle the full story from him and, to Graecus's relief, this was received with sympathy and understanding.

But there was also another matter which was worrying Graecus and that was that he had said to Vulponia that Germanicus was his adopted son. This had, of course, been a lie but it now seemed to him that it was a good idea as it would protect Germanicus and, in any event, Graecus did wish to be his legal father. Whilst this sounded simple, he knew it was not as it would be frowned upon by the Army which discouraged soldiers from having families.

He pondered this for some time and did not know whom to ask for advice – this procedure was so far outside his experience that he did not know where to start.

In the meantime, there were mutterings in the century concerning, 'Waifs and strays,' and 'Mouths to feed' and Graecus knew they were referring to the Stripling who, to be fair to him, was not an idler – he was making himself useful helping Felix by fetching and carrying and chopping and peeling – but this was regarded by the other men as an insufficient contribution to their collective life.

The mutterings grew louder, bolder and more frequent and Graecus despaired of resolving the problem which was not helped by the fact that the Stripling kept himself to himself and was somewhat stand-offish which the other men thought was a bit rich for somebody who had ignominiously been rescued from the Circus and who seemed to have no real purpose in life.

But, just as Graecus was contemplating taking the Stripling back to the town and trying to sell him, there was a remarkable upturn in his fortunes.

Late one afternoon, Graecus and some of the men, including the Stripling, were sitting at the big table in the open air discussing the relative merits of various weapons when Zig came and sat at Graecus's feet just as he was using his hunting knife to illustrate a point but, unfortunately, dropped it only for the dog to pick it up in his mouth and run off.

The knife was a valuable piece of Graecus's equipment and he did not wish to lose it so he shouted after the dog but Zig kept on running.

The Stripling saw the look of loss on Graecus's face and set off after the dog but at such a pace that the men around the table sat open-mouthed in awe that a man could run so fast and seemingly effortlessly then, as the Stripling gained on the dog, they looked at each other in amazement and when he caught up with the dog and wrestled it to the ground, they all sighed incredulously as if their eyes had deceived them and they had not seen what they had all just seen.

The Stripling then took the knife from the dog and, putting it in his belt, ran lightly back to the table arriving there in full wind with no sign of being out of breath.

The other men, including Graecus, were speechless. No-one had ever seen any man or boy run as fast or anything like as fast – it was truly a phenomenon. Such a phenomenon that they all sat silently trying to understand what they had just witnessed.

Graecus spoke first, 'You seem to be an athlete of rare talent,' and the men all chorused 'Aye, aye'.

Then the Stripling said, 'Sir, I was blessed almost from birth with winged feet', and Graecus replied, 'Blessed indeed. Tell me, how far can you run?'

'Why sir, I can run all day.'

At this, the germ of an idea was beginning to form in Graecus's mind and he asked, 'But surely you are able to run all day long only over flat, even ground?'

'No Sir, I am just as able to run over stony ground and up the sides of mountains – I was brought up in the hills in Sparta.'

This brought sniggers from the men as they were well aware of the circumstances of the Stripling's failure to stand up to the tattooed Briton and it was, to them, an amusing paradox that he should have been raised in the very place which was a byword for valour and bravery. Graecus was also amused but felt unable to show it as it would be unbecoming in an officer, so he said, 'Were your family from military stock?'

'No Sir, my father was a man skilled in the law and I was to follow him but first I was to be apprenticed to a Roman lawyer.'

Graecus could hardly contain his excitement and almost whispered his next question, 'And, are you, then, knowledgeable in the matter of Roman Law?'

'Why Sir, prior to my kidnap and transportation to Germania, I studied Law at the feet of a great man in Mediolanum.'

The plan forming in Graecus's mind began to take shape: because the century's camp was some miles distant from the main Legionary camp and messages and information were sent to and fro on a daily basis it had been necessary to divert one or other of the soldiers from his normal duties to undertake what was, to them, the tedious task of trudging over the hills with bits of parchment and wax tablets, waiting around for the replies and then trudging back. And as if this were not enough of a burden, the task of writing up the required daily records was a chore which Graecus himself did not always relish. Now, here before him was a young man who combined the virtues of being exceptionally fleet of foot and very literate and Graecus was overjoyed that the seemingly useless Stripling may, after all, turn out to be quite useful.

He turned to him and said, 'Why, this is good news as we have need of a messenger here.... and a scribe.'

'Sir, I am most willing to perform any task that you give me but it is to those tasks that my talents are best suited.

'That is settled then, and now I must name you – I must think of a name which will denote your place in the century.'

Graecus sat and thought for some moments and scratched his head causing the lock of hair (which happily had now grown back) to fall over his brow, then he sighed, then he crossed his legs, then he uncrossed them, all the while seeking inspiration as to what would be a proper name for this uninspiring youth. He was still scratching his head and beginning to look perplexed when Felix said, 'He runs like the wind, can we not call him Incitatus?'

And Graecus immediately knew that this was exactly the correct name for this rather mysterious person so he smiled broadly and said, 'Of course. So be it. You are Incitatus, the Swift One, our messenger and scribe'.

Having until then been Graecus's servant, it was natural that Incitatus should join Graecus's contubernium which, by now, following the administration to Pneumaticus of a draught of castor oil (with devastatingly explosive results) followed by some of the peppermint oil, was free of the poisonous vapours which had previously filled their living quarters but they were still, at night, assailed by the sound of his percussive snores.

The other soldiers had tried many tricks to try to stop this ruination of their repose – they had tried to make Pneumaticus sleep outside but he would always sneak inside in the middle of the night, they had tried making him drink less but that was a short-lived solution and they had tried throwing their boots at him when he was at his noisiest but none of these provided the long term answer they all now so craved.

Graecus felt this all very strongly, especially as he thought that the lack of sleep made him grumpy and less able to concentrate on his command but he could see no way to resolve it.

Graecus took life seriously and worried about this so was relieved when, sitting one day working on some calculations, he was joined by Incitatus who said, 'Sir, may I be permitted to make a suggestion for the comfort of our colleagues?'

'Please proceed.'

'Sir, it would be for the benefit of us all if Pneumaticus were to be prevented from snoring.'

'Indeed it would.'

'Sir, my Father inflicted such a torture on my Mother but she, using a trick given to her by my Grandmother, at night tied around his neck a thin piece of leather to which was attached a small wooden bobbin which she placed at the back of his neck and this prevented him from sleeping on his back and stopped him snoring. May I make such a piece of equipment for Pneumaticus?'

'You have my permission to make it immediately – go and do it now, so that it is ready for use tonight!'

Off sped Incitatus in search of a piece of wood and a knife and, having procured these from the ever-resourceful Felix, he sat on a tree-stump all afternoon carving and smoothing then polishing the wood and ensuring that it was free of all roughness so that, by sundown, he had made a really rather lovely artefact which he then threaded on the thin strip of leather he had begged from Impedimentus.

Now he found Graecus and showed him what he had made and how it should be used. Graecus marvelled at the fine carving and the finish he had achieved with such rough tools but wondered how best to tell Pneumaticus (whose ego was somewhat bruised by the farting problem) that he must wear this all night. He decided that the brutally honest approach would be best so he sought Pneumaticus where he knew he would find him, gossiping with Impedimentus, and said, 'This is for you. You wear it like this with the bobbin at the back of your neck. It stops you snoring and if you don't wear it every night from now on, I cannot be responsible for the consequences,' before turning on his heel and striding back to his tent.

He was, in truth, quite looking forward to what would happen – the prospect of a good night's sleep was very welcome and he knew that if this neat little device were to silence Pneumaticus then Incitatus would acquire some status within the camp and he himself would be vindicated in his having brought him to the century.

The evening passed and after their supper the men sat about in the torchlight reliving old battles, remembering fallen comrades, good soldiers and bad officers, good times and trying times, good-time girls and bad women, and all the things warriors talk about in front of the camp-fire and then they started to sing.

Singing played an important part in the life of the men. Indeed, they often sang while they were working in the camp, they often sang while they marched and they always sang in the evenings after supper. There were many songs in the communal repertoire – some of which could be repeated in polite company and many of which could not but there were some fine voices among the men, including Graecus's which was a rich tenor and he was well aware of its superior quality which showed itself to best advantage in what might be described as 'sentimental' tunes.

So, it was often the case that when the men had had enough to drink and were becoming maudlin, Graecus would be called upon to sing two or three of his most moving songs about lost love or one's lost homeland and the night air would be filled with the sweetness of his voice, sometimes moving the men to tears as they thought about all the good things in life that they did not have. And this particular evening was no different in that the men had partaken of one of Felix's best creations and had drunk deeply of wine and mead and had had several rousing choruses of various jolly hunting songs when, tiring of that theme, Magnus had asked that Graecus should sing something more peaceful.

Now it might have been that he was feeling particularly morose that evening or it might have been that he had been thinking fondly of Arminia (who often appeared in his dreams) but whatever it was, it was certainly the case that his voice was especially sweet and he chose a very sad, haunting song from Naples all about a sailor who had been shipwrecked and was remembering his beautiful wife who was admired by all, including the rich merchant who bought his fish and who would be consoling her in his absence and the tune was so plaintive and the words so evocative and the sky so starlit and the night so still that some of the men began sniffling as they too remembered women they had loved and lost and, knowing that his song was so effective in unlocking these hidden emotions, Graecus was feeling quietly proud of his skills as a balladeer and preparing himself for the dramatic end to the song when he would need to reach and hold a very high note but, just at that moment, Pneumaticus, who with his usual lack of understanding had fallen asleep, punctured Graecus's triumph by letting out a loud sigh followed by a resounding reverberative snore.

The men collapsed into mirth and Graecus who had hoped for long and loud applause was left gulping wordlessly like a dying fish on a quay.

This was not what he had intended when he got up to sing and he was furious with Pneumaticus for spoiling his performance so he picked him up by the scruff of his neck and frog-marched him to the tent where he forcibly put the anti-snoring device in place before casting Pneumaticus down on his bed and ordering him to sleep silently all night.

Graecus then went back to the rest of the men hoping that they could recapture the earlier magic but the mood had changed and Illyricus was telling an elaborate tale about a woman and a snake he had seen in a Circus in Ostia when last he had been there, which story involved lewd references to the comparative length and girth of the snake and some of Illyricus's own dimensions as later demonstrated to the delight of the Snake Lady and it was quite clear that Graecus would not that night be able to appeal again to the men's romantic instincts.

So off he sloped to bed feeling quite angry that Pneumaticus had stolen his thunder and that, if he heard one more sound from him, he would surely be justified in beating him senseless. His disappointment then, when he entered the tent and there was the wretch......... sleeping peacefully and entirely quietly, was great.

Graecus got into his bed and lay there fuming. Fuming because Pneumaticus had ruined his moment of triumph, fuming because he had wanted to go on to sing some more and because he really enjoyed these performances but, as he lay there, he realised that it was, indeed, quiet and that the snoring problem had been solved and that his prayers had been answered and that all was well after all.

Feeling hopeful therefore the following day, Graecus decided he would discuss with Incitatus his wish formally to adopt Germanicus – having told Vulponia, in an attempt to protect the boy, that he had adopted him, it seemed to Graecus that it would be wise to turn the lie into truth and, in any event, it would give Graecus much pleasure and peace of mind if the boy were his heir. Going to look for Incitatus, he began to try to calculate how long such a procedure would take and thought to himself that, although the Army discouraged men from having families, surely if he were determined, it could not take all that long?

He found Incitatus working with Felix writing up lists of supplies which he needed and it pleased Graecus to see that the young man was at ease in the company of his best friend. Now that he had confessed what had happened between him and Vulponia, Graecus had no secrets from Felix so did not attempt to exclude him from his conversation with the new scribe.

Reflecting later on that conversation, he felt like many a person who has ever consulted a lawyer: he wished he had never asked. He wished he had never asked because it was all so excessively complicated and would take so long and would depend on so many things and would be so costly that it all seemed hopeless and doomed from the start. Well, to be fair to Incitatus, he had not said it was impossible, he had merely said it would be very difficult.

Graecus had had very little experience of dealing with lawyers or the law and did not like long-winded explanations and had, when Incitatus told him for the third time, 'Well, on the one hand..... this, but on the other hand...... that,' switched his mind off completely and stopped listening any more. Indeed, he felt his heart sink to his feet and excused himself as quickly as he could so that he could lick his wounds in private.

He found a quiet place a little way from the camp and sat on trunk of a fallen tree with his head in his hands feeling wretched. He had been there some time when Germanicus came up with Zig and sat beside him on the fallen tree-trunk.

'You look sad,' the boy said.

'Yes, I am sad,' the man replied.

'Why are you sad, Domine?'

'I am sad because I wish that you could call me 'Father' instead of 'Master'. I am sad because I wish to adopt you formally as my son but it appears that it is impossible'

'Oh, but father that cannot be! How can it be that it is impossible when it is what you want and what I want?'

'Well, it would seem that the law is putting obstacles in our way.'

'But how can that be when it is what you want and what I want.'

'Well, it would be very difficult and would take a long time and it is not possible.'

'But how can that be when it is what you want and what I want.'

'Because the procedure is very complicated and we would need to have the Army's permission.'

'But how can it be impossible when it is what you want and what I want?'

Graecus was not normally slow-witted, but on this occasion, he was allowing his disappointment to cloud his thoughts. So Graecus sat, still with his head in his hands, being the adult and the officer and feeling that the situation was hopeless, and that life was unfair and that he could not have the first thing he had really wanted in life..... and then he realised what had just happened. He realised that the boy had just told him, several times, that he wished to be his son, that he had called him 'Father' and that the boy was correct – if it were what they both really wanted then a way would surely be found.

His spirits rose instantly and he clasped the boy to his chest saying, 'You are right! You are right! A way will be found. I will find a way to make sure that you become my son in the eyes of the law and in the eyes of the Army.'

So for the second time that day he went to find Incitatus to discuss how it could be made to happen and this time he listened intently as the lawyer/scribe/messenger told him what needed to be done in order for the adoption to take place.

It seemed to be the case that there were three real problems: the first being that the Army set its face against its soldiers having families, the second being that, in order for Graecus to adopt Germanicus, there would need to be an existing 'Father' to give him up for adoption and the third being that the procedure would need to take place before the Praetor in the nearest large town.

Now that he was determined that he would adopt Germanicus, Graecus had the bit between his teeth and would hear no talk from Incitatus about its being difficult and, in fact, himself thought of the solution to problems one and two: they would seek Flavius's permission for the adoption and would ask him if he would stand in the place of the 'Father' Germanicus did not possess and Incitatus, beginning to be enthusiastic at the thought of solving this problem, said that, although very unusual and irregular, this might indeed be a solution, if only because of the great power and influence of the General.

Graecus felt that he was a legal genius and strutted away from the discussion with Incitatus to tell Felix how he had thought of the solution and, as usual, Felix listened to his friend with interest, patience and understanding.

Graecus was becoming really excited and set about the first step in the procedure by composing, with Incitatus's help, a letter to Flavius asking permission to adopt the boy and setting out the problem of his being an orphan and needing someone to stand in place of his real father in order formally to give him up so that Graecus could take him as his son. The letter took a long time to compose but, when it was finished, each of its authors felt it was a masterpiece of logic, compassion and classic rhetoric; indeed, it would have made a stone weep.

As it was by then late in the afternoon, Graecus could not, in all conscience send the letter using his messenger but told him to set off the following day as soon as it was light and to go with all speed to the main camp and personally deliver the letter to Flavius's own hand.

This done, Graecus felt more content than he had in many long months and was in that lovely state of happy anticipation where one hopes for an outcome and there is at that stage all to play for so he passed a very pleasant evening with his comrades eating, drinking laughing, reminiscing and singing.

The letter was dispatched the following day as he had ordered and all he could do was to wait until Incitatus returned. It was therefore a long day and he tried to distract himself with century business – the type of thing which he normally loved but on this day he could not settle to anything and wandered about the camp in a daze, absentmindedly smiling at people and tickling Zig's ears.

It was at about two hours past the midday when Incitatus reappeared – he was first seen by Illyricus who spotted him running over the southern horizon and Graecus then fixed his gaze on the small figure as it got larger and larger in its approach to the camp.

Incitatus arrived at last and, without pausing for breath, went straight to Graecus with a letter bearing Flavius's seal.

Graecus had, in deference to what was going to be in his life an historical moment, seated himself in a stately manner at his desk, and received the letter most graciously.

The letter lay on the desk and Graecus tried to find the courage to open it but, he who had faced enemies of all shapes and sizes in battle, all of whom wished to kill him, was finding it difficult to open this letter. He looked at it for a while and then decided that it might be a good idea to look at Incitatus's face for a clue as to what he might find within, but all he saw there was curiosity. So there was nothing for it, he would have to open the letter.

He took his favourite knife and slit open the seal, noticing instantly and with surprise that the General had written a very long missive to him.

Puzzled, he knit his brows and concentrated on reading the letter very carefully. The first part of the letter made his heart leap with joy as Flavius agreed to both requests so it was with a light heart that Graecus read on. He read on but the lightness of his heart began to disappear as he learned that Flavius would not be able to fulfil his part of the adoption for some time as he had finished his tour and was required in Rome to attend to the arrangements for the marriage of his niece Julia to none other than Gnaeus Claudius Verus, the bored young equites who had attended the banquet with Rubicundus and Drusilla some months before.

In reading this, Graecus shook his head in disbelief as he knew that Flavius could not willingly give up his niece to someone so unsuited to her. So he read and reread this passage several times and saw that in the careful language was a coded reference to the fact that the marriage was not to the taste of either Flavius or the young woman but that it had been forced upon them by the Emperor Nero whose reasons could only be guessed at but whose whims must be indulged on pain of death.

Graecus knew how repulsive it would be for Flavius to have to give up his close relative into the hands of an epicene dilettante and his own delight in the prospect of actually adopting Germanicus as his son was now overshadowed by his knowledge of Flavius's pain and the uncertain future of his niece.

Graecus carefully replaced the letter on his desk and looked up to see curious faces staring at him and the nearest of them looked as if it was about to burst into tears – Germanicus was standing in front of him and had mistaken his stern looks so Graecus hurried to reassure him that the news was good but was still met with an enquiring look because he had not explained his worried demeanour on reading the rest of the letter.

This caused him a problem as it would not do to let the others know of Flavius's personal tragedy so he had to say that there was unsettling news about developments in Rome and it was not untrue – there was very often these days unsettling news about Nero's increasingly fragile mental state and the strain this put on his more traditional advisers.

So Graecus took up the letter and made to leave his chair but glancing at the rolled up scroll in his hand he saw that there was something written on the back of it which he had not yet read and, on reading it, he fell back in his chair in a daze, all pleasure in the day's good news being overshadowed by what was to come.

For the postscript to the letter told Graecus that the very Verus whom, if he was honest with himself, he rather despised, was being posted to their camp for a short while to give him experience of being in a front line position as this would help his career and he was being groomed for promotion. What was worse was that Graecus was specifically being asked to take the young officer under his wing and to tutor him in soldiery as practised at the frontier of the Roman Army. And what was worst was that Verus would be arriving in about three days' time for a period of about three weeks.

Graecus hoped that he would be able to carry this off without disclosing his dislike of Verus but three weeks is a long time to hide one's feelings when living cheek by jowl with another and he felt very weary at the thought of having to be solicitous of Verus's welfare for such a period.

Well, it must be borne and it must be borne with fortitude for, if Graecus were to fail in any way, this would reflect badly on Flavius and so he squared his shoulders and went to give this news to both Magnus and Felix who would also be expected to assist Verus in learning about life at the sharp end and be involved in the preparations which would need to be made for Verus's bodily comforts.

So Graecus was thrown into a frenzy of activity making arrangements interspersed with moments of doubt as to whether the accommodation he would provide would be met with approval or a sneer and, as the time for Verus's arrival drew nearer, his doubts grew stronger and he kept turning over in his mind that he wished to be successful in this endeavour in order not to make things worse for Flavius.

All in all, therefore, it was a perplexed Graecus who, in his best tunic, went to meet Verus in the middle of the afternoon on the third day after he had received Flavius's letter.

Verus arrived in a chariot with one of Flavius's men and, as it drew to a halt, jumped from it with a sort of flourish which Graecus felt was unnecessary but he gulped down his feelings and went forward to greet the young man with the best humour he could muster, proferring his hand in comradeship.

Verus took Graecus's hand and made a limp attempt at the Cohort's special handshake but said nothing and, after a slightly uncomfortable pause, Graecus felt moved to speak but could think of nothing better to say than, 'Welcome' accompanied by a smile. Unfortunately, this brought no response and Graecus began to feel a mite foolish standing there in the view of several of his men, clasping Verus's hand, trying to elicit some reply but getting nowhere.

Graecus then thought that Verus may not actually have heard him and decided to repeat his greeting but somewhat more loudly so he said, 'Welcome, brother,' in a voice which could be heard across the camp but was rewarded with a reply which was whispered in a hissing tone, 'Just so that you know the circumstances, I did not wish to come here and therefore I do not wish to be here ....and I am not deaf,' as Verus withdrew his hand from Graecus's greeting.

Graecus was taken aback by both the younger man's words and his tone and was irritated with himself for standing there in front of his men with his mouth open so he tried to make it look as if he had opened his mouth to belch and then covered it with his hand in order to close it in private but all that this achieved was to make it look as if he were trying to cover up some secret joke which he did not want to share with Verus.

Verus obviously thought that this was strange behaviour and snorted before handing to Graecus a rolled piece of parchment bearing Flavius's seal and saying, 'Here, you'd better have this, it's from your friend, Flavius. Where am I supposed to be sleeping in this barren place?'

Graecus took the parchment and, essaying a natural and friendly smile which looked more as if he had wind, said that he would show Verus to his quarters so they walked across the dirt clearing to the medium sized tent which Graecus had chosen as being suitable for Verus's sole occupation in the hope that being billeted on his own would make his stay easier for him and because Graecus did not know which of his contubernia could actually put up with him for three whole weeks.

Graecus lifted the leather tent-flap and showed Verus into his quarters which comprised a truckle bed, a trunk for storage, a table and folding chair and on the table was an oil lamp. As he walked into the tent, Graecus said, 'I hope that you will find comfort here and that your time in our camp will be fruitful,' and was again surprised by the reply, 'I doubt it somehow', but, this time, he was at least less openly taken aback and managed to keep his dignity by saying, 'You must be tired after your journey, I shall leave you alone for a while but our best cook, Felix, will shortly bring you bread, cheese and wine'.

This was met with a curt nod and Graecus turned and left with a vague smile. He went straight to Felix shaking his head in disbelief as he recounted in great detail this odd encounter with Verus and his overwhelming rudeness which broke the laws not merely of normal social intercourse but, more particularly, those of behaviour between officers.

Felix, ever good-natured, said that Verus could not be as bad as Graecus was making him out to be and that, maybe he had a toothache or something and perhaps Magnus could help him or perhaps he was just hungry so he would take in the bread, wine and cheese and put a few grapes onto the platter just to cheer him up. So off he went, looking as full of good humour even from the back as he did from the front.

Graecus was ruminating on how he would pass the next three weeks in harmony with Verus when there was a bellowing noise from Verus's tent followed by the sight and sound of the food laden platter leaving the tent and hitting the ground and followed then by Felix hurriedly leaving the tent muttering under his breath.

Graecus went straight to Felix and asked what had happened.

Felix, looking ashen, said, 'I don't know what I did wrong! I went in there, greeted him and put the food on the table and he was taking things from a bag so I went over and said I would help him unpack but he told me to keep away and that he didn't need busybodies like me interfering with his business and I said that all I'd done was offer to help him and I wasn't interested in his business. Then he said that I should be careful how I spoke to him as he is my superior and I said that I was happy to give him the respect he deserved as long as he respected me for being a soldier doing his job in bringing him food and wine after his journey but then he went mad and shouted that I needed to have more care in what I said or there would be serious consequences and he threw the platter out of the tent!'

Graecus did not know what to say to his friend who, like all the men in Flavius's cohort, was accustomed to being spoken to as if they were human beings and this behaviour on Verus's part was a worrying departure from common courtesy.

Graecus passed his hand over his eyes in a weary fashion and said, 'I can explain neither his words nor his actions and I am fearful of men like him who do not come from the same soil as do we. For us, the army has been everything and we have no alternative but to serve our time and retire or be killed in action but for him it is merely a stepping stone to political advancement and he has no true interest in what happens here'.

Felix could see the despair in Graecus's face and said, 'Surely, he is only passing through here and will move on, he is a temporary nuisance who is not important to our lives.'

But Graecus knew better and replied, 'It is more complicated than that. Verus is betrothed to Flavius's niece on Nero's orders and we must not cross him and make things worse for Flavius. Verus may become a very powerful figure in Rome and we do not know what offices of state he may command. We need to tread very carefully. Please treat him with caution my friend.'

Felix, whose colour had not yet returned, said, 'I cannot in my heart give him the respect he requires but, for your sake and the sake of the cohort I shall try to curb my tongue and I will tell the others to keep their distance'.

At these words, Graecus felt that something precious, the freedom that his men had had to speak freely and to feel dignity in the life they lead, had been lost as it appeared to count for so little with this ambitious young Roman.

But Graecus was the officer who had to lead his men including even Felix so, putting on his bravest smile, he said, 'Thank you. It will be for the best if we try to leave him as much to himself as possible and he is here only for three weeks which will soon pass.'

Felix left to go back to his pots and pans and Graecus went to his tent to read the letter from Flavius.

Given recent events, it was not good news: Flavius wrote to inform Graecus that Verus was being considered as their Cohort Commander and that Graecus and his men were to give him all possible assistance to enable him to learn about life in a post at the frontier of the Empire.

The letter was written in formal language but Graecus felt he could detect, between the lines, a sort of resigned despair which was very different from Flavius's usual vigorous enthusiasm and this plunged him further into depression as, if even Flavius, a powerful and popular General, must bend his knee to Nero's caprice, then what hope did any ordinary soldier have of upholding the traditional standards?

He sat for some while, pondering these uncomfortable thoughts while passing and repassing his hand over his eyes as if trying to shut out what was odious to him but nothing he did could quell his unease and he decided that the best thing would be to divert himself with frenzied activity but first he must put away Flavius's letter with all the other official papers so he went to the chest where these things were kept and, rolling up the scroll, he noticed that it had been countersigned by Verus, under Flavius's signature, and that Verus, in signing his name, had put an extra stroke diagonally across the lower horizontal line of the final 's' so that it looked a little like an 'x' – an affectation, which Graecus who was justly proud of his own clear, bold hand, felt really summed up the man in being entirely superfluous.

Graecus then spent the rest of the daylight hours in vigorous physical activity, pushing himself to the extremes of his bodily endurance in squats and trunk curls and weight lifting in the hope that thereby he could quell the unease which was growing in his breast but by sundown he was forced to stop and then, having washed, he went to tell Verus that the men would soon be gathering for the evening repast and that it was the tradition in the camp that they all ate together.

When Graecus entered his tent, he was sitting at the table and was studying important documents by the light of the oil lamp – well, that was what Graecus concluded for, when he entered the tent, Verus hurriedly covered the documents with his hand. Graecus then told him that their supper would soon be ready and was dismissed with a desultory wave of the hand.

Graecus took his accustomed place at the table and the men sat around him, the men who to all intents and purposes were his family and were all people whom he not merely could entrust with his life but had done so on many occasions as they had trusted him, and this thought helped soothe his mind.

Germanicus appeared with Zig and sat next to Graecus. Germanicus then launched into one of his stories about the dog's exploits and Zig, who knew he was being discussed, basked in the glory of his master's praise – today the little animal had excelled himself by hunting a small deer and, as usual, had brought it down in such a way that it was good for the table. Germanicus was very proud of his and his dog's ability to help feed the century and felt as Graecus did that all around him here were his friends and kinsmen.

Looking at Germanicus now in the light of the setting sun and the newly lit torches, Graecus saw how completely at home he was in the century and that he was truly cut out for the life of the warrior. He had grown several inches in the past few months and, due to Felix's tender care and an outdoor life, had filled out and was sturdy and strong. Felix had also cut his sun-bleached hair and he looked like a belligerent cherub.

Verus now joined the table sitting next to Magnus which was just as well because Magnus was the most tolerant of men and probably the only man present who could stomach his ill-grace.

The meal began and Verus tasted some of the dishes with a

bored resignation on his face while Magnus tried valiantly to find a topic of conversation which would interest him and was delighted when, for whatever reason, the subject turned to poisons and the relative speed, efficacy and detectability of the various toxins was discussed and Verus grew quite animated but, after this was exhausted and the men began to talk about the women they had known, he sank in his chair and looked very bored.

Germanicus had finished his supper and was now sitting at the table with a small knife, whittling a stick while whistling softly but tunelessly. Verus looked up to see where the irritating noise was coming from and, noticing the boy for the first time, he asked Graecus if it was the same boy they had met when he had earlier visited the camp and Graecus, gratified by Verus's attention, said that indeed it was the same boy. Verus asked Germanicus to approach him and the boy cautiously got up from his seat and went to stand next to the century's honoured guest.

Verus looked long and hard at the boy as if he were still for sale at the slave market and asked him questions about where he had come from, did he know who his parents were, had he any brothers and sisters and was met with a negative response to all his questions. Once he had finished his questioning, Verus said he could return to his seat but, as he walked back to the other side of the table, Verus's eyes watched him rather too keenly for Graecus's comfort as, since his brush with Vulponia, he was very protective of his would-be son.

The darkness came and the men retired to their tents with a lot of backslapping and shouting of 'goodnight' but Verus went to his tent without wishing anyone 'goodnight' and Graecus felt that this lack of courtesy was consistent with the rest of his unpleasant manners. He decided, though, that there was no point in worrying about a spoiled young man from Rome with whom he would probably never see eye to eye.

As the next day was bright and sunny Graecus took himself off hunting with a bow and a quiverful of arrows soon after breaking his fast and was happily employed almost till the noon day in pursuit of small furry creatures and wild birds. In fact, he had quite a good bag of rabbit and partridge and was looking forward to giving them to Felix when, as he passed close by Verus's tent, he heard a most unaccustomed noise – the sound of Zig's bark coming from inside the tent.

This really caught Graecus's attention as the little animal was normally silent so he went quickly to see what was happening and, not pausing to announce his approach, silently entered the tent.

There are moments in life when a person feels that something really bad has just happened and they would give anything to put the clock back to change what has just occurred. Graecus knew immediately that this was one of those moments as the scene which met his eyes was one which, as far as he was concerned, was straight from the Underworld.

What he saw was Verus, naked from the waist down and sporting a considerable erection, gesturing to Germanicus to come closer while he could tell from the boy's stance that he was confused and angry and that the dog, sensing his master's discomfort, was by his side, ears back, barking at the half naked man.

Graecus instinctively drew his dagger and, telling Germanicus to leave and take the dog with him, he strode towards Verus and put the blade hard up against his throat while staring at him in disbelief mixed with revulsion.

Verus was no warrior and maybe had never before had a dagger held to his throat because he began to snivel quietly and Graecus was as much disgusted with this as with the tableau he had just seen so, putting his face very close to Verus's he said, 'What do you think you're doing, you disgusting pervert?'

Verus looked as if he were going to shit himself and his nose began to run as he said, 'I wasn't doing anything. I asked the slave to bring me water and he came in without knocking while I was dressing and he was staring at my cock'.

This made Graecus all the more angry and he spat at Verus as he said, 'You're a snivelling liar and I don't believe a word of it. Firstly, the boy is not a slave, he is my son, secondly he is not interested in your cock, and thirdly, were it not for my loyalty to the cohort, I'd take your useless head off right now'.

Having delivered this speech, Graecus took a step back and gave Verus his most withering glance and, looking downwards at the offending member, which had lost its former upstanding angle and was drooping forlornly between Verus's thighs, he said, 'It doesn't look quite so impressive now, does it? And if I ever see that thing again in my camp then I'll take it off with my sword as well'.

Graecus then turned to go and was so swift in this that he caused some of the papers from Verus's desk to flutter in front of him and, on catching them in his hand, was surprised to see that, instead of their being the written documents he had thought were secret, they were pictures and from the corner of his eye, he saw that they were pictures of naked people.

Graecus was not a prude – he enjoyed the pleasures of the flesh as much as any man – and he was as much aware of the activities of those men who preferred men as was any man who did not share their enthusiasm – but he was not prepared for the orgy of male penetration which was depicted on the pages now before his eyes. In fact, he had to look quite closely in order to make out what was going on in the pictures but, as soon as he was clear as to what they were, he snorted in derision and, tearing them into pieces, he threw them to the ground saying, 'And that's what I think of your dirty pictures. It might be all the rage in Rome but out here we put our dicks in cunt not up some boy's arse'.

He then turned back to face Verus full on and dropped his gaze to the young man's deflated member and said, 'Cover that thing up, it's making me feel sick'.

Then he left the tent.

And almost fell over Germanicus who was standing outside listening and looking aghast at Graecus's words as it was unknown in the century for Graecus to swear.

Despite its being a warm and sunny day, Germanicus was shivering and Graecus put his arm round the boy's shoulder to comfort him but, after a few moments, Germanicus turned to him and said, 'Domine, I fear I have done something wrong'.

Graecus did not know what the boy could mean, so he said,

'What do you think you have done wrong?'

'I do not know. All I did was to take him the water he asked for but when I went into his tent he wanted me to look at his dick and told me to touch it and I fear that I may have done something to encourage him'.

Graecus was unaccustomed to giving sexual education to young persons and did not therefore have an answer ready for Germanicus but he searched his heart and said, 'My son, you are an honourable member of this century, I have no doubt that you did nothing to provoke what has just happened and I wish you to forget about it. Now, go and help Felix, he is waiting for you.'

This must have been the right thing to say for Germanicus immediately brightened and smiling his best smile nodded his acquiescence. He then whistled for Zig and ran off to find Felix.

Leaving Graecus alone with his thoughts.

And very uncomfortable thoughts they were. By Jupiter what a dilemma he was in! On the one hand, how could he keep Verus in the camp for another two and a half weeks given that he had so broken the Legions' and the Cohorts' code of honour but, on the other hand, how could he return him to Flavius without exposing him as a pederast and torturing Flavius with the knowledge that his niece would, at Nero's whim, be forced to marry such a man?

Graecus abhorred politics but he knew that this was a dangerous problem and that, given Verus's likely promotion, he and Germanicus were in a sticky situation through no fault of their own – Germanicus simply because he was a handsome boy and Graecus because he had sought to protect the boy's innocence.

He could not think of any way in which he could change things so that no harm would come from the morning's events so he decided he would let the problem just lie in his mind until later when he hoped that he would think of a solution.

But now it was time for the noon day meal and he must try to be his normal self, if only to reassure Germanicus. So he adopted a grimace which he hoped passed muster as a smile and went to join his men.

The meal was eaten without incident save that Verus, to

Graecus's relief, did not appear but afterwards, Felix asked Graecus what was wrong with him – he had looked as if he had seen all the shades of the Underworld.

Graecus could not lie to his oldest friend and, in any case, Felix had felt the rough edge of Verus's tongue so he told him the whole story in all its horrifying detail and was not at all encouraged to see that, on knowing what had happened, Felix looked as bad as he felt.

Felix sat with his head in his hands as he tried to find some way of lightening what appeared to be a very dark situation and then he started stroking his chin and this was instantly cheering for Graecus as he knew that Felix stroking his chin was always a sign of impending inspiration.

Nor was he to be disappointed this time for, after a few moments, Felix gave a shout of, 'I know what we need to do! We need to speak to Impedimentus! He knows all the ins and outs of what's happening in Rome and he'll help us think of something'.

Graecus now felt better, knowing that he would see Impedimentus later in the day and Impedimentus duly returned to camp but there was no opportunity for a long uninterrupted discussion with him so Graecus decided to leave it till the next day.

The rest of the day was almost pleasant, marred only by Germanicus cutting his palm quite badly when he stupidly tried to practise juggling with three of Felix's kitchen knives and this earned him not merely the slashed palm but a sharp smack across the head from the cook and an injunction against playing with sharp implements.

It was a blessing that Verus did not appear at the evening repast and so Graecus could retire to his bed feeling that, maybe, it was not as bad as he had at first thought. With this in mind, he fell into a deep sleep.

CHAPTER SIX

Graecus was dreaming of swimming in the warm waters of the Aegean when he became vaguely aware of an unusual noise but he was so enjoying his swim that he tried to ignore it and carry on.

But there it was again.

He was awake enough to want to find out what the noise was and quite quickly identified it as Zig growling. Well, that was unusual but the dog might well be dreaming and so Graecus hoped that he could ignore him and he was just about to go back to sleep when he saw by the small light of the moon, which was coming through the open tent flap, that Zig had sat bolt upright with his ears pricked and was very alert.

Graecus himself was now fully awake and alert.

He was alert because although the Romans had been in control of Germania for some years, it was far from being a settled Roman province and the main camp was stationed at the edge of Roman rule and his century was at the utmost limit of Rome's remit. True, there had been no fighting for many months but he knew that the local population did not like paying taxes to their conquerors and keenly felt the loss of their freedom. This all passed quickly through his mind as he tried to decide whether he should wake the others and sound the alarm.

Zig's ears were still pricked and every muscle in the little animal's body was taut as he and Graecus listened for further sounds.

Then Graecus heard something which was not a natural night time noise – the distant sound of metal clanking against metal and he knew that something was wrong. The next question was why had he been woken by the dog and not one of the men on sentry duty? And the answer was all too clear – they must have been rendered powerless by the enemy. But how could that have happened? How could they not have seen something and raised the alarm before being overpowered by the raiders? He did not yet know the answer to this but it must, in any event wait, because other matters were more urgent.

Graecus swung into action in a way which, through long practice, was second nature to him. He quietly nudged Felix awake and signalled to him that there were enemies outside. Then he did the same to Magnus while buckling himself into his armour. Then he silently left the tent leaving Felix and Magnus to wake the others as he went from tent to tent waking the century, warning them of the oncoming raiders.

The men all knew what this meant – they had been trained to deal with all types of warfare so it was a well-oiled machine which moved swiftly into gear even though they had all been woken in the middle of the night, and in a way which was unexpected.

Within minutes the whole century was awake, alert, armed and ready to repel the raiders whoever they might be. Even Incitatus was to be useful for it was his job to light the distress signal, a ready laid fire at the corner of the camp which was designed to make it visible to the main camp and would, Graecus hoped, swiftly bring reinforcements – but not in sufficient time to deal with this first attack.

Now that the century was ready, Graecus had the time to find out what had happened to the sentries and he sent two men to the gates telling them to approach with great caution.

As his men formed themselves into tight lines in front of the tents, facing the camp gates, Graecus was just silently congratulating himself and his men on this efficient response to a threat when he remembered Verus. Verus who was in solitary splendour in his tent some way away from the rest of the men and was probably still fast asleep. Verus who was therefore in great danger as he would be unarmed when the raiders attacked.

Graecus allowed himself the thought that Verus's murder by insurgents was the answer to his prayers but then he had the further thought that it would take some explaining how the ambitious and rising young man had been left so unprotected by one of the best centuries in the Roman Army.

There was only one thing for it – he would have to warn him.

But that meant he would have to leave the relative safety of the cluster of tents and cross open ground under the light of the moon.

Graecus was not a coward but he hesitated again, wondering to himself whether it was worthwhile to endanger his own life for someone whom he valued so little. But then the answer came to him – it was his job to protect Rome's citizens whoever they were – even prize idiots like Verus.

So off he went – running close to the ground still not knowing what had happened to the sentries and not knowing whether what had happened to them posed a threat to him.

He reached the tent in seconds but it seemed like minutes. Now he was in the tent and had quickly to decide how to wake Verus without making a noise. This was not the time for niceties so he went over to the truckle bed and, putting one hand over the young man's mouth, he shook him awake with the other.

Verus woke and struggled to free himself from Graecus's restraining grasp but Graecus whispered in his ear that they were under attack and that he must arm himself as quickly as possible and come and join the rest of the men.

Verus did not seem to take in this piece of information or had drugged himself or something because he did not react as befitted a soldier – rather he seemed to panic and had great difficulty in even getting his tunic over his head. Graecus felt angry that he had been saddled with such a burden at such a time but whispered to Verus that he should make sure that he had his sword and shield when he left his tent.

As Graecus opened the flap of Verus's tent and ducked his head to the left to leave, the cloud which had been obscuring the moon moved away and suddenly there was enough light for him to see, ahead of him, the cliff at the back of the camp and the two ropes snaking down its face all the way from the top to the bottom.

Now he knew what had happened to the sentries. He knew they were dead. Now he knew that there were at least some of the enemy already in the camp – probably hiding, ready to open the gates when their comrades down in the valley had responded to their signal that the coast was clear and were making their way silently to the top of the hill.

Knowing what the raiders' plan was, Graecus ran as quickly

as he could back towards the gates only to see the crumpled sil-
houettes of the two man search-party he had ordered forward
only minutes before, lying in a shaft of moonlight in the open
gateway. Then Graecus instinctively looked up at the walkway
on the inside of the palisade and, even in the shadow thrown by
the wooden fence, he could make out the bodies of the sentries.

Six good men lost before the century had even seen the
enemy. But he could hear them coming.

He could hear them even though they thought they still had the
element of surprise in their favour. Graecus's mind raced. He
thought about trying to shut the gates but realised that he would be
an easy target for whoever had killed the other men, nor was there
time for him to call for help……and anyway, that would alert the
enemy to the fact that the century had been alerted – better that the
soldiers' readiness would come as a nasty surprise to them.

No, the best thing he could do now was to run back to his
men and give the orders which were most likely to swing the
fight in their favour – swing the fight in their favour, that was, as
long as the enemies' numbers were not overwhelming.

Having decided that this was, in fact, the *only* thing he could
do in this unforeseen circumstance, Graecus turned on his heel
and sprinted back to the centre of the camp where his men were
armed and waiting for orders.

As Graecus approached, the men all turned towards him and
looked surprised as he had set off in the opposite direction.

Graecus had no time for details. He merely said, 'The sentries are dead and the gates are open. No time to close them. The
enemy is upon us. Form four lines, two of spears at the rear,
swordsmen at the front and form the testudo'.

The men quickly got into line and overlocked their shields in
front of them and over their heads so that they were protected
like a tortoise in its shell.

So far, so good. The soldiers were ready for the enemy but
there were only seventy-odd soldiers and there could be hundreds of enemy……which was not lost on Graecus who was
spending these moments of relative calm in berating himself for

not having thought that the camp could be infiltrated by enemy scaling down the rear cliff-face and contemplating the terrible possibility that his would be the only camp in Roman military history which had fallen into enemy hands. This was the first big challenge of his command and it looked as if it could be a shaming failure almost before it had even started. And it was made all the worse for him by the fact that the enemy which might topple his camp were smelly barbarians who put rancid butter in their hair. It was too terrible to even think about.

He would have to hope that the enemy's numbers were sufficiently small to be defeated by Roman discipline and weaponry.

But none of this was allowed to be made knownt to his men. Graecus knew that it was his job to lead and it was his job to put himself first in the line of enemy fire. So he stood slightly apart from his men, holding up his own shield but unprotected by the carapace of their shields. He was not afraid of injury or even death – what really concerned him was the thought that he might have failed in his command of the century – that he might have put the men's lives at risk by his foolishness. Then Graecus had another thought – he thought about the quality of the men beside him and he knew that every man would do his duty, and every man knew he could trust the man next to him, and that he could be proud of all of them.

Now they could easily hear the enemy approaching. Softly at first through the gate and forward into the camp but then the sound of their footfalls and the clanking of their weapons was unmistakable. And then they could smell the enemy and there was a curious comfort in this as the rank odour of those coming with murderous intent meant that they were an undisciplined rabble who probably had had too much beer and could easily be routed by the superior Roman fighting machine.

And now they could see the enemy clearly in the small light of the moon.

Quickly, Graecus scanned them and estimated their strength and effectiveness.

He gave a sigh of relief.

They were a pathetic lot – about two hundred of them, tribesmen, but, as they got nearer, straggling all over the place, and not very well armed.

Graecus ordered Incitatus to go and light the distress flare and told the rest of his men to stand firm and not break ranks until his signal and gave his command loudly so that it would clearly be heard by the raiders in the hope that, once they knew the Romans were prepared for them, they would think better of it and want to go home to their wives.

But the raiders were more determined than that and continued their approach,

This was always a tense moment in any battle or skirmish – the moment when you are waiting...............just waiting. Just waiting for the enemy to make the first move. This is the moment when less disciplined soldiers make mistakes through fear or misplaced valour but also the moment when the iron discipline of the Roman fighting force was at its best – for Graecus knew that every one of his men had experienced this moment time and time again and that there would be no mistakes.

The enemy was upon them.

Graecus kept his men in line until the right moment – until the enemy was so close that the Romans could really smell their animal smell – their dirty clothes, their rancid hair and their beery breath – and the first row of long Roman spears could do their damage while the throwers were still protected by the shields of the men in front.

Graecus gave the order to attack and was gratified that this first sally took down a good number of the enemy whose groans filled the night air.

The enemy was in disarray, it was time for another row of men to throw their spears and he gave the order.

Again, more of the enemy hit the ground.

Now they would have to wait again. Now they would have to wait for the enemy to regroup and make a full frontal hand-to-hand attack.

It was tempting at this stage to push the advantage, to break the formation and go forward but this would, in almost all cases be a disaster as the enemy would the more easily be able to pick off individuals than men in a tight phalanx.

So they waited and although many of the men might have wished that they could get it over with, they stood firm until Graecus gave the order to engage in hand to hand fighting.

He gave the order and his men went forward.

They moved together as one body thrusting their shields into the faces of the enemy smashing their noses and teeth against the embossed insignia, then, while the tribesmen reeled against this assault, driving home their swords into the undefended guts of those who sought to defy Rome.

Smash, thrust, thud as the enemy hit the ground,…. smash, thrust, thud,….. smash thrust….. Graecus was thinking that it was all too easy when, through the noise of the battlefield, he heard an unexpectedly high pitched voice screaming Latin. This was not one of the men engaged in this battle. There it was again and, this time, Graecus identified it as Verus screaming for help.

Graecus really could have done without this and it would have suited him if Verus had managed to get himself killed but it occurred to Graecus that he did not know where Germanicus was at that moment and, although he hoped that he was still in the contubernium tent, he could not be sure. Graecus would have liked to have gone himself to see what was going on behind them but he needed to be in the thick of it to lead the century so he dispatched Illyricus and Litigiosus to go and rescue Verus.

The rest of the fighting was a foregone conclusion with the insurgents making attacks, losing more men, being beaten back, regrouping and repeating this dance of death until they just gave up and the few who were left, about twenty of them, were easily overpowered by the Romans who broke ranks to take them prisoner.

Graecus knew that these men had fought bravely and he had no personal quarrel with people who wanted to govern themselves so he told his men to treat them with the honour due to warriors who had fought fair and square and the captives had their hands tied behind their backs and were put in a tent under guard while a detail went to close the camp gates and Graecus, Magnus and Felix inspected the Roman wounded. At this point, Graecus allowed himself the luxury of wondering whether his colleagues from the main camp were on their way in response to the distress signal and felt that he could do with some direction from a superior officer as to what should happen next.

There were some nasty slashes to arms and legs and one man had lost two fingers but, all in all, apart from a head wound sustained by a young man new to the century, the soldiers had come off lightly and Magnus calmly and quickly took control of the situation, assessing the severity of the wounds and treating them accordingly with salves and dressings.

Leaving the rest of his men to finish off the enemy wounded, Graecus could turn his attention to what had happened to Verus and to find Germanicus so he took a torch and went off to the other side of the camp.

And here he found that the drama of beating off the attackers which had taken place at the front of the camp had been echoed behind because what he discovered was Germanicus, a sword in each hand, standing in front of Verus who was clad only in his tunic, unarmed and backed up against a large rock at the bottom of the cliff-face with the boy guarding him. When he saw Graecus, Germanicus put down his guard and said, 'I am so glad that you have come, Domine, I was beginning to wonder what I should do next. The tribesmen were taunting our friend here and having sport with him and would have killed him but I saw them off'.

Graecus had not yet noticed but now he saw lying face down in the dirt two large dead tribesmen each of whom appeared, from the position of the blood stains in the dirt, to have been dispatched by two sword thrusts to the belly.

Graecus took in the sight of the dead men but could not get it into his head that Germanicus had killed them and stood there looking questioningly at the boy but, eventually, he said, 'My son, are you telling me that you killed these men? Surely Verus killed them?'

'Oh no, Domine, I woke up and you had all gone so I came

to look for you and when I came out of our tent, our friend here was in the middle of a group of tribesmen and they were taunting him and I saw that he was unarmed and so I went and got his sword and I found another sword and I killed one of them and then I killed another of them and then Illyricus and Litigiosus came and the rest ran off and our men ran after them.'

Germanicus was still standing in front of Verus and having heard the boy's story, Graecus held up his torch in Verus's direction and, looking carefully at him, saw that his nose was covered in snot and that he had soiled himself. Indeed, being down wind of it, Graecus realised that the young man from Rome smelled strongly of shit.

For the second time that day, Graecus felt revulsion for Verus but this time it plumbed new depths – here was a man who had ambitions of being a Cohort Commander, a man in charge of 480 or so seasoned fighting men who snivelled like a girl and couldn't control his bowels when confronted by a few crackpot tribesmen. And what was even worse was that he had allowed himself to be rescued by a boy – granted the boy was Germanicus whose ferocity in combat was already well known – but he was still a boy and he had saved the man who one day might be his commanding officer.

At this point, Felix appeared looking for Germanicus and his relief on seeing the boy unharmed would have done credit to any mother – he ran over and ruffled his hair in greeting but then, on learning that the boy had single-handedly killed two large tribesmen, scolded him loudly and boxed his ears saying, 'I thought I told you not to play with sharp weapons!'

Knowing that Germanicus was safe, Graecus told Verus to go back to his tent, clean himself up and get properly dressed.

Then Graecus could purge himself of the dirt and detritus of the battle – he could clean the blood, guts, bodily fluids and bits of flesh from his sword and, in particular his shield and then wash himself and put on a clean tunic. This done he felt refreshed but, feeling that all was in order, Graecus was overcome by concern about what could have happened to Illyricus and Litigiosus and, the more he thought about it, the more concerned he became as they had already been gone for some while and it was night time in what had just reverted into being enemy territory.

If he were being honest with himself, Graecus would have had to admit that he was feeling a little angry with the two missing men for having been so stupid as to run off into the night after the fleeing tribesmen when they could just as well have rejoined their comrades but then he thought about it again and realised that they must have been mortified by Verus's behaviour and had wanted to uphold the standard by pursuing the insurgents so that they could show them how real Roman soldiers fight.

The reinforcements had still not arrived and Graecus, new to command, had to decide what to do. Should he go with say, ten men, with torches, into the forest looking for the two lost men or should he wait until daybreak when they would be less of a target for the tribesmen. It was only a couple of hours until sunrise and Graecus knew that both Illyricus and Litigiosus were old campaigners who would probably have found themselves a cave or a hollow in which to pass the rest of the night before returning to camp when it was light. Graecus wrestled with this decision for some minutes before he came to the conclusion that it would be best to wait until dawn.

Back at the tents, there was the usual post-battle discussion of who had fought well and whether anything could be learned and this was being discussed in a good-natured way until Graecus announced that Illyricus and Litigiosus were missing in the woods but that they would not mount a search party until dawn. This caused an outcry from the men who wanted to go after their comrades immediately but Graecus insisted that it was his responsibility to ensure the safety of the century and, for that reason, they would wait until daybreak. There were cries of 'Shame on you' and mutterings which were very unfair but, as Graecus pondered to himself, this was the price of command.

It was nevertheless, a long wait until daybreak but, having dozed fitfully for an hour or two, Graecus was relieved to see the beginnings of the new day and quickly chose ten men to accompany him. Obviously, Magnus needed to stay in camp to tend to the wounded and Felix needed to be on hand to cook a big breakfast to restore the men's morale but there was no shortage of volunteers to join their Centurion.

There was still no sign of reinforcements and now they must go. Graecus took the lead, marching abreast with Pneumaticus with the others in two's behind them.

They could see footprints in the dust and where the foliage had been disturbed so it was easy to follow the trail and they made good progress for about half a mile into the wood.

Then Graecus knew something was different, maybe it was the excited chatter of the birds, maybe it was some unaccustomed scent on the wind, or maybe it was just his instinct but the hairs on the back of his neck stood up and he felt shivers up and down his spine as if they were being watched by unseen eyes.

They entered a clearing and he signalled the men to stop – he wanted some time to think.

Standing in the clearing, he allowed his senses their full rein and just experienced the feelings in his body for some minutes – listening, looking and sniffing at all the information which was available. Then something told him that they needed to go forward in an easterly direction and he signalled his men to follow him.

They left the clearing and not long after that they left the wood behind and, to Graecus's relief, stood looking into a grassy plain. He was relieved because it was more difficult for the enemy to hide in this terrain but then it also made them more visible so he again signalled his men to halt while he considered what to do.

By now, it was fully daylight and there was no cloud, the sky was blue and it was promising to be a hot day. Graecus was beginning to think that this might all be a wild goose chase and that the two men could well have been back at camp all the time.

He was turning this over in his mind when Pneumaticus nudged him and pointed to a large rock ahead of them in the middle of the plain. Graecus did not see the significance of this and looked quizzically at Pneumaticus who pointed to the bottom left hand corner of the rock and then to his own foot and Graecus understood that he was pointing to a boot-clad foot which was protruding outwards from the bottom of the rock. Even from this distance it was easy to see that that the boot had been issued by the Roman Army.

This could either be good or bad. Good, if it were Illyricus and Litigiosus who had merely fallen asleep at the base of the rock and they could all go happily back to camp but bad if it were a trap.

Graecus quickly concluded that his missing comrades were too experienced to spend any time in the middle of an open plain in enemy territory and thought that this must be a trap.

Then Graecus saw the crows wheeling over the rock.

The birds were excited and were flying lower and lower, calling to each other in anticipation of a feeding frenzy and Graecus and his men knew that their comrades were dead.

The question now was how to recover the bodies which had obviously been deliberately left where they were.

Graecus decided that they needed to know what was on the other side of the rock so he said to Pneumaticus, 'I shall go forward alone. Stay here with the others'

But Pneumaticus had other intentions and said, 'No, Domine, I am coming with you. Whatever is there we can best deal with it together'.

So they went forward towards the rock and the gathering crows, each man conscious that what they would find would not be pretty and each man feeling in his belly every morsel he had eaten that morning. Graecus was the Centurion and he must lead but it was Pneumaticus who was older and had the stronger resolve and walked more determinedly.

It took about two minutes to cross the plain and then they needed to walk round the other side of the rock to see what was on the far side.

Graecus and Pneumaticus simultaneously witnessed the desecration there displayed and Graecus was profoundly grateful that he was not alone.

Illyricus and Litigiosus were seated with their backs supported by the rock, their tunics up around their waists and each of them bore a huge bloody wound at the scrotum matched by a similar clotted grouping at the mouth. There were flies beginning to play around these wounds but they had not yet been dead long enough to stink.

Both Graecus and Pneumaticus stared in horror as, although they had each seen enough blood and guts to last a lifetime, there was nothing personal about a battlefield but what had been done to their comrades was very personal and contrary to the rules of warfare.

Graecus looked at Pneumaticus and said, gesturing to Illyricus who now wore his penis and testicles jutting from his mouth, 'Remember his story about the woman from Ostia and the snake? Remember how proud he was of his dick. And look at what they've done to him'.

Pneumatics nodded and then they looked at Litigiosus who had suffered the same fate. Graecus had been feeling nauseous but suddenly he was very angry.

In fact, he was incandescent. Incandescent because this outrage was all the fault of Verus who could not be trusted to follow simple orders and had to be mollycoddled like a girl and had now caused the horrible and cruel deaths of two of his best men.

And the symbolism of what had been done to them was clear – their killers had sent a message that they thought the Romans had no balls; Rome relied heavily on its reputation for invincibility and this loss of face was almost worse than the loss of the men.

The vengeance to be exacted by Rome would need to be considered but the first thing was to get the bodies back to camp so Graecus called the rest of the men forward and set them to work cutting branches and fashioning crude stretchers from these and the men's cloaks. He knew they were as angry as he was and he could see that some of them were fighting the urge to weep. He felt desolate but this was no time for giving in to his feelings – this was a time for decisive command and Graecus was not going to let the cohort, his men, or himself, down.

The stretchers were finished and the maimed bodies of Illyricus and Litigiosus were placed gently on them and carried deferentially back towards the camp.

As they marched, Graecus shoulder-to-shoulder with

Pneumaticus, the young Centurion thought about the funeral rites which would be given for their lost comrades and this led him to think about what would need to be done to dispose of the dead tribesmen – about 180 of them – who were scattered outside the camp and, no doubt, also beginning to be of interest to the crows.

Normally, he would have allowed the dead men's womenfolk to come and reclaim them so that they could be buried in accordance with the local customs but this was out of the question and Graecus decided that the best thing would be to make a huge funeral pyre and burn them thus sending a pungent message to their kinsmen that the Romans felt they had transgressed the rules of engagement of normal combat.

The sad column regained the camp and as they walked slowly to the centre of the tents, the other men stopped whatever they were doing and fell silent, some shaking their heads in mute sympathy with what their comrades had suffered and others showing their anger in dark looks.

On gaining the centre of the camp, Graecus ordered the men to put down the stretchers and called the other men to him.

When they had gathered round, he said, 'Comrades, you can see with your own eyes what an insult has been made against Rome and its Army. Our friends here died bravely but they were put to death in a manner unbecoming for a warrior. Our enemies think they have made sport with us and they think they have made us look weak. They can think again for we shall not allow this insult to go unpunished'.

At this point, in the past, it would have been Litigiosus who asked the next question but, now that he was dead, the questioner was the young man who had lost his fingers who said, 'But what are we going to do to have our revenge?'

And Graecus replied, 'It has not yet been decided but we must first attend to the funeral rites of our comrades and then we must ensure that these dead tribesmen go to their Underworld by burning them'.

There was a murmur of agreement and Graecus ordered several men to collect wood and make a huge pile of it just outside the perimeter of the camp. Then he ordered the bodies of the tribes-men to be collected and put on a pyre.

In the meantime, Magnus had set to work on the butchered bodies of his colleagues and had, to the best of his ability, restored them to their former glory so that they would be able to enter Elysium and enjoy its delights as whole men.

Graecus had decided that they would be buried at the edge of the camp with their weapons, as befitted fallen warriors, that afternoon so at about four hours past the midday all the men congregated to say farewell to their lost colleagues.

Magnus spoke the words of the funeral rites, as was the custom in the century. He was not a priest, nor was he invoking any particular god but he spoke of the spirits of the air, the wind and the water, the everlastingness of all things, how all things are connected and how, freed from the prison of this world, the dead men could now wander blissfully in the next.

It was then time to ignite the tribesmen's funeral pyre at sunset to ensure that their kinsmen would know what had become of them. This was all accomplished in good time and the pyre was well alight by the time the sun set on this most trying of days.

The pyre was outside the perimeter of the camp but it was large and there were well over 150 bodies on it so it was not surprising that the smell of burning human meat hung over the camp and Felix's cooking, usually so rapturously received, was met with many polite refusals and shakes of the head.

All the men, Graecus included, were relieved to retire to their tents that night but, as he lay on his truckle bed, Graecus was wrestling with three problems – what to do with Verus who was refusing to leave his tent, what to do with the twenty or so tribesmen prisoners who, at the moment were providing an allurement for rescue attempts and what had become of the reinforcements?

CHAPTER SEVEN

The next day was bright and Graecus was up early. He went to the edge of the camp and looked to the horizon, straining to see whether someone….. anyone, was coming to give relief to the century.

Unfortunately, the beginning of the day brought no relief and Graecus had to go about his business, trying to make it seem that he was in command of himself, when, in truth, his thoughts were fractured and incoherent because, much as he wished it were otherwise, he just did not know what to do.

Graecus felt he was at the end of the world both literally and philosophically; there was his century at the very edge of the Empire and he knew he was just about at the edge of his competence – he had little understanding of the wider interests which may need to be taken into account in the big decisions he must make. After much head scratching and thought, he came to the conclusion that there was only one thing to do – he must send a message to the main camp and it must be done that very day.

Now that he had made up his mind, he immediately went to find Incitatus to tell him what needed to be done and together they wrote to the camp commander telling him of the attack, the brutal murders of Illyricus and Litigiosus, the cremation of the dead tribesmen and the problems of Verus and the captive insurgents.

But there was the problem of how to deliver the letter and Graecus knew that there was no easy way to ensure its safe delivery. He was musing on this when Incitatus interrupted his thoughts by saying, 'Sir, I know that you have doubts concerning my ability to deliver this letter but, although I am not a fighter like the rest of the men, I am as speedy as the wind and, if any man wishes to kill me, then first he must catch me. Please let me take the letter.'

Graecus was touched by this show of bravery on Incitatus's part and said, 'You are a credit to the Army in your desire to do your duty but I am not sure that I can allow you to take it on your own. It may be better to send a column of ten men so that they can protect each other.

'But if they are attacked then you will lose ten more men'

'But if you are so difficult to catch, then how were you taken into slavery in the first place?'

'Sir, I was taken at night when the ship I was travelling in was attacked by pirates. As I cannot swim and it was in the middle of the ocean, there was no escape. But the gods spared me and I ended up in the circus in that dirty little town and the gods spared me again by sending you to save my life and it is now my turn to repay the mercy you showed to me. Please, sir, let me take the letter and I promise I shall be back before sundown'

At this, Incitatus went on his knees before Graecus which rather embarrassed the Centurion so, in order to get him on his feet, he said, 'You have my permission to go. Now run as if the Furies are at your back and return here with the answer before night-time'.

Incitatus grinned broadly at being entrusted with this crucial task and set off at his astonishing pace in the direction of the main camp.

This meant that all that Graecus could do until the young man's return was to worry about whether he would be successful in his journeys and it was a very long day spent in turning over and over in his mind what he would do if Incitatus did not return.

All his thoughts that day were uncomfortable.

He felt isolated here at the edge of the empire, he felt vulnerable as his valour and that of his men had been called into question, he felt sick because the smell of roasted human flesh was still thick in the air and he felt…………something which he found it hard to name but in the end, he decided he felt………..lonely.

This was a new feeling because, for many years, he had enjoyed the society of his colleagues in the century and had revelled in their comradeship but now he realised that rank bore its burdens and one of them, especially here at the back of beyond where he was the leader and had no-one to chew things over with, was loneliness.

Graecus was sitting at his desk, trying to make it look as if he were writing a report but was, in fact, deep in reverie, when

Germanicus appeared at his side and gave him a questioning look.

'Domine, you are looking puzzled'.

'I am indeed puzzled. I am puzzled because I have questions to which I do not yet have the answers and, in the meantime, I await Incitatus's return from the main camp which I hope will be speedy and safe'.

'Domine, I do not like to see you worried. Please let me show you how good I have become at juggling'.

Graecus was touched by Germanicus's desire to distract him from his dark thoughts but, at that moment, remembered that he had something important to ask the boy.

'My son, you may show me your skill at juggling another time, although I wish it not to be with kitchen knives, but what I would really like you to show me now is just how you managed to kill the two tribesmen.'

'Oh Domine, it was easy. All I did was get Verus's sword from his tent and then, on my way back to the clearing, I found another sword so I picked that up as well and then when I got to the place where they were taunting him, I entered from behind and tapped one of them on the back and he turned round and while he was trying to work out what I was doing, I thrust the sword in my right hand into his belly and just as he was about to try to take my head off with his sword, I followed through with the sword in my left hand and he fell backwards. I think he was dead.'

Graecus was listening intently to this, so intently, in fact, that he had opened his mouth in amazement, which he realised was not dignified, so he closed it and gestured to Germanicus to continue.

'Well, Domine, what happened then was that the man next to the man I had just killed, noticed that his comrade had fallen and turned to face me but, as I am so much smaller than he was, he was looking in the wrong place and, again, I was able to pierce him in the belly with my right hand and he was so surprised that it was really easy for me to follow through with my left and finish him off then just as the others were about to begin to fight me, Illyricus and Litigiosus appeared and the other tribesmen ran off with our men following them.'

These little speeches of Germanicus were delivered with a breathless enthusiasm which would have delighted any of the Classical poets in epic mode – and any citizen who may have feared that Rome was becoming too soft – and Graecus was not too sure what to make of the boy's evident skill in warfare. He thought for a moment and said, 'My son, you have done extremely well but were you not afraid when you were faced by those who were so much bigger than you?'

'Oh no, Domine, I was not afraid as I have been fighting all my life and everyone I have fought has been bigger than me. I could not stand back and allow the tribesmen to mock our friend, that would have disgraced the century and I would not have wished to let you down, Domine.'

At this, Graecus silently thanked the gods for bringing the boy into his life and thanked them again for letting him restore his faith in the world and the place of the Roman Army in it. He smiled and said, 'My son, you have learned well all the lessons we have been teaching you. I have no doubt that you will be a fine officer in this Army one day, especially if you spend less time juggling and more time practising your mathematics.'

'Oh but, Domine, the juggling helps my balance and you have always said how important that is in swordplay and hand to hand combat.'

Graecus was stumped for he was not accustomed to people answering him back and he struggled for a suitable riposte but, in the end, had to content himself with a sham boxing of the boy's ears accompanied by a 'Be off with you'.

But he had to admit to himself that he felt a great deal better after the boy's visit than before and it was with a lighter heart that he went to check the condition of the stores with Impedimentus and this passed the hours to the mid day repast and then he needed to see Magnus about a rash on his leg which was becoming troublesome. By the time all of this was accomplished it was three hours past the mid day and Graecus began to worry that all that which had been achieved this day would be the receipt of Incitatus's dismembered body. This thought tormented him for the next few hours by which time it was beginning to get dark.

By the time the darkness had closed in, Graecus's agony was overwhelming. How could he have let the unarmed and defenceless Incitatus take the letter? How could he have allowed his desire to share his problems overcome good sense? Why did he not wait until news came from the main camp? Was it his vanity in listening to Incitatus's flattering words which had brought about his stupidity?

Graecus's torment continued through the night which was brilliantly starlit and, every time he heard a noise, he thought it was another group of tribesmen intent on revenge or someone delivering Incitatus's diced earthly remains.

Happily, neither of these things actually happened but it was a heavy eyed Centurion who greeted the next dawn and a grumpy one who sat at the head of the table at the first meal of the day.

But then none of the men was feeling light-hearted as they too bore the scars of the events of the last few days and the smoke from the tribesmen's funeral pyre still cast a pall over everything.

Graecus could not eat anything and had to leave the table to take himself to the bushes urgently to empty his bowels which were also giving him trouble.

He then tried to go back to writing the report he had tried to write the previous afternoon but the words just danced in front of his eyes and he began to get a headache. Then, just as he was feeling really wretched, a bee which had been gorging itself on the flowers of a bush behind him, took a dislike to the back of his neck and stung him.

Graecus flung down his pen in disgust at this new turn of events and went to find Magnus for the removal of the bee-sting.

It was there, as he sat while Magnus probed with his tweezers trying to remove the sting from the inflamed nape of his neck, that he heard the cry heralding Incitatus's return.

Energised by relief, Graecus told Magnus he would be back later and rushed out of the tent to go to look for the slight figure of the messenger who, sure enough, was making his way with astonishing speed across the plain to the west of the hill camp.

Then he began his ascent and, unlike that of most other mortals', his speed did not alter in the least so Graecus had to wait only minutes before the letter from the main camp was in his hands.

Graecus was keen to open the letter but first he must congratulate Incitatus on his safe return so he said, 'Messenger, we are all mightily glad to see your safe return this morning. We were concerned for your safety when you did not come back last night. What prevented your return yesterday?'

'Sir, there was an attack on the main camp two nights ago, the same night we were attacked, that is why they did not respond to our signal. They were attacked by a large force of tribesmen and were taken by surprise while they slept so they suffered more casualties than did we. All is quiet now but the men at the main camp have had their confidence shaken and, now that Flavius is back in Rome, they are missing his skills.'

Much as Graecus was relieved by Incitatus's return, what he had just learned from him was most unwelcome and he wished to be alone when he read the letter so, after thanking the young man for his good work, he went straight to his tent and sat on his stool at his table and looked at the letter.

For some reason, his earlier enthusiasm had vanished and he did not want to open it and then he thought that, maybe if he washed his hands first, he would find the contents of the letter more palatable so he went to the basin in the corner, poured water into it and washed his hands very thoroughly before wiping them on a linen napkin and sitting back at his table. Still he did not want to open the letter and was chastising himself for his reluctance when Felix came into the tent asking what was going on.

Graecus felt a little stupid to be sitting there staring at an unopened letter so he told his friend that he was just about to open the letter from the main camp and, emboldened by Felix's presence, he took a knife and slit the seal.

The letter was quite short but contained all the information for which Graecus had asked but what he read was far worse than anything he might have imagined.

Firstly, Flavius had been called to Rome urgently, earlier than expected and, although no reason was given, Graecus instinctively felt that, whatever the reason, it was not to the advantage of either Flavius or himself. Secondly, the letter had been written by Biliosus, the commander of the camp, who, albeit a campaigner of many seasons and a respected soldier, was known for his ill temper which sometimes overwhelmed his better judgement.

As he read on, Graecus had every reason to wish that it had been Flavius who had written the letter rather than Biliosus – for, in answer to his question as to what to do with the captive tribesmen, Biliosus had written that they must all without delay be.......................... crucified.

Graecus kept staring at the word, hoping it would turn into something else, and the look of horror on his face caused Felix to cry out, 'In the name of all the gods, tell me what it is which so horrifies you. Nothing can be as bad as the look on your face'.

So Graecus gave him the letter and watched his countenance disintegrate.

And each of them sat for a few minutes, deep in his own thoughts.

Then Felix said, 'Can you not write back to Biliosus saying that you do not fully understand his orders and hope that his head may have cooled in the meantime?'

Each man was at that moment thinking that there was a world of difference between spilling a man's guts in hot blood in a battle where he has as much chance of doing the same to you and cold-bloodedly driving nails into someone's flesh so that you can hang them up to die a very slow and agonising death. There is honour in the former but only political expediency in the latter and neither of them had much time for politics.

Graecus thought for a few moments more and then said, 'I think not. He is angry that the other tribesmen found them napping and he thinks he has good reasons for wanting to make an example of these captives'.

'But how will we do it?'

'At the present I have no idea and my stomach churns at the thought of it. Please my old friend, bring me some wine – you know, the warm wine you make with herbs and honey and send Magnus to me.'

Felix left the tent and Graecus did not know whether he wished more to be sick or to relieve his bowels – truly, his digestion had been in a terrible state over the last few days and he had slept little, his eyes felt gritty and the scaly patch on his leg began to itch at the same time as the insect bite on the back of his neck added to his misery by throbbing painfully.

Graecus felt wretched but his physical ailments were as nothing to the mental torture he was enduring at the thought that he could not, as commanding officer, order his men to undertake this gruesome task without himself taking part.

Then as he gave into the misery of the thought of driving nails into an unarmed man's hands and feet, Magnus came in to the tent and said, 'Felix has just told me that we have been ordered to crucify the captives. Is it true?'

'Yes, my friend, we are ordered to crucify the prisoners, this very day.'

'But, Domine, that is a terrible way for a man to die and I have inspected the captives, some of them are no more than boys – indeed, one of them can be no more than fourteen years – hardly older than Germanicus'

'My friend, I have thought about this and I do not see any way round the order that will enable me to keep my command and, if I were to lose it, then I could be replaced by someone more like Biliosus and where would we be then?'

'Yes, Domine, I see. Why did you send for me?'

'Well, I need you to finish taking the bee sting from the back of my neck.'

'I will get my tweezers.'

And Magnus went to get his implements leaving Graecus alone with his uncomfortable thoughts.

Then Felix came back with a flagon of warm wine which he gave to Graecus who gratefully drank deeply from the cup held by the cook and Magnus returned with his tweezers and set to work extracting the bee-sting and putting a salve on his Centurions's neck to soothe the swelling.

As Magnus worked, the three men were deep in thought then Felix sighed and said, 'I do not know how we shall do this thing'.

And Graecus replied, 'Well, we shall try to do it so that they go to meet their gods with dignity. Now, please leave me alone – I must work out how we can actually make the crosses with the materials and the tools we have available'

Felix and Pneumaticus left and Graecus remembered that he had not read to the end of Biliosus's letter so he turned his attention to the final lines and his spirits lifted a little for, in answer to his question as to what should be done to ensure Verus's safety, Biliosus had said that the young man must be taken back to the main camp and that he would send a chariot the next day to accomplish this.

Graecus heaved a small sigh of relief – at least he would not much longer have to breathe the same air as that worthless piece of rubbish who had caused so much trouble.

He needed to think about the practicalities of how the captives would actually be crucified. This was an odd process because although it was a job he did not wish to perform, Graecus was a Roman soldier and he was, in any event, an organised person, so he must ensure that this ghastly task were done with speed and efficiency and, if possible, ...grace.

Firstly, how many of them were there? Secondly, did the camp stores have enough nails to make the crosses or would they need to be held together with rope? Thirdly, where would they actually do the nailing of the men to the crosses? Fourthly, where would the crosses be erected and finally, who was actually going to do the horrible job of the nailing of the flesh to the crosses?

Some of these questions were easy to answer – all he needed to do was to speak to Impedimentus, so he went in search of him and soon found him with a group of men engaged in repairing one of the century's baggage wagons. Impedimentus seemed that morning to be of such good cheer that Graecus could hardly bring himself to tell him what were their orders but the burden of the knowledge must be shared so that the orders could be executed.

Graecus took Impedimentus to one side and told him what needed to be done. He watched the good humour drain from the Roman's face and saw his nose wrinkle in disgust.

Impedimentus was also an organised person – it was the essence of his job in the century that he was so – and Graecus knew that he could rely on him to play his part in this odious task.

The two men discussed the best way to make the crosses given the equipment they had and it was agreed that, given there were about twenty captives, there were insufficient nails which were a valuable commodity and the crosses would need to be held together with rope which was more plentiful and could be used again.

Graecus then asked Impedimentus to find out exactly how many captives there were and he went to talk to the century's carpenter.

The carpenter's name was Nazarenus – this had been a joking reference to the carpenter from Nazareth who was fast becoming famous in Rome and throughout the empire as the founder of a new religion, Christianity, but Graecus now felt, as he explained the situation to Nazarenus, that the joke had become very bad taste.

Nazarenus listened carefully to what his Centurion had to say and agreed that it would be possible to make the crosses using rope. He said that the most suitable wood was pine as it was in plentiful supply around the camp and he immediately set about with three other men chopping down trees and cutting them into thick planks.

So far, only a few of the men in the camp knew what was to happen that day and Graecus must decide how best to tell them all and how would it be decided who would actually do the deed?

He suddenly felt the need to empty his bowels again and went discreetly behind some bushes to do so – this was becoming a problem – he could not shake off this boiling in his belly.

He needed some more time alone to think so he went to his tent and sat down with his head in his hands calling on whatever divine presence might be in this far-flung place to give him strength and inspiration.

He sat for some time with his eyes closed and then it came to him – the only way to decide who would undertake the actual crucifixions was that the men would draw lots. He knew though that in making this decision, he would not be able to shirk responsibility – he would have to do it, anyway. He also decided that, in deference to Felix's good nature and Magnus's role as life-saver, he would ensure that they did not draw any of the marked lots.

Now he must tell the rest of the men about their orders.

He left the tent and called for the rest of the men. Taking them to the centre of the camp out of earshot of the captives, he said, 'You may have heard the news that the main camp was attacked the same night they came for us. This is true, I have heard from Biliosus as Flavius is in Rome. Our colleagues had no warning and suffered many casualties, that is why they did not send reinforcements.'

'Rome has suffered at the hands of the rebellious tribesmen and our dead colleagues suffered most grievously. Rome has been insulted and, to repay that insult, Biliosus has ordered us to crucify the captives we hold here.'

'This is not work which will appeal to all and I do not feel it appropriate to call for volunteers. I have decided, therefore, that we must draw lots for this task. Impedimentus, please tell me how many captives are there?'

'There are eighteen captives, Domine'

'Then every man here must pick up a white pebble and give it to me. I shall mark seventeen of them with a cross and put them in a bag and you shall pick the pebbles from the bag. Any man who picks a marked pebble will be joining me in this task'

The men each picked a pebble and Graecus duly marked seventeen of them and put them in the bag held by Impedimentus.

Then he asked the first man to pick a pebble and pass the bag to the next man. A look of relief passed across the features of the first man but the next looked troubled and so on until the bag was empty.

Graecus asked the men who had drawn the marked pebbles to stay and the others to leave and so he was left with seventeen men, most of whom appeared unhappy at what the rest of the day would hold for them.

Graecus now addressed these men who included Impedimentus

and said, 'What is necessary is for each of us to make the cross on which one of the rebels will be nailed. Nazarenus will help us.'

So the men set about making the crosses and Graecus tried to quell the feelings of nausea which threatened to make him disgorge the warm wine he had had earlier.

The men worked silently, each lost in his thoughts and a heavy atmosphere hung over the camp. As Graecus worked, another detail now entered his tidy mind.

How would they decide which soldier would crucify which captive? This could not possibly be a matter of choice – how could you rationally decide such a thing? No, it must again be by lots.

He finished making the cross and saw that many of the others had also finished.

He called to them, 'Men, you have worked hard, I wish you to rest awhile but then we must draw lots again, to decide which soldier will crucify which captive. It is the only way'.

So the men all sat down on the ground amidst the finished crosses and the smell of newly sawn wood, all of them wondering how they would perform their orders.

Graecus closed his eyes which were hot and gritty from all the sawdust in the air and vigorously massaged the bridge of his nose. His lips were dry and there was an unpleasant taste of bile in his mouth and he was just thinking of getting up to ask Felix for more of the sweetened wine when, on opening his eyes, he saw Felix running towards him with an open book in his hands.

Felix was running very fast and was very red in the face so when he reached Graecus he was out of breath and, not being able to speak, all he could do was point vehemently at the book.

Graecus saw that the book was the classic cookbook by Apicius – the Roman culinary expert and was puzzled why, in the midst of all this misery, Felix would want to discuss recipes with him but Felix was calming down a little now and pointing to the open page.

Graecus took the book and read the passage which Felix had indicated. At first, he could not understand why on earth Felix was so agitated as the passage was about edible mushrooms and how to identify them. Then the book went on to illustrate various species of inedible mushrooms and one forest species in particular which, though poisonous, produced vivid hallucinations. The hallucinations were described as being extremely pleasant and it was even suggested that, despite their being poisonous, it was worth risking eating a very small quantity just to have the experience of Elysium without the necessity of dying.

Then he understood what Felix was trying to say and, deciding that this was not something which it was necessary or desirable for the others to know, he took Felix by the elbow and led him a few yards way from the others and said, 'My friend, how did you come upon this?'

'Well, I was looking for something else and the book fell open at this page and I glanced at it and then it came to me that it could be the answer to our dilemma. I mean, if we can find enough of these in the forest, then I can make them into a dish and the only remaining problem is to get the captives to eat them – they may recognise them and refuse the dish'.

And Graecus replied, 'Truly this was a message from the gods of mercy. We must make haste and get the mushrooms – take Pneumaticus with you and pick as many as you think will be necessary to produce these wonderful dreams in the captives. How will you cook them?'

'Well, I have pig fat, bacon and garlic so they will be quite palatable but, even then, the prisoners may refuse to eat them.'

Graecus thought about this and considered whether it would be possible to force-feed the captives but decided this would be impossible, then he had another idea and, although it would be a difficult, he knew it was the only way to ensure that the tribesmen ate the mushrooms willingly, so he said to Felix, 'Leave that to me, I will arrange it that they will eat what we give them. Now, please go quickly and pick as many as you need.'

Felix left and Graecus sat down again for a few moments as he gathered his thoughts and steeled himself for the next task in this strange day; he passed his hand over the back of his neck where the bee-sting had been and felt the lump left by the bee's venom, then he ran his hand through his hair, pushing the lock that usually fell forward, back onto the top of his head. Then, standing up, he cleared his throat and set his shoulders and walked to the tent where the captives were being held.

The captives were huddled together looking dirty and dishevelled. They were no longer a fighting force but merely a group of men who had sought to assert themselves one night when they had had too much strong beer and now they were in chains. Graecus looked carefully at them, trying to discern whether any among them could be their leader and he saw that, now they had all finished staring at him, the others were all looking expectantly at one of their number, a man with reddish, greying hair and piercing amber eyes.

He was about forty five and, Graecus having signalled to him to stand, he saw that he was very tall – well over six feet. Graecus asked the soldier guarding the prisoners to unshackle the man from his kinsmen and then motioned him to step outside the tent where the guard checked that the ropes tying his hands were secure before Graecus led him a little way from the tent.

Graecus now stood next to the man and, reeling somewhat from the rancid scent coming from his oily hair, said, 'What is your name?'

'My name is Segimer and I am one of the elders of what is left of this tribe. I and my kinsmen wish to know what is to become of us. Are we to be sent to Rome as slaves?'

'No. It is imperative that I am truthful to you – you are all to be executed'.

'Executed? I thought that you Romans liked nothing better than scores of big strong Germans to do your dirty work!'

'That is true in some circumstances but you and your fellow tribesmen tested Rome's patience to the limit'.

'All we did was try to regain our freedom. We've had enough of your so-called Pax Romana – all it means to us is too many laws and too much tax.'

It is not for me to seek to justify Rome to you, my task today is simpler – I require your co-operation'

'I think, sir, that you must be speaking in jest – why should I co-operate with you? Are you going to spare my life?'

'No. I cannot do that. I cannot do that just as your kinsmen did not spare the lives of my colleagues – two of my best men – whom you callously butchered and then left to the crows. No, the reason I require your co-operation is to save you and your men from a similarly cruel and painful exit from this life'.

'I do not understand you sir, what is this cruel and painful exit of which you speak?'

Graecus paused and breathed deeply before he said in a steady voice, 'We are ordered to crucify all our prisoners,' and watched the big man's face crumple as he contemplated this fact.

'That is why I seek your co-operation, Segimer – we have no choice other than to follow our orders but exactly how we do it is up to us and we wish to give you a drug which will render you insensible to pain before we begin the executions – if you follow our plan then you will all be banqueting with your gods and your ancestors long before you are dead'

'What drug is this that produces such wonderful dreams?'

'You probably know of it – or maybe your medicine men know of it. It is simply a mushroom which grows in the forest. It is poisonous and normally inedible but it will serve its purpose this day and I require you to encourage your kinsmen to eat the dish which we will give you. I do not know whether anyone will recognise the mushrooms and try not to eat them but if you, their leader, tell them to eat, then they will be spared the horrors of the death that I have been ordered to inflict on them'.

'But why would you wish to do that, what are the agonies of a few tribesmen to you?'

'I wish to do this not merely to spare you but also to spare my men, and myself, from a task which is cruel beyond our natures and is different from the warfare in which we are trained'.

I see that I have little choice in this matter.'

'You can take comfort from the fact that the last task you have undertaken as your men's leader is to spare them a long and painful death. There is honour in that. Do I have your word that you will encourage your kinsmen to eat the mushrooms?'

'You have my word. For a Roman you seem to have quite a soft streak.'

'I serve Rome but I am not a Roman'.

Graecus signalled to the guard to take Segimer back to the tent and went back to the middle of the camp where he saw Magnus and told him of Felix's discovery and their plan to drug the prisoners with the mushrooms. Then he went back to his tent to attend to the keeping of daily records while he waited for Felix and Pneumaticus to return.

They returned within the hour with two basketsful of the magic mushrooms and Felix immediately set about cooking them, taking care not to lick his fingers while he was peeling them and putting them into the pan.

A very appetising smell began to fill the camp and Graecus went to find out how soon the dish would be ready

He found Felix sweating over several frying pans adding more pork fat or garlic or mushrooms as the need arose. He was more than usually red in the face but, despite the underlying sombre nature of the task he was performing, he was also in a very cheerful state. This puzzled Graecus who would have sworn in the name of any deity you may wish to invoke that his oldest friend was as horrified as he by what was to take place that afternoon. But no, by Jupiter, Felix was even whistling!

Graecus asked Felix when the food would be ready and was told that it could be served within a few minutes so he assembled the requisite number of bowls and spoons while Felix finished cooking.

Felix now broke into song. And not just any song. Certainly not a plaintive song. It was one of the more rumbustious drinking songs that they would resort to round the campfire when they had all had enough wine to float a trireme. Graecus really could not understand Felix's lack of respect for the awfulness of the situation.

Felix had finished stirring the dish in the big pans and began to ladle it out into the bowls. He had stopped singing but was now humming another irritatingly cheerful tune.

Graecus was at a complete loss and stared at his oldest friend in disbelief.

Then he noticed that Felix was sweating profusely and that the redness of his face could not be accounted for merely by standing over the frying pans. Then he noticed that Felix's eyes looked as if he had put belladonna in them – the pupils were completely dilated. Then he understood.

Felix had been inhaling the fumes from the mushrooms and had been poisoned by them.

Ye gods, was he now in the process of killing his best friend?

Graecus immediately ran to find Magnus and, explaining about the qualities of the fungi, took him to look at Felix who was happily spooning quantities of the delicious-smelling mushroom dish into eighteen bowls – humming to himself.

Magnus bent over to look Felix in the eye and, catching the benign gaze of the drugged cook, he smiled at him. In the time it had taken for Graecus to return with Magnus, the potent fumes of the mushrooms had had longer to work and it was quite clear that Felix had left the limited levels on which most of us spend our time and was communing with exalted beings from other dimensions. He appeared so completely blissful that Graecus, fighting to remain in control of himself as melancholy threatened to engulf him, felt almost envious.

Magnus casually took up Felix's wrist and felt his pulse. Then he asked him to put out his tongue. Felix did so and each man gasped as what was unrolled was longer than either of them would have thought possible.

Felix's tongue stayed there, lolling from his mouth in a defiant manner swaying from the left to the right and from the right to the left while he seemed unaware of its activities as he, with exaggerated care, continued spooning the mushroom concoction into the dishes.

At this point, Graecus who had seen Felix in all states of drunkenness and had shared most of them with him, thought that he was about to burst into tears as the real Felix, the person he loved as a friend and comrade, had left this plane and had gone somewhere which was denied to Graecus. It was as if Felix had died. Graecus gave an imploring look to Magnus, begging him to do something to restore Felix to his usual balanced self.

Magnus considered for a moment and then said, 'His pulse is erratic at the moment but basically it is strong and I do not see any critical signs on his tongue. I feel that he is experiencing a very potent vision of Elysium and that it will take some time for him to be restored to us but he has not been mortally intoxicated. I will prepare a tonic for him to help with the headache he will have in about three days' time.'

'Are you sure?'

'Yes, he is in no danger. He has breathed in the fumes from the toadstools and they have intoxicated him to the extent that he is having visions but he has not been poisoned in any life-threatening way. He will feel very sick though when it wears off.'

At least Graecus was to be spared the loss of his best friend so he helped to spoon the mushrooms into the bowls, carefully avoiding the aromatic steam, and when he had done that he called for Pneumaticus so that he, Magnus and the older man could serve the captives with their last meal.

Entering the tent, Graecus again drew the stares of the captives; they would all have known that he was the Centurion, the commanding officer, and they may have thought it strange that he was helping to pass round the bowls of food. Some of them looked at him with curiosity and some with an attempt at hostility but mostly they looked at him with weary resignation.

Graecus looked again at them and saw men who were fathers, husbands, brothers and sons. Here were men who had enjoyed that most precious thing which he had never experienced – the love of a family held together by blood-ties and he thought of the women who would be widowed and the children who would be fatherless. He had to steel himself to carry on. But carry on he must and it helped him to remember the ghastly sight of Illyricus and Litigiosus wearing dark blood clots where their manhoods had been.

Yes, these men might look pathetic now but it was their kin who had butchered two fine soldiers.

Segimer, fulfilling his earlier promise to Graecus said to the prisoners, 'I do not know what this dish is, but it smells good and I am very hungry. Come let us eat'.

The captives took the bowls and the spoons and began to eat. Once they had cautiously tasted the dish, each man ate it with relish and some of them even smacked their lips.

Graecus did not know how long it would take for the intoxicant to take effect but he thought he would leave them for about an hour so that they would be fully under its influence by the time that the dirty work must be done.

So he and the others left the captives in their tent and Graecus went to his tent to pray.

He was not accustomed to prayer, indeed he had never done it before. In fact, he had no specific god or gods to whom he could address himself but he did believe in goodness and he believed in honour and, now that he thought about it, he believed in love.

He believed in love because he had come to love Germanicus and he knew that he loved the boy because, in the essence of his being, he knew that he would willingly give his life for him and that he would always want what was best for Germanicus even though it might not be best for himself.

But this love which had awakened in Graecus so many wonderful new feelings and sensations had also unmanned him. It had unmanned him because, now that he had felt the tenderness of love, it had opened up in him other tender feelings – feelings of understanding for the suffering of others and these new sensations were what were giving him such pain that day. The old Graecus would never have found it easy to crucify an unarmed man in cold blood but this new Graecus was finding it nigh on impossible.

So he prayed. He prayed to whatever it is which gives light and warmth to the sun, he prayed to that something which causes the moon to wax and wane and to the life-force which brings the spring to the land after the winter. He prayed to this universal force that he be given the strength to carry out his orders and that he should disgrace neither himself nor the cohort and that afterwards he would find a way of living with himself.

He prayed and tried to quell the boiling in his bowels. He

prayed and tried to get a grip on himself. He prayed that he would be able to lead his men so that they would be able to find some honour in this undertaking.

It would soon be time to begin the job. But where would they do it? There was every reason not to do it in the middle of the camp but equally there were good practical and security reasons not to do it a great distance from the camp. Graecus considered this for some time before deciding that the best place to nail the captives to the crosses would be at the bottom of the hill on which the camp stood so that the Romans, especially Germanicus, would not have to look at their handiwork but it would be visible to those to whom it was meant to be a deterrent, the tribes-people.

He could not delay any longer – the job must be done today and it must be done in the daylight.

He stood up feeling weary in every bone and sinew in his body. He shook himself and tried to find courage but realised that it was not that which he lacked – it was resolve.

Then he recalled his own words to Magnus – that the job must be done or he would lose his command and perhaps be replaced by someone of more malign tendencies.

He steeled himself and walked out of the tent.

Pneumaticus was standing outside and gestured to speak privately to Graecus.

'Domine,' he said, 'Magnus and I have been in this century for many years – indeed, I have been in this century longer than anyone – and neither of us wish to avoid our duty. We know that you must lead the men in this task and we know that you have no enthusiasm for it. Please allow us, as your longstanding comrades, to be at your side to take the place of the two youngest men who have drawn the lots'

Graecus could have wept with gratitude for the understanding shown by his men for not only were they showing solidarity with him they were also showing understanding for the feelings of the young recruits and this generosity on their part uplifted his heart. It lifted up his heart because it was proof to him that what he had come to think was the spirit of the Roman Empire, the essence of what it was that they all fought for, was still alive and well and had not been destroyed by self-seeking cowards like Verus.

Graecus clasped his old comrade by the arm and said, 'My friend, you are a true soldier and I welcome your suggestion. The cohort is honoured to have men like you and Magnus. You may tell the young soldiers that they are relieved of their part in this.'

It was time to draw lots for the captives and Graecus asked Magnus to go with two other men and mark the foreheads of each of the captives with a number from one to eighteen while he filled the bag with numbered pebbles, this time adding one extra for himself.

Magnus returned and each man then took a pebble from the bag. Graecus's was pebble number twelve.

While other men from the century took the crosses, the hammers, the nails and the shovels down the hill, Graecus and the unlucky few who had drawn the marked lots went to the captives' tent.

CHAPTER EIGHT

Graecus went first and entered the tent cautiously as he had no real idea of what to expect. Pneumaticus was behind him and they stood together at the tent flap looking in amazement at the sight of the tribesmen who were ranged about the walls of the tent, each in a position of exaggerated relaxation and each with a beatific smile. Some of them were already comatose but most of them were awake and it was clear that what they were experiencing in their waking state was not what was visible to the naked eye.

Graecus turned to Magnus who had entered the tent and he nodded, saying, 'Yes, the drug has taken full effect. They are all intoxicated and will know nothing of what we do to them.'

'That is as we wish it to be. Now we must each take the man allotted to us.'

So Graecus began looking for a man with the number twelve on his forehead and could not find him although others around him were raising men to their feet and leading them from the tent.

Then his heart sank as he saw number twelve.

Number twelve was a boy. Number twelve was a boy not much older than Germanicus and he was a boy who had blonde hair and blue eyes. Number twelve was a boy of great beauty whose features had not yet settled into the harsh lines worn on the faces of his older kinsmen.

Number twelve was the boy whom Graecus must crucify.

He was sitting on a bed-roll on the ground and Graecus had to stoop to put his hands under the boy's armpits. He was very light and the Centurion had no difficulty in getting him to his feet. He put one of the boy's arms round his shoulder and began to walk him from the tent while the boy, in his stupor possibly thinking that this was a kinsman intent on some sort of jape, settled comfortably into Graecus's side and started to giggle.

And this pattern was being repeated all around them – as the soldiers lead the drugged tribesmen from the tent, they seemed collectively to have decided that it was all a huge joke and they were snorting and giggling as if they had all just heard the funniest thing.

Graecus did not know whether this improved the situation or made it worse; here they all were going to their deaths and they thought it was hilarious.

One of the captives began to sing. He had no voice and was singing badly out of tune but then others joined in and soon most of them were singing but not the same tune and most of them could had no voice so the progress of this strange caravan – the tall, hairy tribesmen leaning on the mostly shorter smartly-dressed, clean-shaven soldiers all staggering down the hill – was accompanied by a confused and tuneless cacophony.

They reached the bottom of the hill.

The crosses, the nails and the shovels were there waiting. None of the soldiers had ever done this before and so they looked to Graecus to show them how to crucify a man.

Graecus had never done it before either and Graecus's job that day was to crucify a boy so in theory that should be easier.

But it was not.

Firstly, he had to disentangle the boy from his shoulder where he had been leaning in an affectionate manner. Secondly, he had to put him down on the ground and then lay him on the cross.

Then he had to tie the boy's hands and feet to the cross while the boy continued to smile indulgently at him.

Then he had to take up the hammer and a nail and, fighting the urge to gag, he had to hold the boy's small hand against the wood of the cross while he drove the nail into it.

It may have been the effect of the drug but there was surprisingly little blood and, somehow, this made it less hard to repeat the process with the other hand.

The feet were more difficult.

The nails were not long enough to penetrate the feet and pin them to the cross.

Graecus was an organised person. And he was a soldier of many years' experience who was accustomed to improvisation so in order to accomplish the task given to him that day, he had to take the hammer and smash the boy's feet in order to be able to get the nails into them. He did this with as much detachment as he could muster but the bile rose in his throat and, although he was trying very hard not to, he was crying.

Then he had to dig a hole to be able to erect the cross.

He dug the hole then he turned back to the boy lying on the cross on the ground.

The boy was sweating now and, maybe because the toxin in the toadstools was beginning to have effect, his nose was bleeding.

Graecus picked up the cross and, without too much effort as the boy was so light, manhandled it into the hole. Then he took the spade and filled in the hole so that the cross was held upright.

He looked at the boy.

It offended him that the boy's nose was bleeding. It diminished his beauty.

He took off his neckerchief and with great care and infinite tenderness he wiped the number twelve from the boy's forehead and the blood from his nose so that the boy would look his best when he went to meet his ancestors.

The job was done.

Graecus looked around him and saw a forest of erect crosses each with a man hanging from it. Bizarrely, it all looked very tidy as the soldiers had spaced each cross equidistantly from its neighbours.

Graecus looked at the horizon. It was late afternoon on what had been, for those who might have noticed it, a beautiful day. Normally at this time, the birds would be beginning to call to each other but on this day the silence was deafening and there were no birds to be seen.

No-one spoke.

The captives were silent because the poison was taking effect and the soldiers were silent because this was not like the usual discussion after a battle or a skirmish – this time no-one knew what to say.

Graecus least of all.

But he was the Centurion and he must set the tone.

So he said, 'Comrades, we have done this job with dignity. Now let us leave these men to go to their ancestors in peace. We shall return in the morning.'

Then he took one last look at the crucified men and saw that, although they were all well on their way to death, none of them knew anything about it.......... and they were all smiling.

Graecus and his men walked slowly up the hill and rejoined their companions who were also silent.

There they all sat, slumped at the big tables in the middle of the camp – each man lost in his thoughts.

Still no-one spoke.

But then Graecus heard whistling and lifted his head to ascertain the source of this incongruous sound.

In bustled Felix, red in the face, carrying a steaming cauldron of stew.

Graecus blanched at the thought of food and then nearly emptied his bowels at the thought that Felix, in his drugged state, might have cooked some of the toadstools for the men.

Not that any of them seemed eager to eat but, just in case, he signalled to Magnus to look in the pan so the big man gingerly lifted the lid and, trying not to inhale the steam from the dish, looked cautiously into the pot.

Magnus stared for a moment then shook his head and said, 'No sign of any mushrooms. We have boiled pork, garlic, rosemary, leeks, turnips and a hint of fish-sauce for real flavour. On another day we would all be diving into the pot right now'.

'Thank Jupiter. Men you have worked hard. Will you not eat?'

But the man were shaking their heads and gesturing that they were not hungry although some were eating a little bread as they were maybe trying to quell a queasy stomach.

Felix had gone to fetch another dish and was coming back, walking unsteadily across the earthy clearing carrying a tureen. Graecus stared at him as he tottered towards the tables and was trying to work out what it was about him that was different yet again from the Felix he knew and loved.

He saw that he was still red in the face and still sweating and then he looked carefully at his friend below the waist and came to the conclusion that Felix was sporting the most enormous erection.

Really it was quite remarkable – standing away from his

143

body making a huge dent in his tunic like a tent pole.

Felix plonked the tureen unceremoniously on the table and seated himself heavily next to Graecus, leaving his legs open so as to be able to accommodate his magnificently swollen member.

Graecus looked at his eyes and saw that his friend was elsewhere, and, judging from the smile on his face, probably on another of the heavenly bodies communing with as many virgins as his dick could service.

Graecus needed to know that Felix would suffer no ill effects from this and he needed to speak privately to Magnus.

So he rose indicating that he was leaving the table in order to empty his bladder and asking Magnus by way of a raised eyebrow to accompany him.

They walked to the bushes together and stood with their backs to the tables.

Graecus said, 'What in the name of all the gods is happening now? Is this permanent? Will he come back to earth?'

'In truth, Domine, I do not know. This is a plant local to these parts and it is not one whose properties I have studied but I do know that Felix said that his cookbook extolled the virtues of the dreams the plant produces and I think that he is at present enjoying himself in a way we cannot comprehend. He is with the gods.'

'But will he come back to us?'

'I have every confidence that he will but, as I have said, he will suffer badly from headache and sickness before he is fully recovered.'

'What shall we say to the other men who do not know about the toadstools?'

'Tell them that Felix has bought a book from Impedimentus which he got in Rome. Tell them that it contains the most detailed lewd drawings of men and women that you have ever seen and that the women portrayed are the most beautiful you have ever seen but that you have confiscated the book as it has had this extreme effect on Felix.'

'That is an excellent idea, but they will all come to me asking to see the book.'

'Tell them that it was so powerful that you have burned it.'

'Yes, I shall do that and I shall also tell Impedimentus of this ruse but he will have to say that the book cost a year's wages so that the other men will not pester him for copies for themselves.'

'Indeed. Now I think I could eat some of the pork stew and I suggest that you do the same. You are pale and tired and you need to eat'.

So the two men walked back to the tables where some of the other men had begun to help themselves from the dishes and gradually conversations began and the noise level rose and then all the men were eating but, although Graecus had to admit that that the stew smelled delicious and he knew he was hungry, he also knew he could not keep the food down so he sipped slowly at his wine and added some honey to it for sweetness.

It grew dark and the men retired to their tents. Felix lay on his bed still, as far as Graecus could tell, as erect as he had been earlier. He was humming to himself and he was so happy that it was difficult for Graecus to feel angry with him for keeping him awake. Not that he would probably be able to sleep anyway.

In fact, he did sleep but his dreams were bad.

He dreamed of driving spikes into people's heads and having to hold hard onto their skulls to get the purchase to make the spike pierce the thickness of the bone and he dreamed of men hanging from trees with ropes round their necks but smiles on their faces and huge erections and then he suddenly woke up to find a worried looking face in front of his which he then recognised as Magnus who was holding onto his arm and saying, 'Domine, are you alright? You were screaming in your sleep'

'Yes….. yes. I am alright. I was having a bad dream.'

Magnus went back to his bed and Graecus tried to go back to sleep but was afraid that it would mean a return to the horrible place he had been visiting in his mind so he did not return to the arms of Morpheus and lay there thinking about the army, about his life, about Rome and about Germanicus. His thoughts were all a-jumble but the one thread of sense in them was that he must as soon as possible formally adopt the boy.

The next day dawned and there was some comfort for Graecus in the fact that today was the day when Verus would be leaving the camp.

He wearily left his bed, performed his toilette then went to look for Felix whom he found, as usual, bent over a cooking pot.

He was still smiling and whistling and seemed to be sporting another huge erection.

Felix ladled some porridge into a bowl and handed it to his friend with the sunniest smile imaginable.

Graecus sat on a nearby stool and tasted the porridge which was hot, thick and sweet with honey. It was very comforting and he ate it with some enthusiasm.

The men were awakening and beginning to muster and Graecus turned his mind to what would need to be done with the corpses of the crucified captives.

He called ten of the most senior men to him and said that after they had finished breaking their fast, they would all go down the hill, retrieve the corpses and dispose of them. He had in mind that it would be prudent to re-use the valuable nails which had pinned the captives to the crosses and he told his men that they should conserve the nails if possible.

The meal over, Graecus and his men walked down the hill together.

Graecus was not looking forward to seeing the boy again and it was with some reluctance that, as they gained the bottom of the hill, he turned his eyes towards the forest of crosses.

Which were empty.

There was not a corpse to be seen.

Graecus stared for a moment and allowed relief to wash over him. Relief because they would not now need to do the job of taking the cold bodies down from the crosses and manhandling them onto yet another funeral pyre.

The men were also looking at the empty crosses and Graecus said, 'I see that the captives' kinsmen have saved us the task of burning them. They must have taken the bodies in the night'.

He allowed this to sink in before continuing, 'Now we must take

146

down the crosses and save whatever ropes and nails we can find.'

The men set about this and Graecus, feeling that he did not need to take part in this himself was just about to walk back up the hill when he saw in the distance a cloud of dust coming from the direction of the main camp indicating that someone was coming to take Verus.

Graecus sprinted up the hill and went straight to Verus's tent.

He entered without ceremony and found the young man sitting on his bed with his head in his hands but, on hearing that someone had entered the tent, he looked up.

'Oh, it's you'.

'Yes, it's me and I am come to tell you that a chariot is on its way to take you back to the main camp. You look terrible – you are filthy and you stink. I will send some hot water over for you, get cleaned up and put on some proper clothes so that you at least look like a respectable soldier.'

Graecus turned to leave the tent but it occurred to him that there was something else that he must say to Verus so he faced him once again and said, 'During your time here by your conduct and your cowardice, you have disgraced the Roman Army and you have caused the terrible deaths of two of my best men but you may one day be my commanding officer and I have no desire to make these facts known to anyone, but just remember if ever you see me again, that I know what a pathetic coward you really are and that you must stay well away from my son'.

'Your son! Your son! He is no more your son than I am.'

'He is my son because I wish him to be so and I wish only the best for him.'

'Your pathetic sentimentality does you no credit soldier. You are paid to be a hard man and to do Rome's dirty work – having fine feelings is something you cannot afford.'

'At least I have feelings. All you have is naked ambition fuelled by base and unnatural lust.'

'Your 'fine feelings' may have been what moved the City's founding fathers but that is all old fashioned now. Now Rome is about trade and commerce and making money. It is not interested in honour and valour. I know how to make money and I am more valuable to Rome than you can ever be. We need you and your type only to dig ditches and keep our enemies at bay'.

'You are very confident of your place in the world. You are confident in your riches and your place in society. You think you know what is coming and you think that you are part of the new Rome. I am not confident of the future. My world is hard and in it life is short and uncertain. I have not the comfort of riches – all I have is the comfort of knowing that my men would die for me as I would die for them and that what we fight for is the Pax Romana, the ideal that the state is there to serve the people, whoever they may be.'

'If you think that, then you are even more of a fool than I took you for.'

'If I am a fool then I am glad to be so. I could not live with myself if I descended to the depths of your depravity of spirit.'

'Soldier, your fine words do you credit and cut me to the quick but, forgive me, I must prepare for my return to civilisation – away from you and your muscular band of republican thinkers. The Emperor would be fascinated to hear that there are so many in his army who harbour republican sentiments'.

'I fight for the Emperor, he is our commander in chief. Everything I do is in the name of the Emperor so you cannot accuse me of disloyalty.'

'Oh but I can for, although you may not be disloyal in your sword-arm, you are disloyal in your heart. The Rome you think you fight for no longer exists.'

'It exists for me and all the men in the Legions and cohorts. It exists for the men who lay down their lives for it.'

'You do not understand how life has changed. The ideals which made Rome no longer apply and the new force in the Empire is money – pure and simple.'

'Money is rarely pure and never simple. And what you do not understand is that although you think I am here merely to do Rome's dirty work, underlying what I do is an eternal truth and beauty, but you cannot lay claim to any such thing.'

'Oh soldier, your words move me beyond expression but I am anxious now to be rid of you and your tedious adherence to dusty principles. Be gone from me and let me go back to my world where I can unlock the doors to the exotic splendours of the Orient and have Rome at my feet!'

'You make me sick. You make me sick because everything you stand for is base and tarnished but, at the same time, I feel sorry for you because you think that having Rome at your feet will make you feel like a man.'

'I am a man in the new Rome.'

'Remember then, Roman, that it was a boy who saved your life. A boy brought up in the ways of the Army.'

'That was an accident.'

'I think not. The boy killed two grown men while you were shitting yourself in fear. My son is ten times the man you will ever be.'

'Centurion, I am bored with all of this. You have convinced me that you will not forget me and I can assure you that I shall not forget you, nor your blonde boy. Indeed, the two of you are indelibly etched on my brain'.

'So be it'.

The two men squared up to each-other and Graecus quelled the urge to knock Verus's teeth all the way down his throat.

Then in the background could be heard the sound of the approach of the chariots from the main camp and the rallying sound of the horn.

Each man knew it was time to assume a public face so Graecus tried to be calm and look as if he were in command of the situation and Verus tried to look as if he were at home in the middle of nowhere.

There were three chariots.

One with a space for Verus and the other two as outriders.

Verus retired to his tent to prepare for departure while the chariots made their way up the hill and halted in front of Graecus. The senior charioteer saluted and descended from his vehicle.

'Hail! We are come to take Gnaeus Claudius Verus.'

'Hail! He is almost ready for you to take him back to the main camp. He will not detain you long.'

Verus came into view and Graecus had to hand it to him – he looked like everyone's idea of the coming man – clean-cut, erect, bright of eye.

Verus strode into the middle of the camp and smiled at the charioteers who were instantly converted by his charm – a charm which had so far been hidden from Graecus and his men but Verus must be feeling pleased to be going back to a less isolated place and nearer to his idea of civilisation.

Pneumaticus appeared, looking grave, carrying Verus's baggage, and behind him, still humming and almost tripping over his swollen member, was Felix.

It was unfortunate that Felix appeared at that moment, when the charioteers from the adjoining camp were there and seeking to avoid an enquiry from them as to Felix's humour in the face of recent events and, all the more so, an enquiry as to what was happening beneath his tunic, Graecus hurried to ask what was the current state of things at the main camp.

'Oh, Sir, we are struggling to bring ourselves back to normal. The camp lost thirty five men in the attack and Biliosus is in a fit of anger that our sentries allowed themselves to be overcome by the raiders – luckily for them they had their throats cleanly sliced by the insurgents and did not have to face Biliosus's wrath. However, we took many prisoners and we have crucified them to teach these barbarians that it is futile to try to rebel against Rome's might.'

'How many did you crucify?'

'One hundred and twenty three men and boys. You should have heard some of them screaming like girls – it was fit to put you off your supper! And we had a hard job of it getting some of them onto the crosses – we had to cut their hamstrings so they could not try to escape. A mucky business to be sure. But you had to do the same here, did you not?'

Graecus did not wish to discuss this in any detail with the charioteer, so he said, 'Yes, Biliosus ordered us to crucify our captives but there were very few and they were very quiet. Tell me, do you expect Flavius to return from Rome?'

'Sir, I know not exactly but, at the camp, we all hope so and that it will be soon. There is a rumour that he may be away until next spring as he is needed now in Rome and then, once the weather turns, it will be difficult to travel.'

Verus was moving from foot to foot in a sulky way, impatient to be gone so Graecus signalled to the charioteer that he could now depart and with a crack of the reins, he set his horses in motion, wheeled around and, accompanied by the outriders, set off down the hill throwing up great clouds of dust in their wake.

Graecus stood at the top of the hill, watching Verus's departure with a mixture of relief and revulsion.

As the chariots disappeared into the distance, Graecus watched the settling of the dust and thought to himself that it was settling on the events of the past few days and that it was hiding Verus's dirty secrets.

This made him feel very angry and he fought with himself for some time over his feelings but there was one small consolation – Zig had been more effective in sounding the alarm than the sentries at the main camp.

CHAPTER NINE

The next few days were difficult but not as difficult as the preceding ones and each of the two major difficulties was posed by Felix.

Firstly, his series of mammoth erections lasted three days and Graecus was heartily sick of the men sidling up to him and asking what was its cause; he was tired of repeating the story of the graphically lewd book and watching the expressions on the men's faces as he told them. Some of them asked him to describe the scenes in detail and one man even asked if donkeys were featured. Graecus could only assume that their taste in literature was not the same as his own and he took a mild pleasure in telling the more lascivious enquirers that the book would have aroused the desires of an octogenarian eunuch but that it had been burned.

The second difficulty was that, as Magnus had said, on the third day, Felix was restored to earth but was very sick.

Felix's return to earth came with a bump when he collapsed just before midday and this was at first a cause of laughter but his colleagues soon saw that he was ill and picked him up whilst calling for Magnus. As they laid him on a nearby table, his tunic rode up showing his now deflated penis nestling between his legs looking red, wrinkled and rather sore. Magnus arrived and, gently making sure that Felix's dick was not stuck to his leg, replaced his tunic thereby restoring his dignity if not his former state of bliss.

The men carried the senseless Felix to his tent on the table and placed him in his bed before leaving Magnus to tend to his patient and just as he was assessing Felix's temperature by feeling his forehead, Graecus came in.

'How is he doing?'

'Well, I do not think he will suffer any permanent damage but he hit his head quite hard when he fell and it will not help the headache he will have in any event. And he will feel very sick. I have made a tincture which will assist in clearing the   poison from his body but he needs to take it every hour and I am still busy tending to the wounded from the attack the other night.'

'Give it to me and I will ensure that he gets it on the hour.'

'Excellent. He needs a half measure from one of these little cups but it is very bitter and you must make sure that he does not spit it out. You can give him a spoonful of honey afterwards'.

'I will do just that. Should I give him some now?'

'Yes, that is a good idea'.

So Graecus propped his old friend up and put the little cup to his lips encouraging him to drink by telling him it was good for him and that he could have some honey if he drank it all.

And there must have been something in this which reawakened a very distant childhood memory in Felix for he obediently opened his mouth and drank the bitter brew then opened his mouth again in readiness for the honey. Then he settled back on his bed and went to sleep.

Graecus sat and watched him for a while until he was sure that he was peaceful and then he left the tent to go for a walk.

This was an unusual activity for him but he needed to be outside and he needed to be alone so that he could try to marshal his thoughts. So he walked around the camp, strongly giving off signals that he did not wish anyone to approach him or speak to him but after he had perambulated for five minutes or so he realised that he was being accompanied by Zig – the little animal was trotting at his side giving him his most winning look.

At first, Graecus thought he could really do without being the object of the dog's adoring attentions but then he felt that the dog was sympathetic to his dark mood and was, in his own way, trying to cheer him up so he bent down and stroked his ears which were wonderfully silky to the touch. This was surprisingly soothing so he went and found a tree stump nearby and sat there, absentmindedly stroking the dog's head and ears while he tried to make sense of his life.

The truth of it was that his confidence had been badly shaken by the events of the last few days and, what was worse, his principles had been called into question. Yes, even in the middle of the camp, at that moment, he felt lonely and isolated because of the burden of his rank but it went much deeper than that because his sour conversations with Verus had made him wonder what Rome stood for these days and then the awful business of the crucifixions made him wonder if Verus's idea of Rome was worth the wear and tear visited on his nerves.

Still stroking Zig's ears, he thought he came to the conclusion that the world was going mad and that he strongly resented being ordered to crucify boys to ensure that useless pieces of shit like Verus could grow rich and able to indulge their perversions. Looked at in that light, his life made no sense at all.

But that would be an intolerable burden!

So he must look at it another way.

Then he realised that there were many good things in his life which made sense of it: the comradeship of his men, the friendship of Felix and Magnus and, above all, his love for Germanicus. Yes, these were good reasons to feel that his life had meaning but he still had a nagging worry that Rome might now be full of men like Verus and Rubicundus who bribed the mob with free corn and increasingly elaborate, blood-soaked 'Games' so that they could become powerful politicians. Where was the honour in that?

It was time to go and give Felix his next dose of the bitter tincture so he left the tree trunk and went back to the centre of the camp with the dog running beside him. He had found the animal's company strangely therapeutic – the dog seemed not merely to understand the problem but also to avoid making any judgements.

The days passed and Graecus diligently administered the medicine to his friend who suffered badly for a few days and whose groans could be heard in neighbouring tents but the men suffered also as he was unable to see to his duties as cook and, now that Illyricus was dead, the next in line for kitchen duty was Pneumaticus who was out of practice and the men were soon complaining about undercooked or incinerated meat and mushy vegetables. Nor was Pneumaticus any match for Felix in the matter of procurement and, within a very short space of time, their diet reverted to the basic Army fare of bread, porridge, bacon and sour wine. This was almost intolerable for men who had been spoiled by Felix for years and they were all very glum.

During this trying time, the star on the horizon was Germanicus who managed with Zig's help to bring in some game for the pot and to find some herbs with which to season it even if Pneumaticus boiled it until it was a stringy mass of bones and fat.

Eventually, a pale and quiet Felix emerged from his tent and regained control of the cooking pots to the relief of the rest of the camp.

But as Felix got better, Graecus fell into a decline – it was almost as if, now that Felix was cooking again and the camp was back to relative normality, he could give himself permission to fall apart.

It started with the nightmares.

His companions in his contubernium could not fail to notice that he would often wake with a start, mumbling to himself about people hanging from trees and the redness of their lolling tongues. Then they would all try to go back to sleep but Graecus would toss and turn and, on moonlit nights, they could see him lying rigid in his bed, his eyes open and darting about him with fear. Sometimes he would cry out in his sleep and, when it was very bad, he would wake up screaming. The other men in the tent, especially Magnus, would try to pretend that all was well and Pneumaticus even said everyone has nightmares every night but they all knew something was wrong.

And Graecus's nightly journeys to the Underworld began to affect him during the day. He looked drawn and his face became pinched – his olive skin turned sallow and then took on a green-ish hue, his grey eyes which were usually bright and capable of dancing with humour, turned into cold dead metal.

Then, to Felix's consternation, his Centurion's appetite disappeared. Of course, Felix tried to tempt him with his favourite dishes – all generously flavoured with *liquamen*, the poor relation of garum, the highly regarded and highly expensive fish sauce – and, conscious of his friend's sweet tooth, he conjured up wonderful sweetmeats with nuts and fruits and honey. Graecus tried to eat and always, in deference to Felix's efforts tasted the dishes and ate a little, but most of the food was left in the dish and was eaten by Germanicus or Zig. So Graecus grew thin and his fit muscular body lost its tone. He began to stoop.

But the worst thing of all was that he lost his pride in his appearance. He, who had prized cleanliness above almost all things and who had been withering in his condemnation of the laxity of others in this respect, washed less and less often and shaved only when the itchiness of his face was unbearable. He, who had prided himself on being the upright, clean cut young officer with the good teeth, now looked a wreck and he was even neglecting his teeth.

His men did not know what to do. Graecus was pretending that nothing was wrong and was trying to go about his daily business. A few of the bolder men attempted to find out the cause of his decline but each was met with the same, increasingly snappy, response of 'All is well'.

So everyone in the camp pussyfooted around him, trying to behave as if all were normal but their laughter sounded hollow and their words were muted.

There were muttered conversations behind the hands of the men, all speculating what was wrong with their Centurion and all feeling mystified every time they looked at the wreckage of his handsome face.

Despite his youth, Germanicus noticed the change in Graecus and sensibly asked Felix what was its cause and what could be done. Felix told him that Graecus was much exercised by practical difficulties and Germanicus accepted this but tried to be extra helpful and even applied himself to the study of geometry in the hope that this would cheer Graecus.

All in all, it was a grim time for about two months.

But then a letter came from Biliosus.

The men knew immediately that what it contained was important as, on reading it, for the first time in months, their Centurion looked interested in something.

As he sat there with the letter in his hands, musing on its contents, the men looked expectantly at him.

At first he was lost in his thoughts but then, when he saw them all staring questioningly at him, he actually smiled.

This was wonderful because although Graecus's once pristine teeth were now coated with neglect, it was still the first time they had seen him smile in a long while.

'Domine, tell us what it is. What is in the letter?' said Pneumaticus.

'It is good news, I think. From Rome, Flavius has recommended Biliosus to reinforce our camp by the addition of one other century. We are to expect the reinforcements in two days' time. It is the century led by Marcus Caelius Caldus. They are being sent from the garrison at Augusta. Our isolation will not be so extreme once they are here. And we are to fortify our camp –we are to construct a permanent camp for two centuries.'

'Thanks be to the gods for that. I did not relish another winter under wet leather. Marcus Caelius Caldus, is he not known as 'Acerbus'?' said Impedimentus who knew all about the old Roman families.

'Yes, I believe so. I have not met him but his reputation precedes him and he is famed for his caustic tongue.'

They all thought for a moment about what changes this would bring and then Graecus had another surge of good humour and said, 'Send for Felix. We must be ready to welcome our brothers after their long journey and we must hold a feast in their honour'.

This was so much like their old Centurion that the men were similarly enthusiastic at the prospect of reinforcements and a proper fortress and when Felix appeared he was delighted to see his old friend in better form.

'What is the cause of this excitement?' he said

'Felix, we will have guests for dinner two days' hence. We are being joined by Acerbus's century and they will arrive then so we must show them that you are the best cook in the Army.'

'But Domine I do not think I can feed Acerbus and all his men!'

'No, I did not expect that you could but we should be able to feed Acerbus and his senior men, surely?'

'Well, if you limit it to ten extra mouths to feed then we shall be able to manage that.'

'Excellent. Now, Impedimentus, we shall need the best plate

and cups and two big tables so please make sure that all will be in order.'

This was all music to the ears of Graecus's men for the dull-eyed, jaundiced haunted creature they had recently been witnessing seemed to have evaporated and been replaced by the Graecus they knew and loved who was issuing orders and was in his element because he was organising a party.

At that moment, he seemed also to recollect his appearance for he started scratching and feeling the stubble on his chin and running his tongue over his dirty teeth.

'Hmm' he said 'I think I shall change my tunic'.

So later that day it was a much cleaner and happier Graecus who sat at the head of the table and, when someone suggested a song which was one of his favourites, he sang it so very tunefully and with such sweetness, that there were a few moist eyes.

The next thirty-six hours were a flurry of activity to ensure that all the men in Graecus's century and their equipment would all look their best and that the none of the animals was lame, nor dull of eye, nor scruffy of coat.

By the afternoon of the day when Acerbus and his men were due to arrive, Graecus was satisfied that his century would pass muster and he then went to see what progress Felix was making.

Felix was rolling pastry while Germanicus was chopping herbs and what looked like raw chicken livers.

'Is all in order here?'

'Yes, yes. Our guests will not starve.'

'What are giving them to eat?'

'We are having a soup made from ham and turnip then a paste I have made from wild boar meat and mushrooms flavoured with the livers of fowl then we are having boiled fowl with leeks and then a pudding made from dates and hazelnuts, oatmeal and honey.'

'A feast to be sure.'

'The honour of our century is at stake and I shall do my very best to ensure that the meal is memorable'.

Graecus smiled and ruffled Germanicus's hair then went to

his tent to put on yet another clean tunic, wash his face and comb his hair.

Now they could come.

Now that all was ready, now they could come.

Yes, it would now be acceptable for them to arrive.

Well, in truth, it was more than time that they did arrive.

Well, in truth, Graecus was now tired of waiting for them to arrive.

Ye gods. Where were the promised reinforcements? Had they got lost between the main camp and here?

As these thoughts passed through Graecus's mind, he was getting more and more agitated. Agitated because he had felt such deep, sweet relief that the loneliness inherent in being the only officer in an outpost in the middle of nowhere was about to be brought to an end and now he thought that Acerbus and his men were late and he worried as to what might have happened to them. In the light of recent events, this was not surprising but it was still only about the third hour after midday so there was plenty of daylight left.

He must compose himself.

He lay on his bed and closed his eyes.

And then he must have fallen asleep for the next thing he knew he was being woken by Pneumaticus saying, 'They're coming. Wake up! We can see the dust from the vehicles. They will be here soon!'

Graecus stood up and stretched and rubbed his eyes before following Pneumaticus out of the tent.

The men were standing looking at a cloud of dust which was moving towards their camp from the South West and was travelling at the pace of a fast march.

Graecus felt a jolt of joy in his heart that he would soon be welcoming a fellow Centurion to the camp, that his men would soon have more companions with whom to share their campaign stories and that they would all have better shelter from both the elements and the natives.

The cloud grew nearer and nearer and soon they could hear the trundling of the wagons and the sound of the men's feet tramping over the dry dusty ground. Horses whinnied and mules brayed as if they knew that their long journey was about to be over.

The new century was almost here and Graecus felt sick with excitement and relief. But what would he say to Acerbus who was so much his senior in age and experience and, if his reputation were well earned, whose tongue was as sharp as his sword?

The column began its ascent of the hill and then the first chariot was at the top of the hill and through the gate and there next to the charioteer was the famous Acerbus.

Graecus looked the older man over from head to foot and felt................disappointed.

For some reason, Graecus had expected a large man, someone imposing of stature rather like Flavius, someone with presence.

Graecus was horribly influenced by people's looks and Acerbus was, well,.............small: below average height even for a Roman and with a thin, almost scraggy neck set on small shoulders and despite his being at least forty, he looked boyish and not fully grown.

But Acerbus descended smartly from the chariot and, if Graecus was concerned as to what he would say, he need not have worried for Acerbus strode towards him with an outstretched hand and bellowed in a voice that would have woken the dead, 'Hail, brother! We are all exceedingly glad that we have reached your outpost at last. It has been a tedious journey and no mistake. Tell me, where can I take a piss and wash my hands and face?'

And Graecus, stepping forward to take his outstretched arm, loved him from the moment that he opened his mouth.

'Greetings, brother. Welcome to our camp. We are all deeply thankful that you and your men have arrived safely. If you would care to follow me, I shall take you to the pissing place and then show you to my tent where you may wash. Please come this way.'

So Graecus took the older man to the latrines at the edge of the camp and tried not to listen as he noisily and lengthily relieved himself before turning to Graecus and saying,

'You have had a nasty bit of bother I hear'.

'Indeed. We were attacked in the night by about two hundred tribesmen but we were alerted in time to put on our armour and weapons so we were able to kill most of them. The main camp was not so fortunate, I hear.'

'No. Biliosus told me that they were taken by surprise and lost many more men than they should have.'

'Well, we were lucky because my son's dog woke me when the insurgents were still some way off and we had plenty of time to ready ourselves for the attack.'

'Your son's dog, you say. You have a son, here?'

Acerbus said this with some surprise for the Army discouraged its soldiers from marrying and having families and it would have been unusual to find wives and families in such an outpost.

'He is my son by adoption, or rather he will be when we are able to arrange the formalities.'

They had now arrived at Graecus's tent while all around them was the bustle of activity as horses were tethered, wagons unloaded, fires lit, trenches and latrines dug and all the other myriad tasks which are involved in setting up camp for a whole century were being undertaken.

And above all this noise was the buzz of men's voices as some were reunited with colleagues from old campaigns and others exchanged news of mutual friends and acquaintances and yet others indulged in the age-old pastime of character assassination in respect of unfortunates who were not there to defend themselves. All in all, Graecus's men were enjoying the addition to their ranks of this new blood.

Graecus showed Acerbus into his tent and gestured to the bowl of water in which he could wash before leaving him to his ablutions but when the cleaner Acerbus emerged from the tent Graecus said, 'Brother, we have taken the liberty of preparing a meal for you and your senior men and would be most honoured if you could join us at sunset for the evening repast'.

'We shall be delighted to do that, brother. Now, I must go and retrieve my horse and see what my men are about.'

Off he strode. His tunic rode up a little as he turned on his heel, revealing skinny legs and puny knees but, now that he had spoken to the man, Graecus did not care for he could see that, beneath the unpromising exterior, there was something reliable, honest, good humoured and honourable.

He could have wept with relief.

CHAPTER TEN

A few hours later, Graecus and Impedimentus were supervising the laying of the tables for the evening's dinner party as the sun set and the camp was suffused with the delicious smells coming from Felix's kitchen.

Germanicus appeared with the dog and stood at Graecus's side.

'Domine, this is a very exciting day. Is it not interesting to have so many new brothers in our camp?'

'Indeed it is my son but you are not to spend all your time talking to them. You must attend to your studies, especially the mathematics.'

'Yes, Domine. I am trying hard to grasp the geometry but it is very difficult and some of the new men in camp have been to Egypt and Africa!'

'Well, in that case, they will no doubt be able to help you with your study of geography but you must not spend all day gossiping with them or you will stop them from getting on with their work. You can always ask them to tell you their stories in the evening.'

'Yes, Domine. Am I to be allowed to sit with you this evening?'

'I had not thought of it but, now that you ask, yes, you may but only if you promise to let the adults do most of the talking. Now go and wash your hands and face and put on a clean tunic'.

'Yes, Domine.'

When Graecus and Impedimentus were happy that all was ready for their guests, Graecus sat at the table and allowed himself a few moments' reflection.

The evening was warm, the sunset was beautiful, the smells coming from Felix's cooking were wonderful and now that there was a new comrade who was an old soldier and a fine man, for the first time since Verus had been visited upon Graecus and his men, he felt almost cheerful.

The guests arrived, Acerbus leading his men to the table before seating himself next to Graecus and declaring that he was now more than ready for wine.

A most convivial evening followed with Acerbus being mightily impressed with not only Felix's cooking but also his ability to procure ingredients far and beyond the normal Army rations. Many times during the meal, Acerbus smacked his lips and said, 'By Jupiter, this is first rate! Your cook is excellent. He could be the toast of Rome with these skills!'

And his men must have been in agreement for they all emptied their plates in double quick time and wiped them with their bread and sighed when it was all finished.

The conversation during the meal had been about army matters and what was happening within the Legions and the Cohorts but, now that they had all had some wine, and in some cases, too much wine, they began to sing and soon the night air was filled with men's voices recalling the victories of ancient battles from Rome's days as a republic. Then there were calls for Graecus to sing and he was more than pleased to be able to demonstrate the purity of his voice with a haunting love song which, because he was showing off, he sang in Greek.

Germanicus kept his promise and was a credit to Graecus's and Felix's skills as he spoke only when spoken to and was composed and self-assured without being over-confident. In an aside to Graecus, Acerbus remarked on the boy's upright stature and fearless gaze. Graecus smiled fondly and said that he himself had great hopes for the boy who had already proved his worth in battle by having single-handedly killed two of the insurgent tribesmen but then he recollected that he must not say too much on this score as he was in danger of divulging the awful truth about Verus's cowardice – in fact, he thought to himself, the less said about Verus, the better all round.

And even Zig was a topic of conversation as Acerbus asked if this was the dog who had saved the century by waking Graecus and was told that this was the very dog while Germanicus swelled with pride and said that he was also a good hunter and often brought in game for the pot. Acerbus's eyes widened at this, obviously thinking that this was a tall tale but Graecus's men hastened to assure him that it was indeed true and that they often ate rabbit and suchlike which the little dog had cleanly killed.

So successful was this party and so enamoured of Felix's cooking was Acerbus that, in the following days, he would often find something highly important to discuss with Graecus at about the time of the evening meal and would be asked to share the dishes with Graecus's men. It gradually became clear that, for such a skinny person, Acerbus had the most prodigious appetite and it was marvellous to watch him eat as whole loaves and pigeons and legs of pork disappeared down his throat.

After a few weeks of this, Graecus began to wonder what was wrong with the food in Acerbus's own century so, one evening, he decided to turn the tables on the older Centurion and went to find him in his own camp about half an hour before the time of the evening meal. Graecus then engaged Acerbus in a long and complicated discussion concerning the best way to dig ditches in marshy ground and whether they needed to be boarded out if they were of a sufficient depth and whether it made a difference if the soil were full of clay and what to do if the soil were sandy etcetera, etcetera and made no sign of leaving as the dinner hour approached.

Graecus talked on and on as the smell of cooking wafted across Acerbus's camp and, in the end, Acerbus had no choice but to ask Graecus if he wished to dine with his century. Graecus said that would be delightful so they made their way to the centre of the camp where the men were gathering and Acerbus sat Graecus next to him while the other men remarked how unusual it was to have a guest.

Then the first dish was brought in by a cross eyed man who, it appeared was the cook. Well, Graecus thought it was the first dish but, in fact, it was the only dish and, having partaken of it, he was glad that he would not be obliged to eat anything else prepared by the cross-eyed cook.

It was vile and Graecus who was fastidious in these matters wondered how Acerbus and his men could accept this day in and day out and why no-one in the camp was any better a cook than the cross-eyed man.

He could not say any of this, however, as politeness prevented him from voicing his true opinion of the food but, just as he was trying to eat another mouthful, Acerbus leaned towards him and whispered, 'Now you know why I come to your camp every evening. It's absolute shit, isn't it? I wonder that I and my men did not starve to death years ago but, to be frank, we must have become used to it and it was only when I tasted the wonderful food in your camp that I remembered what it should be like'.

'You are most welcome in our camp to share in the excellence of Felix's cooking any time and, in any case, I value your company,' said Graecus and, in saying it, he realised how much it was true.

In fact, he really relied on the older man's wisdom and knowledge and over the coming months, as the days grew shorter, the two Centurions shared many of their innermost thoughts at the side of the fire burning away in its brazier and became fast friends.

It was a source of wonder to Graecus that this man who knew so much about the politicking in Rome and viewed it with wry humour and detachment, was, at the same time, a man of great integrity and personal honour who shared Graecus's values and ideals.

As the oil lamps burned, the Centurions talked and talked and Acerbus began to address Graecus as 'My boy' which pleased the younger man greatly. This was all wonderful for Graecus for, not only had he recently gained a son, now it seemed as if he had gained a father figure of his own, or an uncle at least.

But there were still doubts gnawing at his innards.

Doubts about the rise of idiots like Verus and out and out politicians like Rubicundus and the fact that they could be given positions of high rank in the army, where, as far as Graecus could see, they could do immense harm. There were also the women to contend with – Graecus had been horrified by the behaviour of Drusilla but had comforted himself with the thought that she was a fishmonger's daughter, but then he had been astonished by Vulponia's outburst and could not make any sense of what she had said.

He kept these thoughts to himself for months and pondered them but he was the first to admit that he knew nothing about politics and would probably not be able to make sense of these mysteries without knowing more. He wrestled with these thoughts before deciding that he trusted Acerbus enough to share them with him.

So, one evening, he decided that he would test the ground and he said in as casual a voice as he could muster,

'Did I tell you that we had Gnaeus Claudius Verus here a while ago – when we had the night-time attack?'

'That pillock. I bet he was as useless as a girl.'

'You are correct. I have known many women who have shown more valour.'

'And he's an arrogant pig.'

'Correct. You clearly know him quite well.'

'I know of him – and I hear nothing good about him but it is as well to tread carefully where he is concerned as his cousin, Septimus Pomponius, is as thick as thieves with one of Nero's new favourites and one of his other cousins is a powerful priestess of Isis.'

A cold finger ran up Graecus's spine before he said, 'A priestess of Isis. You do not mean Vulponia, do you?'

'The very same woman. Rather handsome and very noble in her bearing but as cunning as her name. You would not wish to cross her, oh no! Have you met her?'

'I met her some months ago at her temple and had a strange exchange of ideas with her.'

'What do you mean? Did she want to sleep with you, you young ram?'

'No she did not. She very particularly wanted to take Germanicus and train him as a priest of Isis. Funnily enough, she also said she wanted the dog.'

'That is strange. What did you say to her?'

'I told her that she could not have my son – that he would be raised in the Army and that he would become an officer in the Army.'

'Good for you – these powerful Roman women can be all too accustomed to having their own way.'

'That is true for when I resisted her attempts at persuasion,

167

she flew at me in a rage, took several layers of skin off my cheek with her fingernail and told me that I, a mere soldier, should not interfere in matters of high state or I would live to regret it'.

'What did she mean by that?'

'I have no idea but it was definitely something connected with Germanicus – she was extremely keen to have him in her power.'

'What happened then?'

'I know not – she may have drugged me because I passed out and woke up hours later under the moonlight.'

'How strange!'

'Yes, and what's even more strange is that I could swear she took a lock of my hair for this lock here which falls over my brow was missing when I woke up.'

'That is not strange, that is what we would expect from this 'lady' for she is a well-known sorceress.'

'And you say that she is Verus's cousin?'

'Oh yes, on their mothers' side. Despite the difference in their years, they are very fond of each other I hear, but there is no funny business between them because he prefers boys'.

'I know. There was an incident while he was here. Ye gods! It makes me so angry to think of it, even now.'

'What happened?'

I went out hunting one morning and as I was coming back into camp just before the midday, I went past Verus's tent, where he was sulking, and I heard Zig barking. This aroused my curiosity because the little animal never normally barks and, in any event, I wondered what on earth the dog was doing in Verus's tent so I went straight in there without announcing myself and found a scene I wish I had never set my eyes upon'.

Graecus paused here to wipe his brow before continuing, 'What I saw was Verus naked from the waist down, and sporting a huge erection, beckoning to Germanicus to come closer. He had this stupid look on his face as if he were doing the boy a big favour and I could see from the boy's stance that he was confused and uncomfortable and did not know what to do. The dog, who is Germanicus's shadow, knew that the boy was upset and wanted to protect him so he was barking.'

'What did you do?'

'I did what any father would do. I told Germanicus to leave and I drew my dagger and put it to the pervert's throat and told him that if he tried that again with my boy or in my camp I'd have his head off.'

'And what did Verus say?'

'The swine tried to blame Germanicus by saying that he had been staring at his dick which I knew not to be true so I told him to put it away and that, if I ever saw it again in my camp, I'd have that off with my sword as well.'

'What happened then?'

'Well, I turned to leave the tent and, as I did so, I caused the papers on Verus's table to fly up in the air and I caught some of them and could not help but see that, instead of being army documents, they were pictures of the most vile kind imaginable – they were pictures of men buggering each other and buggering boys.'

'Yes, I had heard that he practises the unnatural vices.'

'Well, I told him that I wasn't having it in my camp. But the trouble is – I do not know whether you have heard of this – but Verus is being considered for Cohort Commander and, as far as I can see, that would be a disaster.'

'Ye gods. An idiot like that as our Commander, I had not heard that rumour – he has not the courage of a girl!'

'You never spoke a truer word. You will not believe what happened here the night of the attack.'

'Tell me and I shall try to believe you for I know that you are a truthful man.'

'Well, Verus was in a tent away from the rest of us and I went to him to tell him to put on his armour and get his sword but then I had to go back to organise then rest of the men so I left him to ready himself for the attack. Well, the attack came and we were able to repel the tribesmen fairly easily by killing most of them and taking the rest prisoner but then, when it was almost over, I heard Verus screaming for help so I sent two of my best men to find out what was happening and to make sure that Germanicus was safe. I really need not have worried about the boy because shortly after, when I went to find him, there he was with two swords in his hand guarding Verus who was backed up against a rock and behind my boy were two big tribesmen whom he had killed. Verus was snivelling and had shit himself. It was a disgusting display for a Roman soldier. And it got worse'.

'In what way?'

'The two men I had sent to help Verus went off in pursuit of the tribesmen who had been having some sport with Verus and ran into the woods. They did not come back that night and the following day when we went looking for them we found them behind a rock with their genitals cut off and stuffed into their mouths. It was a terrible sight and a terrible insult to Rome, and all because of that coward'.

'So he was saved by the boy?' Acerbus said this with some incredulity.

'Yes, I know it seems incredible but Germanicus is a true fighter and he has been fighting for most of his short life. What I find incredible is that Verus could be regarded as suitable as our commanding officer'.

'Yes, indeed. But the trouble is that, these days, the rich men and the merchants, the so-called 'equites', have so much more influence. In the days of the Republic, the Army and the Senate worked together for the honour of Rome and the good of its people but now it is all changed and the Emperor wants glory and power and riches and opulence and, to cap it all, he rather fancies himself as a musician'

'You say that Nero has a new favourite.'

'Well, he has them all the time. They're usually from his 'artistic' circle of friends who encourage him to think that he's talented and, as you probably know, he fights against the influence of the old advisers, Seneca and Burrus who counsel caution where he prefers profligacy but, from what I gather, he rebels mostly against the influence of his mother, that old harpie Agrippina.'

'Is it true that she had Claudius poisoned?'

'Who can say? It is openly alleged that she either murdered

him herself or had him murdered with poisoned mushrooms and, ye gods, she had the motive – why would a woman poison her husband when he is the Emperor and she is his consort? Why, when she wants her own son to be his successor! And, of course, when Nero heard what had happened he said 'mushrooms must indeed be the food of the gods''.

'But surely Britannicus was Claudius's obvious heir?'

'Poor Britannicus. He was only fourteen years old when Nero became Emperor. He died not long afterwards – probably poisoned because, being truly of the royal blood, he was attracting political support'.

'But this all sounds like a hot house of murder and intrigue where those in power care only about themselves and their money and indulging their corrupt desires!'

'Yes, that it a fair description.'

'But who then cares about Rome and the Empire and the people in it?'

'That is a good question my boy and I am not sure that I really know the answer but Rome is much more than a city – Rome is an idea, and it is a way of life. Rome brings civilisation to the barbarians and order to a disordered world.'

'But how can that be when the very centre of that idea is beginning to be rotten.'

'Well, that is another good question and I think that the answer is that the idea of Rome is now so big that it has outgrown Rome the city. These days, there are many, many hundreds of thousands of people who have never set foot in the place but they are proud to think of themselves as Romans, in some respects at least'.

'Indeed, I am such a one myself.'

'You understand then that that is the greatness of Rome, that what it does is bigger than those who theoretically are its rulers, even if they behave like demented tyrants'.

'But the founders of the city had lofty ideals!'

'Yes, they did and it is in remembrance of them that our poet Virgil has written, 'Forget not, Roman, that it is your special genius to rule the people, to impose the ways of peace, to spare the defeated and to crush those proud men who will not submit'.

'Ah yes, the founding fathers were men of honesty and had ambitions for Rome, not for themselves but where are their counterparts in modern Rome?'

'Do not be so harsh on them all. There are still men of honour and good standing in Rome – some of the Senators hold true to the old ways and were schooled in the disciplines of public service before private gain'.

'That is not what I hear from Impedimentus. He says they are all rotten and that a fish rots from the head.'

'My dear boy, forgive me if I say this, but Impedimentus does not move in the topmost circles and, through my family connections, I know more than he does about what really happens.'

'Well, name me one, just one Senator who is true to the old ways'.

'Easily done. My second-cousin on my father's side, Sextus Caelius Caldus. He is as honest and as hard-working as even you could wish. Indeed, he is the by-word for honour – so much so that his nickname is Integritus.'

At this point, Acerbus looked as though he were recollecting something and then, as he mused, he began to laugh.

And it was a laugh that was entirely his own.

It started very low down, seeming to come from the stomach but then it burst forth from his lips with a loud shout of 'Hah', followed by spluttering and many more 'Hahs' but these were staccato rather than continuous and Graecus sat in amazement trying, out of respect for the older man, surreptitiously to wipe the spittle from his face.

Eventually, Graecus was moved to say, 'Please share your amusement with me.'

This set Acerbus off again into fresh convulsions and more spluttering so it was a few moments before he was able to say, 'Well, the thing is that my cousin Sextus is a man of the greatest honour but you would wish to be carried straight to the Underworld if you had to listen to one of his speeches. He is the most tedious man in the Empire if he is speaking about one of his pet subjects. I mean, get him to tell you about the problems with Rome's water supply or the dangers of all that wooden-framed housing in the plebeian quarter or the diseases carried by the prostitutes and you would wish for swift and permanent release. In fact, he is so well-known for this that his other nickname is Interminatus.'

This was followed by another explosion of laughter but Graecus had moved away slightly and avoided the spray which came with it. When Acerbus had subsided, Graecus said, 'Well, even if he is dull, I for one would wish to hear him speak and it gladdens my heart to learn that there are still such men in Rome. My dear friend and colleague, it is always good to converse with you. Thank you for listening to me and for your patience with my ignorance of the political ways of this modern world'.

'My boy, you are a good and a brave man and you are a true Roman. Now I must be off to my bed – it is late and in this cold place at the edge of the Empire, my bones ache. Goodnight'.

'Goodnight'.

On reflection later that night in his bed, Graecus did not know whether or not to be comforted by Acerbus's words.

On the one hand, he was disturbed to hear that Verus was so well connected and, even more so that Vulponia was his cousin. Ye gods! What a poisonous duo! On the other hand, he was greatly encouraged to hear that 'Rome' was greater than the city itself. He needed to know this because it was the basis of his whole philosophy – that what he fought for was for the greater good.

Trying to make sense of it all, he concluded that the best thing he could do was just to get on with his job to the best of his abilities and keep well out of the way of those with political ambitions and high connections. Then he fell asleep.

CHAPTER ELEVEN

When the winter came and the fighting season was well and truly over, they reinforced their camp by putting up wood block buildings with thatched roofs. This was very welcome from the point of view of the men's bodily comforts but it seemed to mean that they would remain at the little fort for some time and although this was good news for those men who were making merry with the local women, it was bad news for those who liked either an exciting life or a warmer climate.

In fact, this winter was especially cold and wet and the men worked very hard to put up the barracks blocks – one for each century – an administrative block, a storehouse, a bathhouse and a small infirmary, as quickly as possible.

Then, to deter raiders, the outside of the fort was made more formidable by the addition of two more ditches.

While this work was going on, life was even more uncomfortable than usual but Felix helped to keep the soldiers' spirits up by producing hot, tasty dishes and Zig was in his element going out every day with Germanicus and some of the men hunting for the pot. It was tribute to Felix's skills that, whatever they brought back – moles, voles, badgers, pigeons, even on one occasion a brace of crow – was transformed by him with the addition of well-judged seasoning into a delicious dish and nowhere was this more appreciated than by Acerbus who ate and ate but never got any fatter.

Germanicus grew again and his face began to take on a more adult look – his cheeks lost some of their fullness and became more chiselled as his jaw grew more pronounced. It would not be long before he was a man. In the meantime, he devoted himself to learning all about the various weapons and how to maintain them in good order. He continued to try to learn geometry but with less enthusiasm and vigorously applied himself to physical activities, juggling in particular, and became so adept that he could keep three balls in the air and sometimes throw them behind his back. He was now so good that the men would sometimes ask him to entertain them in the evening and he did this with great pleasure while Zig looked on adoringly at his master.

And at the end of the day, Acerbus would often come to Graecus's barracks and share the evening meal.

Sometimes, Acerbus was accompanied by some of his men and it was on one such evening, as the Feast of Saturnalia again approached, that the men were still at table after the meal was over but they were becoming mellow from the wine.

As the oil lamps flickered in the cold wind which snaked in through the gaps in the windows, a discussion began concerning weapons and swordplay. This quickly became animated with men drawing diagrams on the table with spilt wine and stances being taken as to whether the sword issued by the army was too short and some men saying that it did not matter as the best thing was to have quick reactions.

The debate went on for some minutes and was degenerating into an undisciplined row when, all of a sudden, Germanicus, who had been sitting quietly and attentively, spoke quite loudly, saying to Graecus, 'Domine, may I ask Acerbus a question?'

This was a welcome relief from the previous rabble so Graecus said, 'Of course, my son. I am sure that it will be a good question'.

'Well, I have noticed in weapon training that, time and time again, Acerbus is able easily to deflect the weapons of men much taller than him and, as I am still small myself but wish to be a good soldier, I wish to know how he does it. So my question is, how does Acerbus, being very small, beat bigger men?'

As the boy said these last words, Graecus hardly dared look at Acerbus for, although Germanicus said them politely, in all innocence and had said something everybody knew, he had still said something which could be hurtful to the older Centurion and there was a collective gasp round the table as the boy finished speaking.

Then there was silence as the other men looked at Acerbus, Graecus looked at Germanicus and Germanicus looked blank, then worried.

'Domine, what have I said? I only asked the question.'

But before Graecus could answer, Acerbus cut in and said,

175

'And it was a very good question. You have correctly observed that I am a surprisingly successful swordsman for such a short-arse and I will take much pleasure in showing you how it's done but, for now, just bear in mind three things – the first is always carefully to watch the angle of your opponent's wrist because that is the angle of his sword and you will know where it's coming from, the second is to stand still and let them come to you so that when they go to strike and you deflect the blow, you can use their own momentum to throw them off balance and the third thing is to have long arms. I do not know whether I can help you with the third but I can certainly help with the first two.'

There was laughter at this and relief when the men saw that Acerbus was really quite pleased that his swordsmanship had been admired.

And so for the next few months, Acerbus spent some of his day showing Germanicus how to take on the bigger men in his century. At first, the boy's efforts were no proof against the seasoned Roman soldiers but, as the weeks went by, he learned how to stand, how to use his strong torso, how to turn a man's strength against himself and how to keep calm.

And he became a formidable swordsman as his natural instinct was honed into a potent force by the knowledge and skills of his mentor.

Sometimes, Graecus would watch the boy and the older man – the one eager to learn and the other delighted to teach and his heart turned over with joy that they were such good friends. But he also learned from Acerbus. He saw that Acerbus had a very sharp eye which he used to good effect in all manner of ways – not only in hand to hand combat but also in relation to his camp where he knew everything and any transgressions were nipped in the bud.

In the meantime, Flavius had not returned and there was no news as to when it would be possible to make the journey to see the praetor so that Graecus could formally adopt the boy. This was a source of concern to Graecus who was not happy unless he had something to worry about but, all in all, the winter passed peacefully and harmoniously even though the heavy snows meant that the two centuries in their adjacent camps were cut off from being able to travel and, for several weeks, even from the main camp.

But it is nature's way that the snow recedes and spring comes.

Along with spring came a letter from Flavius.

The letter was short and said that Flavius would be in Augusta the following month and, as the praetor would also be there, then it would be a convenient time to attend to the adoption formalities for Germanicus.

Graecus was overjoyed and having excitedly told Germanicus and Felix and anyone who was within earshot, he went to see Acerbus to tell him the wonderful news that he would be going to Augusta the next month.

Acerbus was, for once, stuck for words and was very excited by this for he said, 'But that is excellent for I also must go to Augusta at some time – there is cohort business with which Flavius wishes me to assist him but I also need to see the praetor myself in connection with my Aunt's will. We must go together – the journey is long and we shall be glad of each other's company'.

'This is indeed fortunate. You are familiar with Augusta are you not? You were recently stationed there?'

'Yes, we were, until we came here. It is quite a fine place, albeit not as civilised as some cities in the far-flung parts of the Empire.'

'Well, I am delighted that we shall be travelling together'.

The time passed quickly and it did not seem long before the two Centurions and the boy set off on their long journey leaving Zig in the care of Felix who, as the source of many tasty treats, was the dog's next best friend. They began with a chariot ride to the main camp where they picked up letters for the General, supplies, horses and a pack-mule.

Then they were really on their way.

The beginning of the journey was on dusty tracks and the travellers did not see many other people on the road but, as they moved further west, the roads improved and became wider and more likely to be surfaced. They spent the nights in little inns at the roadside where they met simple people who led simple lives and ate simple food. The weather was fine for most of the time and they made good progress so that it was about ten days from their leaving their camp before they reached Augusta.

Upper and Lower Germania were military zones and not part of the greater Roman Empire, so they did not possess the colonial administration and infrastructure which could be found elsewhere. This meant that, in order to undertake official or legal business, a Roman citizen in Germania would need to travel to the nearest place where he could have access to a praetor, a magistrate and, at this time, it so happened that the nearest praetor was in Augusta, the city named after the great Caesar Augustus.

The travellers saw the smoke rising from the city whilst they were still some way off and, as it began to get dark and they could from a distance see torches being lit, they wished they had gained the safety and comfort of the city walls but eventually they – travel sore and dusty like their animals – entered the city gates just as darkness finally came.

Acerbus knew the city and, having passed a few pleasantries with the gatekeeper, confidently strode off taking one of the streets to the left leaving Graecus and Germanicus trailing behind him staring at the buildings and the people while trying to accustom their ears to the noise of vehicles and people which was, for them, deafening.

And there was also the smell. The smell of humans living cheek by jowl in small houses in clothes they rarely changed and never washed, the smell of animals and their excrement in the street, the smell of cooking and the smell of fires being lit against the evening cold. It was all very exciting for the young Centurion and the boy and Graecus thought, as he dismounted and passed through an archway that whilst not yet a lavish settlement, Augusta possessed some fine buildings and had a buzz about it which indicated that, as a city, it had ambitions.

Acerbus was still passing determinedly and at a cracking pace leading his horse through the narrow streets but then the way ahead opened into a square which was bounded on each side by handsome municipal buildings.

At this junction, Acerbus paused and looked back at his companions and said, 'Come on you two, stop rubbernecking and get a move on. We're nearly there and I wish to have a bath and rest my bones'.

So the others caught up with him and the three of them walked forward to the largest of the buildings giving on to the square.

'This is it', said Acerbus and it was wonderful for the travellers to feel they had arrived at last.

The frontage of the building was rather fine and impressive being of smooth grey stone and Graecus and Germanicus were somewhat awed by its size but, once they had entered it and walked behind Acerbus through the large hallway with the very tall ceiling into the courtyard beyond, they saw in front of them something more familiar in the simple low structure which was to be their home for the next few days.

This building, cunningly concealed behind the large tall frontage was the barracks and Acerbus was now involved in a loud conversation with one of the men on duty telling him stories of the privations he and his men had endured over the winter and then laughingly turning to Graecus and Germanicus he said, 'And these men here helped to make it bearable by being two of the finest soldiers you could meet but, frankly, the one man who got us through the long cold days is not here.'

'Who is that?' they all said.

'Why Felix of course! The only army cook I know who could make elephants' arseholes into a dish fit for the Emperor.'

And they all laughed, then Acerbus asked where they would be sleeping and having been told they had been allocated rooms in the third dormitory, Graecus and Germanicus sharing, he marched them there telling them to leave their things on their beds and to come with him immediately to the bathhouse as they would need to be clean and well-turned out for their meeting with the praetor the following day.

They emerged some hours later all red in the face and glowing but in high spirits and went to the dining hall for the evening meal where, again, Acerbus was warmly greeted and welcomed back.

The meal passed uneventfully and they gratefully retired to

bed where they fell into oblivion.

The next day they all put on their best clothes – the Centurions in their newest items of uniform and the boy in a clean tunic worn with a belt and a short cloak to keep out the morning chill.

As far as Graecus and Germanicus were concerned, this visit to the magistrate was to be a preliminary to the actual adoption and was for the purpose of providing information so that the proper documents could be drawn up but, as far as Acerbus was concerned, wishing to object to some of the provisions of his aunt's will, he did not know what to expect.

A short while before the appointed hour, they left the barracks and walked straight across the square to another imposing building where, this time, the impressive frontage did not belie what lay behind.

Going up the smooth stone steps and between the columns at the side of the entrance, Germanicus looked about him in awe at the size and splendour of the building. Then they went into the hallway which was tiled and their feet sounded so loud they felt self-conscious. Graecus and Germanicus paused and looked around and marvelled at the splendours of the busts of prominent Romans from history and the present day which were placed in niches in the walls and then their eyes were drawn to the magnificent bronze bust placed in the middle of the hall on a plinth.

Acerbus was not looking at this as he was scurrying off down a corridor saying, 'Wait here. I'll go and tell them we've arrived'

Left to their own devices, Graecus looked more closely at the busts in the niches in the wall while Germanicus made for the bronze in the centre and was stroking its cold, smooth surface and was feeling impressed at the way it really did look like a human being while whistling, tunelessly, as usual.

Graecus noticed what he was doing and had just stepped over to the bronze bust to tell the boy not to leave any greasy fingerprints on it when Acerbus returned and, having witnessed this scene gave Germanicus a long, strange look and went swiftly to Graecus and, drawing him away from Germanicus, hissed urgently in his ear, 'Now listen to me very carefully and do what

I say without arguing with me. Take off your neckerchief and go and put it on the boy's head and tie it under his chin so that you cover his head as much as you can – if you can leave a bit over his forehead so that his face is in shadow, so much the better.'

'What are you talking about?' Graecus protested.

'I cannot discuss it with you now. Please do as I say and if anyone asks you why the boy has his head covered in this way, say that he has the toothache or the earache or both. I will tell you later why this is necessary but do as I say now and, in the name of all that you stand for, do it quickly – the praetor will be here very soon.'

Shaking his head in disbelief at his friend's odd request, Graecus turned back towards the centre of the hallway and went to speak to Germanicus.

'My son', he said 'I think that you must be starting to have a sore throat – your whistling was very tuneless and I do not wish for you to be ill so I am going to put my kerchief over your head to keep it warm for the weather is not yet good and, in this strange place with all its unaccustomed humanity, we cannot take risks with your health'.

Germanicus was astonished by this pretty speech from the man who urged him to bathe in ice-cold rivers and go hunting in all weathers so he said, 'But, Domine, I am quite well and I do not wish to wear the kerchief on my head'.

'My son, I do not think that you understand me. I am telling you that this is what we must do and, if you continue to argue with me, then I must order you to allow me to cover your head.'

Germanicus still did not understand what this was all about but, with the innocence of youth and, because he trusted Graecus to do what was best for him, he allowed him to put the kerchief over his head and tie it beneath his chin even though he knew it made him look foolish.

As he finished tying the kerchief, Graecus noticed that the magnificent bronze bust bore a name plaque which said, 'CLAUDIUS IMPERATOR.'

And then there was the sound of feet coming down the corridor and the praetor appeared.

Graecus knew it must be the praetor for he wore the toga and it had a wide purple edging to it denoting that he was a very important Roman.

The praetor approached them and said, 'Greetings. You have business with me, I think? One of you wishes to adopt a child – is it this boy?'

'Yes it is, Magister and I am he who wishes to adopt him.'

'Ah yes, and is it not the case that your General, Flavius, will stand in loco parentis to the boy for the purposes of the adoption?'

'Yes it is, Magister'.

'Excellent, I will ask my clerk to take your names and other details so that we can prepare the proper documents so please wait here and he will be along presently but, tell me, is there something wrong with the boy? Why does he have that thing on his head?'

At this point Graecus, Acerbus and Germanicus all spoke together.

Graecus said, 'He has the toothache.'

Acerbus said, 'He has the earache.'

And Germanicus said, 'I have a sore throat.'

The praetor gave them a sideways glance and said, 'Poor boy, he must be in need of an apothecary – there is a very good one opposite the statue of Augustus in the forum.'

Then Graecus said, 'And we expect Flavius tomorrow so that the adoption can take place then?'

'Indeed we do. He has informed me that he will be here at two hours short of the noon day.'

'Well, we shall return just before then, if that is convenient to you, Magister.'

'That will be acceptable and my clerk will tell you how much money you will need to bring with you to pay for the formalities and the registrations.'

'Thank you, Magister.'

'Now, Marcus Caelius Caldus, there is a problem with your aunt's will, I understand?'

'Yes, there is. My cousins and I do not wish to sell her properties in Rome. We wish to keep them in the family.'

'I see. Well, if you have a copy of the will with you, then I can give you my opinion on whether you are obliged to sell the properties. Do you have such a copy?'

'Yes. I do.'

'Well, follow me then and I shall consider the matter in my chambers.'

So, off went Acerbus with the praetor, their feet echoing down the corridor leaving both Graecus and Germanicus entirely mystified as to why it was so important that the boy should keep his head covered. Then they heard the sound of other feet coming back down the corridor and they looked and saw another man scurrying towards them.

He was very small. Smaller even than Acerbus and he was very wizened but he hurried towards them carrying several large tomes bundled between his arms and a quill pen between his teeth.

He bustled up to the strangers and, sweeping a glance over each of them, the pen still between his teeth, he said, 'Ah yes, you must be the Centurion who wishes to adopt and I suppose this is the boy?'

'Yes that is correct.'

'My name is Titus Antonius Cunctator and I am the praetor's clerk. Please follow me and I shall make a note of all the details so that I may draft the adoption documents ready for tomorrow. Tell me, is there anything wrong with the boy? Is he sick?'

And Graecus said, 'He has a sore throat'.

And Germanicus said. 'I have the earache and the toothache'.

And the clerk said, 'Poor boy, he must be in need of an apothecary. There is a very good one opposite the statue of Augustus in the forum'.

So Graecus and Germanicus followed the clerk down the corridor to a small, dusty room piled high with books and documents and, sitting on little stools, Graecus gave him as much detail as he could but this was difficult for neither he nor Germanicus knew anything about his antecedents. Indeed, the clerk kept asking awkward questions such as, 'Where and when was the boy born?' and 'What is the date of birth of the adoptive father?' and Graecus was horribly embarrassed to have to keep saying, 'I know not'.

At this point, the clerk gave a loud sigh of exasperation and said, 'You are making this very difficult for me. What *can* you tell me?'

So Graecus sat very straight on his little stool, and in the dusty light of the little room, his grey eyes looked dark and serious as he said, 'Sir, what I can tell you is that neither this boy nor I have any clue as to where we came from, nor who were our parents but this boy was given to me by the gods and I have come to think of him as my own. As both he and I wish that he should be a soldier and as I wish that he should be an officer, it is best that he has proper parentage and I therefore wish to give that to him. Is that sufficient for your purposes?'

The clerk, who had been listening intently, swallowed and said, 'Yes, indeed. I could not ask for any better information to help me prepare the documents and, as long as your general attends tomorrow, then all will be well. All, that is, apart from the money. Tell me, do you have the requisite amount?'

'No-one has yet told me what this will cost.'

'Ah yes. The cost is one hundred and eighty denarii, do you have such a sum in coin?'

Graecus was unaccustomed to the ways of lawyers and could not believe that what to him was such a simple thing could cost quite so much but he did not wish for Germanicus to see his discomfort, so he swallowed hard and said, 'Oh yes. I have the sum in coin and will be happy to pay it to you when the boy is my son.'

'Ah yes. But you do not understand our ways; I need half of that sum now, in order to be able to prepare the documents and to ensure the attendance of the witnesses. You see, you need to have five Roman citizens there as witnesses and a libripens – that is, someone to hold the scales.'

So Graecus took out his purse and counted out most of the coins in it and felt – like many people who have just given money to a lawyer – that he had had his pocket picked but in the most polite manner possible.

Cunctator rose and said, 'Well, that is all for now. I will draw up the formal documents in time for the ceremony tomorrow.'

And Graecus and Germanicus said, 'Thank you' and left.

Not knowing how long would be Acerbus's consultation with the praetor, Graecus decided that the best thing would be for him and the boy to look round the town and then go back to the barracks at noon in the hope that Acerbus's stomach would be in need of food by then.

So the Centurion and the boy wandered the streets looking at the shops and the taverns and the people and the people looked at them for they were a strange sight – the handsome Centurion and the sturdy boy wearing a neckerchief over his head.

They returned to the barracks at noon at the same time as Acerbus who was looking puzzled and Graecus asked if he had had bad news.

'No. I do not think so. Well, maybe it was. In all truth, I am not sure. I gave the praetor my Aunt's will and asked if we are obliged to sell the properties she had in Rome but I do not think that I understand his answer. You see, the thing is that, although the will says that the properties should be sold and the proceeds divided, we, her nephews and nieces wish to keep the properties in the family as we had happy times there in our childhoods and we think that their value will increase.'

'That sounds simple enough to me, if that is what you all want.'

'Well, you would think so. But there are complications because my cousin Helen does wish to sell and the praetor says that her views must be taken into account. And, listening to him was like trying to comprehend a woman's mind – you think you understand but then you know you do not. However, I cannot think any further about this now as I am too hungry. We must eat but, remember, the boy must keep his head covered'.

'I accept your advice and we have been complying with it but you must tell me as soon as possible why.'

'I shall tell you this evening. We shall put the boy to bed in the dormitory where he will be safe and then we shall go to one of the taverns where there will be a lot of noise and we shall not be overheard. Now, please can we eat?'

So, the two Centurions and the boy in the headscarf sat with their colleagues for the mid-day meal where, to avoid the inevitable question, Acerbus said, 'The boy has the toothache and the earache. We will take him to the apothecary in the forum this afternoon'.

Of course, Graecus was impatient to know what was the great secret and thought that the rest of the day would pass slowly but an afternoon with Acerbus would never be dull and, in fact, it was fascinating for his knowledge of Roman history, and especially, military history was great. As they walked around the town, visiting the forum where they saw the shop of the famous apothecary opposite the statue of Augustus, Acerbus pointed out the significance of this building or that column and it was a useful reminder to both the younger Centurion and the boy of the necessity for the presence of the Legions and cohorts in Germania.

And it would have been impossible for Acerbus to relate this history without telling the terrible story of Publius Quinctilius Varus, the then Governor, who, almost fifty years before, lost three Legions in the Teutoburg Forest when ambushed by a German force under Arminius, leader of the Cherusci tribe. And the point of this story was that Varus thought, indeed the Romans had thought, that Germania had been conquered and Varus had set about levying taxes and imposing Romanisation on the German tribes.

But he had underestimated the capacity of 'barbarians' for clever planning and their desire for freedom so that when one of the chieftains, who had become one of his trusted inner circle told him that there was an insurgency brewing within the Chauci tribe, he happily marched west with his three Legions and three cavalry detachments and six cohorts of foreign auxiliaries along with wagon loads of women and children, marching deep into the forest.

The Romans were taken utterly by surprise and the carnage was terrible. When news of the massacre reached Rome, Augustus could not believe that not one, not two but three Legions had been lost. It was said that he kept banging his head against the wall, calling out Varus's name and saying, 'Give me back my Legions!'

The disgrace of losing the seventeenth, eighteenth and nine-teenth Legions and their standards, their eagles, was a stain on the reputation of the invincible Roman army which could not be expunged and the memory of it made the blood of any Roman soldier run cold.

With the thought of treachery and betrayal in their minds, the two Centurions and the boy returned to the barracks at dusk and went to the dormitory.

Germanicus went to remove his headgear but Acerbus told him, quite sharply, that he would need to keep it on, even at night, and that he could not remove it till they had left Augusta. At this, Graecus was even more intrigued and could not even begin to guess what could be the reason.

Eventually, Germanicus fell asleep and, having drawn a blanket over him, the two men shut the door to the room and left the barracks looking for the nearest noisy tavern.

CHAPTER TWELVE

It was not difficult to find, in fact, there was a very noisy place just round the corner where Acerbus ordered two beakers of the local barley beer and he and Graecus sat close together at a stone table.

'Now you must explain to me what this is all about – Germanicus and I are mystified.'

'I do not doubt it, and I am about to explain, but first I must ask you to recall what Vulponia said to you when she scratched your face.'

'Vulponia? Well, I seem to recall that what she said was that I did not know what I was unleashing and that I should not interfere in matters of high state……whatever it was she actually said, it made no sense to me whatsoever.'

'But she said it in the context of your refusing to hand over Germanicus to her?'

'Oh yes, that is what provoked her attack on me. She was desperate to get him in her clutches.'

'Well, bear that in mind now when I tell you what I saw earlier today when I came down the corridor and there was Germanicus, next to the bust of Claudius. What I saw, and I have a good eye, what I saw was a boy who is the spitting image of Claudius.'

Acerbus paused and allowed this statement to sink in. Graecus looked puzzled at first then, as he began to grasp the significance of what Acerbus had said, he shook his head, as if trying to dislodge Acerbus's words, and said, 'What? What in the names of all the gods are you talking about? Have you taken leave of your senses? Have you gone mad?'

In saying this to his friend whom he deeply admired, Graecus had allowed his usual feelings for Acerbus to be overtaken by fear.

Fear, for although he was incredulous and was resisting any thoughts that what Acerbus was saying could be true, deep down within himself, there was a voice whispering urgently and darkly that, if it were, then Vulponia's strange words would have some meaning and some consequences.

'No, my friend, I have not gone mad. I am trying to make sense of a nonsensical world. What I saw was that Germanicus's head is the same shape as Claudius's, his nose is the same, his ears are the same, the contours of his cheeks are the same, the planes of his face are the same, his lips are the same, the set of his head on his shoulders is the same. And now, I must give voice to the real point which is that I fear that Germanicus is Claudius's natural son.'

'Ye gods.'

'Yes, and if we are to keep the boy safe, then we shall need the help of the gods'.

Acerbus was silent again and Graecus was grateful for it gave him time to think. Then, after a few minutes, he said, 'Forgive me, my friend for I do not have your knowledge of the workings of Roman society and politics and I have not had so long to think about this but, firstly – how could Germanicus be Claudius's son and – secondly, even if he were, why would he be in danger and thirdly – supposing he is in danger, what can we do to protect him?'

'Well, he would be Claudius's son in the same way that any-one is someone's son – by virtue of Claudius having pleasured his mother. Now, how that could actually have come about is a matter of conjecture but it is entirely possible that Claudius had a blonde-haired, blue-eyed German slave girl about twelve years ago and that he took a shine to her – some of these girls are very beautiful and that, being the Emperor he could have anyone he wanted, so he and she had sex and in the way of these things she, probably being young and healthy, became pregnant'

'And then what?'

'Well, let us assume that Claudius was actually fond of this girl, he would not have wanted her to incur Messalina's wrath, (you remember she was the wife before Agrippina), so he freed her and sent her home to give birth. What do you know of Germanicus's early life? I mean, would it support my theory?'

'All I know is what the slave master told me and all he knew is what someone told him but the story is that Germanicus was found, aged about eight in the burned out ruins of a village which had been sacked by raiders.'

'Well, that could fit with my hypothesis – the girl went home to her village, let's say it was somewhere near the border, she gave birth to her child and all was well until the village was destroyed in a border raid when Germanicus was about seven or eight when he was taken as a slave.'

'But he says he does not remember having a home, nor where he came from.'

'Well, if you had watched your mother being raped and then murdered, for example, you might blot it out, too.'

'Well, suppose you are correct, why is he in danger?'

'He is in danger because I am not the only person who has noticed his resemblance to Claudius – Vulponia noticed it also. And you can rely on the fact that she will by now have told her cousin Verus who has his own reasons for not having the boy's best interests at heart. Think about it. Just think what great favour they would find with the Emperor and his ghastly mother if they could say that they had found an illegitimate son of Claudius's and could arrange for his quiet disposal thereby eliminating him as a potential rival.'

'But how great a threat would he be?'

'Oh my dear boy, you are quite an innocent are you not? The fact of his being an actual blood son of Claudius, albeit illegitimate, would make him a threat because Nero's claim is merely that he was a step-son and is married to Octavia, Claudius's daughter and those are questionable connections when compared with blood-ties.'

Acerbus blew his nose before continuing, 'Bear in mind also that Nero may fall out of favour with the people. At the moment he is popular enough but there are stirrings of unease. I mean, take all this music and poetry lark – he actually gives performances like an actor and this is not the sort of behaviour expected of an Emperor.'

Acerbus scratched at an insect bite on his knee and thought for a while, then said, 'I mean, not everyone in the ruling class gets to die quietly in his own bed surrounded by his family you know – look at what happened to Caligula, murdered by his own guards – so you see that a living descendant of Claudius –who was, after all, quite a popular Emperor with the people and quite a fair ruler, would be a threat'.

'Yes, I see now. But what can we do?'

'I do not know. I need more time to consider all the ramifications but, in the meantime, I think that the best thing is to keep him as far away from Rome and its rulers as possible.'

'As far as I am concerned, that is no great hardship. Should we keep this a secret to ourselves? Should we tell Germanicus?'

'I am sure that the fewer people know about this the better but you may decide to tell the boy when he is older. You never know, Nero may at some stage fall out of favour and who would be better to succeed him than a young man who is not merely Claudius's actual son but who has been brought up in accordance with the finest of Rome's traditions, is not a spoiled brat and has seen active service in the Army.'

At this point, despite his fears for Germanicus's safety, Graecus could not resist the thought of his son becoming Emperor and restoring proper values to government. Perhaps he would restore power to the Senate? Perhaps he would restore the Republic? All these thoughts were swimming around Graecus's head and then he had another thought.

And he said, somewhat defiantly, 'Well, I am not so sure that Germanicus can be Claudius's son.'

'Why do you say that?'

'Simply because, by all accounts, Claudius was a strange looking man, if not downright ugly and my son is not. My son will be a very fine-looking man.'

'Yes, it is true that Claudius's detractors liked to make much of his speech impediment and his limp and they tried to say he was ugly but it was not so. I am not saying that Claudius was handsome – he was not – but you must also remember that Germanicus's mother was probably very beautiful and, although he looks very like Claudius, he may have inherited a fineness of feature and demeanour from his mother. Certainly, he must have his mother's hair and eyes.'

'Yes, you could well be correct. I see now that it is possible that Germanicus could be the natural son of Claudius and that this would be both a burden and an opportunity. I see also that it is my duty to adopt him and give him a proper status in the world and, having adopted him, it will be my duty to bring him up in a manner becoming of a potential Emperor but above all it is my duty to keep him safe.'

'That is entirely my view and I know of no man who will acquit himself of this difficult task better than you.'

'You are very kind to me my friend and flatter me with your words but I know that in taking on this task, I could ask for no better adviser than yourself'.

'I humbly accept your words and now I think that we had better go back to the barracks and see to it that our young emperor keeps his head covered.'

So the two Centurions left the inn and made their way back to the barracks where they found Germanicus fast asleep still wearing his strange headgear.

Exhausted by all this talk of matters normally outside his knowledge, Graecus nevertheless could not get to sleep and allowed his mind to wander, thinking firstly how it would be the most wondrous outcome if Germanicus could become Emperor and how this would benefit not merely Rome but the whole of the known world as he would be such a wise, fair and incorruptible ruler and then, just as he was imagining himself as the respected father of the Emperor to whom the young man often looked for guidance and counsel, his mind would switch to another train of thought that they would all be murdered in their beds, or worse, in order to keep Nero safely in place.

Acerbus was clearly not having any of these thoughts as, through the wall, Graecus could hear him snoring loudly in a way Graecus had not heard since Pneumaticus had been cured of his deadly night-time habit.

It was an uncomfortable night for Graecus and he was not feeling at his best the following morning but this was a day of such high importance for the boy and for himself that he splashed himself all over with cold water to clear his head and brushed his teeth with such vigour that his gums bled. Having thus purged himself of his confused thoughts, Graecus felt able to face his companions with good grace and properly to perform his part in the adoption ceremony.

The breaking fast meal over, the two men and the boy had hours to spare until their appointment with the praetor and they spent this time looking again at the town until it was nearly time to meet Flavius.

Then they went back to the big building with the imposing columns and stepped into the large tiled hall dominated by the bust of Claudius.

Graecus could hardly bring himself to look at the statue but did not know whether this was because he keenly wished Germanicus to be the dead Emperor's son or whether he felt it was the most terrible thing he had ever contemplated. His mind was in a turmoil again and this made his ears excessively tender so that he could not tolerate the tuneless whistling with which Germanicus was amusing himself whilst stroking Claudius's head.

It was all too much for Graecus so he went over to Germanicus and, taking hold of his hand, in an uncharacteristically vehement manner, told him not to leave his finger marks on the bronze and to stop that infernal whistling.

Just as this little domestic scene was unfolding, there was the clatter of urgent feet on the tiles and they all looked up to see the striking figure of Flavius coming towards them with his hands outstretched in greeting and a wide smile on his face.

He looked older, greyer at the temples and perhaps a little less at ease with himself since Graecus had last seen him but he was still an invigorating and imposing presence and Graecus felt his heart lift at the sight of his General.

'Greetings brothers!' he said and embraced both Acerbus and Graecus before turning to Germanicus and saying, 'What ails the boy, is he sick? Why is he wearing that stupid thing on his head? Can he not take it off?'

And Graecus said, 'He needs to keep it on because he has the toothache'.

While Acerbus said, 'He needs to keep it on because he has an earache'.

While Germanicus said, 'I have a sore throat'.

And Flavius said, 'Poor boy. He needs to see an apothecary. I hear that there is a very good one opposite the statue of Augustus in the forum but, in the meantime, I feel that this is such an important day for him that he should have his head uncovered, at least for the duration of the ceremony,' and in the saying of it, he reached out and undid the knot holding the kerchief at Germanicus's throat thereby releasing it from his head.

So there was the uncovered boy, standing next to the bust of the dead Emperor.

Graecus and Acerbus involuntarily held their breath while Germanicus stood there innocently scratching his head in relief at having its itchy covering removed.

Germanicus was now running his fingers through his hair, trying to undo the restraining influence of having had it subdued for twenty four hours and was unselfconsciously wholly engaged in this while Flavius looked at him.

Flavius at first smiled at the boy's obvious relief in having the head cover removed but, as he looked, his smiling face became more thoughtful and then, positively quizzical. Then Flavius shook his head as if trying to rid it of an uncomfortable thought.

Then he looked up at Graecus and Acerbus and saw that they were having the same thought.

Flavius's mouth, seen by his Centurions but not the boy, then silently formed the words, 'Ye gods. What have we here?'

Then, collecting himself, and speaking directly to the boy, he said, 'Germanicus, this is a very important day for you and for Graecus. I am pleased to be playing my part in it, which, as you may know, is that I stand in the place of your natural father and give you up so that Graecus can adopt you. As it is my privilege to take this role, and as it my wish that you, as my son, even if only for a short space of time, should not be penniless, I wish to endow you with this inheritance.'

Flavius then handed over to Germanicus a leather pouch which obviously contained coins but the boy, unaccustomed to the commercial ways of the world, did not know what he should do with the gift and stood there with the pouch in his hand, looking questioningly at Graecus.

Flavius understood the boy's confusion and said, 'But, for now, it is best that you should give the money to Graecus who will look after it for you'.

At this point, Germanicus remembered his manners and said, 'Sir, you are very kind to me, an orphan of no known family. I am very fortunate that I was taken in by the Roman army and by my father here. In his century, I have learned much of brotherhood, trust and valour but I know that those values come from you, sir, and even though I am your son in the eyes of the law for only a very short time, I am deeply honoured'.

At this speech from the dishevelled boy, there was a collective gasp from the soldiers who were all moved by his mature words and there was a silence for a few seconds as they were all lost in thought but their silence was interrupted by the sound of other feet on the tiles and, as they all turned to see who was making the noise, Cunctator came into view carrying bundles of documents and bristling with pens.

'Oh, there you all are,' he said. 'Thank Jupiter – we have had such a difficult morning! It's been one thing after another – everybody wanting everything now and me only having one pair of hands. People think it's so easy having my job – that all I have to do is sit on a stool all day and copy documents and that it's not as hard as working in the fields or being a soldier, but, I tell you, they don't know the half of it. They don't know how hard it is to make sure that the litigants are kept at bay, that the clerks' lettering is acceptable, that the praetor's wife has due precedence at all social functions, that we have enough pens and ink, that we can send enough tax back to Rome and all the other millions of things I have to do. No-one knows how hard it is!'

This was delivered with great feeling and exasperation but

Graecus, who did not understand the problems of the bureaucrat and was, anyway, feeling less than sympathetic towards official-dom said in a tone of cool sarcasm, 'Is it harder than smashing a boy's feet so that you can nail him to a tree?'

Cunctator heard this and looked as if he wished to vomit and then angrily opened his mouth as if to defend himself but was interrupted by Flavius who said, 'In speaking thus, my Centurion wishes only to allow you to know that it is always difficult to compare the burdens of one walk of life with another. He meant no disrespect to you or to your calling.'

Cunctator was mollified and said, 'Thank you, General, for helping me understand what your Centurion said. Now let us get on with the business of the day. The praetor, the witnesses and the libripens are waiting in his chambers and I have all the documentation ready.'

At this, he set off back down the long corridor and the others followed him, the soldiers' hobnailed feet making a huge clatter-ing noise as they went. Germanicus looked somewhat awed by the magnificence of the building and Graecus put his arm on the boy's shoulder to reassure him.

Then they entered the praetor's chambers where the official and the General greeted each other formally as befitted their respective ranks while Cunctator spread many documents on the table. There were six other men present, one of them holding a pair of weighing scales. They all looked very clean and well-scrubbed as if they had dressed in their best clothes for the occasion.

Having greeted Flavius and nodded to the others, the praetor went back behind his desk and took up an official-looking pose before beginning the complicated procedure of Flavius selling his 'son' Germanicus to Acerbus three times so that the filial ties would be severed and Germanicus would then be in a servile position in relation to Acerbus thus allowing Graecus to claim that he was his natural son and, as Acerbus did not deny this, thereby formally adopting him as his own. This involved sever-al legal fictions, many procedural steps and much signing of documents but, when the last signature was in place, the praetor smiled and said, 'Centurion, embrace your son.'

And Graecus gratefully following the praetor's instructions, said, 'My son, this is the happiest day of my life. There are many great titles in this world but the only one I wish to have is that of 'Father' and the only son I wish to have is you.'

And Germanicus said, 'Father, I am honoured to be your son'.

Cunctator then stepped forward and asked Graecus for the balance of the fees which he paid and, after thanking the witnesses and the libripens and picking up the adoption papers, the soldiers left the room.

As they retraced their steps down the corridor, Flavius spoke quietly to Graecus saying, 'I wish to talk to you in private later today, come and see me this evening in my room at the barracks after supper but, in the meantime, put that covering back on Germanicus's head'.

Graecus had seen the look on his General's face when he had observed Germanicus standing next to Claudius's statue and knew from these words that the evening's interview would be connected with what Flavius had seen but he had no idea what the tenor of the discussion might be so he spent the rest of the day in a see-saw of emotion between extreme happiness that Germanicus was now his son and trepidation as to what the evening may bring and, although he greatly wished to share what Flavius had said with Acerbus, he did not dare to do so in case what he was about to learn would be an unfair burden on his friend.

Germanicus, on the other hand, was in high spirits because, for the first time in that part of his life which he could remember, he actually knew who he was and knew that he had a status in the eyes of the law – no longer was he an orphan or foundling – now he had a father and a fine one at that.

The afternoon passed and then the evening meal was over and Graecus had to excuse himself from both his new son and his friend so he told them that he must go to Flavius to discuss business peculiar to his century and, with a sense of expectation mixed with dread, he entered Flavius's chamber.

'Sit down, my boy', said the General and Graecus sat down.

The General was seated at a table on which were many documents and maps and the proliferation of oil lamps in the room indicated that the older man had been poring over these with some concentration.

Flavius looked tired and he massaged the bridge of his nose between his thumb and forefinger before he spoke again, 'My boy, I am an old soldier and, in the eyes of some, I am a man of the world. I have seen many men live interesting and fulfilling lives and I have seen many men die, some of them bravely and some of them ignominiously. In short, I would say that I have seen most things and, therefore, I am able to deal with most things, but what I saw this morning has left me in a deep quandary. I am, frankly, stumped as to know what to do'.

In saying this, Flavius sat with the palms of both hands turned upwards and slightly outstretched towards Graecus who took this uncertain gesture as a sign that Flavius did not, at least, at that moment, intend to deal with the situation by putting both Germanicus and himself to the sword, so, breathing slowly and trying to find the deeper registers of his voice, he said, 'General, I realise that this is a very important and difficult problem that we are about to discuss, and I therefore wish to know exactly what it is that you saw this morning which caused you to feel as you do'.

'Oh, Graecus, you are such a stickler for precision but I suppose you are correct – in these very unusual circumstances, it is important that we should perfectly understand one another. So, I should tell you that when I took that stupid covering from Germanicus's head this morning and saw him standing next to the bust of Claudius, I saw that his likeness to the dead emperor was remarkable, so remarkable in fact, that I would say that he could well be of the line of the Julio-Claudians, albeit, illegitimate.'

Here Flavius paused for breath, then continued , 'And since this morning, I have been searching my memory for, as you know, I served Claudius in his invasion of Britannia and came to know him a little and all I can say is that my memory also tells me that Germanicus must carry his blood. Why, the way that he stands and the way that he puts his head on one side when he is thinking are identical to Claudius's gestures. I wish it were otherwise but he must be our late Emperor's son!' and in saying this, the General spread his hands at either edge of the table and gripped each end of it as if to try to gain support.

Graecus felt strangely relieved by this and with a sigh which made it clear that he had been holding his breath whilst Flavius had been speaking, he said, 'General, that is indeed what I have been thinking, and Acerbus also. But the problem is that we do not know how best to deal with it....and, before you say anything further, I should tell you that we are not the only people who have noticed the likeness – he has excited the interest of others'

'Ye gods! Who?'

'You may not know her but there is a patrician lady, a priestess of Isis, who has opened a temple to the goddess just outside the town nearest our camp in Germania. The lady's name is Vulponia. Do you know her?'

Flavius groaned and said, 'Jupiter! It could not be worse! How in the name of all the gods did that dreadful woman come to meet Germanicus?'

'Well, it was by accident. I had taken the boy into the town when I went to get supplies and we bumped into her; as we were both obviously strangers to the place and obviously Roman where such are few and far between, it was natural that we should make one another's acquaintance – she saw me in a crowd of local people and made herself known to me. But why do you call her 'that dreadful woman?'

Here Graecus was clutching at straws – hoping that despite what he had experienced and despite Acerbus's strong words in relation to the lady, Vulponia was not quite so bad that she would sacrifice an innocent boy for her own purposes. But he was to be disappointed for Flavius said, 'Because she is cunning, spiteful, ambitious, unscrupulous, vicious, deceitful and any other nasty traits you may wish to name. I cannot emphasise to you how dangerous that woman is'.

'But what does she do that is so awful?'

'Well, she is a sorceress for a start – she uses spells she

learned in Egypt in order to turn people's minds or to send them mad, then she is also a genius at political intrigue, using her very clever tongue to set one person against another whilst appearing to be the friend of both so that they are at each other's throats and fighting to the death while she, having started it all, offers sympathy and succour to both. But what makes you think that she knows anything about the boy?'

'She invited us to her temple but I went on my own and she gave me wonderful wine and food and then she asked me for Germanicus but I told her that she could not have him and she attacked me as if all the Furies were at her back.'

'Why did she say that she wanted the boy?'

'She said she wanted him as a trainee priest for Isis and she said that he could keep the little dog but I thought that she would soon give the dog to the soothsayer and that my boy would be alone.'

'Yes, and at the mercy of that harridan. But did she say anything which made you feel that she suspected what we now suspect?'

'Yes, she did. When I said to her that I would not let her have my son, she scratched my face and told me that I did not know what it was that I unleashed and that I should not interfere in matters of high state..... at the time, I had no idea what she meant'.

'Well, I cannot work out whether that meant that she would wish to keep Germanicus with her so that she could groom him for Emperor or whether she wished to have him with her so that she could easily arrange for his destruction'.

Flavius snorted at either thought and continued, 'Hah. But you can be sure that, whatever it was, it would have been to the benefit of Vulponia and her kind – she is from one of the new breed of families where they do not give anything for the rest of us – all they care about is their enrichment and the gratification of their desires, natural or unnatural'.

This was absolutely not what Graecus wished to hear for it threatened not only his son, but also Flavius's niece and he was thrown into an agony as to whether to tell his General about the shortcomings of his would-be new relative, Vulponia's cousin, Verus.

But before he could decide what, if anything, he should say,

Flavius continued, 'Not that I know anything about her unnatural desires, but I do know about her cousin, that slippery snake, Verus,' and he spat out this last word as if it were itself a viper in his mouth.

Then he said, 'Oh yes, I had almost forgotten, I sent him to your camp, did I not? He was to stay for three weeks but he had to be taken back to the main camp because you were attacked by tribesmen. Did he acquit himself with valour during the attack?'

Graecus wished he had not been asked this question so directly as it made it impossible to avoid giving Flavius the whole sorry story of Verus's time with his century and so, leaning forward towards his General, his eyes locked onto the older man's face, he said, 'General, I am an honest man and I cannot lie, least of all to you so, much as I had not wished to tell you of these events, I now have no alternative', and he proceeded to tell Flavius of Verus's attempted sexual attack on Germanicus and of the man's cowardice in the face of the enemy leading to the unnecessary and terrible deaths of Illyricus and Litigiosus and all the while he was telling this story, Flavius looked ponderous and grave except when Graecus told him that the boy had single-handedly (but using two swords) dispatched the big hairy tribesmen who were threatening Verus and, at this, he had guffawed delightedly and said, 'Did he, by Jupiter. What a wonderful soldier he will be!'

After Graecus had finished, Flavius sat quietly for a while, lost in thought and then he said, 'My boy, how much of this is known to Acerbus?'

'He knows all of it. Indeed, it was he who pointed out to me Germanicus's extreme likeness to our dead Emperor and it was he who explained to me what this could mean in terms both of a wonderful opportunity for the boy and that he could be in great danger depending on what Verus and Vulponia wish to do with their suspicions concerning his parentage.'

'Well, that is to the good because I trust both Acerbus's instincts and his honour so he will be a useful ally. I am glad that you have been frank with me and I know that you would not have wished to make me all the more concerned for my niece and her future as Verus's wife but it is better that I should know all the facts. As it is, I now need time to think about what you have told me and what we may need to do, so I will ask you to leave me now and come back in the morning. Goodnight.'

Graecus bowed to his General and left the room feeling relieved that he had been able to unburden himself to this powerful man and that it now appeared that his assistance and protection had been procured for Germanicus. He went back to the dormitory and found Acerbus who raised his eyebrows questioningly at Graecus who told him all which had passed between him and their General.

Acerbus then lay back on his bed and said, 'Well, that is all to the good. Flavius is a very well respected figure and, if the boy has his protection, then it will be all the more difficult for those who may wish him harm but we must wait and see what he will say tomorrow'.

'Yes, of course, but is not our General a man of great generosity to wish to protect my son?'

'Indeed he is, but do not forget that, if Germanicus were one day to become Emperor, then he would have cause to be very grateful to Flavius so his motives may not be entirely altruistic'.

'Yes, I see that but I prefer to think that our General is a man who is true to the principles of old Rome and that he would be pleased to see a fair and honourable person on the imperial throne.'

'Oh, have it your way, my boy! I am probably just an old cynic. Anyway, let us get some sleep and see what tomorrow brings – if nothing else, we need to set out on our journey back to camp'.

'Goodnight'.

'Goodnight'.

This had been a momentous day for Graecus for not only had he become a father to the son he dearly loved but he had also become the father of a possible future Emperor but despite this, he slept well and woke refreshed the following morning.

Acerbus was up and about and Germanicus was stirring in his bed and, having washed and dressed they all had breakfast together before Graecus went to Flavius's chambers.

'Come in, my boy and sit down', said the General.

Graecus sat and Flavius then said, 'Graecus, I have given our recent conversation much thought overnight and I cannot conclude anything other than that your boy is in grave danger.'

Graecus gasped and Flavius held up his hand asking him to be silent so that he could continue, 'You may feel that I am being melodramatic but I urge you to consider the evidence – Claudius himself was probably poisoned, as was Britannicus, his legitimate son so what chance of survival has the adopted son of a Centurion unless he were to become the protégé of someone with very good connections in Rome but it is unlikely, given what happened with Verus and Vulponia that they or any of their friends would wish to help him become Emperor.'

'I do not think that I properly understand what you are saying.'

'What I am saying to you is that Verus and Vulponia are politically powerful people in Rome by being close to the Emperor's circle of favourites and it is very much in their interests to do away with your son and probably you also. You are both in mortal danger.'

'But I am a soldier, I can protect myself and my son.'

'Yes, Graecus you are a warrior and you can protect yourself with your sword but there are other ways to kill a man and these people are very skilled in them – poison is one of their underhand methods – as the imperial family has found to its cost in recent times'.

'But you make it all sound so decadent and base,' said the Centurion shaking his head.

'Graecus, my boy, despite your having been a courageous soldier for many years, you are truly innocent when it comes to the ways of the world. There are many people in positions of power who are not like us – they do not wish for fairness and justice – they wish only to feather their own nests and be drunk on power. It is these people who would wish to eliminate the threat posed by Germanicus and they would not hesitate for a second to kill a boy.'

'But what can be done? I have only just become his father, he cannot be taken from me!'

'I am not suggesting that he is. What I suggest is that you and he return to your camp and I shall use my position to keep the likes of Verus as far away from you as possible but it is up to you to keep away from the Vulponias of this world and we must hope that, in time, they will forget you and your boy. The other thing is that you must stay away from Rome at all costs as it could be very dangerous for you both.'

'Yes, General, I see that and I see also that, if we are to keep our lives, then I must have no ambitions for my son'.

'I think that is prudent but he is intelligent and will be a fine soldier and he will probably merit promotion. As his father, it is your task to keep him safe but you must allow yourself to hope that the Fates will intervene and make it possible for the boy's talents to find proper expression.'

'General, I thank you for the care you have taken in this delicate matter and for assisting me and my son. I will do all in my power to keep him safe and I feel that it would be safest not to tell him of any of this, at least until he is an adult'.

'Yes, I feel that would be wise. Now, you must leave me as I have a meeting with the praetor – these civil servants and their piddling regulations drive me to the brink of sanity but it seems that I must comply with their pettifogging ways'.

'Goodbye General, till we meet again'.

'Goodbye Centurion, till we meet again'.

Graecus left the room with a feeling of sadness that Germanicus may not be able to fulfil all the promise he showed and how strangely fate shapes people's lives.

Later that day the two Centurions and the boy left Augusta on their long journey back to their camp but it was wonderful dry sunny weather all the way and they reached the main camp in a remarkably short time. Picking up fresh horses from their colleagues, they set off for their camp with great anticipation at seeing their friends again after such a long interval.

It was at about the fourth hour after noon that they saw the camps in the distance, smoke rising from cooking fires and then, as they got nearer, they could hear the distant rumble of men's voices and the sound of metal implements being used and as their approach was noted, there was the sound of cheers coming from both sides of the camp.

As they neared the top of the hill, the cheers became louder as all the men had stopped what they were doing and stood to welcome them back but, for Germanicus, the best welcome was running towards him on four legs barking exultantly; Zig ran straight into the boy's arms where he was held fast until it was time for the evening meal and the prospect of food overcame his delight at being reunited with his master.

That evening, Graecus sat at the head of the table with his men and heaved a huge sigh of relief to be back in the world he understood with people he trusted. He was also very grateful to be enjoying Felix's cooking again; no-one else had his touch and no-one else could produce food which suited Graecus's palate and stomach quite so well and Acerbus, sitting next to Graecus and belching loudly as dish after dish disappeared down his gullet, obviously agreed.

It took some days for the excitement of the visit to Augusta to wear off but, eventually, life returned to normal and it was only occasionally that Graecus would think about Germanicus's heritage and only very occasionally that he and Acerbus would talk quietly about it.

CHAPTER THIRTEEN

Time passed. Summers and winters came and went and Graecus watched as his son grew in stature and maturity. All the while, Graecus enjoyed the company and comradeship of Acerbus and rejoiced that he had so skilful a colleague with whom to share the burdens of command.

Now that the matter of Germanicus's adoption had been resolved, life settled into a happy routine and acquired an almost dreamlike quality for Graecus who loved his role as Centurion and revelled in his role as a father. There were odd scuffles with the locals but nothing as bad as the night-time attack and there were a few incidents among the men but, after all the excitement and incident of the period which had begun with Germanicus's arrival at the camp and ended with his adoption, there was little to disturb the daily routine except that Verus became Cohort Commander but, as a result either of Flavius's intervention or his own inclination, he left the centuries very much to their own devices.

Life went on in this most placid and enjoyable fashion for several years during which time Germanicus became a young man. He grew to be quite tall, above average height for a Roman and was a striking figure with his blonde hair and his piercing blue eyes. Despite Felix's best efforts over a number of years, Germanicus's hair was still untamed and it stuck out from his head in many directions even though he wore it short. Sometimes, Graecus would watch him walking from the camp into the distance with Zig, going hunting, and his heart would turn over with pride and love as the fit, muscular figure walked into the woods and then he would muse that the young man had had a truly wonderful upbringing since his adoption, living a healthy outdoor life full of physical activity and yet learning, at the same time, to read and write and become a good soldier.

On one such day, a hot summer's day, Germanicus had left the camp early in the morning with a quiver full of arrows, whistling to Zig to join him as he went in search of game for the pot. He called to Felix that he would be back at about the midday and that he hoped he would bring back a good bag of meat. Graecus watched him go, watching his light springy step and listening to his tuneless whistling and, if Graecus could have found any fault with Germanicus, it would have been that his whistling was very irritating and, much as he had tried to cure the boy of it or, at least get him to whistle in tune, he had been unsuccessful.

The morning wore on and Graecus, working on documents in his room, was looking forward to one of Felix's dishes when, out of nowhere, a loud cry rent the quiet air. This was followed by other similar cries and Graecus ran from his room into the middle of the camp to see what was the cause of the disturbance.

Pneumaticus and Felix were standing next to the kitchen looking into the distance with horrified expressions and when Graecus turned his gaze in the same direction as theirs, he was similarly distressed for what he saw was Germanicus, covered in blood from head to foot, walking very slowly towards the camp carrying Zig who was also severely bloodstained. As Graecus looked, he saw his son stumble and nearly drop the little dog. Graecus's mind immediately became very practical and he started shouting orders – firstly to Felix to boil a cauldron of water and find clean linen for bandages, then to Impedimentus to saddle two horses and then to Incitatus to run and find Magnus and tell him to scrub the operating table in the infirmarium and to stand by with his surgical instruments.

Then he mounted one of the horses and, signalling to Impedimentus to mount the other, he set off in the direction of his wounded son.

Although there was little distance to cover and his horse was swift, it seemed to Graecus that it was an eternity before he reached Germanicus and in that short space of time his mind had gone through a thousand tortures of how he would try to cope with life without his son and what would happen if he did not die but was terribly maimed or how the young man would cope if the dog died.

Now he was upon him. Dismounting, he said, 'My son, what has happened? Where are you injured? Where are you bleeding from?'

Then he saw that it would be difficult for Germanicus to reply as the lower left hand side of his face was bleeding profusely and seemed to be detached from his jaw. He looked at the dog and saw that he had also suffered a wound to his mouth which was bleeding badly.

Impedimentus had arrived and dismounted and was standing next to Graecus who said, 'Do not try to speak my son, I see where you are wounded and that Zig is suffering also. Please stand still while I tie my neckerchief around your face to keep the wound together and then we will help you onto this horse. I will ride with you back to camp and Impedimentus here will take Zig. Magnus will be waiting for us and will patch you up. You will soon be as good as new'.

Germanicus nodded and, having tenderly handed Zig to Impedimentus, allowed his father to put the makeshift bandage around his face. It was difficult for Germanicus to mount the horse as he was weak but Graecus more or less lifted him onto the beast before himself mounting it and they set off at a walking pace to their camp with Graecus holding his son upright with one hand and the reins with the other. They were followed by Impedimentus who was cradling the dog in the crook of one arm as the little animal moaned softly.

By the time they reached the camp everyone was waiting for them and many hands helped the now ashen-faced Germanicus down from the horse and carried him inside to the infirmarium where they laid him on the clean table and Magnus untied the neckerchief. All then held their breath waiting for the diagnosis.

'Ah yes', he said. 'I see. Hmm. There are two holes in his cheek. They are puncture wounds. He has impaled himself on something and there is an entry wound and an exit wound. It will not be difficult to close the wounds but I will have to sew him up without giving him any wine to dull the pain as he will not be able to drink anything, nor will he be able to bite on anything. You will need to hold him down so that I can work quickly but first I must make the wound clean with this tincture. It will sting like all the bees in a hive'.

At this, Magnus took the cork from a flagon and, tipping it in the direction of Germanicus's face, poured a generous measure over the young man's cheek. Germanicus gasped and shook his head at the onslaught he had suffered from the stinging tincture but he did not cry out and his eyes watered only in response to the sensation, not in self-pity.

Graecus was watching intently and found it hard to bear the thought that his son was in great pain without his being able to relieve it in some way so he leaned towards Germanicus and said, 'My son, it may make it easier if, instead of biting on a wad, that you hold on to my hand as tightly as you wish. Here is my hand, I am giving it to you now – grasp it as hard as you like'.

And Germanicus took the proffered hand and held it very tightly throughout the fifteen minutes or so while Magnus calmly and precisely sewed his face back together. Towards the end of the procedure, the patient became agitated and Graecus was concerned that this was because the pain was unbearable for him as he seemed very keen to say something and, it was, for the moment impossible for him to speak as Magnus had his fingers in his mouth, sewing up his cheek from the inside.

Then, it was over and the surgeon finished off his work with neat knots and another drenching with the tincture but, this time, the young man did not flinch and, indeed, could hardly contain his enthusiasm to speak.

Once Magnus had finished, the others helped Germanicus to sit up and Graecus having asked if it would be harmful for him to speak and having received the reply that it would probably be harmful to try to get him to keep quiet, the young man said, 'Oh father! What an adventure Zig and I have had! How is he? Will he live?'

'Magnus is sewing him up now and he is being as stoic as you were so do not worry about your companion – he will live to hunt another day. Now tell us what happened'.

'Well, we were in the forest when I saw a boar some way in front of us and I crept towards it so that I was near enough to loose an arrow and I got it in the neck but not at that crucial place where you sever the artery, so it was wounded but not mortally.

Then it started running away but more slowly than if it had not been wounded and I managed to put three more arrows in its back and one in the back of its leg and I thought that I had done enough to bring it down but it must have been very strong for it ran off further into the forest and I lost it'.

Here, Germanicus paused for breath and Graecus said, 'But how were you and Zig injured?'

'Well, Zig ran off after the wounded boar and I ran off after him but I lost sight of them both for some minutes and I had to use their tracks to find them but when I did, I found them in a clearing and that the boar had backed Zig up against a rock and he was trapped. When I ran into the space to try to rescue the dog, the boar charged him and although he jumped out of the boar's way, its tusk pierced his jaw and he was impaled on it.'

'What happened then, my son?'

'The boar was very angry because it was injured and because it had a dog stuck on its tusk and I was very angry because I wanted to save Zig so I dived for the boar's neck to try to pull Zig from its tusk and I had my knife in my other hand so that when the boar turned towards me to gore me with its other tusk, I was able to cut its throat quite easily. Oh, father, it is a magnificent boar and Felix will make many wonderful things from it, can we not go now and find it and bring it back to camp before the other wild beasts feed on it?'

'Germanicus, you are a true soldier – even though you are wounded, all you are really interested in is your belly'.

In truth, Graecus was heartily relieved that his son was so pre-occupied as it meant that his injuries were not serious and, having strapped him onto a calm horse, Graecus and two others set off into the forest with him to recover the fallen animal.

It was a magnificent beast and Felix was overjoyed at the many challenges it made to his culinary ingenuity. Furthermore, it had an exceptionally thick hide and Germanicus tanned it and made a strong purse which he kept about his waist. After some weeks, both his injuries and Zig's healed cleanly but Germanicus was left with two scars on his cheek which, whilst not in any way affecting his good looks, made him appear older and more serious.

And there were two other effects of his injuries – one of which was that, possibly as a result of the fact that the shape of his mouth changed slightly, his voice was different and he acquired a slight sibilance in his speech but Acerbus, who knew about these things, said that this was a very fashionable way of speaking among the gilded youth of Rome.

The other effect was not noticeable straightway but, after a few weeks, all of a sudden, Graecus thought that he had not heard Germanicus whistling for some time and felt moved to say to him, 'Why do you no longer whistle as was your wont?'

'Since the injury to my face, I cannot purse my lips in the proper way anymore. I cannot produce a sound'.

And Graecus was more pained by this than he would have thought possible.

Life again went on and the only interruption to routine was that Germanicus was formally received into the Roman Army as a recruit and had the tattoo 'SPQR', 'Senatus Populusque Romanus', showing his allegiance to the Senate and the People of Rome, made on his upper right arm to show that he belonged to Rome.

News came from the outside world from time to time – sometimes in official documents or there would be gossip from the main camp. Then, one day, about the time of Germanicus's recruitment, Acerbus took Graecus to one side and said, 'I have had a letter from my cousin in Rome. He tells me that the story is circulating everywhere in the city that Nero had had his mother murdered'.

'Ye gods, how did she die?'

'Well, he had been trying to poison her for years but she managed to survive but now he has an ambitious new girlfriend, Poppaea, who resented Agrippina so he had her ambushed by the navy in her villa and the admiral, Anictetus, stabbed her to death'.

'I know she was a hateful woman but it is surely contrary to the laws of nature to kill your own mother! Is the Senate doing anything about it?'

'I think not – the Senate is not popular with Nero and the Senators fear the Praetorian Guard and will be relying on Seneca and Burrus to continue to be a restraining influence on the Emperor'.

'Hah! I do not envy them their positions then. And what about this girlfriend, where does that leave Octavia?'

'Well, I would not wish to be in her position either – it's dangerous to be married to the Emperor when he is in thrall to another woman who wants him to marry her. Of course, Octavia is protected by the fact that the people respect her as the daughter of Claudius but, as time goes by, that link is less powerful'.

'What do the people think of all this?'

'Well, I hear that Nero's popularity is in the wane. He's spending too much time with all these actors and other strange types. I mean, there aren't that many people who find it acceptable that their Emperor spends most of his time with musicians, poets, painted boys and all other kinds of fawning hangers-on, just like that idiot Verus and his scheming cousin'.

'Well, if they are his chosen companions then the gods must be laughing at us. The way you put it, it sounds as if his life is dedicated to pleasure and decadence'.

'It is not just the way in which I put it – that is the way it is'.

'Then Rome and the empire will suffer, Rome needs honest leadership – someone who puts the people before himself'.

'That would undoubtedly be a better government but I don't see where such an Emperor could be found – anyone brought up in the court is tainted by its decadence'.

'Then we must ask the gods that such an Emperor be found!'

The news of Agrippina's murder spread through the camp and although there were those who felt that, given her own talents for disposing of those who were in the way of her ambitions, it was only what she deserved, even they had to admit that she had prevented her son from behaving too outrageously.

When he contemplated this latest news of degeneracy from Rome, Graecus did pray to the gods that the empire be given a fair and just ruler – and that that leader should be Germanicus.

But, whatever was happening in Rome, for Graecus's century in Germania, life went on as normal, cheek by jowl with Acerbus and his men.

The life of the little town also was slow to change except that Arminia married a widower and inherited his six children so that now, when Graecus visited the inn, there were small blonde heads bobbing at her skirts but, sometimes, she would wink at him from across the room and he knew that the same fond thoughts were passing through her mind as through his. Looking back over these years of stability as, surrounded by his friends, he watched his son grow into a fine young man, Graecus felt that they had a perfect, idyllic, almost poetic quality to them.

Then, just when it seemed as if nothing would ever change, everything changed.

CHAPTER FOURTEEN

It started in the spring of the seventh year of Nero's reign when a visitor from another cohort brought news to the camp that the Governor of Britannia, Suetonius Paulinus, had taken his three Legions to Mona, the large island off the coast of Wales, and had systematically annihilated the Druids, man woman and child, whose stronghold it had been.

This caused much discussion between Graecus's men as many of the older soldiers came from Britannia and opinions were hotly exchanged. Graecus himself knew little of Britannia but one evening Acerbus, who had served there, was in a philosophical mood after the evening meal, sucked his teeth and said loudly to anyone who would listen, 'You know, this massacre of the Druids will cause more problems than it will solve. When I served Flavius and our late Emperor Claudius in Britannia, I saw that the one thing that really united the warring tribes was the Druids. I mean, you only had to watch how they obeyed the Druids' every word, to know that they will not take this lying down. I think that Suetonius has made a mistake – any surviving Druids – and there must be some – will stir up rebellion in the tribes'.

Pneumaticus had been listening and he thoughtfully stroked his chin before saying, 'I disagree. I am a Briton and I know the power of the Druids – I was brought up with it, but you must remember that the tribes have had years of peace and greater prosperity under Rome's rule and their kings will not welcome interference from the Druids if it affects their wealth'.

'But what about their religion? From what I recall, the tribesmen were very religious and this must surely be an insult to their gods'.

'I am not so sure. Many of the client kings have become rich and have sent their sons to Rome to be educated – they have become Romanised and have turned their backs on the ancient gods'.

'Yes, that may be true of some of them but even you must agree that not all of them are convinced of the benefits of Rome's rule. What about the Welsh tribes, for instance? I would wager that they will take these reprisals very badly'.

'Oh, I have to agree with you there – it is common knowledge that the Ordovices, Silures and the Demetae hate Rome with a vengeance so if Suetonius wants to do this job properly then he needs to take action against them as well.'

Graecus had also been listening and he said, 'But what of the other tribes? I mean, they are not all clients of Rome, are they? Some of them in the north of the country seem to wish to keep their independence, do they not?'

'Yes', said Acerbus 'there are quite a few tribes which resent the yoke of Rome and they bitterly resent paying taxes and I hear that fool of a new procurator, Catus Decianus is making things hotter than they need be with some of the friendly tribes.'

He coughed then went on, 'My cousin in Rome, the Senator, says this is madness – it will alienate those who have been inclined to be Rome's friends, and all of this squeezing more and more money out of the peoples of the Empire is to fund Nero's selfish ambitions. They say he already wants to replace his new palace and to build the palace to end all palaces for himself right in the middle of Rome but the people are tired of all this extravagance and want better houses'.

The latter part of Acerbus's speech was met with a weary chorus of 'Aye, aye' from the men and then Magnus, tiring of the political talk, asked Graecus to sing and the subject of Britannia was forgotten for the moment.

A few days later, Graecus was sitting at his desk trying to add up some columns of figures and was becoming fretful because, every time he added them up, he came to a different total. He was pleased therefore for the diversion of Incitatus bringing in a letter and he was intrigued to see that it was addressed to both him and Acerbus. On opening it, he saw that it was from Biliosus and its contents transfixed him from the start. It read:

'Greetings Brothers!
'I must be the bearer of bad tidings. We have been informed that there has been an outrage committed on Camulodunum in

Britannia by a large force of Iceni and Trinovante tribesmen who are being lead by the Iceni Queen, Boudicca. This horde of barbarians descended on the town without warning and murdered its inhabitants without mercy then they ransacked the buildings before setting everything alight. The town, which as you know, was the provincial capital is in ruins and the Temple of Claudius has been razed to the ground. All of our gallant brethren from the Legions who had retired there with their wives and families have been massacred.

'The barbarians are now marching south but the governor's Legions are still in the western part of the country completing the operation of destroying the Druids. Suetonius Paulinus has taken a small detachment of men on reconnaissance to Londinium but it is not thought that sufficient numbers of troops can be mustered in time to save this city from the British tribes who are rapidly joining Boudicca as she moves south.

'It is not known where the rebels will strike next but we have urgent need of extra troops who have knowledge of and experience in fighting in Britannia.

'Each of you has many men within your century with such knowledge and experience and it is now ordered that you make all ready to leave your camp and to be ready to embark for Britannia on 24-hours' notice.

'Rome has suffered an egregious insult. We know that we can rely on you and your men to deliver retribution against this foreign queen.

'Farewell!'

Graecus read this in a frenzy of uncomfortable excitement and then read it again twice as his mind raced on trying to think of all the matters which needed to be accomplished before his century could be ready to leave but, at the same time, trying to think of what this change in circumstances could mean for him, his men and above all, for Germanicus.

The first thing he must do was to take the letter to Acerbus and share the orders with him so he left his desk and went straightaway to find him knowing that, as it was mid-morning, he would be in the thick of his men keeping their weaponry skills up to his high standards.

And there he was, skilfully deflecting the sword of a much bigger man who was new to the century and had not yet worked out how such a little man could be so effective with his gladius.

Acerbus saw Graecus approach and that he had an important looking letter in his hand. So, pausing only to smash the sword from the bigger man's hand and say, 'Look here, blockhead, you're not paying attention are you? I could have killed you three times over this morning and, if you're not careful, that's what's going to happen to you the first time that we meet an enemy', he then turned to Graecus and said, 'My boy, you are looking very serious and you are carrying a very serious looking letter. Tell me what this is all about.'

Graecus handed him the letter and said, 'Here, read it. It is addressed to us both'.

Acerbus read the letter and then gave a long low whistle through his (rather rabbitty) teeth.

'I knew it,' he said, in a low voice, 'I knew there'd be big trouble. And now it's our job to sort out the mess that they've got themselves into. By Jupiter, I've seen these Britons and they are a very frightening lot. We're in for an interesting time! At least we shall be going together and whatever adventure is coming our way, then it is something that we shall experience together'.

Then to Graecus's surprise, Acerbus embraced him and said, 'But now we must prepare ourselves for leaving the camp. I, for one, do not wish that an incoming Centurion should find any cause for complaint!'

And this was a thought which was also exercising Graecus so, having agreed that they would liaise later in the day, Graecus went back to deal with his own arrangements and went, first of all, to find Impedimentus.

Impedimentus was counting spearheads and marking numbers down with a stylus on a wooden tablet with a waxed surface when Graecus found him in the storeroom.

'I must speak urgently to you', he said but Impedimentus was in the middle of a calculation and did not wish to be interrupted so flapped his hand to his commanding officer motioning him to keep quiet until he had finished. This irritated Graecus who said, 'Impedimentus, when I say that I wish to speak urgently to you, then that is exactly what I mean. Put down the tablet and give me your complete attention'.

'Well, I really do not see what can be so urgent that it cannot wait until I have finished these figures' said the store master testily.

Angered now by the little man, Graecus said, 'This is my camp and I decide what is and what is not urgent. Put down the tablet now!'

And these last words were said in such a loud tone that Impedimentus dropped the tablet so heavily that most of the wax came away and destroyed his morning's handiwork. Graecus then said, more calmly, 'If you would give me your attention, then you would see that what I have to tell you is more important than all the lists you will ever make. Now, read this letter and tell me what you will need to do to be able to be ready in 24 hours and how much help you will need.'

So Impedimentus read the letter and Graecus watched as his face registered firstly surprise, then horror and then concentration.

'Well, I do agree with you that this is more urgent than my storekeeping records. Now, let's see, what we need to do is draw up a list of equipment for every man –weapons, armour, bedding et cetera, a list of supplies – food, bowls, spoons, cooking pots et cetera, a list of tools – spades, hammers, hatchets et cetera, stakes for palisades, a list of administrative needs – pens, tablets et cetera, oh and, of course, we'll need tents and a list of the pack animals we have available and which will carry what and a list of vehicles. Oh, and we shall need emergency fodder for the animals in case there are problems on the way and they cannot forage. Once we have the lists then we can assign men to the different tasks. Assuming that Magnus will organise himself as far as his herbs and medicines are concerned, then I think I shall need the help of five men'.

Graecus was again irritated – this time because he felt that Impedimentus's agreement with his ranking of priorities was patronising so in a cool tone he said, 'Well, I am heartily glad that you agree with me,' and in saying this, he felt that perhaps the men had been languishing in this backwater for long enough and that some action in a different country would sharpen the wits of them all.

So he said briskly, 'Good, I will send five men to you after I have told them of this new situation and I shall expect you to report to me by four hours after the mid-day with your progress'.

Then he went to find Felix.

Felix was in the middle of one of his bouts of coughing laughter, sharing a funny story with Magnus and Germanicus when Graecus appeared.

But they all looked up with alacrity when their Centurion appeared as they knew from the look on his face that he had something important to say.

'Oh, I'm glad that you are all here. We have new orders and they are of the utmost urgency. I can do no better than to read to you the letter we have had from Biliosus.'

Which he did, noticing the expressions on their faces which were a curious mixture of regret and excitement: regret because their happy rural existence was to come to an end but excitement because it looked as though they were about to rejoin the Legions in battle against fearsome enemies.

Felix spoke first and said in a loud voice, 'That's it then. Our time here is done. Britannia and Boudicca had better be careful because if they come across us then they will really know what the Roman Army can do!'

This brought cheers from Germanicus and Magnus and Graecus was pleased that they were all so happy at the thought of action against the legendary warriors of Britannia.

'Well, I could hardly have wished for a more enthusiastic reception to the news. Now, Magnus, you will be responsible for taking all the necessary medicines and, you Felix, will need to agree with Impedimentus how many pots and utensils we can take and you Germanicus must help Impedimentus organise the rest of the men and their equipment when I have given the news to the rest of the century. Come with me now, all of you, and let's enlighten our brothers'.

Off strode Graecus in a determined fashion, energised by this new challenge but, at the same time, a little uneasy as no-one knew what it would entail except that it meant the end of their happy world, miles away from Rome and its politics.

Graecus strode into the centre of the camp and called all the men to gather round. Then he said, 'Brothers, listen carefully. We have important new orders from Biliosus. We must prepare to leave this camp and be ready to go to Britannia on 24 hours' notice. I shall read to you from the letter'.

Then, while he was unfolding the document, the men were beginning to nudge each other and to point into the distance behind Graecus who wished they would pay more attention while he was speaking but Felix spoke and said, 'Domine, there is a chariot approaching with all speed from the direction of the main camp. It could well be Biliosus himself'.

'Thank you, Felix. It could well be that we are to be favoured with a visit from our superior officer but I shall continue to read his letter as it concerns us all'.

He read the letter out loud to the men and it was received with a mixture of groans and whoops of pleasure. The groans were from those men who had formed relationships with and, in some cases, fathered children, with local women and the whoops of pleasure were from those who had not and who relished a fight.

Now the chariot could be seen clearly and everyone knew it was Biliosus. Graecus said. 'It would appear that there is more news. Germanicus, please go and fetch Acerbus and his men, whatever it is that Biliosus needs to say, affects them also,' and Germanicus sped off while Graecus continued, 'Men, I wish that you would hear our officer in silence. We are soldiers and it is our task to obey orders whether we like them or not. Now, form yourselves into lines and stand upright and, when Biliosus speaks to us, look straight ahead.'

The chariot was climbing to the top of the hill and Biliosus could be seen, next to the charioteer.

The chariot stopped in a billow of dust and Biliosus jumped down from it with athletic panache, the scarlet feathers in the crest of his helmet quivering in the breeze and his scarlet cloak billowing behind him. He was an imposing figure – about 48 years old, with a very strong Roman nose and deep, deep, black eyes.

He strode over first to Graecus and then to Acerbus grasping them by the forearm then said, 'Hail, brothers! I am glad that you have your men mustered here. I have more bad news. Boudicca and her stinking tribesmen have sacked Verulamium. There is hardly a stone or a brick left standing, nor a soul left alive in the city. They have taken prisoners and subjected them to the most disgusting tortures imaginable – they have taken our noble-women and stripped them naked and cut off their breasts and stuffed them in their mouths and they have impaled them on poles stuck through their private parts. Men, these outrages must be avenged – Rome and its people have been insulted and what is more, we have been insulted by a barbarian woman!'

Despite what Graecus had said, neither his men, nor Acerbus's, could receive this news without comment and there was a collective gasp at the details of the terrible vengeance wrought on the Roman noblewomen.

Biliosus continued, 'Yes, men, yes. And that is not all! The gallant Petilius Cerealis, hearing that Boudicca was marching south intent on mischief set out with our brothers of the IXth Legion and were ambushed on their way to Camulodunum. I can hardly bear to tell you, brothers, but the IXth were massacred and Cerealis lost fifteen hundred of his best light infantry and cavalry. He was lucky to escape with his own life and, like any Roman now in Britannia, he is in danger from these ungrateful tribes. Men, this carnage cannot be borne and it must be avenged!'

The soldiers were outraged and there were shouts of 'Filthy bastards', 'We'll get them and show them what's what', and, 'They deserve to die, all of them'. Biliosus let them shout for a few minutes and then raised his hand for silence, 'These barbarians think they can murder us and get away with it, well, they must be shown that Rome is all powerful and that they cannot be allowed to thumb their noses at the might of the Empire. We have been asked by Suetonius Paulinus to provide reinforcements for his Legions and we are proud to do so in the full knowledge that due to the experience of some of you in the invasion of Britannia under our late Emperor Claudius, you will acquit yourselves with the utmost valour.

'You will leave here tomorrow morning at sunrise and by forced marches make your way to Gesoriacum on the northern coast of Gaul. From there you will go by ship to Dubris on the south-eastern coast of Britannia where you will receive further orders.'

'Hail to our Emperor Nero and may the gods give you assistance in your enterprises!'

The men all raised their hands and said, 'Aye, aye' in agreement with Biliosus's rousing speech.

Then Graecus addressed his men and said, 'Now we know what we must do, go do it'

And Acerbus said, 'Men, go and do your duty'.

The men left and Graecus and Acerbus were left alone with Biliosus who said to them, 'That was a good display of bravery and enthusiasm from your men but I wish you to be under no misunderstanding as to the likely outcome of this mission. In any engagement with the enemy, you will be greatly outnumbered and it is their land so they know the marshes, the rivers and the forests and, most important of all, they feel they have their gods on their side'.

Having fought in Britannia before, Acerbus knew what could be expected but he also knew that Claudius's invasion had been successful so he said, 'Sir, we have fought them many times before and the valour they have in abundance is weakened by their lack of armour, weapons and, above all, their lack of discipline. I have high hopes of our being successful if we meet them in the right place'.

'You speak well, Centurion, I hope that we shall be able to celebrate your victory with the finest wines and the most beautiful women! Now, brothers, I need only to tell you that your camp here will shortly be filled with a century from Augusta and to wish you the help of the gods with your endeavours. Farewell!'

Biliosus turned on his heel and mounted the chariot. Then with a wave of his hand, he and the chariot were gone, speeding down the hill and leaving the Centurions with their new orders and their thoughts.

Graecus's mind was running quickly over all the matters which needed to be attended to before they could depart but, frantic though he was, he knew that he was not suffering the tortures of those men who would be leaving wives and children, not knowing whether they would ever be reunited.

He thought about this for a moment and said to Acerbus, 'My friend, I have a mind to say to those of my men who have families here, that, once they have finished their tasks, they may go and say farewell to their wives and children. Will you do likewise?'

'I had not thought of it but I feel it is an excellent idea for, although it is outside our orders, the men will at least not be concerned all the time that their families will not know where they have gone. Yes, I shall do the same'.

Then they parted, each to his men and to the many tasks which needed to be done before the following dawn.

The afternoon passed in a flurry of activity accompanied by much sweat and swearing and a palpable sense of excitement. But it was easy to discern those of his men who had local wives for they had stricken faces and were walking about as if they had leaden feet.

Graecus decided he would put them out of their misery so he went to Germanicus and said, 'My son, you know which of the men have local wives and children. I wish you now to go to each of them and quietly tell him that, once he has finished his tasks here, he may go and visit his family and tell them of his imminent departure. But they must all be back here by midnight.'

'Yes, father, I will gladly tell them that they may go to their families, I know they will be relieved'.

'Off you go then,' and, as the young man ran off to his

colleagues, Graecus gave a silent prayer of thanks to the gods that, in the coming endeavour, he would not be parted from that which was most dear to him – his son.

The day wore on and the camp began to look bare as more articles and utensils and tents and tools were packed away.

Then, as the other men were sitting down to the evening meal, the family men crept away to say goodbye to their loved ones.

It was a quiet thoughtful company that evening, each man trying to look to the future and see what would be the outcome of this mission then they went to their beds and tried to sleep.

Graecus lay there listening out for the return of the family men and, when he had satisfied himself that they had all come back to camp, he fell into an uneasy sleep.

CHAPTER FIFTEEN

They were up just before the dawn and, having broken their fast, they set off at first light with Graecus and Acerbus on horseback at the front of the column and the pack mules and vehicles at the back, the men marching four abreast in the middle, Graecus's men in two's behind him and Acerbus's men in two's behind him, marching in the cool dry spring air with Zig trotting at Germanicus's side.

Graecus thought that this column of men must be an impressive sight with him and Acerbus in their figured leather breastplates, scarlet cloaks and their scarlet plumed helmets on their fine chesnut horses and the standard bearer and the horn blower for each century behind, resplendent in the wolfskins worn over their helmets.

They were silent for several miles, no-one speaking just the thump, thump, thump of their feet going over the grass, the creaking of leather and the sound of the metal discs of the soldiers' overshirts chinking against each other but muffled by the tunics they wore underneath. Then they joined the road and the tramp, tramp, tramp of their feet resounded over the dirt, filling the empty countryside.

Acerbus had not said a word since they left camp, other than to his horse, and Graecus had also been silent. Although the centuries had marching practice every month, it was a long time since they had made a forced march and Graecus had forgotten the effect of the repeated sound of all those feet in their hobnailed boots marching absolutely in time together.

It was hypnotic.

The sun rose higher in the sky, there were song birds fluttering overhead and the odd bird of prey wheeling over some movement it had seen in the long grass. The men felt their spirits rise and they began to sing as they marched:

Tramp. tramp, tramp, forward we go, Tramp, tramp, tramp, on to meet our foe, Who is it we defend? What is it we're for?

225

We fight for ROME and the EMPEROR'

This was invigorating and they sang all afternoon, the repertoire going from the bawdy to the rousing to the plaintive and back to the bawdy again. Progress that day was swift and the twenty five mile march was completed well before sundown. Graecus and Acerbus discussed where they should make their temporary camp and agreed that the top of the small hill to their left would be suitable.

At the top of the hill, the Centurions organised their men to dig the regulation ditch around the camp, using the earth from the ditch for the rampart and fortifying it with the stakes they had brought. Then they erected the leather tents, one tent for each contubernium and, as it grew dusk, they lit fires and took out their cooking pots.

Graecus's contubernium was fortunate because Zig had used a short rest period during the day to go off and find a brace of rabbit which Felix now cooked with a few wild herbs he had picked while the dog was hunting but this was washed down only with the harsh army issue beer and was not what they grown accustomed to in their camp.

The night passed uneventfully and they set off the next day in good spirits making rapid progress in their journey to Gaul.

And the days passed in this way, their progress aided by the fine weather and the occasional addition to the basic rations by game they caught en route or trapped overnight. Swiftly they made their way through countryside, villages, towns and forests and across streams and rivers and all was well.

Then the weather became very hot and the men's tempers began to fray. There were harsh words between colleagues and Graecus had to break up a fight between two of his men, caused, they said, when one of them called the other's wife a 'painted whore'. The fight was a disciplinary offence and Graecus had no choice but to give each of the combatants five lashes with his vine staff.

Seven days after they had left the camp, as they were taking a short rest at midday, Magnus came up to Graecus and said, 'Domine, may I have a private word in your ear?'

So the two men walked a few paces away from their colleagues and Magnus said quietly, 'Domine, have you noticed anything strange about Septimus today?'

'No, I cannot say that I have but speak, brother, and tell me if there is anything I need to know'.

'Well, I do not know if it means anything but I have twice today witnessed him stumble as if from drunkenness while we have been marching over good Roman roads and, on the second occasion, he nearly dropped the standard. Indeed, it was only because Germanicus held onto him and to the standard that it was rescued from falling onto the ground'.

'That is most unlike Septimus. He guards our standard with his life. Please ask Germanicus to come to me'.

Magnus turned and went to fetch Germanicus.

'You wanted me, father?'

'My son, I hear that Septimus stumbled badly today while we were on the road and that you had to help him keep hold of the standard'.

'Yes, what of it?'

'Well, Septimus is an old soldier – he was with the century before even I joined it many years ago – and he guards our standard as if it were his only child. Did he say anything to you when he stumbled? Is he sick?'

'I do not know, father. All he said was, 'These stupid bloody boots, they need new studs' and I picked him up and we marched on but, thinking back, he did seem to be dragging his feet'.

'Thank you my son, I wish you to keep an eye on Septimus, without, of course, making it obvious that you are doing so'.

'Yes, father'.

'Off you go now, go and join the others'.

Germanicus turned smartly on his heel and went to sit with Felix and Pneumaticus who were sharing a joke about a pox-ridden prostitute which gave rise to intermittent guffaws of laughter and obscene gestures.

Graecus thought about what both Magnus and Germanicus had said about their standard bearer and decided that, for the moment at least, he would not speak to Septimus himself.

They started back on the road and the tramp, tramp, tramp of their feet filled the hot afternoon. It was too hot now for them to sing so the only sounds were those of their feet and the occasional whinny of a horse or the braying of one of the mules at the rear of the column.

The sun was now high in the sky and Graecus, feeling the sweat slippery on his thighs where his body made contact with his horse and the first intimations of a headache, had just begun to ponder how hot the *signifers* and the *cornices* must be under their helmets and wolfskins when there was a great thud behind him followed by men's voices calling for the soldiers to halt their march.

For a moment, Graecus thought that someone had dropped a heavy piece of kit and that it was over- cautious to call for a halt but then he saw out of the corner of his eye Germanicus kneeling on the road and, signalling to Acerbus to do the same, he put his right arm up in the air calling the column to a halt.

He then turned round and saw Septimus flat on the ground behind him and Germanicus, looking puzzled, holding the century's standard while Magnus put his fingers to Septimus's neck, feeling for a pulse.

Graecus dismounted.

'Magnus, what is happening?'

'Sir, I regret to tell you that Septimus is dead.'

'What? Has he been wounded by an arrow? Are we under attack?'

'No, sir, he has not been wounded. I think that his heart had just given up. He has most likely been overheated by the march and the wolfskin and, let us not forget, he was forty-nine years of age.'

'Are you sure he's dead, is he not just in a faint or a fit?'

'No, sir. I am certain he is dead. There is no pulse.'

Acerbus had now dismounted and was looking over Graecus's shoulder at the sad figure of Septimus lying on his side, with his right arm bent under him and his left frozen in a half wave.

'What in Jupiter's name is going on?' said Acerbus in a voice so loud it should have woken the dead.

'Septimus is dead', said Magnus quietly.

'Ye gods'.

The other men were all gathering round now and Graecus felt that he must take command of the situation. So he said, 'Brothers, Septimus is dead. His heart gave up. We must honour him and his service to the cohort, he was a good man and a courageous soldier'.

The men said 'Aye, aye' and raised their arms in salute to their comrade.

Impedimentus came bustling up.

'What has happened? Is Septimus dead?'

'Yes, he is. His heart failed.'

'Well, he swore me to secrecy but, now that he's gone to meet his ancestors, I suppose I am free of the obligation to keep his secret'.

'Impedimentus, what are you talking about? What secret? As your officer, I command you to tell me'.

'Well, the thing was that Septimus lied about his age when he joined the army. He told me so one evening when we were talking about our families and he told me that he had eight children but, in order to be eligible to join the army, he had lied about being married and he had lied about his age.'

'How old was he, then?'

'He was fifty-nine, not forty-nine and he did not wish to retire. He wanted to remain in the service of the army because it was the life which suited him. He was free but he could send money home to his wife and children.'

Graecus was astonished by this piece of news and felt somewhat cheated that Septimus, whom he had known for over fifteen years, could have kept this secret. But that was all very well, the more pressing problems now were: what to do with Septimus's body and who would be the new standard bearer for the century?

Acerbus immediately answered the first question by saying, 'Well, we can't leave the poor sod here in the middle of nowhere. Why don't we take him with us to Gesoriacum and have him dispatched with proper honours in the camp there?'

'But we're days away from Gesoriacum and the weather's warm – he'll stink long before we get there and be a magnet for the crows'.

Now Magnus stepped forward and said, 'Well, I could wash his body in vinegar and wrap it in vinegar soaked cloths and, if we have a spare tent we could put that around him to keep the sun off so that he'll be reasonably fresh when we get to the port'.

'That is what we shall do then, but we cannot do it here. We must wait until we make camp tonight and do it there. In the meantime wrap him in a tent and put him on one of the baggage wagons.'

'Yes, Domine.'

Two men from Septimus's contubernium picked up their fallen colleague and carried him to the back of the column where, within a few minutes, they fulfilled this command.

Now the column was ready to continue but the century needed someone to carry its standard so Graecus said, 'Germanicus, for the moment, please put on the wolfskin and pick up our standard. You shall carry it until we camp tonight.'

'Yes, father'.

Graecus and Acerbus signalled for their men to begin to march and the column started off again into the hot afternoon sun.

And every man in it was thinking that the sudden death of the *signifer* was a very bad omen indeed.

The column marched silently on until it was nearly sundown when the Centurions called a halt and gave the order to make camp on top of a small hill.

Once camp had been made, Magnus set about preserving Septimus with the vinegar-soaked cloths and wrapping him in the leather tent. Graecus looked on wondering why it had never occurred to him that his old colleague was really too old to have been marching twenty five miles a day, in the sun, wearing a wolfskin.

'Would he have suffered, Magnus?'

'I think he may have felt faint for a while but I do not think that he was in pain for any length of time, it was very sudden, after all'.

'Well, I thank the gods for that. He was a good soldier and a good brother to us all'.

'Yes, he was and he was a good *signifer*. We shall all feel his loss. Who is now to carry our standard?'

'At present, I know not but Germanicus is young and strong. He can carry it until I can think of a permanent replacement for our dead brother'.

'Domine, may I make a suggestion?'

'Yes, go ahead'.

'Well, I know that every one of us is thinking that it was a terrible omen for our standard bearer to drop dead as we make our way to do battle in a difficult land against numerous enemies and I feel it would be best if we had a properly appointed new *signifer* without delay'.

'You make a good point. But who is it to be? I cannot see that anyone really stands out as being the right man for the job'.

'Well, who has been doing it so far?'

'Germanicus'.

'Can he not do the job, then?'

'That would be a great honour for him and a greater honour for me as his father but he is too young and the other men might not think it fair'.

'I am sure that you are mistaken in that view but why not ask for a vote on the matter in accordance with our usual practice?'

'That is a good way forward. I shall do it later this evening.'

So, after the men had eaten and had recovered from the exertions of the day, Graecus stood up and said, 'Brothers, we all mourn the loss of our friend and colleague, Septimus, but we are on our way to meet a fearsome foe and we have a great need of a new *signifer*. It has been suggested to me that my son, Germanicus, will make a good bearer for our standard as he is young, strong and courageous and I cannot disagree with this. I wish, therefore, for the matter to be put to the vote but, before we do so, I must ask Germanicus if he wishes to be *signifer* to this century.'

Germanicus had been listening to this speech intently and had, at first, looked incredulous and then joyful that he might be chosen.

He rose and said, 'Brothers, I am still a young man but all the love and comradeship I have known in my life has been from you. It would be the greatest honour for me to bear our standard and, if that is to be my task, then I shall fulfil it to the very best of my ability'.

Graecus now asked those in favour of Germanicus's promotion to raise their right hands in the air.

A forest of hands shot up.

Then Graecus asked those against the proposal to put up their hands.

Not one hand was raised.

'I now declare Germanicus to be our new standard bearer. May he bring to all of you the good luck he has brought to me.'

A great cheer went up after this speech and there was a lifting of spirits from the gloom of the afternoon.

The night passed without incident and the following morning Graecus watched with pride as his son donned his helmet and then the wolfskin before picking up the century's standard.

They marched off again, each day getting nearer and nearer to Gesoriacum and each day there were more blisters and pulled muscles as the strain of marching twenty five miles a day took its toll.

At last, though, they knew the end of their march had to be soon because they began to see water birds in the skies above them and they could smell the sea.

Then, coming over the crest of a hill, they could see the port below them – the town buildings nestling around the bay and the many moored boats and ships bobbing up and down in the water.

Graecus signalled to Acerbus that he wished to halt the column and they both put up their arms to order the men to halt.

'What is it brother?' said Acerbus.

'I wish to tell my men to take a few moments to brush themselves down and wipe their faces free of sweat and dirt so that, when we enter the town, we look like fresh troops, not dishevelled men who have been marching for weeks'.

'That is a good idea – I am sure that we shall attract a great deal of attention as we march in and I wish us to have our chances with the local girls!'

'You think always about your stomach and your dick!'

'True, but sometimes I think about glory in battle and honour in friendship.'

'Indeed you do and I for one am glad that we are entering this new enterprise together.'

Graecus dismounted and ordered his men to clean themselves up as best they could while Acerbus's men did the same.

Refreshed, they marched down the hill, singing as they went and soon they were passing through the Praetorian Gate into the town making their way to the barracks through the narrow, smoky streets.

As they marched, the townsfolk were drawn from their houses and shops to watch these new men and the stares of the townsfolk were matched by those of the soldiers who were looking out for pretty girls and handsome women.

Then they came to the barracks and marched thankfully through the sentry gate into the area in front of the *praetorium*, the camp's administrative headquarters, where Graecus and Acerbus were greeted by the camp commander and then they were shown to their quarters.

After a bath Graecus and Acerbus were given their new orders telling them to report with their centuries the following morning at the dockside at the ships named 'Nauplius' and 'Obsidialis'.

Meanwhile, their men had set out for a night's enjoyment of the town's taverns and, in some cases, brothels so it was a red-eyed bunch who stood on the quay early the next day.

'Nauplius' and 'Obsidialis' were wooden boats with sails but there was space under the deck for one bank of oarsmen on either side – in this way they resembled a trireme but they were much shallower vessels. For those of both Graecus's and Acerbus's centuries who had not been to sea before, it was awesome to think that these vessels would carry them, one vessel for each century, across the treacherous waters to Britannia.

This thought was passing through several minds when an important looking figure in a strange, front-fastening leather breastplate and leather helmet came down the gangplank of 'Nauplius' followed by four other, less important-looking, individuals.

'Hail', said the leading man with a curl of the lip, 'I am Marcus Quintus Jejunus and I am the captain of this convoy. I do not know whether you are acquainted with the ways of the navy, but, I tell you now that when we are at sea, I am in command of these ships and everyone and everything aboard them, including you and your men. What I say goes, and no arguments. Understand?'

Graecus and Acerbus met this with silence for a few moments but then Acerbus said, 'Sir, we are colleagues in a difficult enterprise, I am sure that we all hope there will be no fighting between us as to who is in command of whom,' and he finished this little speech with his best disarmingly boyish smile, giving Jejunus a full view of his rabbitty teeth.

Jejunus snorted and said, 'Well, we won't be leaving today. The winds are not favourable. Be here tomorrow at the same time and we'll see then if we can leave. Good day to you'.

And he turned on his heel and strode back up the gangplank followed by the lesser mortals.

'And I thought the Army was the senior service!' said Graecus, 'He spoke to us as if we were dirt'.

'The Army *is* the senior service. The rules are that we must defer to him in relation to anything connected with safety at sea but *we* are in charge of our own men and I'm not having a jumped up nobody like him telling me what to do,' said Acerbus.

Given that they were not sailing that day, this meant the men could be at leisure and the day was again spent by many in taverns and brothels.

Graecus and Acerbus spent some time with Germanicus in exercise at the barracks followed by a welcome few hours in the *tepidarium* and the *frigidarium* before finding one of the quieter taverns at the far side of the town.

There they sat and ate and drank and Graecus and Acerbus told the young man tales of old campaigns where they exaggerated their exploits only a little in the interests of dramatic tension.

Fuelled by several flagons of the local wine, they were all laughing loudly at one of Acerbus's stories when a mariner who had been sitting alone at a nearby table came up to them and said, 'Gentlemen, may I introduce myself? I am Xanthippus, first mate on the Nauplius and I could not fail to hear the exchange you enjoyed earlier today with our captain. Have you sailed with the navy before, gentlemen?'

While he was speaking, all eyes were on him and the soldiers noted that he had the black hair of a Roman and spoke Latin like a native but with a surprisingly patrician accent for a mere sailor. They also noted that, although his very dark brown eyes were set deep in his head, they conveyed humour and amiability.

Graecus spoke first and said, 'Yes, my fellow Centurion and I have both sailed with the navy before but my son here has not'.

'Your son? What joy it must be to serve with one's son! I so rarely see my son that he is quite a stranger to me.'

'Where does your son live, sir?' said Germanicus gently, who did not need to refer to the sailor as 'sir' because of his rank but used the honorific in deference to Xanthippus's age .

'He lives in Rome with my wife and our daughter and I see them when we are in port at Ostia but that is not so often'.

'Have you been in the navy many years, sir?'

'Only since my silk weaving business failed five years ago and I could not pay the money-lender and had to sell my fine villa and live with the plebs in a tiny rented hovel'.

'That is a sad story sir.'

'Indeed, but I try not to dwell on it and I take pleasure from the fact that I manage to keep my family out of penury. But, tell me, now, where are you gentlemen from?'

'Sir, please sit with us and we will call for more wine while we tell you our histories,' said Germanicus and so Xanthippus sat at their table and as the afternoon wore into the evening and then into the night, the four men talked and talked and, as is the nature of drunken conversations, between bawdy stories, they spoke of politics and how they would put the world to rights and they spoke of the army and its being infiltrated by soft merchants who didn't know how to hold a sword and they spoke of the navy and how arrogant men like Jejunus made a misery of the lives of those on their ships.

After many hours, the tavern owner wished to go upstairs to his young wife and he threw them out into the street where the soldiers said farewell to their new friend and walked unsteadily back to their barracks.

CHAPTER SIXTEEN

Next day they all lined up again, in the early morning, on the quay waiting for Jejunus to say whether they would sail.

And they waited. And waited. And waited.

After several hours, there were loud mutterings from the men and both Graecus and Acerbus wished to know what was happening.

After even more time had gone by and there was no sign of anyone from whom information could be requested, Graecus and Acerbus agreed that they would go on board 'Nauplius' and find Jejunus.

So they walked up the gangplank and onto the deck.

There was no-one to be seen.

Then they noticed that the hatches leading to below decks were closed, as if the ship were deserted and glancing over to 'Obsidialis' it seemed similarly devoid of activity.

Graecus and Acerbus now scouted round the deck to see if there were any sign of a message from Jejunus or any indication of when they would sail but there was nothing.

They met in the middle of the deck, scratching their heads. Then Acerbus said, 'This is a rum do and no mistake'.

Graecus was just about to reply when he thought he heard a sound from below decks and put his finger to his lips.

They both listened and then they both heard it – a cracking noise.

Acerbus considered for a moment and said, 'Well, whatever is going on, we need to know whether to stand our men down for today so I suggest we go down there.'

'Yes, I agree'.

Graecus opened the hatch and climbed down the rope ladder, closely followed by Acerbus.

After the strong sunlight above deck, their eyes gradually became accustomed to the gloom and they saw many pairs of eyes fixed on them.

Some of the eyes were empty and dead within a living body

– those were the eyes of the men whose job it was to pull the oars which powered the ship. Some of the eyes were still living but were troubled – those were the eyes of the mariners, those like Xanthippus who made a living from the Roman Navy.

And there were two other pairs of eyes.

Those of Jejunus who now stood in the middle of the deck, his tunic unbuttoned to the waist revealing a sweat soaked chest, and holding a long thin whip whose barbed end was trailing on the floor. These eyes were both surprised and ablaze with rage at the appearance of the Centurions.

But the eyes which made the deepest impression on the soldiers were those of the young man whose arms were tied to a beam and whose naked back was the target for the whip.

His eyes, turning towards them as the reason why Jejunus had stopped using the whip, were full of pain but with a spark of hope.

Having adjusted to the gloom, Graecus and Acerbus stepped forward into the space occupied by Jejunus.

Then they saw what he had done to the young man's back.

It was devoid of skin. A bloody mass of raw flesh, cut by the lash and the barbs.

There were stripes of blood across the clearing in which they now stood – stripes left by the lash as it paused on the floor between strokes.

And there were gobbets of flesh encrusted on the stripes.

There was the smell of raw meat but there was also the smell of fear and….. something else. Something Graecus could smell, but could not yet place. Graecus could feel Acerbus's indignation and it matched his own.

A large buzzing fly gave out the only noise.

The fly settled on the young man's back, gorging on the bloody mass.

Jejunus broke the silence, 'What the fuck do you think you're doing, coming on board my ship without my permission? Who the fuck are you to come down here, poking your noses into my business?'

Acerbus strode over to Jejunus and, with his best diplomatic smile, caught him under his right elbow and drew him away from the onlookers saying,'Brother, colleague, my friend, I have need of a word with you, let us just walk a few steps round this corner and we can speak in private.'

As he drew Jejunus away from the crowd, steering him towards the partition which cut off the prow of the ship from its main body, Acerbus signalled to Graecus to cut the young man down.

Graecus called to Xanthippus to help him and they cut the bindings tying the young man to the beam and caught him as he fell, placing him chest down on the deck.

Graecus said to Xanthippus, 'Go and get my son from the quayside and tell him to bring Magnus with him'.

Xanthippus ran to the rope ladder and Graecus called for water for the man who was gibbering away in a language Graecus did not know.

Germanicus and Magnus appeared.

They looked startled to have been asked to come below but, as soon as they saw the young oarsman, they knew why they were there.

Magnus went straight to him and felt his pulse and looked at his eyes which rolled backwards into his head.

'I do not think he will live. He is in such a state of shock that he is unlikely to survive but, even if he lives the night, infection is likely to set in and, by the look of him, he is so underfed that he has not the strength to fight it. Only the gods can save this man but I can make his pain less and ease his passage to the next world'.

'Do what you can for him' said Graecus, 'what herbs do you need?'

'I need my bag. Impedimentus knows where it is'.

'Germanicus, fetch the bag as soon as you can.'

'Yes, Domine'.

Germanicus ran off, scaling the rope ladder as quickly as would a monkey.

Graecus took off his neckerchief and, dousing it in water, pressed it to the young man's forehead which was glistening with sweat even though he was shivering. Graecus now used the water soaked cloth to squeeze a few drops of water into the injured man's mouth while Magnus held onto his legs which were flailing about as his skinny body experienced the agonies of his wounds.

Acerbus's feet appeared within view.

Graecus stood up and saw that his colleague's jaw was registering an implacable resolve. Behind him, looking both murderous and cowed, was Jejunus.

Graecus stood and he and Acerbus went behind the partition.

'What did you say to him?'

'I told him that we have a job to do and that the way he carries on with his crew will not help us to get on with that job. It's quite clear that he starves those rowers and probably pockets the money he doesn't spend on their food.'

'Why was he whipping him?'

'He says it was because he 'stole' some bread but he had another reason as well.'

'What do you mean?'

'I mean that he was whipping him because he enjoys it. He was getting off on it. That's why he overdid it.'

'Ah yes, I knew there was something else, something I could not quite place'.

'Well, it was quite clear when I got near to him – he still had a huge hard-on. Anyway, I told him that we're not going to put up with his perversions when they get in the way of our doing our job. I put my dagger to his neck and told him that *we* are the senior service and that there'll be 80 men on this ship who would gladly cut his throat and throw his useless carcass over the side and that none of his own men would lift a finger to save him so he may as well get used to the idea that we'll be doing things *our* way.'

'And I am sure that he knew that you meant every word of it'.

'Yes, I made it very clear but we shall need to watch him. He's a slippery customer'.

'And a dangerous one'.

'Indeed. Will the young man live?'

'Magnus says not. He is in deep shock and is very undernourished so has no resistance'.

'And these are the wretches who are supposed to row us to Britannia? It makes me sick because, apart from anything else, it's so inefficient'.

'Now we know first hand why the navy is so despised'.

At this, the two Centurions, clasped each other by the arm in tribute to the Army and then they stepped back from the partition.

Magnus was on his knees beside the oarsman, applying a paste to the flayed flesh of his back. He was lying quietly now, almost peacefully, and when Graecus saw this he gave Magnus a questioning look.

'Yes, you are correct. I have given him a very small amount of the mushrooms we discovered in Lower Germania. He's probably dying anyway, and I wished to relieve his pain but this paste will help his back to heal if he survives'.

'What is in the paste?'

'It is a mixture of moss and a special kind of mould which has healing properties. It should help to keep infection at bay and help his skin to grow back, if he is lucky'.

'I am not sure that surviving to go back to being a galley-slave on the Nauplius is 'lucky' but it is all now in the laps of the gods'.

Magnus having finished his work, Xanthippus and one of the other mariners picked up the young man and put him, face down, in a hammock.

Looking at the haunted faces of the other rowers, Graecus asked Germanicus to fetch Felix.

Unused to being onboard ship, Felix came gingerly down the rope ladder but with his usual good humour. Then, as his eyes became adjusted to the twilight and he saw the men and their poor condition, his jaw set in anger.

'What have we here?' he said.

'Brother, we have some hungry men who need to be fed as they are to take us to Britannia. What can we do for them?'

'Well, we have bread and bacon and some cheese but that was to be our ration until we got to shore on the other side'.

'Can we not get more food in port today?'

'Yes, I am sure that will be possible but it will cost money'.

'No doubt, but the important matter now is to get these men fed. Go and get whatever supplies are needed to give them a square meal and ask Incitatus to come to me'.

Felix turned and left and, a few moments later, Incitatus stepped down the ladder with his usual athletic grace. In the six or so years he had been with the Army, he had filled out and acquired muscles but he was still as fast as he had been when he out ran the dog.

'Domine, you sent for me?'

'Yes, I wish you to perform a very specific task for me and I wish to speak privately with you'.

Graecus then drew Incitatus behind the partition and said, 'You have a good head for figures. I want you to look at this ship's books and tell me whether Jejunus has been siphoning off funds for his own use. Will you be able to spot it if he has?'

'Yes, I would think so but how will I get access to the books?'

'Ask Xanthippus. He will know where they are, but you need to be discreet. Jejunus has had a shock today but he's as slippery as a serpent, so watch yourself'.

'Yes, Domine'.

Graecus and Incitatus stepped back from the partition and Incitatus went about his business.

Acerbus was addressing Jejunus, 'When will we set sail for Britannia? My brothers and I are anxious to know when we can wreak revenge on the rebel tribes and avenge the insult made against Rome.'

And Jejunus sullenly said, 'I know not exactly. It will not be today but, if the wind freshens, I may be able to give the order tomorrow, but then again, I may not. The decision is mine.'

'Oh, of course, brother, the decision is yours and we all rely on your superior knowledge of the winds and the tides and the movements of the heavens but we all have a job to do and we in the Army are keen to be slitting British throats.'

'I do not doubt it, brother', Jejunus said with a sneer.

'In the meantime, then, I think that it will be best if our men come on board and accustom themselves to the layout of the ships. Graecus, let us go and get our men'.

Jejunus seemed to be considering whether he should object to this but decided against it and just sat sulking in a chair.

So Graecus's century came aboard 'Nauplius' and Jejunus sat silently in his chair feeling powerless and glowering at every new face.

Then Germanicus brought Zig on board, the dog's nose sniffing wildly at the new smells.

Germanicus was about to let the dog off his lead when Jejunus screamed, 'Get that fucking animal off my ship! You can't bring a dog on board. It's worse luck than having a woman on board!'

'What do you mean' said Germanicus, 'Zig goes everywhere with us. He is part of our century'.

'Zig goes every where with us. He is part of our century' said Jejunus, lisping slightly, in a mocking parody of Germanicus's voice. And then he said in his own voice, 'I don't care if that fucking animal is your fucking father, it's NOT COMING ON MY SHIP!' and his voice reached such a crescendo that, by the time he had finished shouting he had bubbles of spittle at either side of his mouth.

Germanicus was stunned. He could not bring himself to contemplate the thought of leaving his dog behind. He just stood there with his mouth open, gulping air. Zig, meanwhile, knowing that something was wrong, had pinned his ears back and was growling quietly at Jejunus.

Graecus stepped forward, 'As it happens, I am his father and I cannot see why the dog should be banned from the ship. He is a great hunter and is a useful member of our century'.

'He is a great hunter and a useful member of our century' mimicked Jejunus. Then he shouted, 'You don't understand do you? I'm telling you that dog, that lowly cur, is NOT COMING ON MY SHIP. EVERY BODY KNOWS THAT DOGS BRING BAD LUCK'.

There were about ten mariners still present and they had been listening to the exchange between the captain and the Army *signifer* and when he shouted this last statement, they all looked very serious and chorused, 'Aye, aye, it's terrible luck to have a dog on board. We cannot sail with a dog on board'. Emboldened by this support from his crew, Jejunus stood up and facing up to Germanicus he spat the words, 'Throw the filthy animal over the side!' into his face.

Graecus could not stand to see Germanicus so treated and he went over to him and, taking the dog's lead from his hand, he whispered to him, 'My son, this captain is a madman. Much as I do not wish that he should ban Zig from the ship, it may be better for the dog if we leave him here. I am sure that we shall be able to find a good home for him and then you can have him back when we return to Gesoriacum.'

'Oh father, I do not know how I can be parted from him. He has been my companion for as long as I can remember. We are inseparable'.

'It will be better for the dog. We are going on a difficult mission and I would not wish for him to come to any harm'.

'You are, of course, correct father, I see that now but I shall miss him and I know that he will miss the century'.

'Yes, he will but we shall go into the town today and find a good home for him'.

All the while this conversation was happening, Jejunus who had gone back to his chair, was making faces at the two soldiers, pretending to dab his eyes in mock grief.

Graecus took his son's arm and they and the dog left the ship.

It was not too difficult to find a home for Zig – the owner of the tavern they had visited several times while in port said that he would be a good companion for his young wife and that they would look after him until Germanicus could return.

As they would not be sailing until the following day, Graecus agreed that Germanicus could stay at the tavern with the dog until early the following morning and he left his son with a very heavy heart seeing the acute distress on his face.

Graecus was busy all through the day ensuring that the rowers were fed and that the century's provisions were replaced but his mind kept turning to Germanicus's sadness and his heart lurched at the thought of the pain it would cause him to say 'goodbye' to his dog.

Germanicus returned the following morning, looking more wretched than Graecus had ever seen before. His eyes and nose were red and Graecus knew he had been weeping.

'Oh look, here comes the pretty boy' said Jejunus 'and he's *such* a sad boy because the wicked captain says he's got to leave his little doggie behind. Aw, it's such a shame isn't it?'

Germanicus took three strides across the deck and put his fist up to Jejunus's face saying, 'Pretty boy or not, you'd better leave me alone or I'll rearrange your ugly mug with my fist'.

Xanthippus and Felix were near enough to step in and pull Germanicus away from his tormentor.

Everyone was now on board each ship, the rowers were all in place at their oars, the sails were set and Jejunus gave the order to cast off.

This could have been an exhilarating moment if 'Nauplius' and 'Obsidialis' had a different captain. It should have fired the souls of the soldiers with excitement to be breathing the unfamiliar air, feeling the motion of the ships and thinking about the task ahead. Instead, they were all angry with Jejunus and were hanging about the deck in listless silence.

Germanicus just kept looking at the receding port of Gesoriacum, his face a picture of misery.

Graecus looked at him with concern. He hoped that the spirit of adventure would eventually quicken his heart and help him forget his sadness. The rowers were now getting into the rhythm of their stroke and Nauplius's sails filled with the wind which would take them towards Britannia.

Gesoriacum was becoming more and more distant and Germanicus more and more miserable.

Graecus was trying to cheer himself with thoughts of winning battle honours for the century in Britannia, when, suddenly, Germanicus became animated and very quickly took off wolfskin, his helmet, his belt and then his tunic, and boots leaving him in only his undergarment. As he finished undressing, Graecus overcame his astonishment to say, 'My son, what are you doing? What is this about? It is too cold for you to be taking off your clothes.'

Then, without staying to answer his father, Germanicus climbed over the side of the boat and, dropping into the water, began to swim for the shore.

'Ye gods, what is going on? Man overboard!Stop the oars! Stop the oars! Stop rowing!'

Jejunus came and looked over the side and began to laugh.

'Oh what is the silly pretty boy doing? I do hope he's a good swimmer – these waters can be very treacherous.'

'Are you quite mad?' said Graecus. 'That is my son out there and this century's Standard Bearer. Stop this ship immediately and turn around and get him back on board'.

Jejunus put his head on one side and stroked his cheek in an exaggerated way as if he were considering something very carefully. Then he said in an exaggeratedly slow voice, 'I don't think I can do that. You see, it's not really man overboard if the man jumps, is it? So I don't think that as captain of this ship I'm obliged to go after someone who's jumped ship. I'm sure you understand my difficulty'.

Graecus drew his sword and went straight for Jejunus, 'Stop this ship now or by Jupiter, I'll cut your head off and throw it to the fish. And nobody on this ship, or the other one, will be sorry that I did!'

'Oh, I see. Now that you've explained it like that, I understand' Jejunus drawled. 'Xanthippus, go below and tell the foreman to stop the oars. Tell him to turn about for the shore'.

The ship stopped. Then it began to turn. To Graecus it seemed as if the turn were agonisingly slow – an eternity passed before the ship was ready to make its way back towards Germanicus. And this time it was against the wind.

The oars began again, in the direction of the port. And Graecus and all the soldiers looked over the side to see if they could spot Germanicus in the water.

Graecus was beside himself. What if they did not find Germanicus? What if they did find him but he had lost his mind? Why had he taken it into his head to jump overboard? Was madness infectious? Had he caught it from Jejunus?

The sea looked grey and huge. The waves showed white against the choppy water.

There was no sign of a young blonde man anywhere.

Graecus was demented. He could not believe that he could lose his son in this stupid, stupid way. Had he loved Germanicus all these years and taken him as his son, only to lose him to the sea? It made no sense. Graecus thought that he might be sick and was feeling the bile rise in his throat when Incitatus shouted, 'What's that over there?'

Everyone turned in the direction to which he was pointing.

There was certainly something in the water but Graecus could not make out what it was.

Then he saw something else in the water, closing in on the first thing.

They were swimming towards one another.

Neither of them was a fish.

One of them had blonde hair.

The other one was a dog.

Now Graecus understood.

Now Graecus understood and he gave his first prayer of thanks to the gods that his son had not gone mad and his second prayer was that he would be saved from the sea.

Germanicus and Zig were now very close. Graecus fancied that he could see the look of relief on the little dog's face.

Now they had joined each other in the sea and Graecus saw Germanicus take the dog in one arm and start back towards the ship striking out with the other.

The ship was gaining on them and Graecus shouted to the mariners, 'Get a rope! Look to it! Get a rope and put it over the side!'

Minutes passed, the rope dangling over the side, waiting for Germanicus.

More minutes passed as, burdened by the dog, his progress seemed very slow and laboured. Graecus did not dare think about the currents, never mind ask about them. Now that he could see Germanicus and he was so tantalisingly near, it was unbearable to think that the sea might still take him.

Germanicus disappeared from view.

Graecus could not believe that he had swum so close and been so near to safety and then failed to make the ship. How could fate be so cruel as to snatch him when he was so near?

Then he heard the mariners saying, 'Pull, pull, pull' as they reeled in the rope from over the side and then, gasping and shivering but smiling, Germanicus was lying on the deck cradling the dog which was licking his face.

'Get my cloak! Cover him with my cloak! Felix, get him some honeyed wine!'

Germanicus sat up and coughed up some seawater before shaking his head to clear his ears and made to stand up.

'No, Germanicus, I think it better if you lie here for a while and rest after your swim'.

Zig was on his legs, walking around the deck, shaking himself dry.

Jejunus shattered the scene by saying, 'Don't think that animal is staying on board my ship. If it can't be trusted to stay in port then it will have to be put to the sword. I don't care who does it'.

Graecus was thinking that it was all becoming tedious, the number of times that the soldiers had had to threaten Jejunus before he would be reasonable, when a voice came from across the deck. It was Xanthippus, 'Magister,' he said to Jejunus, 'I had a dream last night.'

'What's that got to do with anything? Why should I be interested in your dreams?'

'Well, because it was a dream about a dog.'

'Oh yes?' snarled Jejunus.

'Yes, indeed, Magister. I dreamed that we were in the middle of a huge storm at night off the coast of Britannia and we were lost, we did not know which way to go. We could have been dashed on the rocks but, at the moment when you called the order to abandon ship, there suddenly appeared in the sky above us, a dog made from the stars and it pointed the way to the shore and we were all saved. Not one life was lost and the ship was safe also'.

'And you expect me to believe that, do you?'

'I know not, Magister, it may only have been a dream but it may have been an omen'.

The mariners listening to this were mumbling, 'An omen, an omen. It must have been an omen'.

'I say it was not an omen, I say that the dog dies'.

At this the mariners all began shouting, 'No! No! The dog is our saviour. The dog must stay'.

Graecus now joined the chorus by saying, 'The dog has long been a soldier anyway and carries no ill-luck.'

'The dog must stay. The dog must stay'.

Faced with the prospect of mutiny if he executed Zig, Jejunus had no alternative but to say:

'So be it, but be it on your own heads'.

Colour began to return to Germanicus's face, and for the first time that day, he looked as if he could breathe properly.

'Well, my son, that was a close shave. I thought we had lost you. '

'Oh father, when I saw Zig in the water trying to follow the ship, I had to rescue him'.

'But why did you not answer me when I asked you what you were doing?'

'Because you would have stopped me and I could not allow the dog to drown when he was being faithful and true to those he loves'.

'Yes, I would have stopped you – I would have had you clapped in irons before I would have allowed you to try to rescue an animal, even if it was Zig. But I see that your heart is greater than my head and I can only rejoice with you that both you and he are safe'.

'Thank you, father.'

'Now, you must go below, put on some dry clothes and rest for a while. Magnus, let us also go below and see what has happened to the young rower'.

It was again dark below deck but there were a few mariners moving about engaged in seamanship.

Graecus beckoned one of them and said, 'I require your assistance, brother. Tell me, is the young man still alive?'

'Yes, sir, he is. He has been crying out in pain but he does not have a fever'.

Graecus and Magnus gave each other a surprised look at this, then Graecus said, 'Take us to him'.

They followed the man as he moved aft stepping over coiled ropes and dodging under beams and hanging implements before stopping in a tiny cubby hole in which was stretched a dirty looking hammock.

'Thank you brother, we will attend to the rest ourselves'.

The mariner left and Magnus peered into the gloomy space at the invalid.

'He is asleep. It is best not to disturb him – sleep is the best healer of all. Who knows, he may survive. If he has the will to live then that will drive him on to recovery. If he is in pain when he awakes, I will give him a little more of the dried mushroom.'

'Yes, and Felix will make sure that he gets proper food. Oh! that reminds me, I need to speak to Incitatus'.

Graecus left Magnus below deck, checking Germanicus's lungs after his long cold swim, and went on deck to find Incitatus deep in conversation with Xanthippus.

'Oh Domine, we were just discussing Sparta – our brother here is of Greek blood – his family came originally from Sparta but his grandfather moved to Rome. It is possible that we may be related, albeit distantly.'

'Ah, the gods have many ways of surprising us. I am sure that you and Xanthippus will have many hours to reminisce but I need you now to tell me what you have found'.

'Well, Domine, I went through the ledgers very carefully and I found that a great deal of money has gone missing.'

'How do you know this?'

'Well, there are records of money coming in from government sources, from the procurator, for example, and there are records of money going out – for repairs, new oars, new sails et cetera, and for provisions, but, although crude measures have been taken to try to conceal the fact, there is much more money coming in than is going out and there is a large sum unaccounted for even in just the ledgers I have seen. If this has continued for some years, then the unaccounted sum could be very large indeed'.

'I see. Thank you for your work. You have done well.'

The rest of the day passed pleasantly on the 'Nauplius' with the soldiers and the mariners exchanging tales of life on land and at sea. 'Obsidialis' must have been some way ahead of them as it had not turned back for the shore and it was not visible on the horizon.

Then, as dusk fell, the oars ceased, the sails were reset and the speed of the ship slowed while the mariner on watch kept the ship on course through the calm waters using the stars as his guide.

The soldiers and the other mariners set about the serious business of eating their supper in the lantern light and drinking toasts to the Army and the Navy, trying to outdo each other in singing the bawdiest songs.

Apart from Jejunus who was keeping to his quarters, they were all on deck enjoying the evening against the backdrop of a spectacular sunset of purple, red and gold.

Graecus inhaled the sea air, belched in appreciation of the wine he had just drunk and looked over at Germanicus sitting cross-legged next to the standard on the deck with Zig curled up beside him, his head resting in Germanicus's lap. Then he looked over at Felix, sitting next to Xanthippus, each of them with tears in his eyes appreciating a shared joke. Then he looked over at Magnus, deep in conversation with Pneumaticus. Then he looked over at Impedimentus loudly discussing Greek poetry with Incitatus.

Graecus looked at them all and felt a lump in his throat.

At the end of this day on which he had nearly lost his son, he thought about all the people who were dear to him and, apart from Acerbus who was somewhere over the horizon, they were all here, on the deck of this ship, sailing slowly in the middle of the sea. It was a moment of extreme happiness, for Graecus knew that he was respected and valued by these men and that regard was mutual – they trusted him with their lives and he trusted them with his and he knew this was worth more than all the gold and jewels and finery and fame and power in the world.

In that moment, Graecus knew that he was a rich man in the only way in which riches can truly be counted.

This wonderful thought stayed with him when he went to sleep and coloured his dreams which took him back to Germania and Arminia's embrace.

CHAPTER SEVENTEEN

The following day Graecus went with Magnus to see the young man. He was awake this time but his eyes were heavy with the narcotic which Magnus had given him to dull the pain.

Magnus felt his pulse and looked at his tongue – nodding as he did so, then he carefully lifted the corner of the paste which had dried into a sort of scab on the young man's back and nodded his head vigorously.

'Well? How is he?'

It is little short of a miracle. He has no fever, no infection. The skin is beginning to renew itself. I confess that I am amazed'.

'Well, I am not. You are blessed with the gift of healing. Truly, Asclepius touched you at birth'.

'That may be so. What is worrying me now, though, is that we have saved this rower only so that Jejunus can go back to starving him and his brothers when we leave the ship'.

'Maybe the gods have a plan.'

'We must hope that they do'.

'Be content in the meantime that Felix has the matter in hand. He is using his considerable skills to see that they put on as much flesh as possible while we are on board.'

At this moment, Graecus felt something brush the small of his back.

He turned round to see that it was the young man, seeking to attract his attention.

He was trying to speak but was finding it difficult. It seemed as if his throat was dry and Magnus went to fetch a cup of water which he pressed to his lips. He drank deeply and then said in halting Latin with a heavy foreign accent, 'I do not know who you are but you must be agents of the lord.'

'The lord, which lord? We are Roman soldiers, we answer to the Emperor, not to any lord,' said Graecus.

The young man smiled and said, 'The Lord of whom I speak needs no soldiers. He is the Lord of the heavens, not of the earth'.

'Do you mean that he's a sort of god, then?'

'I mean that he is THE God, the one and only God'.

'The one and only God? How can that be? Surely there are many gods. Where do you come from? I do not recognise your accent'.

'I come from Judea. My name is Gideon and I am grateful for the compassion you have shown me. You may be soldiers of the Empire but you have good hearts'.

Neither Magnus nor Graecus knew what to make of this. On the one hand, it was pleasing to be told they had good hearts, one the other, it was strange – impertinent even – to hear this from someone of such a low rank and even stranger when he had only one god.

'What is the name of your God?' said Graecus

'His name is Jehovah'.

'Now I understand! You are a Jew.'

'My parents were Jews. They were Jews until they met Jesus of Nazareth'.

'Oh, so you are a Christian, then?'

'Yes, I am. My parents heard Jesus preach his message of love and unity and they became followers. I was born after that so I have been a Christian all my life'.

'Are your parents still Christians?'

'My parents are dead. They were executed for their Christianity'.

'That must have been hard for you to bear, but you are still a follower?'

'Oh yes – the truth does not cease to be the truth simply because those who think themselves earthly gods wish to deny the one and only God'.

'But what does your God do? What is your God's purpose? Is he the god of the sun, the god of the moon, or what?'

'My God is the God of love.'

'Like Venus, you mean?'

'In a manner of speaking, in the sense that my God rejoices in the love of husband and wife, yes, but it is much more than that. My God shows us that love is the answer to everything'.

'I do not understand'.

'It is not an easy thing to understand but, for me, what it means is that whatever is happening, whoever is with you, then you try to give them love'.

'Even the man who flayed you alive?'

'Yes, he is one of God's children too'.

'Well, it is a remarkable religion which tells us that we should love those who have tortured us'.

'We love them so that they can learn to love themselves enough to stop torturing people'.

'You have filled my head with strange thoughts and I must try to understand what you have said. Now you must rest'.

'Thank you, Centurion. You and your colleague saved my life. It was a loving act'.

Graecus and Magnus turned to leave, Graecus shaking his head trying to clear it of the strange ideas put there by Gideon.

'What did you make of that?' he asked Magnus.

'I am not sure, yet, but I think that a god who says that love is the answer cannot be all bad'.

'Well, yes, I suppose that must be so'.

They went back on deck where their colleagues were telling each other stories of their exploits with women and there was much loud raucous laughter which Magnus quickly joined in, correcting an anatomical exaggeration made by Pneumaticus, but, after his conversation with Gideon, Graecus did not for the moment have an appetite for this, so he went and sat at the far end of the boat, lost in thought.

The gentle rocking of the boat was soothing, as was the touch of the breeze on his face and he closed his eyes.

He tried to order his thoughts but there were things going on within him which did not submit to order.

Firstly, there was what Gideon had said and, as important, there was Gideon himself. The young man had about him a most unusual presence – a sort of imperturbability, an unshakeable calm which was both impressive and unsettling. Graecus considered this a little further and concluded that it was because Gideon reacted to situations in exactly the opposite manner to what would be regarded as being the norm: when you flogged him to within a finger's breadth of his life, he said that the answer was not to take off your head, the answer was to give you love.

Then there was this business of the 'One and only God'. This really needed thinking about because it was, again, the opposite of what most people thought was normal.

Whichever way you looked at it, most of the peoples on the earth thought there was a whole sky-full of gods and goddesses. And, well, to be fair, you had to accept that the Roman Empire had not sought to destroy the religions of its conquered peoples – in fact, it had added them to its own pantheon. Look at Isis and Mithras, they were foreign gods, but they had become Roman gods as well.

But then he had a thought about the Druids – why, if Rome was so tolerant of other gods, was it busy destroying the Druids? The he remembered what Acerbus had said about the Druids being very powerful among the Celtish peoples and that their word was law. Perhaps that was it – the Druids were so power-ful they were a threat to Rome's supremacy. Where did that leave the Christians then? They were not in the least powerful – they were the exact opposite – they said that love was the really powerful thing.

Graecus wished he could discuss this with Acerbus who would surely be able to help him to understand these things but he was on the other ship and 'Obsidialis' was nowhere to be seen, so stood up and walked around the deck a little – stretching his legs and rolling his cramped shoulders forwards and backwards.

This cleared his head a little and he looked over to where his colleagues were sitting and the same enriching feeling he had experienced the previous evening washed over him.

Then he knew.

Then he knew what it was.

He knew it was love, the sort of love for your fellow man that Gideon had been talking about – the love which makes people's lives worth living. The sort of love which changes people's lives.

This was such a strong feeling that he had to sit down again

for he felt faint. He felt faint because this feeling, this understanding of the power of love was overwhelming. It explained so
many things. It explained how you could be a very rich important person and yet be bitter and cruel, it explained why you
could be a peasant crippled by the harsh toil of living on the
unforgiving land but be happy if you had the love of your family and your neighbours, it explained how he, Graecus, who had
no blood family, could be happy – blissful sometimes, because
he had the love of his son, the century and Acerbus.

Yes, that all made sense. But what about this other love that
Gideon was talking about – this requirement that you love even
those who have been viciously cruel to you?

Graecus thought about this, he tried looking at it from various
angles – he even moved head up and down and from side to side
to try to get a better look at it but he could not make sense of it.
It was all a bit too philosophical for him – he was a soldier and
ideas like that were too fancy for him. Indeed, if you thought too
much about it, ideas like that could be dangerous for a soldier –
it was best to think of your enemy as a barbarian when you were
sticking your gladius in his guts and then you could sleep at night.

Enough, now, of thinking. Too much of it was dangerous in
itself.

Graecus massaged the bridge of his nose and opened his grey
eyes.

Xanthippus was standing above him, looking down at him.

'You were lost to us then. You were somewhere else, communing with the gods'.

Graecus wondered whether Xanthippus had the ability to
read minds but he did not wish to embark on a lengthy discussion with Xanthippus concerning the effect of Christianity on the
mind of the serving soldier so he said, 'I was wondering how
much longer we will be at sea and where the other boat is'.

'Well, the wind has not been strong so we have not made as
good progress as we had expected, even though the oarsmen are
putting their backs into it now that they have bacon and bread in
their stomachs'.

'Ah yes, it is Felix's great talent to feed the hungry! Will we make land before nightfall?'

'All being well. But as for 'Obsidialis', unless it has moved so far ahead of us that the wind is different, it will be making the same slow progress and I expect that we shall catch up with our brothers soon enough'.

'Yes, I confess that I would feel more content if she were near enough for us to be able to see our colleagues.'

'That is one of the difficulties of trying to sail in convoy'.

'Isn't that one of the things that is supposed to be Jejunus's responsibility?'

'Yes, it is, but he's keeping himself below decks, out of the way because you and your colleagues have upset him'.

'I make no apology for that but it may be that now is just the right time for me to speak to him about an outstanding matter. Where will I find him?'

'He is in his quarters – below deck, in a booth just behind the ship's rudder. He may be asleep. He seems to sleep a great deal'.

'Thank you. I will go to find him now'.

Graecus stepped down the rope ladder into the gloom of below deck and let his eyes become accustomed to the darkness.

Then he walked forward towards the prow of the ship past the two rows of oarsmen, one on either side of the ship, and he saw that they were all straining to look at him and to smile their appreciation of his having organised three square meals a day for them.

For a moment, Graecus allowed himself to think that he was a hero but then he realised that he was not heroic – just fair-minded and keen to be able to do his job efficiently.

He passed the last of the oars and went into the narrow passage which led to the prow of the ship but, just before he reached this, he saw a closed curtain which looked as if it were shutting off a small cubicle.

He tapped the mariner who was standing outside the curtain on the shoulder, pointed to the curtain and mouthed:

'Jejunus?'

'Yes' the mariner mouthed back and put his finger to his mouth to indicate that silence was needed because Jejunus was asleep.

Graecus did not have time to pander to Jejunus's siesta habits so he smiled to the mariner that he had understood the gesture and stepped quietly behind the curtain.

Jejunus was wearing a tunic and was lying flat on his back on a divan, snoring slightly with his right hand clamped firmly over his crotch. He seemed to be dreaming as his eyelids were twitching quite quickly.

This was just what Graecus wanted so he crept as close to the divan as possible, drew his dagger and placed it next to Jejunus's throat.

Then he gently moved Jejunus's right hand away from his cock and grabbed his balls so tightly that he woke in alarm and was taking in a deep breath prior to letting out a scream when Graecus quickly removed his hand from Jejunus's balls and covered his mouth with it while keeping the dagger at his throat.

'Keep your mouth firmly shut while I have a little talk to you about money. I know what you've been up to you deceitful piece of shit – I know that you've been pocketing the money you're supposed to spend on food for the oarsmen and I know that you've been doing it for years. All I want to say to you is that it's going to stop – you're going to feed them properly from now on and if I find that you've slipped back to your nasty little ways then I'll have to let your admiral know what you've been doing with Rome's money. And I don't think he'll be pleased with you. Understand?'

Jejunus nodded his head vigorously and Graecus removed his hand from his mouth and put his dagger away before saying pleasantly, 'Oh, and you owe me and the Army for the food we've been giving them for the past three days – I'll take cash when we get ashore. Do go back to sleep now, it's very refreshing to have a nap in the middle of the day, isn't it?'

Then he lifted the curtain and walked back past the oarsmen, up the ladder and onto the deck feeling very light-hearted – as if he had just purged himself of something poisonous.

The day passed but as nightfall came there was still no sign of land and, happily, no sign of Jejunus.

Graecus began to feel a little uneasy that no one really knew when they would hit land and even more uneasy that he did not know where 'Obsidialis' was. Still, it was out of his hands as he was no seaman and it was best left to those who knew the ways of the oceans.

No-one else seemed concerned, so Graecus settled himself down to sleep among his colleagues putting his cloak over his head and his back to Zig to keep warm.

CHAPTER EIGHTEEN

It was not light when Graecus awoke so he thought at first that he needed to empty his bladder but then he realised that it was not the call of nature which had woken him but the call of Xanthippus who was shouting in his ear.

'Wake up, wake up!'

'What's the matter, is land in sight?'

'No, just the opposite. We have run into thick fog and we do not know where we are'.

Graecus rubbed his eyes and looked carefully around him for the first time noting that they were surrounded by a shroud of impenetrable white mist which was so thick that he could not see even the prow of the ship.

'Oh, I see what you mean. What do we need to do? Where is Jejunus?'

'He's in his quarters, asleep. We cannot wake him.'

Graecus was on his feet now and all around him, his brothers from the century were waking up, roused by the sound of urgency in their Centurion's voice.

'Magnus, go below with one of the mariners and see if you can wake Jejunus'.

'You can try but I do not think you will be successful. We'll need to act without him'.

'Are we near land?'

'We think so, these spring fogs come down very quickly when you're nearing the coast of Britannia, especially in these waters'.

'How long have we been in the fog?'

'Only for about one quarter of an hour – we tried to wake Jejunus as soon as it came down but then we woke you'.

'Were we steering for the land when it came down?'

'Yes.'

'Have we altered course?'

'No.'

'So we are still heading landwards?'

261

I'm not sure. The sails are now furled and the tide is probably taking us towards land, but I cannot be certain.'

'I do not know what this coast of Britannia is like, tell me'.

'Well, there are some sandy beaches and coves but there are as many jagged rocks and cliffs and we do not know where we are. It is one hour short of dawn and, even then, it may not make much difference – this fog is so thick that daylight may make it worse'.

Pneumaticus then said, 'He is correct, Domine, these coastal waters are well known for being treacherous in the spring – many ships have foundered on the rocks in these waters.'

But before Graecus could thank Pneumaticus for his helpful observation, Magnus returned alone and said, 'We shall get no help from Jejunus tonight – he cannot be roused – I think he's taken a narcotic. We are on our own.'

'Well, I am not sorry for that.'

Then Xanthippus said, 'The first thing we need to do is get the oarsmen back in their seats and put the foreman on alert for an order to row backwards if we're going to hit rocks.'

'But how will we know where the rocks are?'

'We have to listen very carefully for the sounds of the water but then, sometimes, you just smell them – you just know they're there.'

Graecus allowed himself a moment's annoyance at another of the navy's pathetic superstitions and its reliance on arcane methods which would be treated with contempt in the Army and he was about to give Xanthippus a withering look when he remembered that it was the first mate's intervention which helped save Zig, so he choked back his cutting words and smiled and said pleasantly, 'Oh, of course. Yes, we shall all listen as if our lives depended on it.'

'Our lives do depend on it, my friend'.

'Yes, I suppose you could be right'.

So, the oarsmen were put back in their seats with the foreman on the edge of his seat waiting for the order and the other mariners and the soldiers all stood on deck, listening.

At first, Graecus thought that this was all a waste of time as all he could hear was the sound of the waves lapping against the ship.

Lap, lap, lap, lap, lap.

Then he heard something new. It was the sound of water eddying. He did not know what this meant in terms of rocks or cliffs but it was a change from the monotony of the lapping.

Time passed seemingly interminably. No-one spoke and the men all tried to breathe silently even though many of them were afraid of this foreign sea with its strange tides and its sudden mists.

Then Graecus could hear someone pissing himself onto the deck. He did not turn to see who it was but he hoped it was not one of his men.

Lap, lap, lap, lap, lap.

Graecus was beginning to think that facing a horde of naked, screaming, blue painted Britons would be preferable to this threat from nothingness when there was sudden confusion because Zig had jumped up from where he had been lying on the deck and run to the prow of the ship where he was now standing, barking his head off at the mist as if he wished to frighten it away.

All eyes were now on Zig.

'What's the matter with him?' said Xanthippus.

'I do not know but he never barks, except for a very good reason'.

'What sort of reason?'

'If he thinks that something is going to harm Germanicus'.

Xanthippus ran to the nearest hatch in the deck and shouted down to the foreman, 'Row back! Row back!'

The ship began to move backwards and, as the rowers fought against the tide, a gust of wind blew a hole in the mist and, in the coming dawn, the men saw what the dog had sensed.

It was a huge black rock looming out of the sea, shimmering in the waves, sitting among smaller, jagged rocks each one of which was an invitation to disaster.

The mariners all heaved sighs of relief and shouted out, 'The dog saved us, the dog saved us', but the soldiers, most of whom were unaccustomed to the peculiar dangers of the sea, were silent in tribute to the size of the rock and the damage it could have done to their ship.

Then Xanthippus said: 'We have been spared by the gods

who sent this animal to be their helper. His nose saved us,' and he smiled at Graecus who had no alternative but to smile back even though their confrontation with the rock had unsettled him.

It became fully light soon after that and then, as if by magic, the mist cleared.

They could see the coast.

They could see the tall white cliffs.

Xanthippus was very busy now, calling for the sails to be unfurled and the ship to change direction so that they sailed in parallel with the coast but in a northerly direction.

Graecus felt sufficiently recovered to say, 'Brother, where are we going?'

'We are making for a cove I know which is just up the coast from here, there's a beach covered in pebbles and will be good for landing'.

'Where are we?'

'We're very close to Dubris but I have decided to put in further up the coast'.

'But Dubris is where we are due to meet Paulinus's representative, why are we not going there? It makes much more sense for us to land there.'

'Yes, in theory it does, but Jejunus's brother is Harbour Master there and I don't wish for them to have the opportunity for one of their drunken orgies which always end in trouble for me and the men. I will land you safely at the cove I mentioned and then take the ship off back to sea before Jejunus knows anything about it. That way, I get to keep my job and keep the men happy'.

'You are a diplomat of the highest order, my friend. I should have known that you would have had your reasons and that they would be good ones'.

The soldier and the sailor clasped forearms in friendship and a bond was made between them as each recognised in the other a desire to be honest and upright in a difficult world.

'We need to be ready to disembark quickly so please get your men in order'.

'As you say. Men, make ready to disembark! Germanicus

look to the standard! Impedimentus, look to the horses and the mules! Felix, see to it that the food stores are readily to hand! Magnus, come with me.'

Graecus then led Magnus to the nearest hatch and they went below. Magnus gave his Centurion a questioning look and Graecus put his finger to his lips to indicate silence. They crept forwards until they reached Jejunus's cubicle.

Graecus pulled the curtain aside to reveal the captain, still asleep, snoring heavily despite the dramas of the night.

'Will he wake up soon?'

Magnus lifted one of Jejunus's eyelids and looked at his pupil.

'Hmm, probably quite soon, I think. Do you want me to wake him now?'

'No! I do not. I want you to make sure that he sleeps for many more hours – for half of the day – if you are able to give him as much mushroom as that without killing him'.

I will do the best I can'.

'Do it now'.

Magnus went to fetch his herbs and Graecus went to see Gideon. Gideon was lying in his hammock, fully awake and alert.

'Hail, Centurion'

'Hail, Christian. I wish to ask you something.'

'Yes, go ahead'

'This God of yours'

'Yes'

'Why if he is the God of love – and that means that you love everybody – which sounds harmless to me – why is he so hated by Rome? I mean, why does the Emperor persecute the Christians?'

'Because my God is the one and only God and that means the Emperor cannot be a god, he can only be a man'.

Graecus thought about this for a few seconds and said, 'But if your God is the only God, why does he allow his followers to be persecuted. Why does he not step in to prevent it?'

'Because that would interfere with man's free will and the purpose of our being here'.

'I do not understand. What is our purpose in being here?'

265

'Our purpose in being here is to learn to live in God's way'.

'But that makes no sense to me! If our purpose is to learn to live in God's way, how can we do that when your God allows the Emperor to torture His followers?'

Gideon was enjoying this discussion and his eyes shone with animation as he said, 'I know it seems illogical at first, but the reason why my God allows it is that if He prevented it then the Emperor would not learn – it is only by doing the evil things and suffering the consequences that the Emperor will learn'.

'But what are the consequences for the Emperor? The Emperor is all powerful – he can do exactly as he wishes – the world bows before Nero!'

'The Emperor lives in fear. He cannot know when or where people are plotting against him. He cannot sleep peacefully at night for fear that it may be his last. He needs the Praetorian Guard to keep him safe from attack but, if you recall, it was the Praetorian Guard who did away with Caligula. And the Emperor needs to have his food tasted because he fears poison. What kind of life is it when you live in constant fear?'

'But he has all the riches of the world!'

'Indeed. But they cannot help him if the Roman Mob turns against him. All the riches in the world will not help him then. In the meantime, his life is a constant struggle against boredom – a constant searching for a new way of thrilling his jaded appetites. He has not yet learned that the only way for peace within oneself is to give love to others'.

Graecus shook his head, trying to understand why he should feel sorry for Nero but there were shouts from above and he said: 'I must go now and see to my men. We are disembarking soon. I shall not forget you, Christian, nor shall I forget your God'.

'Do not forget that my God is also your God. He knows you, even though you do not yet know Him'.

'That is a comforting thought amongst all the confusion you have sown in my mind but I do not think that I, a soldier, can afford the luxury of your God'.

'My God, as you call Him, is always with you, whether you

know it or not'.

'Well, if he is here on these far-flung islands then I hope he will not be deaf to the prayers of us foreigners'.

'He is never deaf to anyone's prayers as long as they are moved by love'.

I shall bear that in mind. Farewell, Christian'.

'Farewell, Centurion'.

Graecus moved swiftly to the ladder and on to the deck to see that the ship was now very close to a secluded cove and that the men were all lined up ready to leave. His horse whinnied with relief at the sight of land and he could feel the excitement rising in his men.

He called to Xanthippus, 'Are we leaving in small boats?'

'No, it is shallow enough for you to wade to the shore – the only thing that needs to go ashore on a boat is the food supplies. When you leave, you need to make your way south west to Dubris. It is about three hours' fast march from here. There is a drovers' road at the top of the hill behind the cove, take that'.

'Thank you, brother, you have been an honourable colleague'.

The air smelled different now – it was less salty and had the scent of seaweed in it. The shore beckoned and the men jumped off the side of the boat, making their way to land in an ungainly way, cursing the cold water and swearing when they got to the beach and the pebbles were uneven under their feet.

Graecus and Impedimentus were last to leave the ship, Graecus being lowered into the sea on his skittish horse in a clever sling contraption and Impedimentus leading the placid mules and the baggage wagons from the back of the ship into the shallow water helped by mariners already in the water.

They all now assembled on the beach. Graecus asked them to line up with their comrades from their contubernium, in a column two abreast and he counted them all. They were all present except, of course, for Septimus whose body was now lying at peace in Gesoriacum.

Graecus signalled to Xanthippus that all was present and correct and that the ship could move off.

Xanthippus waved farewell and, soon after, the sails were reset and the oarsmen began their journey back to Gaul.

Graecus watched the ship for a few moments and felt sad that they would not be seeing Xanthippus again. Sad, because he had been an honest and reliable colleague and, Graecus now realised, also because he had filled the space left by Acerbus's absence. This made him think again how much easier life was when Acerbus was around and how much he missed his senior colleague for his advice, knowledge and humour.

He was hoping against hope that Obsidialis had negotiated her way through the fog and round the rocks and that Acerbus and his men were now on dry land but he had no way of knowing where they were and it was pointless to wait on this beach as they were miles from where they should have landed.

The only thing was to go directly to Dubris and see what lay there.

Graecus straightened himself on his horse before addressing his men, 'We are in Britannia. Some of the British tribes have proved themselves to be barbarians and Rome is not liked in many parts of this wild country. We shall need all our courage and resolve to do our job while we are here but I have every faith in you that you will make me proud to be your Centurion and that our name will be a byword for valour in the Army for years to come.'

He finished this speech with a raising of his arm in salute to his men who cheered him for several minutes and then he wheeled his horse round and went to the head of the column and gave the order to proceed.

It was difficult for Graecus to be at the head of this column without the stimulating presence of Acerbus beside him. He felt alone again, as he had felt after the night-time attack in Lower Germania when he had had the burden of command in a remote place and no-one with whom to share that burden. He saw so clearly now, now that he was not here, how much Acerbus had added to his life and, although he was with his century, any one of whom would die for him and he was with his beloved son, he did feel very lonely.

As his horse reached the top of the hill and they saw the drovers' road, Graecus said a silent prayer to Mithras for the courage to do his job well and to be an example to his men and then, for good measure, he said a prayer to Gideon's God asking that they be allowed to gain victory without loss of any man from his century.

Graecus looked behind him to check that Germanicus was holding the standard correctly and that the column was neat and without anyone straggling untidily so that they looked the epitome of an efficient fighting machine. Having satisfied himself that all was well, he set off at a smart pace singing, '*Tramp, tramp, tramp, forward we go, Tramp , tramp , tramp, on to meet our foe, Who is it we defend, what is it we're for, We fight for ROME and the EMPEROR!* and the men all joined in as they marched towards their meeting with Boudicca, the warrior Queen.

CHRONICLES OF ETERNITY II

THE WEIGHT OF TIME

We hope you have enjoyed reading *Moments in Time*. Opposite is a taste of its sequel – *The Weight of Time* – due for publication in Autumn 2009.

In this second book Graecus and his men join the legionary forces of Suetonius Paulinus in fighting the vastly superior numbers of Boudicca's rebellious tribesmen. First they must cross hundreds of miles of unfamiliar territory where local allegiances are unknown and ambush lurks behind every misty clump of trees, but Graecus has enemies even within his own ranks and finds unforeseen solace from a surprising source.

PROLOGUE

The room was warm and the subject lay on the deeply uphol-
stered sofa. The woman's voice was calm as she said, 'Do you
know what year it is?'

The subject thought for a few moments and said, 'Not exactly – I know that Nero is the Emperor ......but we, my century
and I, are nowhere near Rome. We're in the middle of
nowhere......at the edge of the Empire.

'Is anything happening at this scene?'

'Not especially – it's just the normal evening scene with the
men laughing with each other and the smell of food being
cooked but I feel happy. I feel really content'.

'Excellent. Now I want you to go to the next scene. An
important scene in that life. Take your time, there's no hurry'.

The subject's eyes moved rapidly under their closed lids –
searching, searching, searching. The candle guttered in the
breeze coming through the gaps in the shutters.

'We're on a beach'.

'Good', said the woman, 'Who is with you?'

'My century, well most of them anyway. My son is here. My
son – I have a son! He's young and strong and he has bright
blonde hair. He doesn't look like me in any way but I know he's
my son and he's the apple of my eye'.

'Do you know where the beach is? Is it a sandy beach?'

'No, it's mostly pebbles and there's a path up the cliffs to the
headland. It's somewhere in this country. It's not abroad'.

'Why are you there? Have you just landed?'

'Yes. We landed just after dawn – we have an important job
to do inland'.

'Why have you come to this scene in that life?'

'I don't know. I'm feeling relieved that we've landed safely.
I'm with the people I know and trust and I have my wonderful
son with me'.

'Look around you. Can you see anything that tells you why you came to this scene?'

The subject's eyes scanned the scene, searching under closed eyelids.

Well, I feel that something – or someone – is missing – it's more what I cannot see that is confusing me.

'What is it?'

'I'm not sure......I'm looking out to sea and......something's wrong......I'm very concerned.'

MOMENTS IN TIME